The Dissenters
The Beginning

Michael Chapman

Copyright © 2018 by Michael Robert Chapman
ISBN: 9781980722588

CHAPTER ONE

The Sorel moon had just given way to the first faint rays of dawn when Corbin Lockett stepped outside his company-owned prefab. A crisp, cold wind came down from the snow-capped mountains to the immediate north to greet him. Winter was on the way, but then he was no stranger to the cold.

Corbin gently shut the front door then clicked the lock into place so as not to wake his daughter Shara. Her shift didn't start for another two hours. Zipping up his insulated radiation suit, a grimace crossed his face as he started to walk down the gravel road to the trolley station. In his mid-forties, his whole body was one massive ache. For the past two months, he and the other Sorel miners had been forced to work twelve-hour days without a break. All were exhausted. Many had given up, quit. He slowly shook his head, wondering why he hadn't joined them.

Lucian Merrick, Director of Alpha District Mining Operations - Theta Corporation, looked out the window of his drab little office. The first rays of the sun touching the tops of the mountains, he should have seen the beauty of the moment, but… He turned away. He hated Sorel. He had from the moment he first stepped foot on the planet's surface over four months ago. He missed the big city of Edo, the lights and the action but the Director's job was an opportunity he could ill afford to pass up. Only thirty-two, he was pleased with his progress up the corporate ladder but knew if he were to make vice president in the next five years, he needed to up his game. Unlike those who graduated from the Theta Corporation Academy, his future was not set. He needed to show Theta's upper management that he was as good as any Academy grad.

A gentle chime announced an incoming call.

Merrick sat at his desk, his back straight, but not stiff, his hands casually positioned on his desktop. After putting on his best poker face, he activated the com system. "Good morning Mr. Sandor."

The Theta Corporation's Vice President of Operations - Alpha District sat silently at his desk, apparently reading a report. In his late forties with graying hair, T.A. Sandor finally looked up with steel gray eyes. "Mr. Merrick, I see your profit line for the Sorel Mine has improved slightly but is still negative. Care to explain?"

"Yes, sir," Merrick said with a confident nod. "The yield from the recently discovered diamatron ore deposit was less than expected but consistent with our latest projection showing only 1.2 percent of the planet's ore reserves remain. Operating costs for the lower yield kept us in a negative position. Per the guidelines, we should shut down, but there is the miner's contract. They receive six months of severance pay, a contract-end bonus and paid relocation if they are laid off. The estimated cost is, well, prohibitive."

Sandor slowly nodded. "Your predecessor was a fool to sign such a contract."

"Yes, sir."

"And the improvement in your profit line?"

"I lowered overhead another fifty percent and instituted mandatory overtime."

Sandor knit his brow. "Please explain the latter action."

"Yes, sir. Per the contract, if the miners quit, are fired for a contract violation, or for that matter die, they forfeit the benefits."

Sandor looked off, digesting the information. "Interesting... Clever."

"Thank you, sir."

Sandor refocused on Merrick. "How many are off the books?"

As rehearsed, a slight frown crossed Merrick's face. "One hundred and twenty-seven so far, sir."

"What's your breakeven point?"

"Two hundred and two."

"Is that number doable in the near future?"

Merrick nodded. "Yes, sir. It is."

Half dozing, Corbin reluctantly opened his eyes and sighed. The autonomous trolley had moved past the housing area then through the business district and come to a stop at the entrance to the Sorel Mine. Getting up with a groan, he joined the others from the trolley on their way inside the cold, large cavern. Only a few were actually miners in the classic sense. Automation had taken over mining operations a century ago. The crews were now mostly made up of machine operators, maintenance technicians, and programmers. Still, the work was demanding.

Corbin made his way to the coffee pot. In a previous life, fresh out of college, he had been a pilot for the 'Nationals' in the Corporate War. Less than three years later, they had lost to the 'Corporates,' and the Discovered Worlds were placed under Corporate Rule. And, as the spoils went to the victors, there was little meaningful work for those on the losing side. But he had been lucky. He had worked in the mines during the summers to put himself through school, and the Sorel Mine was hiring. He shook his head. That was twenty-five years ago…

When he had first started at Sorel, he had met and married the woman of his dreams only to lose her to a rare disease some eight years later. Still, they had a beautiful daughter, one he had raised on his own after his wife had died. It had been a challenge, but he had treasured every moment of it. Well, maybe not every moment…

"Morning, Corbin."

"Morning, Samuels. How's the coffee today?" he said, pouring himself a cup.

"Like everything else around here lately."

"That bad?"

"Sorry to say."

"Great…" As foreman, Corbin's next move was to the sign-in board for his team. On his way, he found Samuels was right about the coffee. Freet stood next to the board. "Where's Quin?" he asked, noticing her name was missing.

"Said she'd had enough," Freet answered and slowly shook his head in frustration.

Corbin silently nodded, knowing Freet's thoughts, sharing them. He also knew that they had little to no control over what was happening. "Yang, you here?"

"Here," came a weak reply from a man just entering the cavern.

"He doesn't look good," Freet commented.

"Agreed," Corbin replied. He wondered if he should send Yang homesick when a chime sounded. "Gear up, 5A," he shouted out to his team.

Ignoring the moans and grumbles coming from now eleven, Corbin joined them in policing the area then grabbing their hardhats from the assigned pigeon holes. Each checked to make sure their headlamp was working per the safety procedure then formed a single-file line in front of the path to the tunnels below. He took his assigned position at the rear of the procession when a second chime sounded. "5A, head out."

The miners moved single file down into the constant cold of the natural cave where overhead lights locally penetrated the permanent blackness, revealing the narrow, well-worn path. Moving between two massive rocks, the miners continued past numerous pools as well as stalactite and stalagmite formations that had long-ago gone unnoticed.

Corbin unconsciously rubbed his arm in a vain attempt to stay warm. Their insulated radiation suits were old, well past their limits. He had been told replacements were on their way, but given the conditions in the mine and the current treatment of the miners by management, he seriously doubted it. Twelve had died from cave-ins in the last nine months. Twenty-four more had been injured. So much pain and suffering. It was as though the company was trying to purposely get rid of them.

"Corbin, you better get down here."

The request had echoed up from near the head of the line. The procession at a stop, Corbin squeezed past two miners in the narrow confines of that section of the path to find Yang Lee doubled over. A low, throaty cough consumed him. "Sit him down up against the rock."

Samuels and Freet did as asked then stood back to make room for Corbin. As Yang took a deep breath, his head bent back to expose a glazed look in his eyes. Beads of sweat covered the man's face despite the cold of the underground. Corbin knelt down and removed his glove. He felt Yang's forehead with the back of his hand. "You're burning up. You need to go back to the surface."

"I can't, Corbin. I don't have any more sick leave, and," he said before another coughing fit suddenly overcame him. "Please, let me work, for Mi Lin and the kids. Please!"

Corbin looked absently past Yang. He knew all too well that Yang would be fired if he did not show up for work. He also knew that it was his job to look after the safety of his men. And in Yang's current condition...

"He can lay down in that little tunnel off the main, away from the cameras," Freet offered.

"Please Corbin, just this time," Samuels added, knowing what she was asking of her boss was difficult.

Corbin removed his hardhat and ran strong fingers through his jet black hair. He knew what he should do, but... He stood back up and turned to Freet and Samuels. "Keep him in the back and out of sight until we're in."

"Thanks," Samuels said.

"Forget it. Let's just get going before we're late, and management starts asking why."

Hata, the mine's supervisor, checked his watch, then got up and headed out of his office on the surface to a lift that would take him underground. It was connected to a management shack in a lower cavern that acted as the central control point for the mining operations. Two levels of ten tunnels each radiated out from it like spokes of a wheel. Crew start times were staggered at fifteen-minute intervals, eliminating congestion and allowing management to easily take roll before the start of each crew's shift. Corbin Lockett's crew was the first of the day.

As his team entered the lower cavern, Corbin saw Hata come out of the shack with an electronic clipboard in hand. Short and stocky, the man stood on a slight ledge just above the miners and began his headcount when a small tremor shook the area. All eyes darted involuntarily to the metric tons of rock above their heads then to the entrance of Tunnel 5A, where the supports moaned slightly under the shifting load. The experts would have said the tremor barely registered on the Richter scale. But then the experts weren't underground.

"Not this time," Corbin said to himself, the memory of the recent 'unavoidable' cave-in in the tunnel they were about to enter not forgotten. Not this time... "Hata, I want a safety check run on 5A before we go in there."

Some of the miners grunted their approval of Corbin's stand. Others held back in fear, not of a cave-in, but of losing their jobs.

Hata casually looked at 5A then at Corbin. "Forget it. It was checked last week," he said and continued his count.

"That's not good enough."

Merrick suddenly came up from behind Hata. "Problem here?"

Corbin easily redirected his anger to the man he held responsible for the hazardous working conditions in the mine, the injuries, and the deaths. "I want a safety check run on 5A before we go in there."

"Any excuse to keep from working, is that it, Corbin? Well, forget it. I checked 5A last week. It's safe."

"Then I insist on another inspection, this time by someone who knows what they're doing," Corbin said, his eyes flashing an intensity that matched his words.

Merrick's face went red with rage. "I run this place, not you," he shouted, pounding his chest with his index finger. "I'm the one who says what is and isn't around here. And if I say the last safety check is good enough, then it's good enough. Do you understand?"

"According to the contract, you're required to conduct a safety check anytime I decide it's unsafe," Corbin shouted, not backing down. "That quake was here and now, not last week."

"That's not how it works," Merrick said with a sudden, deadly calm. He looked out at the other miners, his jaw clenched. "Get your team into 5A now, or I'll fire all of you for insubordination."

Freet grabbed Corbin by the arm, forcing him to turn and face the crew. "You can't win this."

Gates stood next to Freet. "He's right, Corbin. And we all need the work."

Corbin looked out at the other miners and saw them turn away, saw their beaten-down acceptance of the situation. Still... "Alright, we'll go," he said calmly, then viciously turned back on Merrick, his eyes ablaze with contempt. "But you haven't heard the last of this Merrick!" he shouted, his index finger stabbing the air with each word.

Merrick exploded. "Just who in the hell do you think you are?"

"I'm the one who's going to bring you down," Corbin shouted back. "When the Mining Board hears about this-"

"Get him out of here! Get him out of here, now!" Merrick yelled.

Gates and Freet grabbed Corbin by each arm and forcibly escorted him to the entrance of 5A. Struggling the entire way, but unable to break free, his angered shouts continued to echo off the cavern walls while Hata and Merrick headed back to the shack. "When the Mining Board hears about this Merrick, your days of playing God will be over. You hear me, Merrick? You hear me?" he shouted before disappearing inside the tunnel.

"Yeah, right," Merrick said, slamming the shack's door behind him. "I want Corbin Lockett gone. I want him gone now!"

"And the others?" Hata asked with a neutral face.

Merrick's eyes narrowed. "Whatever it takes."

"Yes, sir," Hata said with an ever-so-slight grin. He headed to the controls for each of the mine's tunnels. Sensors showing the location of Corbin's crew in 5A, he deactivated the force field for that section of the tunnel. Then, with 5B located directly under 5A, he increased the force field for the corresponding section of that tunnel to well beyond the suggested maximum.

Tunnel 5A was one of the first dug, the signs of age and abuse obvious as was the lack of maintenance. And the latest tremor had done little to help the miners inside it forget about the cave-in that occurred there three months earlier killing seven.

"Damn it, let me go," Corbin shouted before finally wrestling free of his escorts.

"I'm sorry," Freet said, "but you have to understand, we have no choice. They own us."

Corbin knew that all too well. Freet's wife had died after battling cancer for the last two years. She had left behind two little boys and a mountain of bills, all payable to the Theta Corporation. Still... He began to pace. "Nothing will ever change if you're not willing to stand up for your rights. Together, and only together, can we change the way things are around here. Together," Corbin said when an intense rumble suddenly drowned out his words and brought to consciousness each miner's primal fears. Freet's eyes grew wide as the floor began to pitch violently. Then the overhead lights went out. Headlamps instantly on, Gates struggled to suppress the rising bile, hoping the tremor would soon pass. He was wrong.

With savage intensity, columns of rock suddenly slashed up through the floor of 5A. Samuels screamed then fell silent, caught in the mid-section by a column that crushed her against the ceiling above. Aging supports moaned briefly under the compressive load then buckled before the floor gave away. Those still alive screamed as they fell. It was as though the planet was seeking her revenge for the atrocities she had suffered over the years at the hand of the Sorel Mining Company, and she was not to be denied.

Thirty seconds later, the horrific violence had passed. In its wake lay the dead and dying miners. Trapped, randomly pointed beams of light pierced the eternal blackness of the miner's self-created grave.

Pinned under a section of support, his leg broken, Corbin was unable to move. His breathing labored, he could taste blood in his mouth. He hovered between pain and unconsciousness when somewhere in the darkness, he heard Yang's voice among the screams and cries of the others.

"Corbin! Corbin!"

CHAPTER TWO

Shara Lockett bolted upright in bed. The siren! A cave-in! She checked the clock. Her father and his team were to be the first in. They would be in the tunnel by now. "Oh God!" she said, getting up, fearing the worst. Quickly dressed, she raced outside to catch the trolley. Finding the track deserted, not willing to wait another moment, she took off running to the entrance of the mine.

Liam Chandler and his team were just short of the lower cavern when they heard a rumble followed by the siren. They raced for the assembly area.

Merrick and Hata came down from the shack to meet Liam's team. "Sensors show a cave-in in 5A!" Merrick exclaimed, apparent concern in his voice. "Lockett and his team are in there."

Liam stared at Merrick in anger, feeling one way or another the man was responsible, but... He turned to one of his crew: "Chu, go to the shack and make sure the force fields are up and running. Hawkins, you and three others get dollies out of 6A. Roberts, get a mining laser from there as well. The rest of us will start clearing the tunnel as soon as it's confirmed the fields are in place."

Out of breath, Shara entered the upper cavern to find both friends and family of those known to be underground inside. Many were crying. Others just stared absently off into the distance. "Shara," Keira Chandler called out.

Shara saw her best friend come toward her as if in a fog, tears in her eyes. "Oh, Keira," she said, hugging her. "Has management said anything yet?"

"No... Wait, here comes Merrick."

Merrick entered the upper cavern looking sad and concerned. Those inside formed a semi-circle around him. "The mine was hit by a quake this morning," Merrick began. "Corbin Lockett and his team are trapped inside Tunnel 5A. We don't know their status yet. Liam Chandler and his team are conducting the rescue operation. I'm headed back down to provide whatever assistance they may need. As more information becomes available, I will return and inform you," Merrick said then headed back out of the cavern.

For those whose loved ones were not involved, fear gave way to ultimate relief. For Shara and the families and friends of eleven others, the nightmare intensified. Tears filled Shara's eyes.

"There's still hope, Shara," Keira offered.

"I know."

"We're through!" Hawkins announced.

A collective cheer echoed down the cleared portion of Tunnel 5A from Liam Chandler's team. They had quickly cleared the first section of the tunnel before coming to a wall of stacked rock. One by one, those rocks had been carefully removed to expose an opening on the other side where sensors had last put Corbin's team.

"Careful," Liam cautioned. He unconsciously held his breath while Hawkins carefully removed another rock from the breach. He knew the slightest imbalance could trigger a cascade of loose rock on the other side that might further endanger the trapped miners if they were alive.

"Got it," Hawkins said and handed the boulder to another of his team, who in turn, passed it down the line to be cleared from the tunnel in a dolly.

Chu, Yang's younger brother, put his ear to the wider opening.

"Anything?" Liam asked.

Chu pulled back and brushed a tear from his eye. "No, but they could still be alive, couldn't they?"

"They could," Liam said, fearing the worst, but forcing himself to remain hopeful. "Set up a force field projector on the other side."

"On it."

"Roberts, ready the camera."

"It's all set."

"And the bio scanner?" Liam asked the former medic.

"Mounted on the camera pole."

"The force field is active," Chu reported.

"Alright. Let's see what we've got."

Roberts fished the pole-mounted camera through the opening while Liam manned the system's monitor. "Looks like 5A fell into 5B, giving us plenty of room to move around inside... There are bodies on the floor... I don't see any movement."

"Any bio-readings?" Chu asked, trying to cover the strain in his voice.

Liam shook his head, the motion exaggerated by the arc of his headlamp. "No, none."

"But, you might not get any if they were buried, right?" Chu asked, hopeful. "Wouldn't that prevent you from getting a reading?"

Liam nodded. "It would... Roberts, prepare two climbing ropes. Hawkins carefully create an opening large enough for us to get safely through it."

"Right."

Hata entered Merrick's office to find his boss working at his desk. "They've broken through into what appears to be a chamber," he reported, his face expressionless.

Merrick casually looked up from his desktop monitor. "Did they find anyone alive?"

"Preliminary bio-readings did not detect any survivors."

"That's good to hear," Merrick said with a grin. "Let me know if anything changes."

"Yes, sir."

Liam Chandler was a seasoned veteran of the mines, which meant he had been unfortunate enough to have been on more than one rescue mission. Still, the horrific sight that greeted him made him sick. He had known most of the miners that now lay dead before him. He had laughed with them, drank with them, and shared their sorrows and dreams. Now their crushed and mangled bodies were so utterly destroyed that many could only be identified by their DNA.

"No," Chu suddenly moaned, finding Yang among the dead. "No...."

Liam started toward Chu to comfort him when he was stopped by an electronic beeping. "I'm getting a bio-reading. It's faint, but..." Roberts reported.

"Where?"

"Over there," he said and pointed. "By the fallen support."

Hawkins was first to the area. He carefully removed several rocks to expose the victim. "It's Corbin!"

"My God," Liam exclaimed, seeing one of his best friends pinned under the failed support structure. His breathing was shallow, raspy. Dried blood covered most of his face. "Can you save him?"

Roberts checked the data from his bio-scanner and shook his head. "The damage is too extensive for me to do anything here, but I can put him in stasis," he replied and removed a small device from the medkit he had brought with him. Placing it on Corbin's forehead, his patient suddenly stopped breathing.

"What just happened?" Liam asked, alarmed.

"The stasis field puts the body in suspension," Roberts explained. "Corbin will remain as he was when we found him, but he doesn't need to breathe, and his heart doesn't have to beat as long as the device is active. He'll become no better or no worse until we can get him to the hospital, and the field is removed."

"Amazing... If only we would have had that capability during the Corporate War," Liam said. "Millions of lives could have been saved."

"If only the war had never been fought," Roberts offered.

"Really..."

"Mr. Hata," Merrick said, finding his supervisor at his door once more. "Any news?"

"They found one survivor: Corbin Lockett," the man reported straight-faced.

"You're kidding," Merrick said with a laugh.

"No, sir," Hata replied impassively. "Do you think that will be a problem?"

"Are all the others dead?"

"Yes, sir. It has been confirmed."

Merrick thought for a moment then smiled. "Then no, there's no problem. No problem at all."

Shara paced back and forth inside the mine's upper cavern, her pensive dark eyes framed by her raven hair. Merrick had returned as promised and delivered the latest status. For the family and friends of her father's team, even hope had disappeared in a trail of tears.

"Shara!" Keira said, a stretcher suddenly appearing from down below.

She ran to her father's side. Tears filled her eyes on seeing his bruised and broken body. "Father?"

"Shara," Liam Chandler said, drawing her aside, allowing the stretcher to continue on to a company hovercraft that would take her father to a hospital off-planet. "Your father is in stasis. He can't hear you."

"Is he going to be alright?"

"They won't know until they get him to the hospital."

"Can I go with him?"

Liam paused, wondering if Merrick would allow it or even fire her for doing so. "Certainly," he finally said, more than willing to take responsibility for his decision.

"Thank you," she said before running off.

"Mr. Merrick, a Mr. Levine from the Theta Corporation's Accident Review Board, is here to see you," his secretary announced over the intercom.

"Please send him in." Merrick got up from his desk to greet the representative. He was surprised to find a slight, pale, nervous man wearing round-rimmed glasses and carrying an old fashioned briefcase. "Mr. Levine, nice to meet you," he said, extending his hand.

"Mr. Merrick," he replied with a limp handshake.

"Please have a seat."

"Thank you. Thank you very much."

Merrick moved back behind his desk and took his seat. "We just cleared Tunnel 5A and have exposed the chamber where all but one of the miners died. Would you like to inspect the site?"

"Oh, dear me, no. No, no, no. That will not be necessary. I am only interested in the events that led up to the cave-in," Levine said, fidgeting, seemingly unable to sit still. "As such, I read the report you provided my office on my way out here. Very nice. Yes, very nice, indeed. Everything seems quite straight forward. You said all but one?"

"There was one survivor, Corbin Lockett."

"The foreman?"

"Yes."

"How ironic. What is Lockett's condition?"

"Unknown at this time."

"I see, I see... Then would you like me to file charges against him?"

Merrick thought for a moment then shook his head. "No. Let's wait to see if he recovers first."

"Yes, yes. That would certainly be best. Yes. Yes, indeed."

Shara checked her watch again. It had been four hours since her father had gone into surgery, but it seemed more like years.

"Ms. Lockett?"

As the Doctor approached, every muscle in her body was suddenly tense. "Yes," she said, then held her breath.

"The surgery went very well. Your father should make a full recovery."

"Thank God," Shara said exhaling. "When can I see him?"

"Not until tomorrow, I'm afraid. We want to keep your father in ICU overnight to monitor his recovery. After that, he'll need about a week of physical therapy before he's out on his own once again."

Words suddenly failed her. Shara simply nodded to the doctor with tears in her eyes.

"Mr. Bradstreet, a Mr. Merrick is on line one for you," an unseen voice announced over the intercom.

The lawyer smiled on the way to his desk. "Thank you, Debra. Computer, activate the viewscreen." Sitting, he watched a wall panel opposite him lower. Merrick appeared on the previously hidden viewscreen. "Lucian, how are you?"

"I'm well, Brad. You?" he replied to his former college rowing partner with a smile of his own.

"Couldn't be better. I bought a new single racing shell the other day. Man, is she ever fast."

"Rub it in, why don't you."

Bradstreet chuckled. "Not my fault you got yourself assigned to places without any decent size lakes or rivers."

"True, true. But if all goes as planned, it shouldn't be for much longer."

"Good to hear. So what can I do for you?"

"I'd like you to take care of a little matter that's come up here at the mine."

"Officially?" Bradstreet asked.

"Very much so."

Shara entered the hospital room to find her father resting in bed, his left leg, and chest surrounded by electronic casts. His color had returned, but she found the blank stare on his face worrisome. "Father?"

"Shara," he said with a smile that was replaced by a grimace as he tried to sit up. "They told me you were here."

"They told me you were still here too," she said with a chuckle.

"I was the lucky one," he replied, withdrawing.

She quickly countered. "Is it too early to talk about it?"

Corbin looked back at his daughter, knowing what she was doing, loving her for it. "There was a minor quake just before we were ready to go in. I requested a safety check, but it was refused."

"What?"

"Merrick said he had just run one. I protested, but my crew didn't back me up."

"Why not?"

"Merrick threatened to fire us all for insubordination if we didn't go into the tunnel. Instead, my crew lost their lives," he said and slowly shook his head.

"And you think that's your fault?"

Corbin quickly refocused on his daughter. "Yes," he said with force. "If I would have only stood my ground."

"If you had, you would have been fired, and someone else would have taken the crew in," she said, matching his tone. "They would still be dead."

"But…"

"You know all too well one of the stages of grief is to falsely believe you could have done something to prevent what happened. You couldn't," she said, taking his hand, holding it tenderly. "Sorel management could have. That's the path you need to go down."

Corbin slowly nodded, then squeezed her hand lightly. "How'd you get to be so smart?"

"My father was a good teacher," she said, kissing him on the forehead.

Leaving his own office above ground, Merrick headed down the hall to Hata's. "Busy?"

"No, sir. What can I do for you?"

"I was wondering how many more are off the books."

"It turns out the cave-in was good for business," Hata said, his face impassive. "Not only do we get to count the eleven dead miners, but thirty-seven more who claimed the risk wasn't worth it and quit. One of those was Shara Lockett."

Merrick smiled. "Excellent."

"Corbin Lockett?"

He sat up in his hospital bed with less effort than the day before. "Yes."

"My name is Terrell Bradstreet. I'm a lawyer for the Theta Corporation."

"And?" Corbin replied, suddenly on guard.

Bradstreet purposely positioned himself at the foot of Corbin's bed to look down on him. "The Theta Corporation's Accident Review Board is prepared to level charges against you for gross negligence in the death of the eleven members of your team in Tunnel 5A of the Sorel Mine."

Corbin's eyes narrowed. "On what basis?"

"That you should have requested a safety check of the tunnel after the quake that occurred just before you and your crew entered Tunnel 5A."

"I did request a safety check," Corbin said, his voice low, menacing.

"Not according to Mr. Hata and Mr. Merrick. Both men have stated that you failed to do so. Mr. Merrick further said that he advised you to delay entering the tunnel until a safety check could be performed, but that you felt the check was unnecessary."

"They're lying," Corbin said in anger, his eyes boring in on the lawyer.

"Do you have any proof?" Bradstreet asked with a grin.

Corbin continued to stare at the lawyer. "Why are you really here, Bradstreet?" he finally asked, his voice once more calm.

"To tell you that you have been fired for violation of the contract."

"Of course," Corbin said, the pieces of the puzzle starting to fall into place. "But that certainly can't be all."

Bradstreet nodded slightly. "If you pursue the matter of your innocence, you will be charged."

Corbin stared back at the lawyer with the hint of a grin. "Right…"

"Well, that's the last of it," Shara said, closing the lid on the final packing crate in the living room. The prefab she and her father had called home was now empty.

"How long will the company keep your things in storage for you?" Keira called out from the kitchen.

"Up to six months."

"That's good to hear," she said, coming forward with two glasses of wine. She handed one to Shara then sat across from her on one of the crates. "So, are you going to miss this place?"

"The mine, definitely not. Friends, maybe."

"What?"

"Just kidding..." Shara raised her glass. "Thank you for being my friend."

Keira raised hers then started to tear up. "To that never ending."

"Agreed."

"Corbin?"

"Hawkins!" he replied with a broad smile from his hospital bed. "Aren't you supposed to be working?"

"Aren't you supposed to be out of the hospital by now?"

"Tomorrow," Corbin replied, "and you didn't answer my question."

"You're right. I quit," Hawkins said with a shrug. "After the last cave in, I just couldn't stay there any longer."

Corbin's smile gone, he could only nod his understanding. "I'm sorry."

"Hold on, Corbin," Hawkins said. He leaned up against the window's ledge, next to the side of the bed. "We all know Merrick's story about you not requesting a safety check is bull."

"Thanks for that."

Hawkins nodded. "Also, a number of us believe the cave-in was not the result of a quake."

"What?"

"After the bodies were taken out, a few of us started to look around. Nothing made sense. The damage was too localized. The pattern of fallen rock was all wrong."

Corbin forced himself to once again review the horror of that day. He slowly, unconsciously nodded. "I remember shafts of rock coming up through the floor."

"That explains a lot," Hawkins said, his knuckles going white as he grabbed the window ledge. "The top of 5A was basically intact."

"But, we were buried..."

"By the floor," Hawkins exclaimed. "We found you in 5B, not 5A."

Corbin stared at his visitor, his eyes narrowed. "How is that possible?"

"I don't know. It was like nothing any of us had ever seen before."

CHAPTER THREE

Sea birds screeched, disturbed from their resting place on the mag-lev track support tower by the approaching car. Inside the soundproof private vehicle, their protests went unheard as the craft rushed across the bay to the island ahead. The sun's reflection off the water caused Sandor's chauffer to dial up the shading on his windscreen before he activated the car's intercom. "We will be arriving at Theta Corporation Academy in five minutes, Mr. Sandor."

"Thank you," he replied from his private compartment. Putting his book down, he leaned back in his chair and closed his eyes. In one way, he hated his annual visit to the Academy to give the graduation address. In another, it provided him a much-welcomed break from the demands of the office.

The Academy, he mused. To even be considered for a nomination to there, one had to have a Bachelor's degree from an accredited university with at least a 3.85-grade point average and two years of exceptional service within the Theta Corporation. Of those who applied, less than one-tenth of one percent were admitted. When he was among those selected, he had been told he was lucky. When he was part of the twenty percent of his class that was still around for graduation, he had again been told he was lucky. A smile crossed his face. He did not believe in luck.

A blond, blue-eyed Thomas Chandler entered his dorm room wearing only shorts and a towel around his neck. He headed to his closet and a freshly laundered shirt and dress uniform. Thankfully, it was the last time he would have to wear it. His remaining two years of service after the Academy would be spent in space exploring the cosmos.

"That took longer than I thought it would," his roommate and best friend Wendell 'Toa' Alesana said rushing in from the dorm's central shower. From the mid-Pacific region of Earth, he was the same age as Thomas at twenty-six, slightly shorter and slightly heavier, the difference certainly all muscle.

"I know. We don't have much time," Thomas said as he swiftly buttoned his shirt.

Toa dressed even more quickly. "You don't think they would get rid of us on graduation day, do you?"

"I wouldn't put it past them," Thomas said while putting on his jacket.

Dressed, Toa moved to the mirror to comb his hair. "Damn, Thomas."

"What's wrong?"

"Not a thing. I am perfect."

Thomas picked up his and Toa's hats and headed for the door. "I'm going to miss rooming with you."

"Really?"

"No."

"Mr. Sandor, welcome."

"Professor Greer. It is good to see you again," he replied, exiting the mag-lev car and shaking the woman's hand. She was one of a select few from the Academy that he actually enjoyed being around. "Thank you for meeting me."

"My pleasure," she said with a smile. "Dean Mayer extends his apologies for not greeting you personally, but he had some unfinished business he had to attend to."

"Then it's my lucky day," Sandor said with a sly grin.

Greer just slowly shook her head.

The reflective glass lecture hall was set amongst the tall palm trees and pools that figured so predominantly in the architecture of the Academy's campus. Thomas and Toa fell in line with the other graduates on their way inside for the ceremony. Family members were not invited. Only select Theta Management was.

Inside, per the rules, Toa removed his hat. Thomas did as well then followed Toa down the descending aisle to their assigned seats in the mid-center of the hall. Thomas knew the two of them were fortunate to be there. Two years ago, the hall had been full. Now only a fifth of their incoming class remained. The others had been dismissed based on their lower marks per the structure of the school. The reason offered was that Theta only wanted the best of the best. He couldn't help but think it was because there was only so much room at the top. You might as well cull the herd early....

He unconsciously shook his head. Was it worth it? Only time would tell. Hopefully, they would have a chance to effect change in Theta, a corporation that was desperately in need of it. Hopefully...

"There's Sandor," Toa said, taking his seat.

Sitting next to him, Thomas looked down to see those on stage. "He looks better in his picture," he said with a laugh, one that quickly disappeared as his focus shifted. "Toa, see the man just to the left of Sandor?"

"Early thirties, well-groomed?"

"Yeah. That's Lucian Merrick."

"I don't recognize the name."

"He took over as Director of the Sorel Mine awhile back."

"I thought Lin Soo was next in line."

"So did everyone else," Thomas said, slowly shaking his head. "God knows he worked hard enough for it, but, one day, he was mysteriously gone, and Merrick was put in charge."

Those on stage began taking their seats behind a center-stage podium.

"I take it you're not really fond of this guy."

"My dad says a lot of good people have quit or been fired. Then there are all the cave-ins and the deaths."

"But is that Merrick's fault?"

"I don't know. Apparently, Merrick is a real hard-ass, especially when it comes to making a profit."

"All rise," was suddenly heard.

The cadets in the auditorium came to attention in unison. Those on stage stood respectively while Dean Mayer slowly made his way from the left wing to the podium. His pace befitting his eighty-some years, he was dressed in the traditional black gown with black stripes, a burgundy hood, and black tam. Finally arriving, he adjusted the microphone to accommodate his slouched form. "Be seated," he commanded in a strong voice, one that told you right away that he was a man who had power and was not afraid to use it.

All sat in unison.

"Members of this year's graduating class of the Theta Corporation Academy, the road you have traveled to this point has been long and hard. It was meant to be. For if the Theta Corporation is to maintain its position as the leader among the corporations of the Discovered Worlds, the decisions you make must be the right ones. What you have learned here these last two years has given you the tools you will need to make that happen. Use them, and Theta will prosper. You will prosper. Fail to use them, and Theta will suffer. You will suffer."

Not a sound was heard while the Dean took a drink of water, giving time for his comments to sink in. Toa carefully turned his head and looked at Thomas with raised eyebrows. Thomas slowly shook his head.

"Now, it gives me great pleasure to introduce this year's commencement speaker, Mr. T.A. Sandor, Alpha District Senior Vice President of Operations. A former graduate of the Academy, Mr. Sandor, is an example of the possibilities that await each of you as you continue to apply yourselves. Mr. Sandor." The Dean motioned for Sandor to take the podium then took his reserved seat while the assembly politely applauded.

"Thank you. Ladies and gentlemen," Sandor began. "I would first like to take this opportunity to congratulate all of you on completing the academic portion of your training and wish you continued success on your respective assignments within the Theta Corporation.

As you know, it was inevitable that the corporations of the Discovered Worlds would dispose of the outdated national governmental structure and assume the leadership role as a logical extension of an inter-global economy. Throughout history, however, many corporations have come and gone. Those that were content to stay the course and continue producing the same products or services, in the same manner, were soon replaced by others that were more aggressive and/or visionary, other corporations that had the talent to take on the competition and best them.

"The purpose of establishing this great institution is to keep the Theta Corporation at the forefront. We have gathered you together, the best and the brightest. We have given you the tools that will enable you to become the talented visionaries and managers who will not just maintain Theta, but will propel her even further beyond the competition," he said in anticipation of the applause he received.

Sandor continued. "The corporate structure is the most efficient and economical system to satisfy both private and public needs. To demonstrate this, let me cite an example from early Earth history. A private business had overextended itself. It had a large inventory of merchandise and no ready market." Sandor paused while he examined his notes. "Mr. Chandler, as number one in your class, please speculate on what the owner most likely did aside from declaring bankruptcy?"

In retrospect, the graduates should have anticipated a question being asked during the ceremony, as it was true to the nature of the program. In reality, it caught most of the class off guard. They held their collective breath while Thomas stood confidently, at attention and in control. "The most likely scenario, sir," he said, his voice strong, "would be for the owner to burn down the building and its merchandise and collect on the insurance money."

Sandor remained expressionless, staring at Thomas, waiting for him to show some sign of breaking under pressure. After an awkward silence, he was forced to conclude it was not to be. "Very interesting, Mr. Chandler and also quite correct. Please be seated."

Without a change of expression, Thomas took his seat while Toa carefully shook his head.

"By destroying the merchandise and, as a result, the business, the public would not have benefited. Now had that business been a member of a corporation, it would have had the leadership required to be effectively managed, a financial base for development and growth, a marketing group, and so on. Benefit for both public and business alike.

A corporation's success is based on profit, and profit is associated with a quality product and/or service that is economically managed. This brings me back to the Academy and, in particular, to this class. You have been specially selected and trained by the Theta Corporation to be its future management. It is now up to you to put what you have learned into practice. To that end, I wish you continued success. Thank you."

Thomas and Toa joined the class as well as those on stage in giving the obligatory standing ovation to Sandor. He nodded his acceptance then joined the Dean in walking off stage, the ceremony over.

"Dismissed."

Thomas and Toa joined the others in making their way out of the hall.

"Thank you, T.A., a well-pointed speech," Dean Mayer said.

"Thank you, Dean. As always, my pleasure."

"I understand you won't be able to stay after the banquet tonight."

"That's correct. I'm afraid I must give my attention to some rather pressing business back at the office," Sandor replied, secretly thankful for any excuse to leave, still loathing the Dean from the days of his own education.

"The monthly report?"

"Why, yes. I'm surprised you remembered."

"They were usually not something I looked forward to back in the day."

"That's still true," Sandor said and offered his hand. "To that end, there are a few things I need to take care of before dinner. If you don't mind, I will meet you there in say one hour?"

"One hour then." He shook Sandor's hand then watched him walk off to his private mag-lev car. He had never liked Sandor. And he couldn't help but question the man's rise to power without his help. Of course, he never would have given it to him.

Thomas and Toa exited through the lecture hall doors with the other class members. Putting on their uniform hats, they headed down the path through campus back to their dorm before marching to dinner.

"Did you know Sandor was going to ask a question?"

Thomas grinned. "No, but given all we've been through…"

"Agreed. I wonder if you should have given him the right answer."

Thomas looked off. "Good question... How did you like being referred to as an investment?"

Toa shook his head. "That's something I will definitely change when I'm in charge."

"Right…" Thomas said when his wrist communicator vibrated. "My orders just came in for Space School," he said. It was the unofficial name for the six-week orientation each graduate, who had elected to serve the next two years in space, was required to attend. "I've been assigned to the Centurion, a communication's ship after that."

Toa's communicator vibrated. Reading the text, he smiled. "Want to share a room again?"

After nearly four days on three different spaceliners, Corbin and Hawkins had finally made it to the space station above Chu's home planet of Arcturus. They had questions that needed answers. The hope was that Chu might just have them.

As the shuttle entered the outer atmosphere, Corbin was amazed at how each of the Discovered Worlds neatly fit the blueprint of Earth: its position from their respective sun being at the same ratio as that of Earth from its sun based on the intensity of the planet's star, its single moon creating tides in saltwater oceans that surround large landmasses, its tilted axis of rotation providing seasons, and most importantly its strong magnetosphere shielding the planet from solar and cosmic particle radiation and preventing the erosion of the atmosphere by solar wind.

So, too, had human life developed much like that on Earth. There were subtle distinctions, but for the most part, the people looked pretty much the same. They also behaved pretty much the same: good, bad and everywhere in between.

"I'm glad that's over," Hawkins said, the shuttle coming to a stop just short of the terminal.

Corbin stood up and flexed his knees. It had only been a little more than a week since the cave in. His body was still sore. "I think I've had enough of spaceflight for a while."

"Me too," Hawkins said on his way outside to the hovercraft rental counter with his carry-on bag in hand. "Is this what they call humidity?"

Corbin, carrying his bag as well, smiled. "Yes. You've never experienced it before?"

"No," he said, wiping his brow as he walked up to the counter. "Hovercraft for Hawkins," he said in English. It was the universally accepted language, although many of the inhabitants of the Discovered Worlds, especially those in the service industry, had implanted translators.

"Thank you, sir," the attendant said and handed over a key fob, the arrangements already made and paid for. "It's the second vehicle on the right, parking stall eight."

"Thank you." Hawkins led the way to the vehicle. "I've never really experienced humidity or even tropical vegetation before. My family has always lived up in the mountains."

Corbin put his bag in the back next to that of Hawkins then got in the front passenger seat. "It's early still. Wait until mid-day when it gets really hot."

"Great."

Corbin checked the map on his portable computer as Hawkins pulled the hovercraft out onto a four-lane highway. "We're surprisingly close to Chu's house. Turn right here," he said, putting them on a two-lane road that was carved out of the surrounding foliage. "I grew up in an area much like this as a kid. We didn't have air conditioning. You just had to put up with it. The first time I knew any different was when I joined the Space Force right out of school."

"Just before the Corporate War?"

"Unfortunately… Turn left just up ahead."

Hawkins slowed, the growth so dense, he had to strain to find the drive until he was almost on top of it. "You sure about this?"

"Says the house should be seventy-three meters down the drive."

"Alright," Hawkins said and made the turn. The dense vegetation eventually gave way to white sand, leading to a very blue ocean. On a rock bank, high enough to avoid any storm surge, stood a large, stylish house of glass and concrete with massive wooden beams and doors.

"Wow," Corbin exclaimed. "Whatever drove Chu and Yang to work in the mine?"

"Their parents," Hawkins replied, pulling to a stop under the shade of a portico. "They wanted their sons to appreciate manual labor before they took over the family business."

"I applaud them, and yet it seems like that only compounds their loss," Corbin said, getting out, welcoming the salt-laced breeze coming in off the ocean, the sound of the waves crashing in the distance.

"Agreed," Hawkins replied, joining Corbin when Chu opened the front door.

"Gentlemen," he said, coming forward and shaking hands. "I must confess I was intrigued when you asked if you could drop by. We're a little off the beaten path, not to mention on a distant planet."

"Thanks for seeing us," Corbin said with a smile.

"My pleasure. Come inside where it's cool. Something to drink?"

"Ice tea would be great if you have it," Hawkins said, parched.

"Corbin?"

"The same."

Chu smiled. "This way…" He headed into the kitchen, where they found Mi Lin and her two daughters.

"Corbin, Hawkins," she said, coming forward, hugging them. "How nice to see you both again."

"Mi Lin," Corbin said. "After the hospital, I asked about you, but no one seemed to know where you and the girls had gone."

She nodded. "After Yang died, we were left with nothing, not even relocation money. Fortunately, his parents reached out to me, asked us to come and live with them as part of the family. Honored, I accepted. Some two hours later, a private shuttle arrived and took us away before I could even say goodbye."

"My parents adore her," Chu said, handing his guests their drinks. "And the grandchildren can do no wrong."

"If only," Mi Lin said, shaking her head. "Speaking of which, it's time for their nap, so if you would please excuse me."

"Certainly," Corbin said then turned to Chu. "Is there somewhere we can talk?"

"How about the living room?" He led the way to where a glass wall provided a one hundred and eighty-degree view centered on the ocean.

"This is a bit of a step up from the prefabs on Sorel," Hawkins said, looking out.

"My parents started a space salvage business before the Corporate War. It turned out to be rather profitable."

"I can see that," Hawkins said.

"So tell me, why are you here?" Chu asked, taking a seat. "Is it about the cave-in?"

Corbin nodded somberly. He and Hawkins sat opposite Chu. "As you were part of the rescue effort, we'd like to pick your brain. I'd like to see if you agree with our observations and conclusions or have any thoughts of your own before we go forward and try to get the Theta's Accident Review Board to reopen the case."

Chu smiled. "Fire away."

Corbin began. "We believe a quake did not cause the cave-in."

Chu stared at his two guests. "Interesting. What evidence do you have?"

Hawkins leaned in. "First, it was too localized."

Chu nodded, recalling the rescue effort. "Agreed. There was only loose rock leading up to and after the chamber."

"Second," Corbin said, "during the cave-in, shafts of rock came up out of the floor of 5A before it gave way and fell into 5B."

"Shafts of rock up from the floor," Chu echoed, contemplating what he had just heard.

"Yes."

"That explains the debris pattern we saw after the rescue in the chamber."

"Agreed," Hawkins replied. "What we don't know is how any of that could have happened."

Chu stared off, studying the problem. "The force fields," he finally said, turning back to his guests, his eyes narrowed in anger. "For the shaft of rock to move up, there had to be a force pushing them."

"And another one not resisting them," Corbin said, shaking his head in disgust with the sudden understanding of what had really happened.

Chu nodded. "Exactly. Sorel's tunnels are reinforced by connected force fields spaced down their length. Sensors would have shown where you were in the tunnel. With 5A directly above 5B, dropping the local force field in your section, then boosting the force field in the corresponding section below it to well beyond its limits would have caused what you described and what we saw."

"Could what happened to the fields have been accidental?" Hawkins asked. "A malfunction of the system?"

Chu shook his head. "No. The way the system is set up, it had to have been a deliberate act. He looked directly at Corbin. "Your team was murdered. My brother was murdered."

CHAPTER FOUR

"Mr. Merrick," Mr. Lavine is on line one for you," his secretary announced over the intercom.

"Thank you, Mary." He activated the viewscreen in his Sorel office. "Mr. Lavine, what can I do for you?"

"Pardon me for bothering you, sir, but I have received further communication from one of your former miners, Mr. Hawkins. He claims he was part of the team that rescued Corbin Lockett," Lavine said, his body twitching slightly.

"And?"

"And, well, well, he's claiming the observed debris pattern could not have been initiated by a quake. He claims it was deliberately induced by manipulated force fields."

"I see," Merrick said with a slight nod. "And does he have proof?"

Lavine wiped the beads of sweat forming on his forehead with a handkerchief. "Well, well, he says there is another member of the rescue team, a Mr. Chu Lee, who will come forward and provide his observations regarding the debris pattern as well, but other than that, no."

Merrick leaned back in his chair. "So Mr. Lavine, does either man have any photographic evidence to support their claim?"

"No, no, sir. They have none."

"And do you think they would be considered expert witnesses in a court of law."

Lavine rapidly shook his head. "No, no, I think they would not. No, of course not."

Merrick leaned forward and stared at Lavine. "But you would be considered an expert, would you not Mr. Lavine?"

"Yes, yes, of course, but I, I don't understand, Mr. Merrick."

"You would be considered an expert, but as I recall, you did not enter the chamber after it was exposed, did you, Mr. Lavine?"

He again mopped his brow, his hand shaking. "Ah, no, no. There was no need."

Merrick continued to stare. "Mr. Lavine, the debris field in question is long gone. As such, it would be your word against theirs if you were to reopen the case. That would mean you would have to testify, under oath, that you did not go into the tunnel and observe the debris field that you did not adequately perform your duties. You would then be fired or perhaps even put in jail. But if you do not reopen the case, none of that will happen."

"Fired? Jailed?" Oh dear me," he said wide-eyed, barely able to sit in his chair. "I, I will most certainly deny their request. Most certainly. Thank you, Mr. Merrick. Sorry to bother you. Sorry, very sorry."

"Not a problem. Have a nice day, Mr. Lavine." Deactivating the viewscreen, Merrick sat back in his chair and laughed out loud.

Hawkins and Corbin came from the guest house to join Chu on the main house's deck that overlooked the ocean. The day had just started. The temperature and humidity were both bearable.

"Good morning, gentlemen. Mi Lin was kind enough to make us all breakfast," Chu said, sweeping his hand toward the buffet.

"Fantastic," Corbin said on his way to the plates. "And thank you for putting us up last night."

"Yes, thank you," Hawkins said, getting in line behind Corbin.

"It was the least we could do."

Hawkins's communicator suddenly sounded. "The Theta Accident Review Board has refused to reopen the case."

Chu led the way to an outdoor table. "Not unexpected. One does have to question the objectiveness of the 'Theta' Accident Review Board."

Hawkins laughed. "Agreed. So, where does that leave

us?"

"In that Merrick will block our every move to expose the truth," Corbin said, slowly shaking his head, "our only hope is to make our case known to Theta's upper management. But I'm not sure how to do that."

"We could mount an old fashioned protest," Hawkins suggested.

"And be immediately arrested for violating Corporate Rule," Corbin countered.

"Ah… That would not be good," Hawkins said with a laugh.

"Agreed… Any ideas, Chu?"

He paused between bites. "How about we do something to get upper management's attention, without getting caught, then present the reason why we did it?"

"We?" Corbin asked.

"My parents and I would like to do everything we can to bring Yang's killers to justice."

Corbin nodded. "Thank you… So what do you have in mind?"

"I'm not sure, but once we survey our assets, something should come up."

Hawkins finished his glass of juice. "What assets?"

Chu smiled again. "Up for a little trip?"

"Mr. Merrick," Hata said, entering his boss' office.

He looked up from his monitor. "Yes?"

"I contacted Theta's Tactical Squad. They were able to trace Hawkins's movements to Arcturus then from there to the spaceport near Chu Lee's parent's home. Corbin Lockett appears to have traveled with Hawkins."

Merrick nodded, his suspicions confirmed. "Contact Mr. Lavine. Have him issue a warrant for Lockett's arrest. Once that's done, contact the police department on Arcturus and have them arrest him."

Hata cracked a rare smile. "Yes, sir."

Hawkins had driven Chu and Corbin in the rented hovercraft back to the local spaceport. Returning the vehicle, a tram took them to a terminal reserved for private space shuttles. Mr. Lee was waiting for them there.

"Father, this is Corbin Lockett and Hawkins."

"Mr. Lee," Corbin said, extending his hand as did Hawkins.

"A pleasure," Mr. Lee replied, shaking hands. "My son speaks very highly of both of you. And I would like to thank you for helping my family understand what really happened the day our son died."

"Yang was a good man," Corbin said. "He didn't deserve to die that way. None of them did."

"Thank you," Mr. Lee said with a slight bow, "but it must not stop there. Those who did such a heinous act must be brought to justice. To that end, I wish to help you create a situation where your message will get through to Theta's upper management."

"Thank you," Corbin said simply.

Mr. Lee smiled. "Please follow me." He headed out of the terminal building and onto the tarmac where an older, pristine space shuttle was parked.

"She's beautiful," Hawkins said, staring at the classic craft.

"Thank you," Mr. Lee replied, the door opening automatically. "Please have a seat. We will be at the salvage yard shortly."

At the Lee house, Mi Lin answered the doorbell. "Yes?"

A large man held up his badge. "Lieutenant Logan. I'm looking for Corbin Lockett," he said, his tone forceful.

"He's not here."

The detective took a step closer and looked down on her. "I need to come in and verify that."

"Do you have a warrant?"

He took another step forward, dwarfing her. "Why? Do you have something to hide?"

Her eyes narrowed. "Do you really think you can intimidate me? You're sworn to uphold the law, so do so. Get a warrant, if you can," she said and slammed the door in his face.

"Who was that, my dear?" Mrs. Lee asked, joining her in the hall.

"Police," she said, fighting her adrenalin surge. "He's looking for Corbin."

"Interesting," Mrs. Lee said. "I shall notify father."

"I don't know if that is a good idea, mother. They probably have set up electronic surveillance and will monitor all incoming and outgoing transmissions."

Mrs. Lee smiled. "During the Corporate War, father and I had our own code based on a mixture of three ancient Chinese dialects. Hopefully, the police are monitoring us. It will drive them crazy."

"Interesting," Mr. Lee said after listening to what was obviously a coded message on board the shuttle. "The police are looking for you, Mr. Lockett, as you thought they might."

"It was a risk worth taking," he replied with a shrug. "Who knows, it may actually work to our favor in revealing the extent of the cover-up."

"Hopefully," Mr. Lee said, taking the shuttle to the dark side of the Arcturus moon. Pulling to a stop, he remotely activated the salvage yard lights inside a surrounding cubic shaped force field that was a kilometer on all sides. Inside the field were hundreds of ships, experimental, commercial and military, and/or parts thereof.

"Very impressive," Hawkins said. "Is everything held in place by tractor beams?"

"Yes, but because continuous beams would require a significant amount of energy, they are pulsed. Everything is basically floating in place most of the time."

"Clever."

"Thank you. I designed this system some forty years ago and ended up patenting it. After the Corporate War, I sold a similar system to the new corporate government. They still pay me to store their surplus," Mr. Lee said with a chuckle while he entered a code that opened a gate in the force field. He powered the shuttle into the yard before the opening closed. "Fortunately, the system has continued to work ever since."

"If you don't mind my asking, Mr. Lee," Corbin said, "how were you able to bring this all about?"

"As with any salvage business, we make our money by selling used replacement parts at a fraction of the cost for new parts from the original manufacturers or for parts no longer made.

Before the Corporate War, all the signs were there that it was coming, so we shifted our focus from commercial to military. We were able to build up quite an impressive inventory of National products before the shooting started. As anticipated, the Corporates' strategy was one of National attrition. With military replacement parts no longer being supplied to the Nationals by the corporations, we were able to fill a good portion of the void. The business flourished even though we did not increase our prices to take advantage of the situation."

"As one of those who fought for the Nationals, thank you," Corbin said.

Mr. Lee nodded. "It was the right thing to do."

"I'm surprised the Corporates didn't discover your operation and try to destroy it," Hawkins said.

"They tried, but we decentralized our stock early on and essentially hid it in various asteroid fields. At each site, we used windships to move our merchandise around. With their collapsible solar sails and gas jets, they could easily operate in tight spaces and leave no wake or electronic signature in the process."

"Clever," Corbin said, noticing an ion cannon mounted on the transom of two windships to port. "And the ion cannon?"

Mr. Lee smiled. "They were there just in case. Fortunately, we never had to use them."

"Fortunately… And the business after the war?"

"It was a buyer's market," Mr. Lee said while he headed toward a small freighter, "but we were selective, buying mostly for the peacetime market. Our competition was not. That is why they no longer exist," he said with a sly grin.

Corbin's eyes suddenly grew wide. In front of them was a freighter, a relic from the Corporate War. Some one hundred meters long and half as wide, she had definitely seen her days in combat. "Do you know if that is the Copernicus ahead of us?"

"Yes. Why?"

Corbin began to chuckle. "I was in command of her during the war."

"Lieutenant Logan?"

'Rizzoli,' he said from his desk, a cup of coffee and a donut at the ready.

"Hawkins's rental hovercraft was turned back in at the spaceport."

"Any record of Lockett or Hawkins leaving or purchasing tickets?"

Rizzoli shook his head. "No, but the Lee's do own a shuttle."

"Really? Where is it now?"

"Unknown. It's gone, and the family doesn't have to file a flight plan."

Logan looked sideways at Rizzoli. "What?"

"Given the nature of his business and the frequency of his trips, all agreed it was a waste of time, so Mr. Lee was given a waiver."

"Great," Logan said, shaking his head. "Get in touch with the control tower. I want to know when Mr. Lee's shuttle is on its way back so we can meet it."

Rizzoli grinned. "Will do."

The Copernicus consisted of two cargo bays, one large and one small with overhead doors. Her flight deck and crew quarters were forward. Her engine pod was aft. In the Corporate War, she had been used for close-in support. Seeing her again after so many years with all her patches and repairs, Corbin wondered how it was he was still alive.

Mr. Lee had remotely opened the cargo doors of the smaller bay then expertly landed his shuttle inside the ship. Once the atmosphere in the bay had been restored, Corbin exited the shuttle as though he had just come out of a time machine. Looking around, his memories were mixed and a bit distorted. His crew had been his family for two years. Too many had died in a fight all soon knew they could not win. Still, they had tried…

"Welcome back," Mr. Lee said, coming up alongside him. They were joined by Chu and Hawkins.

Corbin shook his head. "In a strange way, it's like I never left…. Is the ship operational?"

Mr. Lee shrugged. "No, but there are enough parts in the yard to bring her back to life. Obsolete systems can also be replaced."

Corbin nodded then turned his attention to the articles

stored to the side of the bay. "Transmitting lasers?"

"Yes. Three units should yield two that will work."

"And do you have a collector dish?"

Mr. Lee smiled. "Four… Do you have a plan, Mr. Lockett?"

A grin crossed Corbin's face. "Can we borrow the Copernicus, two windships, two lasers, one relay dish, thirty spacesuits, cloaking devices, and a shuttle?"

"Certainly."

"Then, I have a plan."

Chu looked around and shook his head. "It will take time and talent to make the repairs to the ship and equipment."

"And manpower," Hawkins added.

Corbin nodded. "A number of the Sorel miners that quit are mechanics. If say twenty-five or so are willing to join us, we should be able to have everything ready to go in four weeks once they get here, don't you think?"

"Can we pay them?" Hawkins asked

"Minimum wage?" Mr. Lee asked.

Hawkins nodded. "That should work."

"And Mr. Lockett, can you execute your plan in say six weeks total time?"

"Yes."

"Then I will provide the funding as well, in cash, of course."

"Of course," Corbin said with a laugh. "Thank you."

"No. Thank you. As I said before, the truth needs to be known."

"Agreed. So Chu, are you in?" Corbin asked.

"Definitely."

Mr. Lee turned to his son. "You will not be paid."

Chu smiled. "Understood."

Detective Logan watched the Lee shuttle taxi to its assigned position on the tarmac then waited for the door to open. "Mr. Lee?"

"Yes," the elder Lee said on exit.

"I'm detective Logan." He held up his badge. "I'm looking for Corbin Lockett."

"He left the other day," he replied plain-faced.
"Do you know where he went?"
"No."

Logan took a menacing step forward. "I need to look inside your shuttle to verify your claim."

"I need to see your search warrant. And no, I do not have something to hide," Mr. Lee said with a grin.

CHAPTER FIVE

"Corbin, Corbin!" Yang screamed from the blackness.
Corbin woke with a start and bolted straight up in his bunk onboard the Copernicus. His face was covered with sweat, his breathing heavy, rushed. He fought to pull himself out of the recurring nightmare that had haunted him over the past weeks. He glanced at the clock. He was due to record his message to Theta's upper management in the mess hall in five minutes.

Getting up, already dressed, he headed out of his small cabin. Over the past month or so, a team of thirty volunteers had somehow managed to resurrect the Copernicus. Each had lost someone they knew or loved to either injury or death at the hands of Sorel management. And when told what really happened in Tunnel 5A, they had gladly joined the cause to expose the truth.

Non-functioning and outdated equipment had been replaced with newer technology from throughout the salvage yard while the ship's structural concerns had been eliminated. The Copernicus certainly wasn't pretty, but she was space-worthy once more.

"Father."

Corbin turned to see Shara come up from behind him in the corridor. In her early twenties, she reminded him so much of his late wife. So, how could he possibly put her in harm's way? Then again, how could he keep her from not being involved? She possessed the same inner strength and drive that her mother had had. And, if possible, her sense of right and wrong was even more intense than his. "Is everything okay?"

"Cali asked me to ask you if it wouldn't be better for her to be the one to record the message to Theta's upper management."

"Oh?"

Shara smiled. "She said that it's not that you wouldn't do a great job, but she's worried that with the warrant out for your arrest, our credibility will be questioned when they discover who you are. Her doing it will also minimize my risk when I return to Sorel after we're done."

Corbin slowly nodded. "Agreed. Is Cali the right choice?"

"I think so. Her last name is not the same as her brother's, so there's no direct connection to him being one of the miners lost at Sorel. She's also never had any contact with the law, so she won't be in any facial recognition database."

Corbin thought for a moment. "Does she know that if this goes south, Theta will come after her?"

Shara couldn't help but laugh. "If this goes south, Theta will be coming after all of us."

Corbin smiled. "Alright. Have her take my place."

"Will do."

"And tell her thank you."

"I will," Shara said before heading off.

Thomas laid back on his bed in the hotel room he and Toa shared, a pleasant tiredness consuming his entire body. Space School's simulator training was expected. Combat was not. But in retrospect, it made sense. The possibility of encountering others who were unknown and less friendly existed. They needed to be ready for any eventuality.

Toa entered the room, looking exhausted and unceremoniously flopped down on his bed. "Man, did I ever get my butt handed to me on the urban combat range."

"It gets worse. The zero gravity range was next to impossible and extremely frustrating."

"I can't wait."

Corbin entered the cramped flight deck where Chu sat in the copilot's seat. "How's it going?"

Chu looked up from his calculations. "Given the required tenth normal speed limit through the channel, a two-second burst should certainly do it."

Corbin ducked to avoid a newly installed electronic box patched into the overhead console then straddled a reworked center console before sliding into the pilot's seat that had been commandeered from a scrapped fighter. "What's your margin of safety?"

"1.26."

Corbin shook his head. "That's too tight. We're just trying to get upper management's attention, not put one of their ships on the rocks. What would it be for a second and a half burst?"

Chu input in the new number into his laptop. "1.85."

"Let's go with that," Corbin said and activated the monitor in front of him. Installed over original obsolete gauges, it showed the Copernicus positioned just outside Buoy 19 of 220 for the Theta Shipping Lane, a manmade channel through the Sea of the Giants Asteroid Field. A fitting location, he thought as he activated the com system. "Hawkins, what's your status?"

"Stand by." A distorted image of Buoy 19 was reflected in the mirrored faceplate of his twenty-first-century spacesuit. Three-quarters of the way up the structure, an intense blue laser beam rotated every two seconds. Working with the other buoys, they navigated spaceships safely down the lane. The buoys also maintained the spacing and position of the lane through the asteroids through a series of tractor/repulser beams.

Using a tractor beam of his own, a modification to his spacesuit, Hawkins stabilized himself just outside the buoy's maintenance door then pulled in a tethered combination targeting/transmitting laser. Taking hold of it, judging the approximate line of sight to a nearby asteroid, he attached the assembly to the buoy with its own tractor beam. "The targeting laser is in a rough position."

"Roger that," Corbin said, then looked out the port window to the asteroid Hawkins had aimed his targeting laser at. "Lindsey?"

In a spacesuit like that of Hawkins, she floated down toward a control panel with an electrical cable in hand. The other end was connected to a relay dish mounted on top of a two-meter-high tower anchored to the rock. Halfway between, a transmitter laser was aimed at the entrance to the shipping lane. The connection made, a green light appeared on her panel. "Ready here as well."

Corbin checked the data on his screen. "Hawkins, rotate your laser 15.43 degrees to port, 2.72 degrees up."

"Adjustments complete," came over the Copernicus' speaker seconds later.

"Hawkins, activate the targeting laser. Lindsey, start the dish search pattern."

She pushed the appropriate button then watched the dish move in a slow spiral pattern. The tracking laser beam acquired, both the dish and the beam moved to where a red laser dot came in from the upper right quadrant and worked its way to the center of the dish. She checked her monitor. "I show the signal to be within 99.3 percent of the center. Do you want any further adjustment?"

Corbin couldn't help but chuckle. "No. I didn't think we could get that close. Adjust your transmitting laser 77.35 degrees to port, 3.55 degrees up."

"Adjusting," she replied over the com system.

"Hawkins, activate the laser bypass program. No telling when we'll have visitors."

"On it." He opened the buoy's maintenance door then plugged a cable into the buoy's computer. A smile crossed his face on seeing a green light appear. "The bypass is activated."

"Right. Stand by," Corbin said before an awkward silence filled the flight deck. Both he and Chu knew they were about to cross the line.

"We're doing the right thing," Chu finally said.

Corbin stared blankly out into space. "I know... Even so, I'm about to put all of you at risk."

Chu slowly shook his head. "You may have organized us, but we all agreed to do this, need to do this."

Corbin looked at Chu and nodded. "Thanks."

"Father," Shara called out as she approached the flight deck. "We're all set below."

He turned and smiled. "Hopefully, we won't need to use you," he said when the sound of a sensor suddenly filled the flight deck. Chu immediately accessed the data from a long-range scanner they had placed earlier near the entrance to the shipping lane. "Looks like a large cargo ship headed this way."

"I need an ID on that ship now. Shara, get ready to launch, just in case," Corbin said, his voice strong, any indecisiveness gone.

The Pride of Theta's Captain felt truly blessed. He was the head of a select crew chosen to serve on the largest ore ship ever built by any of the worlds' corporations. She carried forty 10 x 10 x 35 meter diamatron ore containers. Arranged in groups of four, they were mounted down the length of a truss that ran between her command module and her engine pod. She was also capable of reaching speeds considered impossible just ten years ago with only a crew of eight to handle her. Incredible....

"Captain," the helmsman said, "we're coming up on the outer marker for the alpha entrance to the Theta Shipping Lane."

He walked along the raised rear deck of the spacious modern bridge with a cup of coffee in hand. His first command had been with the Theta Corporation during the Corporate War. Almost thirty years later, the Pride was like a dream come true. "Helm, slow to one-tenth normal," he ordered on his way past the Engineering and Communications stations. He headed to the central command chair located directly behind the ship's Helmsman and Controller. A massive viewscreen mounted to the forward bulkhead showed the opening of a channel through the asteroid field ahead.

"Yes, sir."

For what seemed like an eternity, Chu's laptop worked to process the oncoming ship's code without success. The delay only raised the anxiety of both men. "Well?" Corbin finally asked.

"Still nothing."

"How's that possible?"

Chu shook his head. "I'm not sure. I'll input her physical shape."

Seconds later, both men stared at the picture on the screen. "Are you sure about the ID?" Corbin asked, shaking his head in disbelief.

Chu nodded. "Verified. It's the Pride of Theta. Her code wasn't in our database because she's too new."

"The Pride of Theta," Corbin said with a laugh. "It can't get any better than that."

Chu smiled. "No, it can't."

Totally committed, Corbin brought the Copernicus engines to life and took the ship further into the field where the composition of the asteroids and their size made her detection by the Pride's sensors impossible.

In the Copernicus' cargo bay, the lights changed from white to yellow. Two crews of eight ran to their respective windships. A pulsating alarm warned of the upcoming depressurization and atmosphere extraction.

The Pride's Captain looked at his ship's viewscreen and the approaching entrance to the lane.

"Ready to transfer ship's control over to the shipping lane, sir," the Controller announced.

"Make the transfer."

"Yes, sir." He pushed the appropriate icons on his screen then cautiously sat back in his chair.

"Not very comforting letting another system take over the ship, is it Control?"

"No, Captain, it is not."

"Stand by for activation countdown," Chu said over the com system.

Hawkins's breathing suddenly quickened. Ever since his eighteen-year-old brother's legs had been lost from a cave-in on Sorel, he had longed for justice. So much life literally crushed out of the boy.

Corbin sat transfixed by the icon representing the Pride as it moved ever closer to the intersection point with the transmitting laser. He was certain they were doing the right thing.

"Five," Chu said with more calm than he felt.

Hawkins's mind raced. Had he made the right connections? Of course, he had, but what about the laser itself? Would it work? He had checked it three times before transporting it. But what about the transport itself?

"Four," echoed in Lindsey's helmet. A quick scan of her control console told her all was ready. Her thoughts once more returned to her husband, dead because of Sorel management's negligence.

"Three," Chu said, thinking of Yang, murdered.

Shara checked her team in one of two windships. All were nervous. Hopefully, they would not be needed.

"Two."

Hawkins felt a rivulet of sweat run down his forehead despite his air-conditioned suit. He placed his gloved finger over the toggle for the laser.

"One."

Corbin unconsciously nodded. They were doing the right thing.

"Activate! Activate!"

Hawkins pushed the toggle down and held his breath. The buoy's lighted ring went dark, but... After an agonizing two seconds, a pulse of blinding blue light finally shot out of his laser toward the relay dish.

Lindsey watched the transferred collimated beam of light race toward the entrance of the shipping lane. She smiled.

The Pride of Theta suddenly, violently lurched hard to starboard. A collision alarm sounded while all struggled to regain their seats. The Captain quickly checked the viewscreen. They were rapidly headed toward the asteroid field. "Control, manual override! Helm, hard port! Full deceleration!"

The ship shuddered then started to slow, but the check of a navigational screen showed it would not be enough. The Pride's projected course was well inside the field. "Control, thrust reversers!"

"Sir, the engines will burn up at this speed," the Engineer protested.

The Controller hesitated.

"Do it now, damn it!" the Captain shouted, angered at the loss of precious seconds.

The force of the thrust reversers rocked the ship, throwing the crew forward, some onto the deck, while multiple alarms sounded over the protests of the engines. One by one, overloaded systems failed. Fire erupted from the center control console. Then all of the bridge's viewscreens went black. "Control!"

"On it, sir," he shouted, feverously inputting the commands on his panel.

"Captain, the engines won't last much longer," the Engineer shouted over the din.

"They have to," he yelled when a new collision alarm sounded. "Control!"

The viewscreen suddenly came back to life to show an asteroid dead ahead, only seconds away. "Helm, hard starboard, 6 degrees down now!"

The Pride dove as best she could to the side, but even at her ever-decreasing speed, she still raced up upon the asteroid. The ship flashed by it to port, missing the rock by mere meters when another collision alarm sounded.

"Helm, Hard port, 21 degrees up!" the Captain shouted over the alarm and the painful protest of the engines.

"Captain, I can't clear her!"

"Brace, brace, brace!"

The Pride's starboard side slammed into the asteroid. A jagged outcropping of rock slashed into the third and fourth container bays, ripping four of the containers from their attachments in a series of violent electrical explosions. Three more containers in the following fifth and sixth bays were gashed open, causing their precious cargo of diamatron ore to come spewing out.

The collisions altering the ship's course, a new alarm sounded. The Captain recovered his seat to find them headed for yet another asteroid when a series of explosions rocked the vessel.

"Captain, the engines are gone!"

"Captain, I've lost steering control!"

"Helm, what's our speed?" the Captain asked.

"Thirty meters per second, sir."

"Still too fast..."

The viewscreen showed an asteroid growing ever larger dead ahead. The Controller checked his board. "Impact in ten seconds!"

The Captain searched his mind for the impossible. "Control, launch the two escape pods on the starboard side, now! Everybody hold on!"

"Where is she?" Corbin asked in fear.

"I don't know!" Chu yelled just before the Pride suddenly came out of nowhere and flashed overhead. The ship in a flat spin, what was left of her engine module rotated into a nearby asteroid, the collision marked by a massive fireball. Most of the remaining cargo containers flew off in all directions. One container was sent spinning end for end on a direct collision course with the Copernicus.

"Corbin!" Chu shouted over an alarm.

Not enough time to spool the engines up, Corbin quickly activated the port bow thruster, pivoting the nose of the ship, putting her in line with the path of the approaching container.

"She headed right for us!" Chu shouted the container almost all that could be seen out the front windows.

Corbin next activated the port stern thruster. Working in tandem with the bow thruster, the Copernicus moved ever so slowly sideways.

"Corbin!" Chu shouted again just before the cargo container passed by the port side of the Copernicus with a good ten centimeters to spare down the length of the ship. "How did you do that?"

"I'm not sure," Corbin replied before quickly turning his attention back to the Pride. "My God, where's her command module?"

Still shaking, Chu scanned the wreckage. Most of the ship's engine pod was buried in the asteroid. The rest of the Pride's stern was a blackened mass of twisted metal flayed open by countless explosions. Further out, a few cargo containers remained partially attached to the truss, which ended in a severed stub. "It must have broken off during the collision."

"I pray you're right," Corbin said. He anxiously powered the Copernicus forward, closer to the wreckage. Both men desperately scanned the surrounding space. "Do you see her?"

"No... Wait, there!" Chu shouted, pointing to an asteroid coming out from behind another. "Oh my God!" The command module's bow was embedded in the rock.

"Are they alive?" Corbin asked, his voice trembling.

Chu entered the query into his laptop. "There's no way to tell from here."

"Damn," Corbin said and activated the com system.

"Launch the windships."

CHAPTER SIX

So this is what death is like, the Pride's First Engineer thought in the back of her mind, for some reason no longer afraid. Was I crushed under a beam, or did I suffocate in the vacuum of space and my brain or soul or whatever survived? And what about heaven and all the not so good things I have done or said or even thought... Damn, I mean darn, I hope God has a sense of humor...

"Engineering, emergency power."

What was that? It sounded like the Captain's voice, but how could that be?

"Emergency power, Engineering."

"Yes, sir," she said weakly, reacting more from her training than conscious thought. She got up off the bridge deck in the dark and felt around for her chair. Finding it, sitting, she located her console then input the proper commands. Life support, then lights and computers suddenly came active before it dawned on her that she was alive!

The Captain surveyed the bridge as the cook, off-duty Second Engineer, and First Officer entered, shaken. Everyone appeared unhurt. "Damage report."

Each member of the crew knew the job of survival took precedent and quickly responded. "Captain," the First Engineer said, "emergency power is fully functional and should provide us with life support and communications for about four days. The only major damage is to the bow, but the pressure bulkhead is holding."

"Alright... Set up a force field around the bulkhead, but don't activate it unless it's needed. I don't want to waste the power."

"Yes, sir."

"Communications, notify Sorel Colony of our situation," he ordered when the viewscreen went active.

All stopped to stare in disbelief at the surface of an asteroid only centimeters from the ship's forward pressure bulkhead. Those who had religion came closer to their deity. Those who didn't suddenly considered the wisdom of that choice.

"Control," the Captain said, slowly shaking his head. "I want to know what the hell just happened to my ship."

The Copernicus main cargo bay depressurized, the atmosphere recaptured, her massive overhead doors started to open. Mooring clamps were released, and the two windships activated their downward-facing jets.

From the flight deck, Corbin watched the ancient vessels each spread its solar sail then use their jets to accelerate toward the Pride of Theta's command module. He had almost laughed when he had first seen them in the yard. Now, the stubby, sailboat-like spacecraft with their open cockpit astern and a large cabin forward would hopefully save those on board the Pride, if anybody was still alive. He activated the com system. "Shara?"

She moved forward between the opposing benches holding her team. All were in spacesuits with helmets in hand. The Controller handed her a headset. "I'm here."

"God knows we never meant to harm the Pride crew, but if they are alive, they probably think otherwise," Corbin said. "I think it best you go in armed, just in case."

"Understood... Roberts, did you copy?"

Roberts looked out the front window of his windship as the command module came into view. He slowly shook his head. He wasn't sure anyone could have survived. Still... "Copy," he said then turned to his crew. "Secure helmets. Set disrupters to stun."

Shara's windship pulled up to the portside transfer chamber of the Pride's command module while Roberts' ship headed for the starboard chamber. She made a quick check of her crew. All helmets were secure. "Control, prepare the cabin to open the hatch."

The Pride's Controller studied his screen. "Captain, it looks like Buoy 19 overrode the others, but I don't see how," he said when a sensor suddenly sounded. "Captain, the portside transfer chamber's outer door has just been opened!"

"Engineering?"

"Confirmed, Captain. "The same is true for the starboard door as well."

"A malfunction?"

"I don't think so, sir."

"Control, can you put the outer doors on the viewscreen?"

"I'll try, sir. The system is pretty torn up." First bypassing the burned-out primary circuits, he next rerouted the power to the aft-mounted cameras to produce a viewscreen image. It was more static than a picture, but... "It looks like we're being boarded, sir."

The Captain looked at the ion cannon on the transom of each ship and suddenly went cold. A memory, no, a nightmare long-suppressed, came screaming back to his consciousness.

"Are they here to rescue us?" the Communications Officer asked.

"No," barked the Captain, his voice threatening, his eyes narrowed, his thoughts consumed by his past: the violence of war, the loss of his first command at the hands of a vile foe. The torment he had almost escaped through time and treatments came crashing back, welling up inside of him, uncontrolled, unchecked. The pain was real, the rescue that wasn't, the torturous years in the prisoner of war camp. His mind snapped. "Never again."

The First Officer looked at the Captain. "Sir?"

"They're not going to take us prisoners again," he said, reaching the only conclusion his past would allow him to, all others not to be considered.

"What?" the First Officer asked eyes wide. "Sir, that doesn't make sense."

"Never again," he said with venom. He marched to a rear locker. Inputting a secret code, he opened the door to reveal an armory of disrupter pistols, their existence previously unknown to the crew.

"My God!" the Helmsman caught himself saying out loud. The Pride was a commercial ship, and he was certainly no soldier.

In fact, he had never fired a weapon in his life and wondered seriously if any of the others had either.

"They're not going to take my ship without a fight," the Captain shouted, forcing the weapons into the hands of his crew after setting them to kill. "Follow me."

The external door of the Pride's transfer chamber closed. Shara checked a wall-mounted monitor while the chamber's pressure and atmosphere were being restored. "They're on emergency power, but all values inside read normal," she said over her suit's com system to the five others inside. "We can take our suits off."

Marsh removed his helmet. "That's a good sign, right?"

Shara nodded hopefully. "Right."

The Pride Captain quickly stationed his people at the intersection of two corridors, one of the corridors connecting the opposing transfer chambers.

"Roberts?" Shara was heard to say over his communicator.

He looked at the other five with him. All had their suits off. All had their disrupters ready, just in case. "We're ready."

"So are we. Activating our door."

"Fire!" the Pride's Captain shouted.

In shock, four of Shara's team quickly took cover behind the chamber door supports. Caught in the open, Shara and Marsh raced forward for the cover provided by the first available corridor support. She just made it before a disrupter blast struck Marsh in the leg, dropping him on the deck, screaming. "Cover me!" she yelled to those behind her.

A hail of disrupter blasts flashed overhead, giving her the precious seconds she needed to crawl out and pull Marsh to safety. "What are they doing with their weapons set on kill?" he yelled, fighting against the pain.

"I don't know," she replied in anger. "You're lucky. It just grazed you." She pulled a hypo from her pants pocket and jammed the needle into his leg. The narcotic took immediate effect. "Can you still fire your weapon?"

"Yes."

"Then, cover me."

Pinned down in the starboard transfer chamber, Roberts saw the Pride crew shift their focus to Shara as she raced to the next corridor support on the opposite side. "Now!"

Roberts' team raced forward, firing.

"Captain!" the Pride's Communication's Officer yelled before being struck in the chest and thrown hard against the wall, unconscious. Wide-eyed, the First Engineer turned to see Roberts' team advancing when she was suddenly lifted up off the deck from three separate shots. She flew backward, stunned in a crumpled heap.

Enraged, the Captain fired on Roberts' team with unrelenting fury. A sick smile crossed his face on seeing one of the enemy fall screaming. On the deck, writhing, his second shot silenced the man forever.

Appalled, both Shara and Roberts' teams rushed forward, firing upon the Captain and crew of the Pride of Theta. The Second Engineer took aim at Shara's team, but in the process, he exposed himself to the other end of the corridor. The first blast struck him in the back. A second hit him in the leg, dropping him into unconsciousness.

"Captain, there's too many of them," the Helmsman shouted, cowering from the incoming disrupter fire that struck all around him.

"Keep firing, damn it. They're not going to take my ship," the Captain shouted when a blast from Shara's team ripped the weapon from his hand. He screamed from the pain, from his failure or both before dropping to his knees, his arm useless.

"Surrender, damn it," the First Officer screamed at the Captain over the incoming hail disrupter blasts.

"No!" he shouted back. "Not the POW camp again!"

"Oh my God!" The First Officer quickly threw down his weapon. "We give up!" he shouted, his hands in the air. "We surrender!"

The few of the Pride's crew that were still conscious gratefully followed his lead.

"Ceasefire," Shara ordered.

Both teams approached with caution, weapons aimed, covering one another against any eventuality. Roberts moved to his downed man then looked at Shara. "It's Ali Khan. He's dead."

Angered, she made her way to the Captain only to find him babbling, his mind gone. "Who's second in command here?" she demanded.

"I am," the First Officer replied, defiant. He looked at her over his shoulder through angered eyes while his hands were being bound behind him. "What the hell are you doing killing our people."

Shara slammed the man hard up against the wall. "Our weapons are set on stun. Yours were set on kill! You killed one of ours!"

"The Captain ordered-"

She slammed him up against the wall again. "Did you refuse the order? Did you even question it?" she demanded, her eyes bearing down on him.

The First Officer looked away, unwilling to face the truth.

"I thought so," she said with disgust before throwing him to Roberts. "Get him out of here."

"With pleasure." Roberts pushed the First Officer down the corridor and into an aft escape pod where he joined the rest of the Pride crew.

"Shara," her Controller called out, coming from the transfer chamber with a package. "It's a follow-up message."

"Thanks." Taking it, she headed to the escape pod and the Pride crew. She tossed an original package plus the new one in. "Deliver these to Theta upper management when you are rescued."

"You won't get away with this," the First Officer said.

A grin crossed her face. "We already have."

Corbin paced back and forth outside the Copernicus cargo bay's pressure door, keeping an eye on the indicator, wondering how anything could take so long. The pressure finally stabilized, the atmosphere restored, he heard the lock bolts for the door withdraw. A hissing sound was followed by the door starting to move.

Squeezing through the increasing opening, he ran to his daughter's windship. Her communication from the Pride said their messages had been delivered, but little more. He knew something was wrong.

First off her ship, Shara ran into his waiting arms.

"What happened?"

"They fired on us. The Pride's crew's weapons were set on kill."

"What? Why would they do that?" he asked before the color suddenly drained from his face.

Shara followed her father's stare and saw the shrouded stretcher being taken off Roberts' ship.

"Oh my God…"

"It's Ali Khan. There was nothing we could do. We were committed by the time we found out."

"But we're trying to prevent death, not cause it," he said in a distant voice. "This is all my fault."

She forced her father to look at her. "No, it's not."

"Yes, it is. If I had just left everything alone…"

"You would have condemned those in the mines to the increased possibility of injury or death."

He looked past her to the stretcher and slowly nodded. "You're right, still…"

"I know…"

"Shara," the shuttle pilot called out on his way to her. "We're ready."

"Thanks. I'll be right there," Shara replied and then turned her attention back to her father. "Will you be alright?"

He gave her a slow, unconvincing nod. "Given what's just happened, do you still think it's wise to go to Sorel?"

She nodded. "We need to monitor Theta's reaction first hand. You said so yourself. Being on Sorel is the best way to do that."

"But if they discover you had anything to do with this…"

"I don't see how that's possible. With Cali having delivered the message, I'll just be visiting an old friend. Besides, it will only be for a couple of days," she said then kissed him lightly on the cheek.

"Alright," he replied, unable to refuse her. "But be careful."

"I will," she said before jogging off.

Corbin watched her go then turned his attention back to Ali Khan.

Merrick checked his watch then sighed. His spaceflight to Sigma Three Station still had another three hours to go. Besides hating the travel, he wasn't sure which planet he despised more, Sorel or Sigma Three.

"Mr. Merrick, a call for you from a Mr. Hata," the Business Class flight attendant announced. "Booth One."

"Thank you." Getting up from his seat, Merrick moved to the small, soundproof room and activated its viewscreen. "Hata."

"Can you secure this line?"

"Certainly," Merrick said, pulling a standard-issue thin black box out of the inside pocket of his jacket. He activated it. "The line is secure."

"The Pride of Theta went off course inside the Theta Shipping Lane and crashed in the asteroid field. No one was injured, but the loss of the ship and her cargo have been assigned to Sorel."

"Damn."

"There's more. An unknown group tried to rescue the crew, but the Pride's Captain, a former POW in the Corporate War, mentally lost it. He thought they were Nationals coming to take him prisoner again. He made the crew attack the rescuers, killing one."

"You're kidding."

"I'm afraid not. But it doesn't end there. After the Pride's crew was defeated, they were given a packet by the rescuers to give to Theta's upper management. I'm onboard the command module now. They gave it to me unopened. It contained two videos I think you'll find of interest…

The screen went momentarily blank before a young woman dressed in all black was seen seated behind a desk. "Management of the Theta Corporation, we claim responsibility for momentarily altering the course of your ship to bring to your attention the hazardous working conditions that exist at the Sorel Mine. Twenty-two have died this year alone from avoidable cave-ins due to negligence on the part of Sorel Mine's management. Now, another eleven have recently been murdered in a cave-in brought on by the deliberate sabotage of the mine's force field system by the same management. Our protests blocked at every turn by Lucian Merrick and his Supervisors, the ones who have committed these crimes, you are our only hope. We implore you to investigate our claims. The guilty must be brought to trial. The current policies and practices at the Sorel mine must change. For until even basic safety demands are met, the lives of the people who live and work at the Sorel Colony will remain at risk. If immediate action is not taken by you, it is almost a certain more miners will die."

Hata reappeared.

"Interesting," Merrick said, contemplating all he had just seen.

"Here is the second video."

The picture changed to show the same woman rushing back to the chair behind the desk. "Theta management, we never meant to cause the destruction of the Pride of Theta. We only meant to alter her course for a moment to gain your attention. Please believe me," she pleaded before the recording ended, and Hata reappeared.

"Are you the only one to see videos?" Merrick asked.

"Yes, and now you."

"Good. I want to keep it that way... What was the cause of the crash?"

"The crew reported a buoy malfunction. The video would suggest the rescuers caused that to happen."

"Agreed... Where are the Pride's Captain and crew now?"

"With me on board the command module."

"And beside the crew, are you alone?"

"Yes."

Merrick nodded, excited. "Can you make sure there is a bad circuit board in the buoy in question before the investigators showing up, one they will use to confirm the malfunction?"

Hata nodded. "Easily."

"And the Pride's command module, can it be destroyed to hide any evidence of the attack?"

"With or without the crew on board?"

Merrick smiled. "I'd rather not have any loose ends."

Hata nodded. "That will not be a problem, either."

"Good. Where do you stand on the monthly report?"

"A draft awaits your approval. I included the videos, but they can easily be taken out."

Merrick smiled. "Excellent. Call me at my office on Sigma Three in four hours. I'll update the report based on your progress."

"Yes, sir," Hata said and terminated the communication. The Pride Crew recovering in their rooms or the ship's mess, he found himself all alone. Getting up, he moved aft to the two escape pods. Disabling both, his next move was to pick up one of the Pride's disrupters left on the deck after the battle. Heading to the controls for the emergency power reactor, he input a series of commands then fired the weapon at the console to prevent its further use. He then ran to the transfer chamber and his shuttle amid an alarm and flashing lights.

"Warning," the ship's computer stated, "loss of containment will result in the destruction of the command module. Warning."

The First Officer ran from his room to the bridge, the First Engineer just behind him. "You need to reestablish the containment!"

"Yes, sir," she shouted over the alarm, quickly taking her seat. She input a series of commands then looked at the First Officer with abject fear on her face. "I can't access the containment field."

"Oh my God!"

From his shuttle, Hata watched the uncontained reaction rip the command module apart in a series of violent explosions. With a slight grin, he headed for Buoy 19.

CHAPTER SEVEN

Thomas sat next to a sleeping Toa on the Theta Spaceliner. Space School was over. They were ready, if not excited, to start their next two-year assignment.

A soft female voice was heard over the cabin's speakers, one designed to gently wake those passengers who had elected to sleep during the long flight. "Ladies and gentlemen, we are approaching Sorel Station. Please fasten your seatbelts, secure your tray tables, and place your seatbacks in an upright position."

Two attractive female flight attendants started down the twin aisles of the second cabin in preparation for docking. The pleasant, bodiless voice continued. "For those passengers continuing on Flight 509, we will depart Sorel Station at 10:30 hours. For those passengers traveling to the planet Sorel, the shuttle will leave from Gate 27 at 11:00 hours. For those passengers traveling to Taos Station, Flight 644 will depart Sorel Station from Gate 17 at 16:00 hours. Thank you for flying Theta Spacelines."

Lightly dozing himself, Thomas suddenly sat straight up. Had he misheard the announcement? With Toa still asleep, he turned his attention to the approaching attendant. "Excuse me, miss, but I thought the flight for Taos left at 21:30 hours."

"It did," she replied with a cute little flip of her long hair, silently declaring her interest in Thomas. As corny as it sounded, she had always been attracted to a man in uniform, especially if they were as cute as this one with his military-cut sandy blond hair and his blue eyes. "We've had a schedule revision go into effect starting today as part of our total quality improvement program."

"Great," Thomas said in disgust, slowly pounding his fist on the armrest.

"Please place your seatback up in preparation for docking," she ordered with a painted-on professional smile, one that hid her true hatred of her job and the people she had to put up with. "You too, sir," she said to Toa in a voice loud enough to wake him.

"Huh?" He pulled himself out of a deep sleep, not quite sure where he was at first.

"Your seatback, sir. Please move it into an upright position for docking," she ordered before continuing down the aisle.

"Friendly little thing," Toa said, complying with her demand.

"Really," Thomas replied in a low voice, slowly shaking his head.

"Something wrong?"

"They've changed the flight schedule as part of some stupid total quality something or other. We've got less than four hours on Sorel."

"You've got to be kidding. When did that happen?"

"Today."

Toa stared blankly out the window. "Well, at least you'll have some time at home."

"True," Thomas said, suddenly feeling guilty. Toa hadn't seen his family in five years, and he was complaining about losing a couple of hours.

Sandor entered his outer office on the one hundred and twenty-fifth floor of the Theta Towers, headquarters for Alpha District Operations. The building was just down the road from the corporate headquarters in Edo. He had been away for the week successfully negotiating a new contract for an ore processing plant on the planet Taos before visiting the Academy. It had been a long trip. He was glad to be back home.

"Welcome back, sir," his secretary said in greeting. A matronly woman, she had been with him for fifteen years and was the epitome of efficiency. She literally ran the office, allowing those to enter who should and politely refusing those who should not. She used his power in the process but was very careful to never cross the line and abuse the privilege.

"Good evening, Helen. Are there any messages?" he asked, taking off his overcoat and hanging it up.

"Yes, sir," she said, coming forward. "Your All Managers Meeting has been changed to tomorrow, and your appointment with Mr. Cantu has been canceled per your request. Also, Mr. Maas has a conflict and won't be able to attend your staff meeting," she said, purposely holding that information for last. She had tried to advise Maas against not showing up, but the man had belittled her. Fine, he was obviously as stupid as all the others said he was. He deserved what she knew was coming next.

Sandor's steel-gray eyes narrowed. It was the third time Maas had dared to miss his staff meeting. The excuse no longer mattered. "Draw up his termination papers for my signature in the morning."

"Yes, sir," she replied with a small, satisfied smile.

"Just who does he think he is?" Sandor said in a low voice, shaking his head on his way into his inner office.

Closing the door behind him, his mood changed almost instantly. He was once again surrounded by the things he loved, treasures of the past. The hardwood shelves that lined the far wall were filled with his priceless collection of first edition books. His matching desk and leather chair sat alongside a window wall from where he could look down on the city below. Ancient oils hung on rich paneling, and his bar was stocked with the finest imported liquor housed in crystal containers. Power truly had its rewards, he thought, passing by a table and chair arrangement on his way to a glass of scotch. Pouring it over ice, he headed to his desk, ready to take on the business of the worlds. "Computer, initiate the monthly report. Display it on the main viewscreen."

A section of paneling slid effortlessly away, and the screen behind it came alive. The title slide for the Alpha District Monthly Report was centered over the Theta Corporation logo. "Computer, graph the overall profit percent for the last month."

Sitting, Sandor saw the picture change to show a column graph. Each column represented the percent profit for a week for all companies under his control. Weeks one through four were shown moving from left to right. A low of 11.5 percent was shown in the first week, with values steadily increasing to 13.7 in the third week. The fourth week, however, showed a decrease to 11.7 percent. "The average percent profit for the month was 12.2," the computer announced.

Sandor nodded, overall pleased, but curious about the drop in the fourth week. Patience, he reminded himself. "Computer, compare current month-end profit for each company against the value posted for the previous month."

The screen changed to show a table with three columns. For each row, the company name appeared in the first column. The second column contained that company's previous month-end profit and the third column, its current month-end profit. Major improvements were shown as green in the third column. Minor improvements to minor losses were colored yellow. Significantly negative performance was marked by red. Company 120 jumped off the chart. "Computer, provide additional information on company 120."

The screen changed to show company 120 to be the Sorel Mine. The change between the two months was a negative 25.78.

Sandor shook his head. Was his memory failing him? "Computer, list the reasons for company 120's last month profit loss."

A pie chart was shown with only a sliver of ore remaining. The caption read Ore Depletion. "98.8 percent of the theoretical amount of available ore has been mined to date," the computer stated. "Recovery of the remaining 1.2 percent of ore represented a profit loss of 1.58 percent for the last quarter."

The screen again changed to show what was left of the Pride of Theta's engine module. The caption read Equipment/Ore Loss. "Loss of the Pride of Theta and its cargo of diamatron ore accounted for a profit loss of 26.14 percent for the last month."

Sandor's instant anger was as quickly replaced by curiosity. "Computer summarize all additional information on the Pride of Theta."

"The ship was damaged beyond repair, and her cargo lost when a malfunctioning navigational buoy in the Theta Shipping Lane caused her to run off course and crash in the asteroid field. All hands were lost."

Sandor slowly shook his head.

Karin Chandler stood alone outside the one-room building that was Sorel's spaceport terminal. It had been over two years since she had last seen her son. And although the separation had been hard on her, it was nothing like what she had experienced over the last week knowing Thomas was finally coming home, if only for a visit.

Seeing the shuttle on final approach, her heart began to pound with excitement. As it touched down and taxied forward, she removed her compact and checked her hair and makeup for the tenth time. A frown crossed her face again. Age was not kind. Still... She returned the compact to her purse and pulled out a handkerchief. There were a million things to say, an equal number of questions to ask. "I will not cry," she said to herself when the shuttle came to a stop, and her son appeared at the door. "Thomas!"

"Mom!" He took two steps at a time down the stairs and hugged her.

"Oh, honey, it's so good to see you again."

"I've missed you."

She held him at arm's length and examined him with a mother's pride through tear-filled eyes then hugged him again. "I missed you... Well, I guess I'm being a little silly, aren't I?"

Thomas smiled. "No, not at all."

"Good," she said and hugged him a third time. It was then that she noticed Toa standing off to the side. "I'm sorry. Where are my manners?" Breaking free of her son, she wiped her tears away and extended her hand. "You must be Wendel."

"No need to apologize, Mrs. Chandler. It's a pleasure to meet you. People usually call me Toa though," he said, shooting a sideways glance at Thomas. He hated the name Wendel. Thomas knew he hated the name Wendel.

"Well, Toa, it's a pleasure to meet you. I've heard so much about you."

"All good, I hope."

"Of course. How was your flight?"

"Great, I slept the whole way."

"That's good because I've got quite a full day planned for the two of you."

"Mom, I'm sorry, but Theta Spacelines moved up our departure time up. We only have about three hours before we need to be back here."

"Oh, honey," she said deeply saddened. "Can you take a later flight?"

"No. The next one's not for two days, and we're to be on station tomorrow."

"Well then, we'll just have to make the most of the time we've got," she said, maintaining the logic that allowed her to be a miner's wife and a mother. "I had better call Keira and have her get lunch ready. I hope the two of you are hungry for a home-cooked meal."

"Oh God, yes," Thomas said while his mother moved to a vid-link on the station's wall.

"I can't remember the last time I had one," Toa said when he was suddenly distracted by an approaching vehicle. "Is that a trolley?"

Thomas turned to see the single-car, its contact pole running across a junction, causing sparks to shoot out. "It is indeed. It's also our ride home or, for that matter, to almost anywhere that is worth going to on Sorel. You remember your ancient history, don't you? Well, here you can live it."

"Why?"

"The colony is the only inhabited part of the planet, so to simplify things, everyone agreed that a trolley would be the only means of transportation allowed, except for the ore trains and a handful of company-owned hovercraft."

"That would be hard to get used to."

"At first, but it eliminates all the hassles of owning a vehicle, insurance, traffic control, and the like."

"Logical."

"Very. And it works," Thomas said, leading the way to his mother.

The vid-link established, a distorted image of his sister appeared on the screen amongst a great deal of interference.

"Sor-- -aycare. ---lo," was heard.

"Keira?"

"--ng on - seco--, an ore ship---- is go--- by."

Karin waited patiently.

"What's with all the static?" Toa asked.

"An ore train must be going by. The radiation causes it," Thomas explained.

"Is it harmful?"

"The corporation says no."

Toa couldn't help but laugh. "Based on your development, I would have to challenge that ruling."

"I'm going to tell my mom you said that."

"Ah, no, that's okay."

When the interference finally cleared, Toa was amazed at just how beautiful Keira was with her long red hair and bright green eyes that sparkled above high cheekbones. Behind her were twenty or so children ranging in age from two to four, running in all directions, yelling and shouting as they played.

"Hi mom, I thought that was you. Did Thomas make it? Oh!"

A blonde, blue-eyed, four-year-old suddenly jumped into Keira's lap unannounced and stared blatantly into the camera. "Hi, Mrs. Chan-ler," the girl said with a bubbly smile that instantly melted your heart.

"Hi, Sasha. How are you today?"

"Fine," she said, drawing the word out before burying her head into Keira's shoulder with instant bashfulness.

Keira smiled and stroked the youngster's head with affection. "So I take it Thomas made it in."

"He did, but he has to leave earlier than planned to make his connection. Can you go home and get lunch ready?"

"Sure. Parker just came in, so I'm on my way."

"Thanks, honey," Karin said and ended the call. She headed to the trolley stop. "Shall we?"

The trolley car was configured in separate compartments where one bench in each faced forward and the other bench faced aft. The only passengers, Karin, sat in the lead compartment with her back to the front giving Toa and Thomas the bench with the view forward. "Hold on," she cautioned after entering the destination code.

Toa did as instructed. Thomas did not. "Mom, I'm not four anymore," her son said when the car jerked to a sudden start, throwing Thomas roughly back into the bench. His head hit with a resounding thud. "Ouch!"

Toa couldn't help but laugh. His mother couldn't help but smile. "I told you to hold on honey, but then you never did do what you were told."

"That's still the truth, Mrs. Chandler."

"Alright, you two... So, Mom, what's Keira doing at the daycare?"

"She took the day off so I could come to meet you."

"You're working at the daycare?"

Karin suddenly turned serious. "Mi Lin, the lady who used to run it, well her husband, Yang, was killed in a cave-in, so she and her children left the planet. In that we still need a daycare, a few of us volunteered to run it in our spare time until a replacement can be found."

"Sounds like a lot of work."

His mother shrugged. "It is, but it's nice to be around children again. It also doesn't hurt to know that you can leave them when it's time to go home," she said with a laugh while the trolley ran alongside a small lake at the end of the tarmac on its way to the housing sector. "Oh, Thomas, I forgot to tell you, Keira has a friend of hers visiting from off-planet, Shara. Well, you remember her, don't you?"

"Was she that skinny little girl with pigtails that lived two blocks over to the north?"

"That's the one, although she's changed a little since you went away to the university."

"I'm sure... So why did Shara leave?"

Karin looked off. "Her father, Corbin, was fired."

"Really?" Thomas asked, taken aback. In his time on Sorel, people were typically never fired from the mines. He then remembered what his dad had said about Merrick. "Why?"

Although alone, Karin looked around to make sure no one was listening, then leaned in closer and lowered her voice. "Awhile back, Corbin and his crew of eleven were caught in a terrible cave-in. He was the only survivor. Later, the company said the accident was his fault, that he should have requested a safety check of the tunnel before taking his team in."

"You sound like you don't believe it," Toa said, his voice lowered as well, caught up in the intrigue.

"No, not for a moment. Corbin is one of the most caring men I know, but it was no good to say anything. Those who did were later fired for reasons that just don't make any sense."

"Weird," Thomas said. "What did dad say?"

"Well, you know your father. He really doesn't talk much about work, but when he found out what they did to Corbin, he was really angry. He would have quit then and there if it weren't for our contract being up in two months. The contract-end bonus and paid relocation make it just barely worth staying on."

"It sounds like you've made the right decision, mom."

Karin stared off into the distance again. "I don't know. I just don't know."

Toa sat back and slowly shook his head. "Thomas, given all we learned at the Academy, this doesn't make sense. I think it warrants investigating."

"Agreed," he replied as the colony's identical prefab homes now lined either side of the tracks before those on the right-hand side gave way to a park. Thomas looked out and smiled, the memories of growing up there coming back. Early summer, the children that were too young for school were hard at play, seemingly filled with endless energy. But something was different. The park was almost empty. A check of the houses showed many of them to be empty as well.

"So, is this where you grew up, Thomas?" Toa asked.

"Yes and no... Mom, where is everyone?"

She again shook her head, trying to be strong. "Since Merrick took over, things have really been bad. Initially, hours were cut back so far that a number of families could no longer afford to stay and quit. Then Merrick ordered mandatory twelve-hour workdays, seven days a week. After a couple of months, all the miners were exhausted. Many couldn't take it anymore and quit. Others were fired for violating the mandatory order. Then there are all the accidents and deaths. So many deaths."

Thomas knit his brow. "But why? Why deliberately destroy the mining operation? It goes against every principle the Theta Corporation was built on."

His mother shrugged. "I don't know, Thomas. We don't know."

The trolley suddenly jerked to a stop at an intersection on the far side of the park, just short of the business district. At the same time, the front door of a corner house flew open, and Keira ran out.

"Thomas!"

"Keira!" Out of his seat in an instant, he met her halfway and hugged her. "How's my baby sister?"

"Well, I may be your sister, but I ain't no baby," she replied with hand on hip, using her best Mae West imitation learned from hours spent with the archived videos.

"Oh Keira, I just don't know where I went wrong with you," her mother said with a smile on her way past her children and into the house.

"And you must be Wendel," Keira said, unable to suppress a laugh.

Toa again shot a sideways glance at Thomas.

"I'm sorry, Toa," Keira said, "but Thomas told me to call you that."

"No, I didn't," he replied and quickly positioned himself behind Keira, using her as a human shield.

"That does it," Toa said, moving toward Thomas in mock anger.

Grabbing his sister from behind by the arms, Thomas steered her from side to side to fend off Toa's false advances.

"Thomas, no, no, you don't," she yelled over her laughter. "Settle down, you two... Shara... Shara..."

"Keira?" Shara called out the front door.

Both Thomas and Toa instantly ceased their false hostilities, each man appearing slightly embarrassed by their behavior as Keira's extremely beautiful friend approached.

"Shara, thank God." Keira stumbled toward her, doubled over with laughter.

"It sounded like you could use some help," Shara said, looking at the two officers, flashing a perfect smile.

Toa came forward to shake her hand. "Hi, I'm Toa."

"Nice to meet you, Toa, but I was told your name is Wendel," she said innocently, not in on the joke.

"My friends call me Toa."

Shara shot a glance at Keira and shook her head. "Then, may I call you Toa?"

"I would like that very much. Thank you." He looked back at Thomas and Keira with a self-satisfied grin.

"Shara, I don't know if you remember me or not," Thomas said.

"Vaguely, Thomas," she replied then laughed. "I'm sorry, but Keira told me you were short, fat and balding."

Toa turned to Keira. "Not bad."

"Why, thank you," she replied with a smile.

Thomas looked at his sister. "Yeah, thanks, Keira."

"No, Thomas, it's not her fault," Shara said with a straight-face. "You see, it's just that you're such a disappointment. I prefer men who are short, fat, and balding."

Thomas shook his head. The others couldn't stop laughing when Karin appeared at the front door. "Time to eat."

Keira dragged Shara away from Thomas. "Coming, mom."

Toa followed. "Home-cooked food, Thomas."

Thomas stopped staring after Shara and joined Toa. "I can't wait."

Inside, Toa closed his eyes and inhaled deeply. The aroma of an apple pie filled the room. "I must have died and gone to heaven."

Thomas moved past his friend to find a buffet of baked beans, cornbread, and a mountain of barbecued ribs. He went weak in the knees. "Toa, you're not going to believe this."

"Oh my God!"

"Thomas, Toa, you don't have much time, so please eat. You too girls," Karin said, bringing out a bowl of coleslaw.

"You don't have to ask twice, Mrs. Chandler," Toa said first in line.

Shara followed. "This is fantastic, Mrs. Chandler."

"I couldn't agree more," Toa said.

"Thank you both."

Keira was last in line. "Mom, where's dad?"

"I don't know. Your father was supposed to be here by now," she said with a touch of concern in her voice on her way back into the kitchen.

Toa quickly filled his plate and headed to the dining room table.

"So tell me about the Academy, Toa," Shara said as innocently as possible, joining him at the table. She wasn't sure if he and Thomas being there was a coincidence or part of an investigation by Theta Corporation looking for links to the attack on the Pride. Either way, she needed to be careful.

"The competition was both fierce and unrelenting. The professors were always trying to expose any weakness they could in you. If you let up, even for a second, you were basically gone."

"Is that true, Thomas?" Keira asked, following her brother to the table.

"Unfortunately, yes. It was probably the worst two years of my life. Some say that the ends justify the means, but if I had it to do over again, I wouldn't."

"But your futures are set, aren't they?" Shara asked.

"That depends on what you value," Thomas replied. "If it is money or power you're referring to, then the answer is probably yes. But that pretty much means you have to sacrifice everything else in the process."

"I didn't think about that," Shara said, impressed.

"We didn't either until later. Hopefully, we can change all that," Toa said with a smile, having already finished his third rib. "But enough of us, what do you two have planned for today?"

"We're going explore the caves near the great glacier," Keira said.

"Really?"

"Well, it was either that or play dolls."

"I ah..."

"I'm sorry," Keira said with a laugh. "Want to join us?"

Toa smiled at his former roommate. "What do you think, Thomas?" he asked, knowing the torment associated with the temptation.

Thomas unconsciously shook his head as if to clear the devils that lurked within. "I think Theta would probably kick our butts... Dad!"

His father entered the room and smiled, despite his right arm being in a fresh sling. "Thomas. It's great to," he started to say when Keira saw him.

"Dad, are you okay?" she asked, unable to hide the fear brought on by the condition of the mine.

"I'm just fine. It's nothing."

"Liam!" his wife said on her way out of the kitchen. "Oh my God, Liam, are you alright?"

"Now, now everyone, I'm fine. It's just a sprain, nothing more."

"Was it another cave-in?" his wife demanded.

"A minor one, Karin, but no one was seriously hurt, and the problem has already been corrected. There's nothing to worry about."

"What do you mean there's nothing to worry about? That's the second accident this month. Don't try to make it something it's not. You know those tunnels are unsafe."

"I know, but Merrick announced today that they will be upgraded starting next week and that everyone will get a ten percent pay raise retroactive to last quarter."

Shara was barely able to hide her shock and joy. They had done it! They had really done it, she thought to herself, suppressing the urge to tell the world.

"That's great news, dad," Keira said.

"But Liam," his wife started to say.

"Karin, things will be alright."

"We'll talk about it later," she said and stormed back into the kitchen.

"I'm sure we will," he said in a low voice with a slight chuckle, "but first, I would like to meet Toa, isn't it?"

"Yes, sir," he replied, somewhat in shock.

Mr. Chandler grinned. "Did Biffy and Bunny give you the complete tour of our little colony?"

"Dad!" Thomas and Keira shouted simultaneously.

"Most people around here still call them that," Mr. Chandler went on. "I think it's kind of cute, don't you?"

"Oh, Yes, sir. Very much so, sir."

"I thought you might... Are those ribs I smell?"

A Theta Power shuttle came in over the mountains and landed at the Sorel spaceport. Two men got out wearing Theta Power uniforms and sunglasses. One, Pendrac, was very tall. The other, Yates, was large, powerfully built. Without a word, they got in a company-owned hovercraft and made their way to the colony's power plant.

"How long do you want to set the delay for?" Yates asked, free from being overheard.

Pendrac through for a moment. "Four hours. That will give us more than enough time."

"Agreed."

"Thomas," his mother said, her children having finished clearing the dishes from the table, "you and Toa had better get ready if you're going to catch the next trolley. You too, girls," she said on her way back into the kitchen.

"Right, mom," Keira said, she and Shara heading to a back bedroom.

"I thought your flight wasn't till later, Thomas," his father said, confused.

He shook his head. "It was moved up starting today of all days."

"I'm sorry to hear that. Had I known, I would have tried to get here earlier." He then looked at his arm. A grin crossed his face. "Well, I would have tried."

"I'm just glad I didn't miss you," he said when his mother returned with two small boxes of food. "Mom, I forgot to tell you. The ship we've been assigned to is home-ported at Taos Station, so I should be able to make it back here in about a month for a couple of days."

"That's great, honey," she said, a broad smile on her face. "Toa, you have an open invitation as well."

"Why thank you, Mrs. Chandler. You don't know how much that means to me."

"It will be our pleasure. By the way, I packed some food for the two of you, including that apple pie you never got to try. This box is for you. The other one is for the girls."

"You're a saint, Mrs. Chandler," Toa said, relieving her of both boxes when Keira and Shara came out of the backroom. Each carried a backpack and hardhat with a headlamp. Keira also had a climbing rope.

"Mom, how about we see Thomas and Toa off at the station," Keira said, staring at her father. "That way, you can stay here and take care of dad," she continued, pleased to see the pained look on her father's face, her revenge for his Bunny comment complete.

"Thank you, honey. There are a few things I'd like to discuss with your father, in private," she replied with a no-nonsense look at her husband.

"Yes, dear," he said sweetly. He put his good arm around his wife and gave her an affectionate hug in hopes that it would change her mood. It didn't.

"Thanks again for everything, Mrs. Chandler, Mr. Chandler," Toa said on his way out the door, following Keira and Shara to the trolley stop.

"You're more than welcome," Karin replied, moving out onto the porch. Thomas and his father joined her. She hugged her son once more. "I wish you could stay a little longer."

"So do I, but... I'll call when I get settled."

"You better," she replied with a tear in her eye.

"Thomas, the trolley," Keira shouted as she stepped into the car.

"Be right there... Dad, be careful."

"I will," he said when without notice, the trolley started to move.

"Thomas!" Keira called out.

He kissed his mother then took off running after the moving trolley car. Halfway down the block, he jumped on board with a helping hand from Shara. "Thanks," he said, slightly winded. "I don't remember this thing being that fast."

"It's not," Keira said and laughed.

Toa looked at Thomas. "It runs in the family, doesn't it?"

"I'm afraid so," he replied, the trolley headed toward the spaceport.

Looking out past the housing toward the mountains, Toa saw the effects of man: countless piles of crushed rock and dirt brought up from below then unceremoniously dumped after the diamatron ore had been extracted. He knew that the chances were good the residual radiation had already poisoned the area. He also knew the realities of business. But the exploitation of the planet, the associated destruction of the land, did not seem right. Nor did the treatment of the miners as described by Thomas's mother. It strengthened his resolve to look into what was happening on Sorel.

"The news about the upgrades and the raise is great, isn't it," Keira said.

Thomas nodded. "Agreed. The Theta Corporation is pretty good about things like that."

Shara's head suddenly snapped around, her eyes narrowed. "Good? How can you say that?" she said, throwing caution to the wind. "Theta has a duty to provide a safe environment for the workers, and yet thirty-three miners have died this year alone. Nearly twice that number have been injured!"

"Nobody ever said mining wasn't dangerous," Thomas argued, a conditioned reflex from his days at the Academy.

"Come on, Thomas. The death rate here is over four times the average for all the Discovered Worlds' mining operations. Theta's just in there for the almighty profit. Damn the workers. They can always be replaced."

"That's not how Theta operates."

"Tell that to the families of the dead and injured miners. I'm sure they'll find comfort in your statement."

Thomas looked at Shara then slowly nodded. She turned away and stared off, leaving an awkward silence in the trolley car.

Keira looked at Toa, silently asking what had just happened. He shrugged, unsure. Ah... Isn't caving pretty tough, Keira?"

"No, not really. We're very careful and have all the right equipment."

"Then, ah... What about wild animals and such?"

"There are none on Sorel, except for an occasional drunken miner. Right, Shara?"

"What?" she asked, turning her attention back to her friend, having failed to hear the question. She was still hot from her 'discussion' with Thomas when the trolley came to a sudden stop in front of the spaceport terminal.

Saddened, Keira reached over and hugged her brother. "Be safe and make sure to send a com when you're settled," she said before pulling back. She brushed a small tear from her eye. "I'm as bad as mom."

"Yes, you are," Thomas replied, getting out, joining Toa, who was already standing beside the trolley.

"Keira, Shara, it was really nice to meet both of you," Toa said.

"And you," Keira replied, then noticed the package. "Wait, don't forget this." She handed it to him.

"Oh my God, thank you."

Thomas turned his attention to Shara. "I think I've been out of touch with reality a little too long. What you said makes a lot of sense. The next time we meet, I promise I'll listen and not say something stupid first."

A smile crossed Shara's face. "Next time?" she asked, impressed by his honesty and offer, but doubting their paths would ever cross again.

"Well, you never know," he said with a smile of his own when the trolley suddenly took off down the track toward the mountains as programmed.

"Remember, call mom," Keira called out.

"I will. Bye," Thomas said just before the vehicle disappeared behind the building.

Toa led the way to the terminal. "So, I thought your little exchange with Shara went well."

"Really?"

"No."

CHAPTER EIGHT

Surrounded by snow-capped mountains, Shara and Keira stopped at the mouth of the cave. Slightly winded from their hike up from the valley floor, they removed their backpacks and paused to take in the view.

"I forgot just how beautiful it is up here," Shara said, tracing the path of the great glacier down from above to a natural bowl some thirty meters below them. In the far distance lay the Sorel Colony.

Keira nodded. "It kind of makes you wonder about, you know, life."

"Life?" Shara asked with a smile.

"Yeah, like have you made the right choices or what would have happened if you had made others."

"But sometimes you just don't have a choice," Shara offered.

"I don't know… You could still choose to do nothing or the wrong thing. Then, of course, there's always the other person's point of view where you think you're right and they think you're wrong. What do you think?"

"I think it is good you don't come up here too often," Shara said with a laugh.

"You're probably right," Keira replied with a chuckle of her own while putting on a radiation suit from her backpack. It would provide protection against the cold of the cave and any stray diamatron ore deposits.

"How much time do you think we have underground?" Shara asked, fastening a climbing harness over her radiation suit.

"I'd say three hours max if we're to get back before dark," Keira replied, her suit and harness on. Her backpack followed.

Shara put on her pack then activated her headlamp. "Should be more than enough. Want to lead the way in?"

"Sure." Her headlamp on and showing the way, Keira entered the narrow cave. Forced to crouch under numerous low bridges, she led the way single file to the first of two caverns. "So, what did you think of Thomas?"

Shara ducked under an overhang. "His corporate attitude was a little hard to handle."

"Agreed, but he's really not that way, or at least he wasn't before he left. Even though it was an honor for him to be accepted to the Academy, he wasn't going to go."

"Why not?"

Keira entered the first cavern. Her headlamp showing ample headroom, she stood up and removed her backpack. "He didn't like the way Theta operated," she said and activated a light stick. It showed a narrow shaft some four meters from her near the cavern's west wall. "He thought they were too hung up on making money at the expense of the people and the environment."

Shara removed the climbing rope from her pack. She handed one end to Keira while keeping the other. "So why did he go?"

"Probably because of my dad," Keira replied on her way to the east wall. Finding one of many pitons they had left in place from earlier trips, she clipped a carabiner to it then passed her end of the rope through it. "He agreed with Thomas that Theta's policies need changing, but felt that it had to come from within. He convinced Thomas that the Academy would be the best chance to bring about that change."

Shara attached a carabiner to a piton near the shaft on the west wall. To that, she clipped the sling that was attached to the back of her harness to act as an anchor. She next threaded the rope through a belaying device attached to the front of her harness with a locking carabiner then tied a stopper knot at the end of it. "And how many more will die in the meantime?" she said softly to herself.

Keira clipped a carabiner to a piton in the ceiling of the cave just above the first shaft. Passing the rope through it, she secured the end to the front of her harness then sat on the edge of the shaft. "I'm sorry. I didn't hear you."

"I said, it sounds pretty idealistic to me."

Keira nodded. "I guess. Only the future will tell."

"True."

"Ready?"

Shara pulled in the slack. "Ready."

"Ok. Just so we're on the same page, it's about eight meters down to the ledge that runs seven meters to the second shaft. From there, it's about another seven meters down to the second cavern."

"Got it... Break a leg," Shara said with a grin.

Keira looked at her friend and slowly shook her head. "Ah, I think that's for the theatre."

"Be safe?"

"I like that much better."

Shara started to lower Keira down the shaft, controlling her rate of descent through the amount of friction on her belaying device.

"Half a meter to the ledge."

"Got it," Shara yelled back down, playing out the amount of rope to where she felt Keira's weight come off it.

"Okay, I'm at the ledge and, whoa," she said, slipping slightly on loose rock.

Shara instantly stopped the rope's advance. "Are you okay?"

"Yeah," Keira replied, carefully turning around so she could look down at the ledge. "The beginning part isn't as firm as I remember it being." Using only part of her weight, she tested the surrounding area for secure footing before committing. She found it firm. Attaching a carabiner to a piton a meter above the base of the shaft, she passed the rope through it to again prevent any interference with the rock. "Okay, I'm ready to head down the ledge."

"Alright," Shara said and once more fed her the rope, this time without the friction.

"I'm at the second shaft."

"Right."

Keira attached a carabiner to a piton in the ceiling above the second shaft and ran her rope through that. "Ready."

"Ready here as well," Shara replied and lowered Keira down once more, leveraging the friction caused by her belaying device.

"I'm in the second cavern," she shouted. "Give me the slack, and I'll set an anchor."

"You got it."

Able to stand up in the domed cavern, Keira switched roles with Shara after running the rope through a carabiner a meter above the base of the second shaft.

Above, keeping the original reaction point in the first cavern, Shara disconnected her anchor sling then attached a carabiner to a second piton over the first shaft. She next ran her end of the rope through it before tying it off to the front of her harness. "I'm all set here," she said, sitting on the edge of the shaft.

Her anchor set, the stopper knot tied after she had run her end of the rope through her belaying device. Keira pulled in the remaining slack. "Ready here as well."

"Okay, here I come."

Shara couldn't help but smile as Keira lowered her down the first shaft. It had been a couple of years since they had last come up to the cave. "I'm at the ledge."

"Okay. The tension is off."

"Right." Shara started to walk to the next shaft when what felt like a magnitude seven quake suddenly blasted the cave. In a heartbeat, the ledge disappeared out from underneath her. "Keira!"

"Shara!" Keira screamed, instantly feeling the strain of her friend's full weight on the rope. She belayed her fall when a second shockwave hit. More powerful than the first, Keira was thrown off her feet then drug down the cavern floor before her anchor caught and jerked her to an abrupt stop. Barely managing to work her way up into a sitting position on the violently pitching ground, she desperately struggled to regain full control of the rope. The friction of its advance burned through her gloved hands before she was finally able to create a full belay when the shaking finally stopped. "Shara!" Turning, fearing the worst, she saw a swaying shaft of light pointed up at an angle almost directly across from her! "Shara! Shara!"

"I'm... I'm alright," Shara moaned in a weakened voice that echoed in what appeared to be a single, larger cavern.

"Thank God," Keira said, still breathing hard. "The rope slipped, and I wasn't sure for how long."

Hanging from her harness, Shara's headlamp showed her to be below where the ledge was. Looking down, she found she was two meters off a debris-laden continuation of the second cavern floor Keira was standing on. "No complaints here. Can you lower me down?"

"Hold on," Keira said and eased her down. With Shara on the floor, her weight off the rope, she was finally able to get to her feet again. "If it's okay with you, I suggest we get out of here."

"I'm good with that," Shara replied, standing opposite her. "We should be able to," she started to say when another tremor suddenly blasted the cavern with sheer, unrelenting force. Both women screamed as the floor on which they were standing disappeared beneath them. Shara found herself in freefall before an abrupt stop knocked the wind out of her.

Twenty seconds later, all was still again.

Keira shook her head in an attempt to separate dream from reality in the dark. She went to move only to find herself suspended by the rope caught in the belay device on the front of her harness and from the anchor attached to the back of it. Shara! "Shara!" Her voice echoed and re-echoed. Turning her head, she finally saw the shaft of light from Shara's headlamp some ten meters below her. "Shara! Oh, God, Shara, please answer me. Shara!"

"Keira," she moaned.

"Shara, are you alright?"

"I'm not sure. I think so," Shara said, gasping, trying to regain her breath. Once again, righting herself, she fought against the pain that wracked her entire body. Looking down, she saw she was less than a meter above the point of one stalagmite and in between three others. "Okay, that about does it for me. I'm definitely ready to go now," she said, trying to ignore the terror that filled her.

Keira managed to retrieve a light stick from her pocket. She instantly regretted activating it. A third cavern floor was some fifteen meters below her. "How are we going to get out of here?" she shouted, starting to shake uncontrollably.

"I can climb up the rope then... Keira, do you hear something?"

"It sounds like water falling," she said, "but how is that possible?"

"I don't know..." Shara redirected her headlight up to the cave's mouth to find a torrent of water racing into the cavern, the volume increasing exponentially. In a matter of seconds, the entire entrance was engulfed, the sound deafening. Looking down, she saw the cavern filling at an incredible rate to the point where she suddenly found herself floating in warm water. The tension on the rope relieved, she got out of her harness and swam as best she could to Keira.

Suddenly dangling from just her anchor, Keira could only watch in horror as the water level surged upward. The anchor that had saved her life earlier would soon keep her from her next breath.

Seeing Keira's head go underwater, Shara dove down. Her headlight showing the way, she swam to the anchor and pulled on the sling. With enough slack in it, she released it from the carabiner then joined Keira in bolting for an air pocket that had formed just above them.

"Thanks," Keira said between gasps, the top of the dome only about a meter above the water level.

"Not a problem," Shara replied, trying to catch her breath as well. "What is a problem, however, is that we will soon suffocate."

Keira saw the rope floating next to her and grabbed it. "Is your harness still attached to the other end?"

"Yes. Why?"

"I'll pull in the slack so that it jams against the reaction point," she said while doing so. "We can then use the rope to pull ourselves to the first cavern."

"That's got to be forty meters or more to the outside!" Shara exclaimed.

"There should be another air pocket."

"Should?"

"Like you said, we can't stay here."

"Agreed."

"That's it," Keira said, the end of the rope stuck. "I'll tie off our end to the anchor to tension it."

"Good thinking, but not too tight."

"Right." Keira took a deep breath then went back underwater before returning to catch her breath once more. "We're good."

"Do you want me to lead?"

"Sure."

"Taking a deep breath, Shara went underwater. Upside down, pulling as hard and as fast as she could hand over hand, she used her headlamp to search for another air pocket above on the way. But what started out as optimism was quickly replaced by desperation. None were to be found. Her lungs about to burst, she continued forward, past the point of no return. With increased terror, she tried not to exhale. To inhale would mean her death, but…

The muffled sound of an aftershock was suddenly heard. Seconds later, the water level began to drop. On the surface, gasping for air, both women suddenly found themselves slowly spinning inside the cave.

"What's happening?" Keira shouted.

"We're in a whirlpool. Take a deep breath," Shara shouted just before she was sucked down into the giant vortex.

Keira wanted to scream but inhaled instead just before the water violently pulled her down then pushed her forward. In total darkness, moving at breakneck speed, she suddenly found herself in the blinding light outside the cave. Airborne, she crashed down into a warm water pool. Struggling to the surface, she spotted Shara lying face down, unconscious some three meters away. "Shara!" With renewed strength, Keira swam to her friend. Turning her over, she quickly brought her to the nearby shore. Aided by fear, not wanting to believe Shara was already dead, she started CPR. "Come on, Shara," she said between rescue breaths, the time seeming like an eternity. "Please."

Shara suddenly awoke with a start and began to cough before bringing up what looked like half the pool in the process. Keira quickly turned her on her side then collapsed next to her, totally exhausted. It was several seconds before either woman was able to speak.

"Keira... I... Thank you," Shara said weakly.

She looked at Shara and smiled. "I think we were both lucky."

"Agreed... Where are we?"

Keira sat up. "As near as I can tell, the pool is in the bowl at the end of the glacier, but instead of being filled with ice, it's filled with warm water like in the cave."

Shara's eyes suddenly went wide. She quickly scanned the trees above the shadow of the natural bowl. All were scorched. "Oh God, no! Please, Lord, no!" With a strength born from fear, she ran up the bank to the edge of the bowl facing the valley.

"What? What's wrong?" Keira asked, following, afraid.

From the rim, Shara turned back to Keira with tears in her eyes. "Oh God, I'm so sorry."

Confused, afraid, Keira moved to the top of the bowl and looked at a mushroom cloud over what used to be the Sorel Mining Colony.

"No!"

CHAPTER NINE

The spaceliner from Sorel Station was right on time. With traffic in the pattern minimal, the ship had proceeded directly to Taos Station in orbit above the planet with the same name. Her onboard computers, working in consort with those of the stations, the spaceliner was swiftly guided to Gate 10 of Concourse B. It was one of twelve concourses that extended out perpendicular from the station's large outer ring. It was also one that appeared to house half the population of the Discovered Worlds.

"I've never seen so many people," Toa said, following Thomas off the ship and into a sea of humanity. "I'm glad we checked our bags directly to the Centurion."

Thomas shook his head in dismay. They were literally surrounded by people, all of whom seemed desperate to get to where they were going as fast as they could. "Delta must have lowered their fares again."

"They're just cutting their own throats."

"And everyone else's, but the passengers don't seem to mind."

"Why should they?" Toa said. "Of course they have to fly on older equipment and receive less service, but when price is everything…"

"I guess. There's an information center." Thomas led the way through the crowd. Ten minutes later, he was in position to access the machine. "Computer, display the location of the Centurion."

A schematic of the station appeared in a simulated three-dimensional representation. Three decreasing diameter rings surrounded a central cylindrical core. All were connected by transfer tubes that looked like spokes. The outer ring was for the passengers. Flashing arrows showed the location of the Centurion and their own. "The Centurion is currently docked at Gate One, Concourse H," the computer announced.

Thomas moaned. "That's on the other side of the station."

"It gets worse," Toa said and pointed to a second screen for departures/arrivals for Concourse B. "There are ten ships all leaving within an hour of one another."

"Starting when?"

"Good evening, ladies and gentlemen," a uniformed woman manning the desk at gate B6 droned. "Delta Corporation's flight 796 for Matee Station will begin general boarding shortly. At this time, we would like to pre-board all those who require assistance or who are traveling with small children. Thank you."

"Any other questions?"

Thomas watched the waiting passengers abandoned their terminal seats and move into the already crowded concourse, each jockeying for position in line. "I love traveling, don't you?"

Toa slowly shook his head. "Hard not to."

Pendrac entered a bar on Sorel station to find Merrick in the back, alone, out of earshot. "Were any survivors reported?" he asked, joining him.

Merrick took a sip of his drink. "The news people don't believe so."

Pendrac nodded. "Good. I was able to identify the woman on the Pride as Cali Benton. Her brother was Richard Freet."

"Was?"

"He was part of Corbin Lockett's crew."

Merrick looked at Pendrac and shook his head. "Lockett? Really?"

"Really."

He sat back in his chair and laughed. "This just keeps getting better."

"Can we rest for a minute?" Keira asked, nearly spent from the climb up the mountain, the cave far behind them. She knew they had been lucky, very lucky. They had somehow managed to survive the cave that ironically saved them from what appeared to be an uncontained reaction. Still, the ordeal coupled with the walk up the mountain had her on the brink of exhaustion. Every joint in her body protested with each step.

Walking single file, nearly spent, Shara turned to see Keira some three meters behind her. She stopped and called back. "The sun will be down in the next half hour. If we're going to survive, we need to find the weather station while there's still light."

"How much further?" she asked, catching up.

"It should be in the valley just above us, but it's been a couple of years since I was last up here."

"God, I hope you're right," Keira said when a smattering of freezing rain swept over the area from an inbound storm. She wanted to stop, to give up, but... She had to survive. She had to find out what had ultimately caused the destruction of the colony.

Shara reached the valley rim first and desperately scanned the horizon. Before her lay nothing but rock and grass. "It should be here."

Joining her, Keira started to cry. She had reached her limit. Her family, her friends, the children, all gone. Oh, God, the children...

Shara took her in her arms. "Hold on, Keira, just a little longer."

"I don't think I can take anymore."

"I know..." Shara let her cry for a bit, knowing it was the best thing she could do. Then... "Hey, how are you ever going to get Thomas and me together if you give up now, huh?"

Keira managed a small laugh. Pulling back, she brushed away her tears with the back of her hand. "Well now, that's certainly true."

"So, are you ready to press on?"

"Yeah, I'm ready," Keira said with uncommon force.

"Oh, so you think you're tough enough?"

"Hell, yes. Where did you put that damn cabin you promised me? I paid good money for this vacation, and you're telling me I don't have a place to stay? What gives around here, huh?"

"Well, excuse me. I know I put it somewhere around here."

Both women began to laugh. Keira hugged Shara again in true appreciation of their friendship. "Thank you."

"We're going to make it out of here."

"Only if you find that damn cabin."

"Oh yeah, right..." Shara scanned the horizon to the west, squinting against the setting sun. "It's here somewhere. I know it is."

Keira looked to the east as a fast-moving storm cloud momentarily blocked the sun. Seeing nothing but a rock-strewn landscape, she started to look to the north when her peripheral vision caught a brief flash of reflected light. She quickly turned back to the east, but the sun had gone behind a cloud again. "Shara, I thought I saw something over there," she said, maintaining her focus, pointing to two monstrous rocks one hundred meters away. Everything else was bathed in indistinguishable shades of gray and shadow.

"I don't see anything."

Keira turned and looked at the sky behind her. The clouds were increasing, but moving quickly. They would have only a few seconds of exposure. "You should be able to see it... now."

"That's it!" Shara shouted, the sunlight reflecting off a satellite dish next to the weather station. "That's it!" she shouted, then joined Keira in jumping up and down in a dance for joy. They were safe. Thank God, they were safe.

Over an hour after they had docked, Thomas and Toa finally entered Concourse H. Exhausted, their spirits picked up when they rounded the corner and came face to face with their new home.

The Centurion was the first of a new galaxy-class communication ship. Equipped with the TX7 dual-drive system, the latest advancement from Theta Technologies, she was light years ahead of the competition. She could reach speeds equal to that of a fighter, but at half the operational cost of the conventional CS8's. Radically different from the older designs, the forward command module was connected to the rear engine pod via a 100-meter long truss. Mounted to it were two hundred plus quasi-geometrical appendages. Amidships was an especially impressive fifteen-meter diameter dish that was capable of receiving and transmitting to all parts of the Discovered Worlds.

"This could be fun," Toa said.

THE DISSENTERS

"I wonder if you'll say that in another year or so."

"Really... You ready?"

"Might as well. It's what we came here for," Thomas said on their way down the ramp to a security checkpoint.

They were greeted by a Theta Security guard's salute. "May I help you, sirs?"

"Lieutenants Chandler and Alesana reporting for duty," Thomas said, he and Toa returning the guard's salute.

"Welcome," he said and activated a security field behind both men.

Thomas looked at Toa with raised eyebrows. After all, the Centurion was a communications ship, wasn't she?

"Lieutenant Chandler, please stand where you see the footprints on the deck and open your eyes for a retinal scan."

Familiar with the routine, Thomas did as instructed. A second later, his picture appeared on a monitor located on the backside of the counter for viewing by the guard only. Listed were Thomas's name and physical characteristics. The guard closely compared the computer readout with the man standing before him before handing him a badge. "Please wear this chest high at all times while onboard the ship. It's both an ID badge and a communicator. Remove it when not on board and keep it hidden from public view. Is everything I have told you clear, sir?"

"The instructions, yes. The reason, no."

"Security, sir. The Centurion conducts several highly classified missions. Lieutenant Alesana."

Toa repeated the procedure. "Our briefing didn't mention anything about secret missions."

"It wasn't meant to, sir. We're on a need to know basis, so the people who briefed you earlier were not capable of conveying that information to you. You will receive the full briefing once you're on board. At no time will you be allowed to discuss any of the information you will receive when you are off the ship unless you are in a designated Centurion secure area within a Theta Corporation building or vessel. As both of you have top-secret, level-four clearances, all areas of the ship will be open to you, but at no time is any material to be removed from those areas without following the proper procedures posted at that location. Thank you, sir," the guard said and handed Toa his badge/communicator.

"Do either of you have any questions about what I have just told you, or are you in any way unwilling to comply with the rules or regulations as I have described them?"

"No," both men replied in unison.

The guard nodded then pushed a button on his control console. The Captain of the Centurion appeared on his monitor. "Yes?"

"Captain, Lieutenants Chandler, and Alesana have arrived, sir."

"Good. Send them to my cabin."

"Yes, sir." The screen going blank, the guard opened the outer door to the ship. "The Captain's cabin is down the corridor in front of you, fourth door on the port side. Welcome aboard," was followed by a rigid salute.

"Thank you," Toa said as both men returned the salute then boarded the ship. Down the corridor, he looked at Thomas. "What have we gotten ourselves into?"

"I'm not sure. Think it's too late to head back to Sorel?"

"Now there's a thought."

With a normal ship's complement of fifty, Thomas thought the command module appeared spacious from the outside but found the inside to be a different story. Actual crew space was restricted by banks and banks of electronics and systems, way more than seemed necessary to support the ship and its function as a communications vessel. There was also a large number of the crew on duty for such a late hour. Men and women of various ranks passed by them in obvious pursuit of their tasks. He couldn't help but wonder what kind of ship the Centurion really was.

Toa stopped in front of the Captain's cabin door and knocked before he and Thomas became rigid.

The door automatically opened to reveal the Captain seated at his desk, working. Thomas and Toa saluted. "At ease, gentlemen," he said, rising from his chair. He half-heartedly returned their salutes before offering his hand. "Dirk Bryant."

"Thomas Chandler."

"Wendel Alesana, but people call me Toa."

"Thomas, Toa, nice to meet you both," the Captain said and motioned to a table and chairs that were near the door. "Please, have a seat."

"Thank you, sir," Thomas replied.

"Beer?" the Captain asked on his way to the small refrigerator located on the other side of the door.

"Yes, sir," Thomas replied, somewhat shocked.

"Thank you, sir," Toa said, amazed by the offer.

The Captain took out three bottles and handed one to each to his new officers before sitting opposite them. "I think you'll find your tour of duty on the Centurion to be both challenging and enjoyable. She's the finest communications vessel in the fleet with all the latest equipment. We also have a damn fine crew, and if you two are as good as your files read, it should be even better."

"Thank you, sir," Thomas replied. "It will be interesting to see how much of what we've learned is actually applied."

"Then you couldn't have landed a better ship. However, I'm afraid you're going to find a lot of what they taught you at the Academy is outdated." The Captain took a pull on his beer while waiting for his statement to take hold. He was not disappointed to see the look of surprise on both men's faces. "The Centurion's technology is so advanced that our knowledge of this portion of the galaxy alone has grown at a rate mankind has never seen before. Just the new mineral deposits we've discovered alone will keep the Theta Corporation well ahead of the competition for decades to come."

"I thought the Centurion a communications ship," Toa said.

"She's registered as such and is more than capable of performing that mission, but, and this is classified, she is also the finest research vessel ever made. It took us nearly two full days to download all the information we discovered on our last voyage, one I might add was accomplished in a quarter of the time it would have taken a Star Class vessel."

"Captain, if I might ask, with all this need for security, one would think the ship would be capable of defending herself, and yet I saw no weapons before we boarded. Why is that?"

He slowly shook his head. "The thinking of the upper brass is that adding weapons systems to a communication's ship would make someone suspicious. So, based on their infinite wisdom, we don't have any."

"Isn't that risky, sir?"

"In my opinion, it's damn risky, but then I guess we're never really alone. Theta Tactical continually monitors us and can respond with a squad of fighters within a maximum of twenty minutes at the first sign of trouble."

Toa looked uneasy. "It could be all over by then if someone was serious."

"I said the same thing to the upper brass," the Captain replied with a shrug. "But orders are orders."

"Yes, sir," Thomas stated flatly.

The Captain finished his beer. "Another?"

Toa finished his. "I'm good, sir."

"I am too," Thomas said, putting his empty on the table. "It's been a long day."

"I bet," he said, getting up and collecting the empties. He put them in the nearby recycling. "I'll show you to your quarters."

"Thank you, sir," Thomas said.

The Captain led the way out the door and down the corridor. "After morning mess, I'll arrange for a security briefing, a ship's tour, and introductions to the crew and your duty stations."

"Thank you, sir," Toa said.

They entered a second corridor and stopped at the third door on the port side. Nameplates with 'Lt. Chandler' and 'Lt. Alesana' were located on the wall beside the door that automatically opened as they approached. "It's been programmed to respond to your com badges," the Captain explained. "Well, gentlemen, I'll see you at 06:00 hours in the mess and again, welcome aboard." He once more extended his hand.

Thomas shook it. "Thank you, Captain."

"Yes, thank you, sir," Toa said, doing the same.

"You're welcome," he replied before heading back down the corridor.

The two entered their new home for the next two years to find a bunk located against each sidewall separated by one meter of deck. An individual desk and computer terminal were at the head of each bunk. Behind the desks was a central viewscreen that also acted as a 'porthole.' Opposite, closets framed the cabin's door.

"I thought our Academy dorm room was small," Thomas said, shaking his head.

"Makes you wonder what the enlisted have."

"Stacked bunks with curtains, I would imagine… So, which bed do you want?" Thomas asked, flopping on the one on the right.

"Ah, the left?"

"Good choice. I'm too tired to move."

"Right…" Toa found the remote for the viewscreen and changed the porthole to the Theta Nightly News. "You should have slept on the flight in."

"If only I could," Thomas said, seeing Byron Walker at the anchor desk with a picture of the Sorel Colony over his left shoulder. Below was written 'Sorel Disaster'. "Toa, turn up the sound."

"… breaking news," Byron Walker was heard to say, "the Sorel Mining Colony was destroyed today by what is believed to be an uncontained reaction. At this time, it is also believed that there are no survivors. And now for the details…"

Thomas sat up, numb. It couldn't be. It had to be a mistake. They were just there, his mind screamed as his emotions surged. Pain, fear, disbelief, confusion… Oh God... My family!

Toa looked at Thomas in total shock.

"We now go to Michael Brannon at the Theta Corporation Headquarters for a live update. Michael."

"Thank you, Byron," the young investigative reporter said from a balcony that overlooked the stage of the Theta Corporation Headquarters – Alpha District's theater. Below was a sea of reporters and video crews. On stage, two large viewscreens were set up behind a podium with the Theta Corporate seal on it. "A statement is about to be made by T.A. Sandor, Vice President of Operations – Alpha District, concerning the tragedy that unofficially claimed the lives of the 1640 people on Sorel earlier today. Here now is Mr. Sandor."

The camera moved to show Sandor walk across the stage to the podium. The audience grew silent.

"I am saddened to report to you today," Sandor said, "that the diamatron power plant at the Sorel Mining Company experienced an uncontained reaction. Subsequent satellite scans from above the Sorel Colony lead us to believe that the colony has been completely destroyed and that all those on the planet at the time have perished."

Toa slowly shook his head. Men aren't supposed to cry; he remembered his father saying to him. He was seven, and his grandmother had just died. The circumstances were different now, but not the emotion.

Thomas remained motionless, transfixed.

Sandor continued. "Our deepest sympathy goes out to the surviving friends and family of the people of the Sorel Mining Colony as well as our pledge to apprehend and bring to justice those responsible for this act of infamy."

Thomas and Toa looked at one another, brows knit in obvious confusion.

Sandor again continued, the anger in his voice apparent. "We earlier received a recording from a group of dissenters. In it, they take credit for the destruction of the colony to demonstrate their opposition to the Theta Corporation. I offer it to you now for your judgment."

The stage lights dimmed. Cali appeared on the viewscreens seated at a desk. "Management of the Theta Corporation, we claim responsibility for the destruction of the Sorel Colony. Change your current policies and practices. If immediate action is not taken, more will die."

The screens went black, but not the message. It was burned into the minds of everyone watching. As the lights came up, so did the voices of those present, angry voices from people who understood a new malignancy had been born and needed to be removed at any cost. Their shouts rose as one, demanding justice.

Sandor stood silent, feeling the power of the moment. His hands finally up, he motioned for quiet. "The Theta Corporation condemns these dissenters for this murderous act and vows to commit whatever resources necessary to bring about their apprehension and conviction. Thank you," he said, then walked off stage, ignoring the shouted questions from the audience, knowing the value of speculation to be far greater.

Toa looked at Thomas, who remained motionless, staring blankly at the screen. "Is there anything I can do?"

"Ah... I'd just like to be alone for a while, if that's okay?" he said, his voice hollow.

"Sure, not a problem," Toa replied and left the cabin.

Thomas continued to stare blankly at the screen, the light of the changing pictures highlighting his rigid face.

"Once again, of the 1640 people on Sorel at the time, there are no known survivors."

CHAPTER TEN

"Heat? Power?" Keira said, entering the weather station.

"Geothermal," Shara explained, having serviced the station two years back as part of her job in Maintenance for the mine. "There are coils in the floor and a generator out back. There's also a hot springs bath and a flush toilet in the next room."

"Are you serious? Tell me you're not joking..." Keira opened the rear door and went weak. "There is a God!"

With a smile, Shara moved past a bank of instruments to a small kitchenette. "There are also enough provisions up here to last a month," she said and held up a bag of dehydrated food. "How about some stewed Brussels sprouts?"

"You really didn't have to go to all that trouble."

"It's nothing."

"I believe you."

"Are you hungry?"

"I'm starved," Keira replied, "but I'm more disgusting. If you don't mind, I'll take the first bath."

"Dinner will be ready when you're done."

"Thank you," she said when her face suddenly clouded over with concern. "Do you think they will be able to find us up here?"

"Easily. Search and Rescue should be here tomorrow," Shara said with an assuring nod. "The next day at the most. We'll show up on their infra-red scanner."

"That's great." She sat down on the side of one of four bunks and started to take off her radiation suit.

"After your bath, I think it best we continue to wear our radiation suits," Shara said. She regretted bringing Keira's attention back to the colony, but their survival was paramount.

They needed to find out what had happened to the power plant. Things just didn't add up.

"You're right," she replied, the grief suddenly like a weight around her neck. Life would never be the same. She needed to deal with what had happened and somehow put it behind her. Somehow, she said to herself as she lay down. "I just…"

Shara turned to find her friend fast asleep.

Transfixed, Thomas watched Byron Walker once more reappear at the Theta Corporation News anchor desk. This time, a picture of Corbin appeared over his left shoulder. "In breaking news, the manhunt for the Dissenters has shifted focus to Corbin Lockett as their alleged leader. Lockett, a former employee of the Sorel Mine, already has a warrant out for his arrest, where he is accused of negligence that killed eleven in a cave-in at the Sorel Mine. His suspected destruction of the Sorel Colony is being viewed as an act of revenge."

The Search and Rescue Captain and his Lieutenant checked the equipment they would need for their upcoming mission to Sorel. They were to be the first in, and although no one was believed to be alive, both men had been witness to some amazing acts of courage and outright luck in the past. If someone did survive, they would be ready.

"Splints?" the Captain asked, going down his checklist.

"Four sets," the Lieutenant replied.

"Freshwater?"

"Excuse me, Captain," the youngest of three men said, coming up from behind him. Of the other two, one was very tall. The other was large, powerfully built.

"I'm sorry, gentlemen, but this area is off-limits to civilian personnel."

"Captain, due to the sensitive nature of this mission, I have been put in charge. My men and I are to go with you."

A scowl crossed the Captain's face. "This is highly irregular, Mr.?"

"Merrick, Lucian Merrick, and yes, Captain, it is, but I assure you that your superiors are in full agreement."

He stared hard at his unwanted guest. "Then you won't mind if I ask them personally," he finally said, more a statement than a question.

"No, not at all," Merrick replied in a less-than-friendly tone of his own.

Keira looked out one of the cabin's two windows. The morning had dawned white. The mountain storm had hit just as they had reached the cabin. In its wake lay a twelve centimeter blanket of snow. Thank God they had found the station. It had probably saved their lives.

"Good morning," Shara said, coming out of the bathroom, a towel wrapped around her.

"Good morning," Keira replied. "How did you sleep?"

"I passed out right after you did then woke up in the middle of the night thinking about the colony. After that, I pretty much tossed and turned until about a half an hour ago."

"I know. Me too. There's breakfast on the table, if you can call it that. I already ate."

"Thank you."

"You are welcome." Keira suddenly groaned as she tried to walk. "Oh am I ever sore."

"I suggest a bath. Mine was glorious."

"Sound great," she said, moving slowly, stiffly toward the bathroom and the thought of the hot steamy water that awaited. "I just hope I can make it that far."

Headed for what was left of the Sorel Colony, the Search and Rescue Captain brought his ship in low over the ruins. He and his copilot were hardened veterans, but still… Most of the buildings had either been flattened or torn apart by the shockwave that had radiated out from the power plant. "Anything?"

The copilot shook his head. "The radiation levels are too high. The sensors won't work."

"Then let's check the surrounding area. Maybe someone was outside the blast zone."

"Agreed."

"Captain," Merrick said from behind them, sitting next to Pendrac and Yates, "there's a weather station in the mountains to the north. I suggest you start your search there."

The Captain looked back at Merrick, suspicious. "Why?"

"It's the only place still habitable on the planet," he said with a straight-face.

"I've got the station's coordinates, sir," the copilot announced. "They're on your screen."

The Captain turned back to the ship's controls. "Then let's go have a look." He banked the ship, and in seconds, they were hovering over the station. "Anything?"

"Possibly," the copilot replied. "There appears to be some IR movement inside. It's certainly worth checking out."

"Right. I'll put us down." The Captain looked for a place to land then selected an area in a lower part of the valley that was free of rocks. Seconds later, the ship was on the ground. Two minutes after that, the Captain and copilot were outside. Dressed in yellow environmental suits, they moved twenty meters away from the ship and directed their portable bio-scanners toward the weather station. "I'm getting two life signs," the copilot announced.

The Captain checked the readings on his unit. "Confirmed. Let's get," he started to say when he saw Merrick and his men coming forward. Dressed in orange environmental suits, they were carrying disrupter rifles. "What do you think you're doing?"

"What have you found, Captain?" Merrick asked.

"I want to know what the rifles are for."

"There may be Dissenters on the planet. Did you consider that possibility?"

"Yes, and I dismissed it as being totally illogical."

Merrick's eyes narrowed. "What have you found?"

"Two life-form readings, definitely human."

"Interesting. I'm going to have to ask you and your copilot to remain here while we go and investigate."

The Captain shook his head. "That's not going to happen."

"Why am I not surprised..." Merrick nodded to Pendrac and Yates, who aimed their weapons at the officers.

The Captain's eyes flew open wide. "Oh my God, you can't just," he said before two shots ripped through the silence of the morning, killing them. Blood stained the pristine whiteness.

"Let's go see who's up there," Merrick said with a grin, the thrill of the hunt beginning.

Keira couldn't remember the last time a bath had felt so good. The penetrating warmth of the hot springs soaked away her aches and pains, revitalizing her body. It also helped cleanse her mind. Or was it just that enough time had passed to ease the shock. It was hard to say. The loss of her parents was beyond measure, but to feel guilty for being alive when they were dead was wrong. There certainly wasn't anything she could have done to save them or the colony. And that she and Shara were still alive was only by the grace of God.

But what had caused the disaster? She and Shara had been part of a team that had just run a safety check on the power plant and given it a clean bill of health. So, what were the possibilities? The system could have failed, or someone could have caused the system to fail. If it was the latter, then was it an accident or deliberate? And if it was deliberate, were she and Shara somehow in harm's way?

An unexplained sound suddenly came from the main cabin. "Shara? Shara?" Receiving no answer, concerned, Keira got out of the tub and draped a towel around her. "Shara?" Opening the door, she saw a figure with its back to her clad in an orange environmental suit. She screamed.

"What, what?" Shara shouted as she quickly turned to defend herself.

"Shara, Oh God! I heard a noise and called your name, but you didn't answer. Then when I saw the suit and didn't know who you were. I... I'm sorry," she said gasping.

Shara fought back her adrenalin rush. "I heard a ship go over and thought I'd go investigate. With the suit's hood on, I didn't hear you."

"A ship?" Keira asked, eyebrows raised.

Shara nodded. "Yeah. Want to go see?"

"Is there another suit?"

"There is."

"Two minutes…"

Pendrac took a reading with the Captain's bio-scanner while he and Yates waited for Merrick. The two had gone ahead up a path that was both steep and winding while Merrick retrieved a medkit from the ship just in case something happened to one of them. "The readings seem to be moving this way," Pendrac said and pointed up the hill in front of them. "Fifty meters ahead."

Yates activated his rifle then used its scope to scan the rise.

Shara and Keira looked over the ridge to see a shuttle in the distance and two orange-clad Search and Rescue just below them.

"Hey, up here," Keira shouted. She began to wave her hands over her head when Shara rudely yanked her back down on the snow-covered ground. A split second later, a disrupter blast flashed overhead. Both women backpedaled from the edge, then got to their feet and started running back to the weather station. "Why did they fire on us?" Keira shouted, fearful.

"I don't know."

"You idiot," Pendrac yelled.

Yates glared back at the man. "I had a shot and took it."

Merrick rounded a large rock formation and rushed up with his pistol in hand. "I thought I heard a shot."

Pendrac stared at Yates. "Two people, looked like women, appeared on the ridge and numb-nuts here starts blasting them."

"I had a shot," Yates stated in anger, not backing down. He didn't like Pendrac, and, unlike others, he was not afraid to stand up to the man.

"Right," Pendrac taunted.

"That's enough," Merrick ordered, the need for team unity essential. "You say two women?"

Pendrac nodded. "Yes."

"Then this should be easy."

Scrambling back into the cabin, Keira locked the door while Shara secured the shutter for the window to the right of it.

"It could have been an accident," Keira said, the fear in her voice acute.

Shara removed a mining laser from a storage locker. "Maybe, but I don't feel like taking any chances." She handed the laser to Keira, then turned the locker over and pushed it under the left window for additional cover.

"Can the mining laser be used as a weapon?" Keira asked.

"It has the punch. I just don't know about the range."

Concealed from view by the massive rocks in front of the weather station, Merrick and Yates waited patiently while Pendrac scanned the area. "Still only two readings."

"Okay," Merrick said, "I want you two to go in peacefully. Remember, you're Search and Rescue. Have your rifles lowered, but ready to fire."

Both men nodded and moved out.

Shara carefully peered out the left window. "They're coming down the path, armed."

Behind Keira, one of the station's multitudinous instruments began to beep slowly. She quickly studied it. "According to the label, this machine monitors external energy levels. The value is up over twenty points above normal."

"Is it a malfunction?"

"I don't know. Activate your laser's power pack."

"Right."

Keira watched the value on the screen jumped another seven points. "That's it."

"That's what?"

"Their weapons are active. And from this reading, I'd say they're also set on kill!"

Pendrac and Yates stood directly in front of the weather station some ten meters from the door. "In the cabin, we're Search and Rescue," the taller of the two shouted.

"Then why did you fire on us?" Shara yelled back through the open window, staying hidden.

"It was an accident. My partner tripped and his rifle accidentally discharged."

"Why was his rifle even activated?"

"We were receiving two life form readings, but couldn't verify if they were human or some kind of predatory animal."

Keira slowly shook her head.

"I assure you, we're very much human," Shara said with a cute little laugh. "Hang on, I'll open the door."

Pendrac turned to Yates and grinned. "Once inside, kill them fast so we can get out of this God-forsaken place," he said in a low voice.

"You got it," he replied and led the way to the station.

Keira opened the door. "We're sure glad to see you," she said then stepped sideways to give Shara a clean shot.

An intense blue laser beam flashed through the air and struck Pendrac in the shoulder. The impact blasted him backward onto the snow-covered ground. Yates returned fire, but not before the station door was closed. More rounds followed from Merrick while Yates helped Pendrac back behind the rocks.

Inside, both women had taken cover behind the overturned locker.

Sitting down, Pendrac fought against the pain while Merrick unzipped the man's suit and exposed the wound.

Yates used a scanner from the medkit. "The blast missed anything vital and cauterized the wound in the process," he said, replacing the scanner with an injector containing a pain reliever.

"Do you think you can make it back to the ship?" Merrick asked, looking down at the wounded man as the narcotic started to take effect.

Pendrac's eyes narrowed. "I want the one who shot me."

"That's not what I asked."

Pendrac stared hard at Merrick then thought better of his next answer. He did not respect Merrick as a person, but he did respect the man's position. "Yes."

"Then do so. Yates and I can finish up here."

"Yes, sir. Hey Yates, make it slow and painful for the one who shot me."

A sadistic grin crossed Yates' face. "My pleasure."

Shara and Keira dove behind the metal locker for protection as a new round of incoming fire pierced the corrugated walls of the station.

"Why are they doing this?" Keira shouted in panic.

"I don't know," Shara said and checked the laser's power meter. The needle had just moved out of the red, the power source almost dead. "Keira, quick! Look for another energy pack."

"Where?"

"Try the other lockers."

Merrick surveyed the ground between the rocks and the weather station. "Yates, do you think you can work your way to that pillar in front of the door?"

He assessed the request. He'd be out in the open, totally exposed for four, maybe five seconds before reaching the cover of the pillar. And the women in the cabin were good. But he was quick and had surprise on his side. The challenge was stimulating. "I could, if"

"Don't worry. You'll be well taken care of," Merrick said in anticipation of the request.

"Then it will not be a problem."

"Good." Merrick lowered his mirrored goggles then put on his hood against the worsening weather. "Give me your rifle. I'll provide cover fire. Use your pistol to burn through the door lock. Enjoy yourself, but don't take too long."

"Damn it," Shara cursed, her shot missing the darting figure, allowing him to take cover near the door. She quickly bolted the left window's shutter then crawled toward Keira amidst the incoming disrupter fire from the rocks. "The power pack is dead," she shouted and joined Keira in her frantic search for another.

"I'll try the next locker," Keira yelled, fighting both fear and frustration.

Yates turned the intensity of his pistol to the maximum and aimed at the door lock. The blast continuous, he began to cut between the handle and the jamb.

"Shara!" Keira shouted and handed her an energy pack.

Without comment, she slammed it home, but a check of the meter told her it too was old, taking what seemed like forever to move from red to green. The lock almost compromised, she pivoted and aimed at the door. "Come on... come on…"

The door slammed open, and a shape appeared. A split second later, the meter crossed over into the green, and she fired.

Yates suddenly appeared from behind the jamb with a scorched piece of corrugation in one hand and his pistol in the other. "Drop the laser, now."

Shara did as ordered then looked at her potential executioner with a strange calm. "Why are you doing this?"

Yates chuckled as he threw the metal down. "For the good of the Theta Corporation, of course."

"What is that supposed to mean?" Keira shouted, almost hysterical.

"You know too much already."

"But we don't know anything!" she pleaded.

"Possibly, but now you never will. Stand over there," Yates commanded and motioned with his pistol for Keira to move to her left to separate the two women. He then turned to Shara. "I'm going to let you watch your friend die first. Then I'm going to take you apart joint by joint for what you did to my partner."

Shara started to come at Yates with her bare hands, but a warning shot at her feet stopped the advance. "Move again and your friend dies slowly. Understand?"

"I understand." Consumed by rage, she backed up toward the kitchen table.

Yates turned his attention to Keira. He saw her shaking uncontrollably and found it exciting. He had killed before and liked it, but never had he been this close to his victim. This was much more exhilarating. Keira's fear and his heightened sense of power were an intoxicating combination. That was it, wasn't it? The power…

Shara suddenly rushed at Yates, a kitchen knife in hand. He instinctively pivoted then fired. The blast struck her in the shoulder and sent her flying into the station wall, where she fell unconscious.

Keira raced for the mining laser when a second shot from Yates blasted it away. On the floor, she tried to scramble away from him, but there was nowhere to go. Yates came at her like an animal moving in for the kill. Their eyes met. Hers were filled with tears. His were cold and penetrating with a sick smile to them. She couldn't move. She could only watch in horror as he aimed his pistol at her head. Before her stood the face of an executioner, set in an unholy grin. She saw the strangely beautiful light, heard the evil sound it made and felt... Nothing!

Her mind raced. Had her attacker missed on purpose? Was he playing some kind of sick, perverted game to torture her further? Or was she dead, and her brain was trying to convince her body that it didn't really happen?

But no, something was very wrong... with her attacker! His face contorted in confusion and pain, he stumbled forward, unable to break his fall. He hit the floor unchecked, triggering his weapon. The blast ripped through his heart, killing him instantly.

I'm free, she told herself then she saw another figure standing in the doorway. Dressed in a hooded orange environmental suit and mirrored goggles, a disrupter was in his hand.

"You there."

She tried to scream but couldn't. A thousand different questions consumed her, questions she knew would never be answered, her death imminent once more.

"Keira?" the man called out, his voice reflecting his shock and surprise. "Keira?" The man ripped off his hood and goggles on his way to her. He reached down to help her up.

"Corbin? Oh God Corbin, is it really you?" She hugged him with all her heart. She could barely believe it was true.

"We thought there might be survivors, but I never dreamed that it would be you."

Keira suddenly pulled back. "Shara's alive too, but she's been shot!" she said on her way to Corbin's daughter. "I need the medkit on the far wall."

"Oh my God!" Corbin ran for the kit while Keira carefully exposed his daughter's wound. He handed her the kit, still in shock. When he had learned of the destruction of the Sorel Colony, he could not accept Shara's death. Logic suggested otherwise, but a father's love defied logic. All onboard the Copernicus had agreed that they needed to journey to Sorel despite the danger. Now...

Keira studied a bio-scanner. "She's lost a lot of blood already."

Tears filled Corbin's eyes as he knelt next to his daughter. "What can I do?"

Keira activated the kit's med-light. "Point this directly at the wound about twenty centimeters above it," she said, handing over the instrument before reaching back into the kit for an injection of blood multiplier.

"Understood..." Within seconds, the instrument's healing rays miraculously cleaned the wound and stopped the bleeding.

Keira gave Shara an injection then checked the scanner. "We need to," she started to say then suddenly gasped on seeing two others enter the cabin.

Corbin put his hand on her trembling shoulder. "It's alright. They're with me... Roberts, its Shara. She's been shot!"

"Shara? Really? My God!" Roberts quickly scanned Shara with a probe of his own then turned to Keira. "You did a great job, probably saved her life."

"Thank you," she replied with a smile. It felt good to smile again.

Roberts turned to Corbin. "Shara is stable, but we need to get her back to the ship as fast as possible."

"Right. Marsh, the stretcher," Corbin said and moved to the far wall where it hung. "What about her attacker?"

"Dead," Roberts replied.

"That's too bad," Corbin said. "It would have been nice to find out who sent him."

Roberts and Marsh carefully loaded Shara onto the stretcher under Keira's watchful eye. Corbin covered her with a blanket from one of the bunks before all headed outside.

"Corbin," Hawkins called out, he and his team coming up from the direction of the Search and Rescue ship.

Corbin stopped while the others headed to the Copernicus' shuttle. "What did you find?"

"The Search and Rescue pilot and copilot are dead. Shot. Two men took off in their ship before we could catch them."

"My God," Corbin said, appalled by it all. And mankind thought itself civilized. "Let's get out of here while we still can."

CHAPTER ELEVEN

Finding sleep difficult, Toa got up early and headed to the Centurion's mess for a cup of coffee. Alone, he sat at one of the tables. Pain, anger, and frustration consumed him. It was the reason for the attack that fueled his rage. Innocent people had been murdered by a group of fanatics whose sole intent was to gain attention for some futile cause only they cared about. But he knew that power was like a narcotic, the more obtained, the more required. And after a while, they began to believe their own lies and their solutions, even though they could only result in the death of innocent people and then ultimately their own.

Toa saw the mess door open, and Thomas enter. He stared at his friend, not sure what to do or say.

"It's okay. I'm alright," Thomas said. "Is that coffee?"

"Yeah. Want some?"

"Please."

Toa got up and headed to the coffee pot when the mess door opened again, and the Captain entered. Both Thomas and Toa came to attention.

"Relax... We're a little less formal around here, remember?"

Toa smiled. "Sorry, Captain. Force of habit."

"I know... Thomas, I wanted to tell you how sorry I am to hear about what happened on Sorel."

"Thank you, Captain."

"If you like, you can go ashore now and arrange for transportation to Alpha District Headquarters on your own, or we can drop you off there after a repair job that has just come up in the Theta Shipping Lane."

"I'll stay on board, sir. The work will be good for me."

"Good. Then how about you two follow me. I'll give you that tour I talked about last night."

"Yes, sir," both replied.

Keira sat with her eyes shut, her head back up against a Copernicus bulkhead. The hour she and Corbin had spent waiting outside the sickbay was unbearable. The fate of Shara was still unknown.

Corbin stared absently at the deck. He felt the same as Keira did, but his own time in the hospital had taught him all too well the futility of letting one's emotions take control. He had learned to avoid it by consciously focusing his thoughts on a given issue, forcing himself to examine it from all sides and not accept the conclusions so easily offered up by others. And so it had been with the destruction of Sorel Colony. His questioning of Keira about everything that had happened, including the attack at the weather station, had been demanding. He had asked her to recall even the minutest of details, going over it all point by point. And the pieces of the puzzle started to fall into place. He rubbed his eyes. He felt old, tired.

"Corbin," the Doctor said, seeming to appear out of nowhere.

Both he and Keira were instantly alert, focused.

"Shara will be just fine," he said with a smile, pleased to see the relief come over the two of them. Her shoulder will be a little sore for a few days, but there's no permanent damage. By the way, Keira, is it?"

"Yes, sir."

"You did an excellent job down on the planet. You probably saved Shara's life."

Keira couldn't hold back her emotions any longer. Her tears came freely, joyfully. "Thank you."

Corbin placed a fatherly arm around her shoulders. "When will we be able to see Shara?"

"How about now?" his daughter said, moving past the Doctor. Her arm in a sling, she carefully kissed her father. "I knew you would come."

"I didn't want to believe you were dead."

"I'm glad you didn't," she said, then clumsily hugged Keira next.

"I'm so glad you're alive," she mumbled through her tears.

"I told you we'd make it, didn't I?"

"Yeah, but next time, I think I might ask for a few more details," Keira said with a slight laugh.

"I'm not sure why, but…" Shara said with a smile before turning back to her father. "Any idea who attacked us, and why?"

"We believe they were from the Theta Corporation. As to why, the only thing we can come up with is that they thought you might be potential witnesses to what we suspect was their sabotage of the power plant. As such, you needed to be eliminated."

"Theta?"

"Our message to them was altered to make it appear that we claimed responsibility for the sabotage of the colony's power plant."

"So, murder by neglect wasn't good enough. Now it's mass murder for profit. Damn Theta. They have to be stopped."

Corbin nodded. "We earlier induced a malfunction in one of the shipping lane's navigation buoys thinking Theta will send a communications ship to make the repairs. When she arrives, we plan to commandeer the ship then use her dish to broadcast live to the worlds our innocence and Theta's guilt."

Shara nodded. "At this point, there really is no other way to clear our names."

"That's the conclusion we reached as well," Corbin said then turned to Keira. "But first, we need to get you to someplace safe."

Keira defiantly shook her head. "Yesterday, Theta killed my parents and all the others who lived in the colony. Today, they again tried to kill Shara and me... I want to do whatever I can to help you and your people bring the guilty to justice."

Corbin smiled. "Then welcome to the Dissenters."

"Who?" Shara asked.

"That's what Sandor called us."

"Interesting," Shara said when Chu's voice came over the intercom. "Corbin?"

He moved to a wall unit. "Go ahead, Chu."

"Long-range scanners at the entrance to the shipping lane have just picked up an approaching communications ship."

"Initiate phase two."

"Roger."

"Initiate phase two. I repeat, initiate phase two," echoed over the ship-wide com system. The announcement was followed by a pulsing alarm.

Corbin looked at Shara. He was concerned about her health but knew they needed her skills. "Can you handle your ship?"

"Yes," she replied without hesitation.

"Alright... Keira, do you know how to fire a disrupter?"

She nodded. "My father taught me. I shoot expert."

"Then go with Shara," he said then looked back at his daughter. "Roberts will fill you in on the mission once you're on board."

"Right." She kissed him before running off with Keira to the cargo bay.

Manning the helm of the Centurion, Thomas found the ship to be far superior to anything he had ever seen or even read about. She really was the embodiment of the forefront of technology. "Captain, I'm reading a black hole at 123-045-678."

"Any previous record, Mr. Chandler?"

"Negative, sir."

"Then, you have the privilege of recording it, in your spare time, of course."

"Thank you, sir."

Sitting next to Thomas at the controller's station, Toa couldn't help but smile. He and Thomas had expected to be phased in, but it was obvious that the Captain had other ideas. He did not mind in the least.

Thomas did his best to ignore Toa. "Passing the outer marker, sir. Heading for the alpha entrance."

"Mr. Alesana, slow to one-tenth."

"Slowing to one-tenth, sir." Toa skillfully executed the maneuver finding the controls familiar and yet different at the same time. The extra hours both he and Thomas had spent in the simulators were turning out to be well worth it.

"Mr. Chandler, what's our ETA to Buoy 127?"
"Twelve minutes, ten seconds, sir."
"Engineering, have your repair crew standing by."
"Yes, sir."

Corbin took his seat on the flight deck of the Copernicus. Just off the port bow was Buoy 127. Its transmitting ring was at less than half intensity. "Status?"

"Everything is set," Chu said. "The windships are concealed in the asteroid field, and the cargo doors are closed. We are drifting into the field, though. Do you want me to compensate?"

"Have we been spotted yet?"

"No."

"Alright, do so, but make it quick."

Chu powered up the ship's engines while Corbin activated the communication system. "Lindsey, do you read?"

"Loud and clear," she replied, once again in her spacesuit. She stood next to a similarly attired Hawkins on an asteroid that was recessed from the perimeter asteroids. With a clear shot into the section of the shipping lane in front of them, they stood next to an antique missile launcher. Long since bypassed by modern technology, the system contained four heat-seeking solid fuel/oxidizer rockets. Despite their age, they were still an effective kinetic energy weapon if used correctly. She and Hawkins were going to make sure they were.

"Standby to launch on my command."

"Roger that."

Corbin turned down the intensity of their communications transmitter. "Chu, activate the emergency rescue beacon."

"Captain, I'm showing a ship just off Buoy 127," Toa said. "She's registered as the Copernicus, a D-class freighter."

"I'm surprised a ship that old is still space-worthy."

"Captain, I've got an emergency beacon and an audio-only distress call coming in from the freighter," the Communications Officer reported.

"On speaker, Mrs. Pham."

"Yes, sir."

"Emergency, emergency, this is the freighter Copernicus," Corbin was heard to say, his voice barely audible, the transmission filled with static. "We have experienced engine failure after trying to avoid a collision with an asteroid near Buoy 127. Life support is failing. Emergency, emergency."

"Ship to ship, Mrs. Pham."

"Go ahead, Captain."

"Copernicus, this is Theta Corporation's communication ship Centurion, do you read?" came in over the com system.

Chu looked at Corbin. "Shall I acknowledge?"

"No. We need to make the Centurion think we're completely helpless. Cut all power except for communications to Lindsey and Hawkins."

"Is that wise? We're drifting back toward the asteroid field again."

Corbin grinned. "I'll let you know."

"No response from the Copernicus, Captain."

"Keep trying, Ms. Pham."

"Yes, sir."

"Engineering, sensor readings."

"I show multiple life forms, and the ship's power levels are below the minimum, sir."

"How much time do they have?"

"I'd say fifteen minutes max, sir."

"Any sign of structural damage?"

"Negative, sir, but with a ship of that age, several things could certainly have gone wrong."

"Understood," the Captain replied as the Copernicus appeared ahead, drifting in space. He rubbed his chin. "I don't like this... Mr. Alesana, any other traffic in the area?"

"Negative, Captain."

"Damn..." His obligation was to his own ship, to protect her secrets. He should defer the rescue to the Tactical Squad, but by the time they got there, those on board the Copernicus would most likely be dead. "Mrs. Pham, notify the Tactical Squad of our situation. Mr. Chandler, bring us alongside the Copernicus nice and slow," the Captain said, then activated the ship's internal communications from his command chair. "Prepare for rescue operations. I repeat, prepare for rescue operations."

"Now, Corbin?" Chu asked, beads of sweat forming on his forehead. He was awed by the enormous size of the ship approaching.

"No, let's bring her in a little closer."

"She's nearly on top of us now!"

"We've got to give Lindsey a clean shot," he said with a blinding searchlight suddenly shot out from the Centurion.

"Play dead!"

The light moved across the bow, illuminating the bridge through its windows. As it passed, Corbin carefully opened one eye to check the Centurion's position.

"Captain, nothing visible on the port side."

"Alright, Mr. Chandler, move us further out in the channel."

"Yes, sir." Thomas entered the appropriate commands and unknowingly exposed the stern of the Centurion's engine pod to the field where Lindsey and Hawkins lay waiting.

"Lindsey, fire!"

Two of the four missiles ignited, shooting flames out of their exhaust nozzles. Racing off the launcher, they headed straight to the Centurion's engines.

Onboard the Centurion, a collision alarm started to sound the warning, but the missiles were too quick, and the distance was too short. They slammed into the ship's engines before anyone could react. Bridge lights flickered then went out. Backup lighting went active. The viewscreen stayed dark.

"What the!" the Captain said.

Toa quickly scanned his board. "Captain, two missiles from the field have struck the engine pod."

"Engineering, status?"

"The main engines are down, sir. We're on emergency power."

"Ms. Pham, notify the Tactical Squad that we are under attack and activate the emergency beacon. Engineering, get the viewscreen back online," he ordered when another alarm sounded.

"Captain, I show two windships headed this way from the asteroid field. They are armed with aft-mounted cannon," Toa reported.

"For want of a weapon," the Captain said and activated the com system. "Stand by to repel boarders. This is not a drill. I repeat this is not a drill."

The windships headed straight for the aft opening in the Centurion command module for her landing bay. They folded their sails like a fan into the mast that then hinged back over the cockpit. The mast ended just short of and below the ion cannon giving each weapon 360 degrees of range.

Shara looked at her crew. She could see the anxiety on their faces. They thought they knew what to expect on the Pride and were still surprised. The Centurion was different. Those who had recently been to Taos Station had reported her guarded while there. She was also rumored to have members of the Tactical Squad as part of her crew. It would not be easy. "Control, status on the entrance?"

"Standard field, but on emergency power, they can't keep us out."

"Good." She scanned the inside of the landing bay through the windship's forward windows. It had a balcony in the back with stairs to the port side. To starboard was an adjacent hanger with a supply barge. It was equipped with a small aft-mounted disrupter cannon and was manned by two Tactical Squad soldiers. "Everyone, mirrored goggles on now," she ordered, then winced as she took off her sling to put on her goggles as well. "Weapons, take out the barge's disrupter as we land," she said, then activated the com system. "Roberts, we'll take the starboard side."

"Copy that." He looked back at his team. Silence filled the ship. All knew what they now must do for their own survival. "Activate disrupters. Set on stun. And make sure your mirrored goggles are on."

The Captain led his armed bridge crew onto the balcony of the Centurion's landing bay, where they were quickly joined by the Head of Security in full battle dress. "My people and the crew are positioned on the lower deck as well as can be expected, Captain."

"Where do you want us, Lieutenant?"

"Right here on the balcony would be best, sir. It will give you an overall view of the situation and act as our fallback position if need be."

"Nothing we can do with the shields, then?"

"Not on emergency power, sir. We're lucky just to maintain the atmosphere in the bay as is."

"Okay. So how bad is it?"

"Well, sir, our only real hope is to stall the attackers long enough to give the fighters time enough to get here."

"Right," the Captain said dryly.

"You never know, sir, these situations will surprise you. I don't think anyone likes what those bastards have done to the ship."

"True. Better get back to your position."

"Yes, sir," the Lieutenant replied. Lowering his mirrored visor, he ran off.

The Captain activated his wrist communicator. "Captain to crew, keep them pinned down inside their ships. The fighters are on the way."

Roberts' ship executed a controlled crash onto the landing bay's deck while his ion cannon blasted away on its stun setting.

Shara's ship followed seconds later. Her initial ion cannon blast slammed into the barge, sending the crew flying backward, stunned while ineffective disrupter fire came from throughout the bay.

Thomas looked down on the windship below him. Toa was next to him. "We've got to take out their cannons."

Toa glanced over the rail then ducked just before an ion cannon blast roared overhead. He looked down again then pulled back. "Thomas, there's something on the deck of the windship."

"I can't see it from here."

"Here, switch places with me."

Thomas slid over then ducked just before another ion cannon blast from the portside ship slammed into the Captain's position. He rose up and quickly glanced below. "Close your eyes and cover them now!"

Two Dissenter mortars fired their charges simultaneously. The bay was suddenly filled with a brilliant white light. The Centurion's technicians screamed, temporarily blinded. All instinctively dropped their weapons to cover their eyes with their hands.

"Go, go, go!" Shara shouted. Her team rushed from the ship and joined Roberts' crew in taking up positions behind support beams and cargo containers throughout the landing bay. As the Centurion technicians and crew stumbled from their places of concealment, they were quickly stunned. But that was not the same story for the six remaining members of the Tactical Squad. Protected by their mirrored visors, they fought on with new intensity.

Thomas looked over to see the Captain and the rest of the bridge crew unconscious. It was up to them… "Toa, we need to get to the barge's disrupter cannon."

"That should be fun."

"Really…" Thomas led the way down the stairs two at a time. At the bottom, each man rolled into a firing position. Two of the attackers in front of them fell stunned before a third man was struck in the chest. His unconscious body flew backward, opening a path to the barge. Taking it, Thomas and Toa raced through a hail of Dissenter fire. Somehow unscathed, Thomas dove behind the steering controls while Toa made it safely behind the disrupter cannon's shield.

"A little forward, Thomas and I can get a clean shot at both windships."

"Alright," he said and brought the barge to life.

Shara looked out from behind the cover of a storage container to see the barge bearing down on her and two other members of her team. She quickly activated her com system. "Control, the barge, the barge!"

Toa set up to target Shara's ship first then froze on seeing Keira standing in the cockpit, waving her arms. "Toa!"

"Targeting the barge," came from inside Shara's ship.

"No, wait," Keira shouted before the ion cannon blast struck the barge point-blank, launching Thomas and Toa out of the vehicle. Both men's bodies slammed into the bulkhead behind them then fell stunned, unconscious.

"Hold your fire," Shara shouted, the last of the Centurion crew including the Tactical Squad members down. "Search for wounded and weapons. Bind everyone's hands."

Keira raced to her brother and Toa with the Doctor and Medic in tow. The Doctor scanned Thomas. "He'll have a headache when he wakes up, but other than that, he's fine."

Keira exhaled. "Thank God."

"Doc, I've got a bleeder over here," the Medic shouted, a jagged piece of metal lodged in Toa's leg.

He moved quickly to his new patient, amazed at the amount of blood on the deck. Pulling a med-light from his kit, he activated it before removing the implanted metal. "I need some plasma."

"I'll get it," Marsh said and ran back to the windship.

The Medic activated his scanner. "His readings are still too low. There must be another bleeder."

"Check the other leg," the Doctor ordered.

The Medic cut away the fabric of Toa's pants to expose the broken end of his femur sticking out through the skin. "Damn. Doc, we better change places."

"Right." He handed over the med-light to the Medic then turned to Keira. "I need your help."

"Anything."

"Sit at his head and grab him under the arms. I'm going to set the leg."

Without hesitation, she quickly moved into position and dug her heels in. "Ready."

The Doctor grabbed Toa's knee then pulled. The bone slid back inside with a slight sucking sound. Moving forward, he probed the wound with his fingers. "Okay, that should be good enough for right now." He turned to the Medic. "Shine the light over here."

"Right."

Cutting off the sleeve of Toa's uniform, the Doctor gave Toa a shot then inserted a catheter in his arm in preparation for the plasma.

Marsh ran forward with two bags. "Here you go, Doc."

"Tape one to the bulkhead about a meter off the deck."

"Right."

The Doc connected the bag's tube to the catheter and started the flow of plasma. "How's he doing?"

The Medic checked the scanner. "Everything looks good."

"He was lucky," the Doctor said with an exhale. His adrenalin rush subsiding, it was replaced by a sudden wave of tiredness. "A couple of minutes more and he would have bled out."

Keira leaned against the bulkhead, her own energy reverses spent. "Thank you."

"Thank you, Keira. You know, you should consider going into medicine."

"Sounds good, if we ever get out of this mess…"

The Tactical Squad Lieutenant lay face down on the deck, unnoticed between two cargo containers. Pretending to be stunned, he cautiously concealed his disrupter. Only two meters away from him was the woman who appeared to be in charge. As soon as he had a shot, he would take her out.

"Shara," Roberts called out, coming toward her. "Corbin and the com-team are inbound in the shuttle."

"Good. Get the Centurion crew into the escape pods as fast as possible. We probably don't have much time."

"Right," he said running off.

The Lieutenant remained motionless. Were they talking about the leader of the Dissenters? Corbin Lockett's death would make him famous, jump-start his career. He weighed the odds. The wait was worth it. He covertly advanced the power settings on his weapon to kill.

Coming forward, Shara was startled to see Thomas and Toa, wondering what the odds were. "My God, are they alright?"

"Toa's stable for now, but needs hospitalization," Keira replied, having left him to be with her brother. "Thomas was just knocked unconscious. He's starting to come around."

"Keira, Shara, are you? Am I?" Thomas stuttered as he worked his way out of the fog in his head.

"You're alive, Thomas," Shara replied with a pleasant laugh.

"I don't understand... The news said there were no survivors."

Keira helped Thomas to sit up. "We were in the cave when the colony was destroyed. It," she said, stopping in mid-sentence, seeing a look of hate cross Thomas's face. Turning, she saw Corbin approaching.

"You murderer!" Thomas shouted. He tried to get to his feet and attack Corbin but was easily restrained by his sister in his weakened state.

"No, he's not," Keira said.

"He destroyed Sorel!"

"No, he didn't, Thomas. Theta did."

"What?" he asked with a shade of doubt in his voice.

"You saw what they wanted you to see," Corbin said.

Thomas looked at Keira, then Corbin confused. "And why would I believe anything you have to say?"

"Because I'm telling the truth. Ask your sister and my daughter."

"Who?"

Shara smiled. "Thomas, Corbin is my father."

"What?"

"Think about it, Thomas," Keira said. "Do you really think Corbin would murder his own daughter?"

"And this morning," Shara added, "we were nearly killed by men posing as Search and Rescue. Theta is the only one powerful enough to pull off something like that."

"But why? Why would Theta destroy Sorel then try to kill you?"

"The mine was running out of ore," Corbin began to explain.

Opening one eye, the Lieutenant saw Corbin. He would only get one shot. It had to count.

"So why didn't they just shut the mine down?" Thomas asked.

"It was better to work it at a loss rather than pay the miners the contract-end bonus and relocation if they were laid off. Later, by destroying Sorel, all costs were eliminated."

"And they probably collected on the insurance, too," Thomas said, lost in thought.

Corbin nodded. "A sizeable amount, I would imagine."

"So, why did you attack us?"

"With your ship, we can broadcast live the truth about Sorel without the Theta Corporation altering the message as they did with our first one."

"This is all so hard to believe, and yet it isn't," Thomas said, shaking his head. He stared absently forward, trying to find a flaw in the logic Corbin had presented but was unable to do so. "I always," started to say when he saw the Lieutenant rise up with his pistol aimed at Corbin's back. "No!"

CHAPTER TWELVE

Marsh desperately dove for the Lieutenant's disrupter. His muscular body slammed into the man's arm, deflecting the shot. But the officer was well trained and used Marsh's momentum to throw him aside before re-aiming.

"Corbin!" Keira shouted while drawing her own disrupter.

The leader of the Dissenters turned and looked into the eyes of his executioner. Those on Sorel hadn't had the chance to face their enemy. At least he would, he thought when his chest suddenly exploded with searing pain.

Keira fired a split second later, stunning the Lieutenant.

"Doctor!" Shara screamed on her way to her father. Down on her knees, she applied direct pressure to the wound as best she could, her eyes filled with tears.

Corbin screamed in agony, his face distorted by excruciating pain as he writhed on the cold hard deck. As blood flowed freely over Shara's hands from the burning wound, he struggled just to get his next breath before forcing himself to focus on her face. "Shara, I'm so sorry," he said, seeing her for what he knew would be the last time. "I love you," he breathed before the pain again wracked his body once more.

"I love you so much," she whispered.

Corbin screamed again as his body contorted in a final death throw. Then it went suddenly limp, the life passing from it.

"Doctor!" Shara screamed.

The Doctor racing up, Shara sat back while he scanned her father's body. Looking back at her, he slowly shook his head. "I'm sorry, Shara."

"No," she moaned, taking her father's hand in hers.

"Doctor! Over here!" Keira yelled, ripping away Toa's shirt, exposing a disrupter blast to the man's chest.

He quickly moved from Corbin to Toa's side with his scanner. "Keira, shine the med-light on the wound."

Finally able to stand, Thomas headed over to Toa as the Doctor gave him an injection. "Will he make it?"

"I don't know yet."

The Dissenters present gathered around Corbin. Each struggled to hold back their own tears when a pulsating alarm from Roberts' windship suddenly filled the bay.

"Shara!" Roberts called out as he ran to her. "Long-range scanners have picked up four Tactical Squad fighters headed this way. Oh my God!" he said, seeing Corbin for the first time.

She looked up at him with forced calm. "Is there time to get the windships back onboard the Copernicus?"

Roberts tore his focus away from Corbin. "No. They'll be here in about ten minutes. We can only load the shuttle."

"Then have it take our wounded back to the ship," she ordered, knowing it was now up to her to save the Dissenters. "Get everyone else into the windships as fast as possible. We'll take them into the asteroid field."

"And your father?"

"Will there be enough room for him in the shuttle?"

"Yes."

"Then take him there as well."

"Right."

She kissed her father lightly on his forehead before releasing him. Standing, numb, she watched while others carried his body away before becoming aware of the activity around Toa. She headed to Thomas. "What happened?

"The Lieutenant's first shot."

"Will he be alright?"

The Doctor looked up at her as Toa regained consciousness. "Fortunately, the shot missed all the vital organs. He's stable now, but can't be moved without anti-gravs, and ours are on the Copernicus."

"Thomas, save Keira and Shara," Toa said in a weakened voice.

"Shara, we've got to go now!" Roberts yelled from the deck of his windship.

"Alright," she shouted back. "Doc, you and the medic get on the shuttle. Thomas?"

"Help them, Thomas," Toa said. "There's plenty of help for me on the way."

He knew Toa was right. He also knew he needed to do everything he could to save the people he would have killed only minutes earlier. "Alright, but if you die on me…"

"Then I'll come back and haunt you," Toa said with a smile before passing out again.

"Shara, now!"

Thomas turned to her. "How many fighters are on their way?"

"Four."

"How far out are they?"

"About seven minutes... Thomas, we can't outrun them, and we certainly can't outgun them,"

"No, but we might be able to beat them with their own arrogance."

"Interesting… Do you have a plan?" Shara asked, willing to put her trust in Thomas.

"Shara!" Roberts shouted again.

"I think so. How about I go to the other windship and fill you in as soon as I see a chart of the area."

She nodded. "Go with Roberts. He's the one yelling."

"Right."

She kissed him on the cheek, then ran to her ship. He couldn't help but smile before he ran off to Roberts' ship.

Four sleek, lethal, pod wing fighters raced for the entrance to the shipping lane. A downward curved wing ran from port to starboard and blended into outboard engines. A reverse curve formed the lower fuselage weapons bay. In the lead ship, the Tactical Squad Commander shook his head in frustration. The distress call had come in just as his team was relieving the first shift, putting them the maximum distance away from the Centurion in their coverage pattern. Now there was nothing over the com lines. Whoever had planned the attack was either very good or very lucky. Either way, he would be ready for them.

"Anything from the Centurion, Control?"

She sat next to the Helmsman, just below the command chair. "Still nothing, sir."

"Damn."

Roberts secured the windship's hatch then turned to Thomas. "Like it or not, your training makes you the expert, so as far as I'm concerned, you're in command. Tell us what to do, and we'll do it as best we can."

"Thanks, I think."

"Yeah, really."

Thomas followed Roberts to the bow and a navigation table just short of the Helmsman and the Controller, who activated the windship's bottom gas jets. Coming up off the Centurion's deck, then rotating, aft jets took the ship through the force field toward the asteroids.

"Do you have any other ships?" Thomas asked Roberts.

"A freighter, the Copernicus."

Looking through the bow windows, Thomas saw Lindsey and Hawkins standing on an asteroid next to the rocket launcher. "Are those your spacesuits?"

"Remember your ancient history?" Roberts replied with a chuckle. "Well, here you can live it."

"Fascinating... Control, how much time do we have before the fighters get here?"

"I estimate four minutes."

"Fire a ten-second extended ion cannon blast down the channel away from the Centurion before we enter the field," Thomas said.

"On it."

"Roberts, can you call up a chart of the area?"

"Sure." He opened up a laptop.

"Is that your computer?" Thomas asked, somewhat shocked.

"I think you'll be surprised at what we can do," Roberts shouted over the sound of the outgoing ion cannon fire.

"I was on the Centurion. I know what you can do," he said as he studied the chart. "Do you have any ordinance on board?"

"We have a couple of mining lasers and some contact mines."

"Where are they stored?"

"In a locker in the cockpit."

"Perfect. Helm, take us to 289-776-988 and stop near the asteroid on the starboard side. Roberts, when we get there, we'll need to go outside for a bit."

"Not a problem. Löfven," he called out to one of his crew, "get a spacesuit for Thomas, will you?"

She sized him up, then nodded. "On its way."

"Control," Thomas said, "can you raise Shara for me?"

"Sure. Hang on."

Roberts handed Thomas a headset with a microphone then laughed at the puzzled look on his face. "Here," he said, putting it on Thomas's head. "Just talk naturally."

"Go ahead, Thomas," the Controller said.

"Shara?"

"I'm here, Thomas," she replied into her headset, anxious.

"Call up grid D-7," came over the ship's speaker.

"Stand by." She looked on while one of her team, Rachael, pulled it up on her laptop. "Got it."

"Position your ship in the recess of the asteroid at 289-775-986. The fighters' sensors won't be able to detect you," Thomas said. "We'll draw them past you from left to right on the chart. It will be up to you to take them out as they pass."

"But Thomas, there's four of them."

"There are now, but by the time they get to you, there should only be one or two."

"Should?"

"Well..." she heard him respond with a laugh.

"Okay," she replied uneasy. Her crew looked at one another with equal concern. "We'll be ready."

"Right. Out. Control, switch me to the Copernicus."

"Go ahead."

"Copernicus, this is Thomas Chandler."

"Thomas, this is Chu," he heard over the headset. "Shara briefed me on you helping us. Welcome."

"Thanks. What's your status?"

"The shuttle has been loaded, and the cargo doors are closed."

"Alright. Activate your emergency beacon then patch me into your emergency channel. Then move your ship into the channel headed toward the alpha entrance."

"Wait five seconds."

"Commander, I have an emergency beacon and incoming message from D class freighter, the Copernicus. The message is audio only."

"D-class. Really?"

"Yes, sir."

"Strange... On speaker."

"Emergency, emergency. This is the freighter Copernicus," Thomas was heard to say.

"This is the Theta Tactical Squad," the Commander responded. "What is the nature of your emergency?"

"We are alongside the spaceship Centurion. She is motionless in the shipping lane. Sensor readings show she is on emergency power. Do you want us to provide assistance?"

Roberts stared wide-eyed at Thomas. He just smiled.

"Thank you, Copernicus, but we are just outside the alpha entrance to the shipping lane," came over the windship's speaker. "We will take it from here."

"Understood."

"Copernicus, did you see any other ships in the area?"

"Only a glimpse of something small racing down the shipping lane toward the beta entrance."

"Roger Copernicus. Please vacate the area for your own safety."

"Will do. Copernicus out," Thomas said then looked at Roberts. "Don't you just love the arrogance?"

"They do have the firepower to back it up."

"Good point. Control, can you get the Copernicus back?"

"Go ahead, Thomas."

"Chu, head toward the fighters at normal speed. We will rendezvous at 287-778-990. If we're not there in two hours, assume the worst and protect those on board."

"Understood. Good luck."

The Commander barely saw the Copernicus pass by them on its way out of the shipping lane. His focus was on the Centurion and what had become of her. "John, board the Centurion. Eric, provide top cover. Kavos, run a scan of the surrounding area to the port side of the ship. We'll do the same starboard."

"Coming up on position," the windship's Controller announced over his suit's com system.

All wearing spacesuits with helmets, the air inside the windship's cabin captured, the pressure zero, Roberts activated the hatch. "Roger that. Ready, Thomas?"

"I am. Are you sure this suit is?" Thomas asked, finding it odd he could turn his head inside the helmet.

"Well, we haven't tested that one, but most of the others have worked pretty well, all things considered," Roberts said with a laugh while he moved outside.

Thomas couldn't help but mentally monitor his suit's performance with each step. "You should really go into public relations."

Roberts chuckled. "I need you to get us out of this first."

"Right." Out on the deck of the cockpit, Thomas was in awe. He had been in free space numerous times before, but it was nothing like this moment. Then he had literally been surrounded by the latest in advanced technology. Spacesuits had become obsolete, replaced by the SS-TXB micro-electronic force field. Housed in a backpack, the total unit provided a fail-safe barrier for the containment of pressure, atmosphere, atmosphere regeneration, temperature maintenance, and tractor beam control. The latter provided either artificial gravity or the ability to pull oneself in any given direction. His spacesuit was very much different. The element of danger made the experience almost exhilarating. It was also extremely restrictive, inconvenient, and frustrating.

"Is this your first time in a real suit?" Roberts asked.

"Yeah. I'm surprised how awkward it is to move."

"You should have seen it before we installed the tractor beams. We had people floating all over the place."

"I bet. So how do I itch my nose?"

"Turn your head and use the ear padding. Using the faceplate makes a mess."

"Find that out the hard way?"

"Unfortunately..." Roberts opened an aft locker door in the stern of the cockpit and removed two mining lasers. He handed one to Thomas before joining him in taking cover behind the starboard rail. Both aimed at the mammoth asteroid seven meters away.

"Fire."

After a ten-second blast, they ducked to avoid the shower of rock fragments that came floating back at the ship and into the channel formed between the other asteroids.

"Wow, I actually hit something," Roberts said.

"Not exactly a good shot?"

"That would be an understatement." Standing after the last major pieces of rock floated by, Roberts exchanged the lasers for contact mines. He handed one to Thomas. "The mine has a weak surrounding force field after you activate it, so it would be good to make sure it doesn't hit anything with too much force."

"If you insist," Thomas said, releasing two more. "Helm?"

"Go ahead, Thomas."

"Take us down to the end of the corridor and come to a stop just short of the asteroid. Position the ion cannon dead astern. Target the fighter's engines if you can."

"Understood."

"Commander, I'm picking up the end of an ion trail headed further down the shipping lane," his Controller announced.

"That fits with the report from the Copernicus. Let's get after them," he said and activated the ship-to-ship com system. "Kavos, you're with me."

"Roger that," came over the com system.

The two fighters raced down the lane. The Commander checked a chart to the right of the viewscreen. "Computer, extrapolate distance of the spacecraft in front of us based on ion density."

"The trail does not emanate from a spacecraft of any known origin. Disbursement is indicative of ion cannon fire."

"Really?" the Commander said out loud. Ion cannons had been obsolete for decades.

"Sir, incoming message from Beta Two."

"Go ahead, John."

"Sir, the Centurion's Captain said they were attacked by the Dissenters in two windships," came over the ship's com system.

"Dissenters in windships?"

"Yes, sir."

"Did the ships have ion cannons?"

"Yes, sir. They did."

The Commander nodded. "What is the status of the Centurion?"

"Her main engines are down. Repairs are estimated to take about forty-eight hours. Emergency power is stable and well capable of supporting the ship during that time. The Dissenters used light grenades, so most of the crew are temporarily blind. Three have significant injuries. One requires immediate transport to the hospital. There is also one man missing, a Lieutenant Chandler. The Captain says he's from Sorel."

"A hostage?"

"Sounds like it, sir."

"Damn... Are any of the Centurion crew capable of flying the injured to the hospital?"

"No, sir, not until the blindness wears off. I could take him in a Centurion shuttle if you like."

"Do it."

"Yes, sir."

"Eric?"

"Yes, Commander," he was heard to say over the com system.

"Hold position above the Copernicus. We'll set up for triangulation."

"Then you think they're in the asteroid field, sir?"

"I'm sure of it... Kavos, reverse course. We'll go upper starboard of Eric's ship. You go lower starboard."

"Yes, sir."

Back inside the windship, the cabin pressurized, the atmosphere restored, Thomas took off his helmet, but left his suit on and awkwardly made his way to the headset. "Control, can you raise Shara again?"

"Go ahead."

"Shara, we're in position to draw the fighters past you. Be ready."

"Standing by," came over the com system.

The Commander watched his three remaining fighters form a triangle to pinpoint the location of any perturbation above background radiation levels. The composition and size of the asteroid field made the task difficult, but not impossible.

"Sir, probable bogy at 289-775-987," his Controller announced.

"Computer, tactical. Download the best possible path to target for each fighter."

"On screen."

A graphic of the local asteroid field appeared along with the target. Three intercept courses were displayed. The Commander activated his com system. "All ships attack, weapons on stun."

With a smile, he watched his fighter race into the asteroid field, the speed, and closeness of the rocks heightening his excitement. He scanned his tactical display. "Control, shields up. Helm, nice and steady. Keep scanning for that second bogy. I don't want any surprises."

"Yes, sir."

Eric's fighter rapidly entered the gap between two asteroids then turned starboard to go just in front of the Commander's ship.

Kavos' fighter joined from above, taking the lead. He smiled, knowing he had truly been blessed. He would be known as the man who captured the Dissenters. No longer would he have to toil at his lowly station. Fame and fortune would soon be his. And the women. Oh, yes, the women.

"Light debris ahead, sir," his Helmsman reported after turning hard between two asteroids at high speed.

"Asteroid fragments?"

"It appears so, sir, but with all the sensor interference from the asteroid field, I can't tell for sure."

If he slowed, Kavos knew the sod-eating Commander would take the lead and the glory. "Maintain present speed."

The space around Kavos' ship suddenly erupted in a series of explosions, one of which blasted his starboard engine. The power suddenly unbalanced, no room to maneuver, the ship slammed hard into an adjacent asteroid before being redirected back toward the channel.

"Evasive!" Eric shouted.

His helmsman slammed the stick back and hard port. The fighter responded, roaring up and away only to have her starboard wing tip strike Kavos' crippled fighter. The collision instantly threw his ship off course.

"Helm, pull up! Pull up!"

"Captain, I can't," he said before the fighter drug her port pod along the face of an asteroid where a fiery explosion blasted her fuselage back into the channel.

"Hard starboard!" the Commander shouted then watched as Eric's ship flashed just overhead when a threat alarm sounded.

"Fire!" Thomas ordered.

"Dive!" the Commander shouted a split second before an ion cannon blast flashed overhead. "Helm, get us out of here!"

"I missed!" the windship's Controller exclaimed.

"Damn," Thomas said. "Helm, take us hard starboard then down to where you clear the asteroid to port."

"Kavos, status?" he heard the Commander asked over the ship's speaker system. The officer stumbled to his chair through the smoke-filled flight deck and activated the com system. "We're a little shaken, but alright, sir. Both engine pods are gone, but emergency power is holding."

"Do you need our help?"

"Negative. We've issued a distress call back to base and can make it until backup arrives."

"Roger, stand by."

"Eric, status?"

He handed his Controller a bandage for the cut on his head then activated the com system. "Commander, all we have left is life support. Hansen has suffered a minor injury, but he'll be alright."

"Do you need our assistance?"

"Negative, sir."

The Commander checked his tactical display. "Alright. Notify Kavos that we're going in."

"Make them pay, sir," Eric said.

"My thought exactly... Helm, plot an intercept course."

"Course plotted and laid in, sir."

"Control, set disrupters to kill."

Having positioned Roberts' windship near the shipping lane at the end of a corridor formed by the asteroids, Thomas knew the odds had improved, but still... The remaining fighter suddenly came out from behind an asteroid at the end of the channel. "Fire!"

The ion cannon erupted, but the blast missed the fighter astern.

The Commander's ship responded with a deadly pattern of disrupter blasts spaced at five-degree intervals as she made a turn then disappear behind another asteroid.

Thomas watched one of the beams flash just over the ion cannon and slam into the windship's mast, ripping it from its supports and creating a half meter wide hole in the roof of the ship's cabin. Löfven, standing next to the breach, screamed as she was sucked stomach-first through the opening, ironically plugging it long enough to give the others inside the time to secure their helmets. "My God," Thomas said, stunned by the brutality of her death.

The Commander checked his tactical screen. They were headed between two asteroids toward a passage that led to the disabled windship. "Helm, let's have a nice, straight shot now."

"Yes, sir. Target in," he started to say when an alarm suddenly sounded.

"Evasive!"

Shara watched her ion cannon blast flash just over the top of the descending fighter. "Oh no! Thomas, we missed! We missed!"

"Control, do you have the fighter?" Thomas asked.

"No!"

"Helm, take us out into the shipping lane as fast as you can."

Roberts looked at Thomas wide-eyed, the ship leaving the cover of the asteroid field. "We're a sitting duck out here!"

"I'm counting on that."

"What?"

"Sir, one of the windships is in the shipping lane," the Controller announced.

The Commander smiled, "Then they're as good as dead. After her." He watched his ship exit the field, saw the enemy when a harsh alarm suddenly filled the bridge. "Helm, evasive," the Commander roared again. "Full power to," he started to say when a heat-seeking missile, less warhead, suddenly ripped through one of the fighter's engines, sending the fuselage spiraling down the shipping lane, leaving a trail of sparks in her wake.

CHAPTER THIRTEEN

Shara sat alone in the observation lounge of the Copernicus. A small room with a viewport, a bench, and plants, she failed to see the universe passing by. Her father was dead. The only family she had ever really known was gone. She felt sad, empty, and angry. The Lieutenant didn't have to set his disrupter on kill…

But Corbin was more than her father. He was the leader of the Dissenters. Was it now up to her to carry on? Would the other Dissenters follow her? Or should they run and hide in their anonymity? Could they really win against the most powerful corporation in the Discovered Worlds?

"Shara?"

She turned to find Thomas at the door.

"Keira said you wanted to see me."

"If you don't mind." She slid to one side of the bench to make room. "I wanted to tell you how sorry I am for ruining your career."

"Actually, I should be thanking you," Thomas replied as he sat down next to her.

She slowly shook her head in confusion. "That certainly begs for an explanation."

Thomas chuckled. "During the first few days at the Academy, we were repeatedly told the way things had to be to make Theta greater than she already was. Then one day, someone dared to question what was being taught. Another suggested there may be a better way to do business. The following day, both cadets were gone, dismissed from school. The rest of us found it an easy lesson to learn, but… I went to the Academy, hoping to change Theta from within. After learning the truth about Sorel, I realized all I had really done was to condemn myself to a life of false hope and frustration. Now, I'm free."

"If only that were the case, Thomas. Now, you'll be hunted like the rest of us," she said and slowly shook her head.

"Then, we need to prove your innocence."

"If only that were the case… In the back of my mind, I can't help but think that our action against the Pride caused the destruction of the colony."

Thomas slowly shook his head. "The sabotage of the colony was always an option. The Dissenters were, *are* just a convenient scapegoat."

She stared at him, the past few days playing out in her mind before she slowly nodded. "I never looked at it that way."

"That's because you're a good person," he said with a comforting smile. "Part of the corporate culture is the quest for power. It can consume those who seek it beyond all else. It blinds them to the point where they convince themselves it is okay to break the rules, that the ends justify the means. History is littered with such people and their willingness to sacrifice others so that they can reach their ultimate goal, power. Those are the people responsible for the destruction of the colony, not the Dissenters. You need to look at yourself and your people as victims, just like those who died that day on Sorel."

"Including your parents," she said softly.

"Including my parents… For the 1638, the Dissenters need to continue on, need to expose the truth."

Shara slowly shook her head. "But with Theta's unlimited resources, the odds are not exactly in our favor."

Thomas smiled. "No, but the only way we will ever be free is if the truth is known."

"That's the second time you have said we."

Thomas smiled. "I'd like to join the Dissenters if that's alright with you."

She managed a slight smile. "Thank you, but…"

"But?"

She looked off. "I'm not sure I can be as strong as my father was."

"You already are."

Merrick knew the mission to Sorel had gone poorly, but not only could he explain it, but he could also turn it to his advantage.

"Incoming call from Mr. Sandor, sir," came over the intercom.

"Thank you." Confident, he moved to his chair, assumed the correct posture then activated the viewscreen on the far wall. "Mr. Sandor."

Sandor sat at his desk. "Mr. Merrick, I see you have filed an insurance claim for the Sorel Mining Colony."

"Yes, sir. The lawyers feel that the Dissenter recording is evidence enough to qualify for such a claim."

"Yes. I quite agree. And were you successful in your Search and Rescue efforts?"

"Unfortunately, no. Two survivors were located, but our attempt to rescue them was met with opposition. We believe they were Dissenters, the saboteurs themselves. After we arrived, the main Dissenter force landed and attacked us. Yates, the Search and Rescue pilot and copilot, were killed by them. Pendrac and I barely managed to escape. A press release stating what I have just told you has been prepared and awaits your approval."

Sandor paused to consider what he had been told, then nodded. "Please issue the release."

"Yes, sir."

The viewscreen going black, Merrick sat back in his chair and smiled.

"Clear shuttle area for chamber isolation. Repeat, clear shuttle area for chamber isolation," the Chief announced over the Copernicus bay's com system.

Flashing yellow lights encouraged the Dissenter support crew to head quickly for the pressure doors that separated the shuttle bay from the windship bay. The Chief checked and rechecked his headcount. All hands present, he triggered the atmosphere to withdraw.

Chu checked his computer then activated the com system. "Shara, orbit has been established around Sorel. Opening forward cargo bay doors."

"Initiating launch." She moved the shuttle up off the deck, having learned to fly from her father after he had first formed the Dissenters. She found the experience enjoyable.

Thomas sat next to Shara in the copilot's seat. Six others were behind them, Keira and Roberts included. All wore radiation suits. In the aisle between them was a make-shift coffin carrying Corbin's body. "We're clear of the Copernicus."

"Roger." She activated the shuttle's engines and headed the ship down to the planet's surface.

Despite the number of times he traveled, Thomas couldn't help but marvel at how pristine everything looked from space. He knew the colony would be a much different story. "Shara, after we lay Corbin to rest, I'd like to check the power plant's security room. There may be a chance the recordings will show who sabotaged the reactor."

"But wouldn't everything have been destroyed?"

"Possibly not. The room was designed to withstand even an uncontained reaction."

"It would be good to know the truth," she replied as she brought the shuttle in over the mountains, the weather station appearing below. The recent memory made her uneasy. The colony ahead, or what was left of it, made her sick. The structures that immediately surrounded the power plant had been leveled as were the prefabs. The office and warehouse buildings were a mass of broken concrete, twisted rebar, and shattered glass. Most disturbing were the shadows of the people that had been burned onto the ground before they were vaporized by the intense heatwave. It was all she could do to land in what used to be the park.

First down the aft ramp, Keira staggered a few steps before falling to her knees, sobbing. "Oh dear God..." Roberts came up behind her and stood silently by.

The others on board exited in silence, each with his or her own thoughts upon viewing the horrific destruction of what had once been their home.

Thomas followed Shara. "There was so much life here," she said, slowly shaking her head.

He looked off in the direction of his parent's house. "I know."

"Excuse me, Shara," Roberts said, coming up, Keira by his side. "Where would you like the gravesite?"

She looked at the park and saw the remains of a single tree. She remembered her mother and father used to sit under it on warm summer evenings while she played with her friends. She recalled the smiles on their faces as she ran with the other children, her energy seemingly endless. Then, strong arms picked her up, held her tenderly before she fell fast asleep, her head on her father's shoulder. "Under the tree, please."

"Perfect," Roberts replied then turned to Keira. "Will you be alright?"

She kissed him on the cheek. "I will. Thank you."

He nodded with a smile, surprised, and pleased at the same time. He turned back to Shara. "It's going to take us about twenty minutes to dig the grave and set up a hardwired relay far enough outside the radiation zone for the Copernicus to share in the remembrances."

"Will our communicators work?"

"They will work over a limited range. The shuttle's been set up to act as a local receiver/transmitter."

"Thank you."

"Not a problem," Roberts said and ran off to meet with the other Dissenters.

Keira watched him go then smiled at herself for doing so. Thomas and Shara couldn't help but notice. "What?" she said, having turned back to see the look on their faces.

"Nothing," Thomas replied, his grin fading as he turned serious. "Keira, where do you think the power plant's security room is?"

She surveyed what was left of the office buildings further to the west. "In the basement of the first building on the right or the next one up on the same side. It's so hard to tell."

"Ok, I'll take the far one," Thomas said. "How about you two check the near one?"

Keira looked at Shara, who reluctantly nodded. "Alright."

"Call if you find anything," he said and jogged off.

Keira exhaled then joined Shara, who led the way up the road to the first building and an exposed stairwell. "After the cave, I'm not sure I particularly like this."

"I know what you mean..."

The upper part of the building completely destroyed, sunlight filtered down through fallen beams onto a flight of stairs that provided a debris-strewn path down to the concrete basement floor. There, communicator flashlights took over.

Keira carefully led the way along a partially blocked corridor to find a crevasse crossing their path. A third of a meter wide, some three meters deep, they easily jumped it then headed toward two doors on the right-hand side of the hall.

"How about you take this room? I'll take the next," Shara suggested.

"Are you sure we should split up?"

"We don't have much time," Shara said and continued on.

"Great..." Keira carefully entered the room and cautiously probed the dark with her flashlight. What damage there was came mostly from the fallen structure from above and not fire.

Ducking under a downed beam, she balanced herself against another when it suddenly let go. With a yell, she fell and landed next to the body of a dead woman, her face only centimeters from that of the corpse. The woman's eyes were gone. Her skin was drawn tight and paper-thin around her skull. Screaming, Keira scrambled to her feet then turned to come face to face with the desiccated corpse of a man, his body inadvertently suspended in an upright position by a coat rack, his arms reaching out toward her. She screamed again when a hand grabbed her shoulder.

"Keira."

"Oh, Shara, oh God. I'm okay, it was just that, well, well..."

"I know. The other room is filled with bodies as well."

"Sha--, do y-- read?" Thomas was heard to say, his words barely discernible due to the static on her communicator. "--ara, I've --und --- -onrol --om. Ba---ent fl--r, se---d ---r on th-   -ight."

"It sounded like he said he found the security control room," Shara said.

"Then let's get out of here."

"I'm okay with that."

Thomas sat at a desk in front of a large viewscreen. On it played the surveillance video from the Sorel power plant's control room.

"Thomas?" Keira called out.

"In here."

She and Shara entered the room through a half-meter thick door to find it undamaged.

"Power?" Shara asked.

"An emergency generator."

"And the recording?"

"According to the time stamp," Thomas said, "this should be just before the uncontained reaction."

They watched in silence as two technicians casually left the power plant control room. A subsequent lack of motion caused the recording to stop before the next segment started with two different technicians entering. Wearing Theta Power uniforms, one man was very tall. The other was large, powerfully built. Each man moved quickly to a separate console and began to input data when one of them turned toward the camera. Keira gasped. "Shara, that's the one you shot at the weather station."

"My God! You're right. Thomas," she said, then stopped on seeing a look of pure anger on his face. "Are you alright?"

"The man's name is Pendrac. He works for Lucian Merrick."

"Merrick?"

"Merrick," Thomas said in a low voice.

They watched the two men leave the room, and the recording momentarily stop. The next segment was activated by four panicked technicians and Hata rushing in amidst the sound of alarms.

"The field is jammed!"

"So is the coolant flow!"

"Activate the manual override," was heard before a blinding flash caused Thomas, Keira, and Shara to instinctively look away before the screen went totally blank. Nothing more remained on the log.

"Damn him," Keira whispered, brushing the tears from her eyes.

Thomas stared blankly at the screen, lost in thought. Shara broke the momentary silence. "Can we use this to expose Merrick and clear our names?"

Thomas shook his head. "I'm not sure. Our credibility isn't exactly the best right now."

"That's an understatement," she said when Roberts was heard over her communicator.

"Shara, we're ready for you."

"We're on our way," she replied as Thomas pocketed the recording disc then followed the women out of the room.

Roberts had set up a camera for the others onboard the Copernicus to share in the service. The coffin had been placed in the ground and covered over. Now, at the base of the tree rested a single tombstone, one they had brought with them.

Thomas and Keira walked up and joined the others in the burial party, standing solemnly at the foot of the grave.

Shara moved behind the marker to deliver the eulogy. "I would like to thank all of you for your prayers and kindness. They have been of great help to me in coping with my father's death. But then Corbin was much more than just my father. He saw the pain and suffering on Sorel, the wrongful injuries and deaths, and tried to do something about it. We are a result of that effort. God knows it would be easy for us all to stop now and grieve, but we can't. We must put aside his loss as we have had to do for so many others and carry on. For if we quit now, all of our efforts will have been in vain, and what you see around you here will happen again. We cannot allow that. We need to make sure that those responsible for the deaths of the colonists, of family and friends, do not go unpunished. Again, I thank you from the bottom of my heart for your kindness. We have all felt my father's loss, but we must go on."

Those on the planet struggled with the emotion of the situation but gained renewed strength from Shara's words. Filing past the grave, they silently bid their last respects, then moved to Shara and thanked her. Thomas was the last. He tenderly embraced her. "I never really had a chance to know your father, but if he was anything like you, he must have been very special."

"He was… Thank you, Thomas, for everything. I really couldn't have done this without you," she said, looking up at him, succumbing to tears at last. She gently laid her head on his shoulder, drawing from his comfort, his strength.

"Yes you could have."

"Thank you," she said when the moment was broken by a signal from her communicator. With difficulty, she pulled herself away and addressed the camera. "Chu."

"Shara, on behalf of the crew here on board, I would like to say how sorry we all are at the loss of your father. I would also like to thank you. There have been many times when each of us has questioned our ability, and each time, Corbin's strength was there to keep us going. You possess his same strength, and for that, we are all thankful. We will continue on."

She slowly nodded. "Thank you so very much, everyone. Together and only together, can we succeed. And we will succeed. I promise," she said, then nodded to Roberts to end the transmission before activating her communicator once more. "Chu, we'll be finished here in a couple of minutes. Have the shuttle bay crew standing by."

"Will do."

"Shara, is there anything else you'd like us to do before we load up?" Roberts asked.

"No. I really appreciate all you've done… You know, there is one thing."

"What's that?"

"Could you check out my communicator when we get back onboard the Copernicus? It worked fine just a minute ago, but earlier I was getting a lot of break up."

Thomas's head suddenly snapped around, his attention completely focused on Shara. "What did you say?"

"Nothing really. It's just that there was a lot of interference on my communicator when you called before. It seems fine now, but earlier, I was getting a lot of breakup."

Keira looked at her brother, wide-eyed. "You don't think?"

"Come on. Show me where you were!" Thomas said and ran off with his sister.

Shara looked at Roberts, confused. "Do you know what's going on?"

"No, but…" They took off after Thomas and Keira.

Keira led the way down the stairs to the basement floor of the first building, her flashlight on. "We were down the corridor, first door on the right. Careful of the crevasse."

Thomas easily jumped over it then entered the room. "Keira, call me on your communicator. I'll follow the interference."

"Right."

He pushed past the dead man on his way to the other side of the room, where the crevasse became visible again. The interference on his communicator continued to increase.

"Thomas, Keira," Shara called out, Roberts behind her. "What's going on?"

Standing by the edge of a continuation of the crevasse, they turned and smiled as the two approached. "Just this…" Thomas shined his flashlight down to where the ice blue diamatron ore crystals multiplied the light, reflecting it back in a maze of brilliant sparkling patterns.

"There must be billions here!" Roberts exclaimed.

"Easily," Shara replied, 'but legally, it's not ours."

"But it can be," Thomas said. "Every mining claim requires those who own the claim to maintain a constant presence. If they fail to do so for ten days or more, their claim becomes invalid."

"So, this deposit can be ours?" Keira asked, excited.

"If we're first to file," Thomas replied. "We need to make sure that happens."

"And what about proving our innocence?" Shara asked.

Thomas smiled. "I have a plan…"

CHAPTER FOURTEEN

Sandor sat alone in his office, his focus on the viewscreen in front of him. The Theta Corporation News was on with Byron Walker at the anchor desk.

"A new deposit of diamatron ore was discovered at the former site of the Sorel Mine," Byron said, a graphic of a Phoenix rising out of the fire displayed over his left shoulder. "The discovery is rumored to be one of the largest in history and was made by a group calling themselves the Phoenix Mining Company. The claim comes after the Theta Corporation failed to maintain their exclusive mining rights to the planet by allowing their claim to go unmanned for more than ten days after the colony was destroyed by the Dissenters."

"Computer, viewscreen off," Sandor said in anger, slowly shaking his head.

Merrick sat alone in his Sigma Three office as the Theta Corporation News played in the background. The discovery of ore on Sorel was unbelievable. All the data from the planet had shown it to be played out. The whole idea was to get out of there. There's no way Sandor could blame him, and yet… The sound of the com system startled him. "Yes."

"Mr. Sandor, on line one."

"Thank you," Merrick replied in a voice that sounded stronger than he felt. He activated the viewscreen. "Mr. Sandor."

"Merrick, are you aware of the recent claim on the planet Sorel by the Phoenix Mining Company?" Sandor asked, his tone hostile.

"Yes, sir. It certainly exceeds any projection we had."

"Did you fail to maintain a crew on the planet after the disaster?"

"Yes, sir, but that was our plan all along."

"So, the Phoenix Mining Company's claim is valid?"

"Yes, sir. It is," Merrick replied, frustrated.

Sandor slowly shook his head, his jaw set. "Damn it, Merrick," he said when the screen went black.

Sandor was still shaking his head when his office intercom sounded. "What?" he almost shouted.

"I'm sorry to interrupt you, sir," Helen said, "but there is a Mr. Thomas Chandler here from Phoenix Mining Company. He would like to see you concerning their find on Sorel."

"Interesting," Sandor replied, his mood changing instantly, his anger replaced by curiosity. He activated a hidden outer office camera and scanned his patiently waiting guest for a computer ID. The readout included Thomas's resume at Theta. The last two entries showed he had been taken prisoner by the Dissenters then resigned from the Theta Corporation shortly after that. Sandor's mind raced with all the possibilities, but in the end, he knew his best course of action was personal contact. "Please, send him in."

"Yes, sir," his secretary said, her voice reflecting her relief. She had made the right decision.

Attired in a very expensive business suit, Thomas entered the office and shook hands. "Thank you for seeing me without an appointment Mr. Sandor."

"Not a problem, Mr. Chandler. Please have a seat." Sandor motioned to the chairs and coffee table combination near the bar. "May I offer you a drink?"

"No thank you, sir."

Sandor nodded, then sat opposite Thomas. "So tell me, why are you here?"

"I represent the Phoenix Mining Company. Our find on Sorel is substantial, but we lack the equipment and manpower necessary to mine it efficiently and economically," Thomas said, getting straight to the point. "We would, therefore, like to subcontract the Theta Corporation."

"I see..." Sandor pondered the proposal. "Well, Mr. Chandler, quite frankly, I'm not sure Theta is all that interested in just the mining phase of the operation."

"Forgive me, Mr. Sandor. We would like to subcontract the entire package, including transportation and refinement."

"And who would have control over production quantities?"

"We would require two hundred metric tons of high-grade ore per month as a minimum shipment with increased production when the market favors it."

"And what would be the profit percentage realized by Theta?"

"What would you require?" Thomas asked straight-faced.

Sandor's suspicions were running high. Much of his life he had spent negotiating contracts. His skill at doing so was evident by the position he now held. But this session was like no other. Chandler was either being extremely clever or incredibly stupid. "Computer," he said after moving to his desk, "calculate the profit percentage required for a subcontract agreement for the mining, transportation, and refinement of diamatron ore from Sorel on a two hundred metric tons per month basis. Display the response on my desk monitor. Assume standard variables."

A series of figures flooded the screen. At the bottom, a final value of 15.48 percent was shown. Sandor contemplated the number carefully before speaking. "We would require a 19.54 percent profit share, Mr. Chandler."

"Interesting," Thomas replied with a poker face. "I would have thought the value to be more like 15.5 percent. Still, I will accept your offer under three conditions."

"And those are?" Sandor asked, the negotiations taking an unexpected, if not an interesting change of direction. But he was very good at this facet of the art as well. And in light of the increased profit associated with this particular deal, he knew he would be the victor.

Thomas looked at his opponent, calmly and professionally. "The first is that you clear the Dissenters of any wrongdoing, especially the sabotage of the Sorel power plant."

Sandor knit his brow. "And why would I do that?"

Thomas took a disk out on his jacket and handed it to Sandor. "This is a copy of the original message sent by the

Dissenters where they discuss their attack on the Pride of Theta, not the Sorel Mine and its colony. If you examine it closely, you will see the recording you showed the Discovered Worlds was constructed from it."

"Interesting," Sandor said. "But then that begs the question, who destroyed the Sorel Colony?"

"Lucian Merrick and his supervisor, Pendrac," Thomas said, "which brings me to my second condition. "I want them arrested for the crime."

Sandor sat back in his chair. "Do you have proof?"

"I do. Also on the disk is a copy of the Sorel power plant's security log. It clearly shows Pendrac sabotaging the controls before the uncontained reaction. Pendrac would not have acted on his own. Lucian Merrick would have had to have given him the authorization."

"And if I choose to believe they are not guilty?" Sandor asked innocently.

"It's a simple matter of economics. The profit you will derive from our contract will be of far more value to the Theta Corporation than the two men and the insurance money Theta received from the colony being destroyed."

Sandor nodded. "And your third condition?"

"You and I will sign the final contract on Sorel with Merrick and Pendrac present in seven days."

"An odd request," Sandor said.

"Perhaps, but I want you to witness firsthand the result of Merrick and Pendrac's warped business sense and hope that you will take steps within the Theta Corporation to make sure 'Sorel' will never happen again."

Sandor silently studied Thomas. He assumed a well-rehearsed deliberate pose in an attempt to make Thomas feel uneasy and give something up to better his own position. After a short while, it became obvious the ploy had failed, just as it had at the Academy during graduation. Once again, the next move was his. "I accept your conditions, Mr. Chandler, with one proviso."

"And that is?"

"That you provide to me the original recordings during the contract signing so that I can use them to make a case against Merrick and Pendrac."

Thomas nodded. "Agreed."

"Then we have a deal," Sandor said, getting up and offering his hand. "Now, how about that drink?"

Thomas stood and shook Sandor's hand. "Again, no thank you. I look forward to seeing you on Sorel," he said on his way to the door.

"In seven days, then," Sandor said, opening it.

Thomas nodded. "Good night, Mr. Sandor."

Pendrac logged off on his computer then got up and stretched. Night came early on Sigma Three this time of year. He considered going to the local bar, but then thought the better of it. Management and the miners did not mix, especially when alcohol was involved. Instead, he left his office building and walked the short distance to his prefab in the management section. Opening the door, he was surprised to see an uninvited guest sitting in his lounge chair holding a pistol. "Who the hell are you?"

"Your executioner," he said and shot him dead.

Merrick had decided to take some well-deserved time off at one of his favorite haunts in Edo. The music loud, the drinks flowing, he had managed to hook up with an old friend who suggested they go to her place for a nightcap. With a smile, he got up to pay his tab when a man moved in behind him and, unseen, stabbed him with a needle in the middle of the crowd. The injection's drunken effect instantaneous, the man quickly supported Merrick. "Here, let me help you, old buddy," he said, helping him walk.

"Thank you," Merrick slurred on his way to the club's back door.

Their radiation suits covered with a mixture of dirt and sweat, Thomas and Roberts strained to roll yet another dolly full of ore by hand down Main Street from the 'Crevasse Building' to a nearby staging area. Shara came out from under a canopy to help them.

"A little further… That's it," Shara said and set the brake.

With the dolly resting on a scale recovered from inside the mine, both men staggered to the shade while she recorded the weight before transport of the ore to the Copernicus. Both men grabbed a much-needed bottle of water.

"I can't remember the last time I had so much fun," Roberts said, collapsing in a chair next to Thomas. He was exhausted. All the Dissenters were exhausted, having worked around the clock in advance of Sandor's arrival. But no one seriously complained. All knew this was their best chance, if not their only chance, to prove their innocence.

Thomas downed half a bottle before pouring the remainder over his head. "Me either... Shara, when are Keira and Hawkins due in?"

"Keira is on final approach," she replied on her way back to the canopy. "Hawkins should be here an hour later."

"And the trench?"

"A couple more hours and it should be done," she said while checking her totals, six other dollies full of ore parked off to the side. "So are we. This one puts the Copernicus at maximum capacity."

"That's all right," Roberts said with a grin. "As near as I can tell, what we found was only a localized deposit. There are a few more veins left, but I'm not sure they amount to much."

"Oh," Shara said, grabbing a bottle of water for herself. "Now, what will Sandor say?"

"One can only imagine," Thomas replied with a chuckle as the Copernicus shuttle came in over the mountains. Clearing the lake at the end of the runway, the ship headed down Main Street before transitioning to a hover. Rotating, she put her stern to the staging area before landing.

Keira came down the lowered aft ramp. "You all look good."

Shara wiped the grit off her forehead. "We try... So, how did it go at the Black Market?"

"You would have loved this place. After several starts and stops with bags over our heads to make sure we didn't know where we were going, Hawkins and I ended up in this warehouse that was like a giant high-tech toy store for the insecure. In exchange for surprisingly little ore, we got everything on the list."

"Excellent," Shara said then turned to Roberts. "So, how long do you think it will take to get everything in position and operational?"

"Maybe three hours after we get it all unloaded."

"Then, should I assume my non-union negotiated break is over?" Thomas asked, getting up with a groan.

"I'm afraid so," Shara replied with a laugh. "Keira, after the dollies are loaded on the Copernicus, bring the shuttle back. We should have time before Sandor shows up for everyone to take a hot bath up at the weather station."

Keira nodded. "I know of three who could certainly use one."

A Theta Tactical Squad transport streaked past the Sorel Station and prepared for its final approach to the planet. Inside, Sandor sat in a private compartment reviewing the mining contract when the com sounded. "ETA for Sorel orbit is five minutes, Mr. Sandor."

"Thank you, Captain."

The Copernicus and its shuttle hidden in a nebula, Thomas and Shara stood alone on Main Street. Once again clean, wearing new two-piece radiation suits, all trace of the Dissenters' mining activity was gone.

"Here he comes," Thomas said just before a Theta Tactical Squad transport touched down less than one hundred meters in front of them. "Certainly an interesting choice of ships for just Sandor and his two managers."

Shara slowly shook her head. "Surprised?"

"No, not really," he said, adjusting his suit's jacket.

Three large figures in radiation suits were first out. Surveying the surroundings, one man motioned to another inside. Similarly dressed, Sandor emerged.

"This is getting more and more interesting," Shara said in a low voice as the party approached.

"Very," Thomas replied in an undertone then moved forward to shake hands. "Mr. Sandor, it's nice of you to come."

"Mr. Chandler," Sandor said, coming forward while the others stayed back out of earshot.

"May I present my partner, Shara Lockett."

"Lockett, you say. Mr. Chandler never told me he had such an attractive associate."

"Why thank you, Mr. Sandor," Shara replied, barely masking her disdain. Instead, she smiled too sweetly. "It's not often one meets someone who can so quickly recognize that one quality that leads to a successful business relationship."

"Yes, well..." Sandor turned coldly back to Thomas. "About the contract."

"Where are Merrick and Pendrac?"

"They appear to have literally gone missing," Sandor replied with a grin.

"Of course..."

Ignoring Thomas, Sandor took a military-grade communicator out of his pocket, one designed to work in high radiation zones, and turned to the transport. "Colonel, deploy your troops now."

"Thomas?" Shara asked, staying by his side. He slowly shook his head while twenty members of Theta's Tactical Squad wearing full battledress with radiation protection exited the aft ramp of the transport. They were accompanied by four open-air hovercraft, each with a pilot and a gunner standing behind the ship's aft-mounted disrupter cannon.

Sandor smugly turned his attention back to Thomas and Shara. "Excuse me, what was that you said earlier, Mr. Chandler?"

"I was going to congratulate you on eliminating your liabilities."

"I don't understand," Sandor said with a grin.

"Merrick is, or I should probably say was, typical of so many in Theta seeking power: ambitious, arrogant, above the law. He could justify murdering the eleven miners in Tunnel 5A on his own, but not the entire population of the colony. For that, he needed permission, your permission."

Sandor smiled. "I'm afraid you have it all wrong, Mr. Chandler. You see, I believe the recordings you gave me are fake. As such, that leaves the Dissenters responsible for the destruction of the colony. And your claim provides the true motive for that action, greed. Tell me, Mr. Chandler, what kind of man sides with the people who murdered his own parents for money?"

"You son of a," Thomas said and took a menacing step forward, his fists clenched.

The bodyguards pulled out their disrupters.

"Thomas, no!" Shara shouted, holding him back.

"What's wrong Chandler," Sandor said, "hiding behind a woman?"

"Why you," Shara said, Thomas now restraining her.

"A nice try, Sandor," Thomas said, collecting himself, "but you'll have to kill us outright instead of claiming self-defense."

"Careful what you wish for."

"Besides," Thomas continued, "you have no evidence to support your allegation that we are Dissenters."

Sandor smiled and activated his communicator once again. "Mr. Alesana, if you would join us, please."

"Yes, sir."

Shara looked at Thomas in shock as Toa made his way out of the transport to stand by Sandor's side.

"Mr. Alesana, was Ms. Lockett one of those who attacked you onboard the Centurion?"

"Yes, sir. In fact, she was one of the leaders."

"And was Mr. Chandler forcibly taken off the ship, or did he leave voluntarily?"

"He left on his own free will, sir."

"Thank you, Mr. Alesana," Sandor said then turned back to Thomas and Shara. "Anything else?"

"The rest of the Dissenter force?" Thomas suggested.

Sandor stared hard at his opponent, then suddenly burst into laughter. "Excellent. I must confess I would have been disappointed if you had not tried such a gambit. Unfortunately for the both of you, our scan of the planet and surrounding space showed no other life forms other than the two of you. But just in case, I felt my little display of force to be a sufficient enough deterrent for even that to happen."

"Can you be sure?" Thomas asked.

"Yes, very... Well, it's getting late, and I really must be going." Sandor turned to head back to the transport, then stopped and looked back at Thomas and Shara. "By the way, I have no intention of killing the two of you. That's why I brought these men along," he said with a laugh before moving on. Toa followed him. The three bodyguards did not.

CHAPTER FIFTEEN

Shara put one hand on Thomas's shoulder while holding onto his arm with the other as Sandor started back to his transport. "Thomas?"

Not answering, he continued to silently stare forward as Toa passed within centimeters of the last bodyguard.

"Now, Thomas!" Toa shouted and lashed out with a devastating right uppercut to the unsuspecting bodyguard's chin. The man fell unconscious.

Shara instantly removed a concealed disrupter from the back of Thomas's jacket and dropped the bodyguard nearest her before he could react. The third bodyguard was not as slow. He fired at Thomas, but the shot missed just wide as he dove to his right. Pulling a second concealed disrupter out from inside his jacket in the process, Thomas fired. The third bodyguard fell unconscious before he could get off a second shot.

"Roberts, now!" Shara yelled into her wrist communicator as Sandor ran off to his left for cover.

The ground behind her literally opened up as a cloaking device was deactivated to reveal a heavily armed Dissenter force strategically positioned in a trench with makeshift battlements across Main Street. "Fire!" Roberts shouted.

"Take cover!" the Tactical Squad Colonel yelled while heeding his own advice. "Fire as our people clear. Sergeant, get the transporter out of here."

Shara raced for the trench but fell screaming from an incoming disrupter blast, striking her in the leg. Toa scooped her unconscious body up then jumped into the trench with her. Thomas landed next to them a second later. "I'll get a medkit."

Toa exposed Shara's wound then shook his head in disbelief. The Tactical Squad had set their weapons on kill.

"Launch the recon," Roberts shouted over the incoming fire.

The hardwired probe sped five hundred meters up, then maintained its position over the battlefield. "We're online," Rachael shouted from the bottom of the trench, her monitors coming alive. They showed both real and infra-red signatures for men and machines. "I've got two hovercraft coming up on us behind the ruins. One is one street over on the right, the other one street over on the left."

"Bring the rocket launcher online," Roberts shouted on his way to the weapon.

Thomas scanned Shara's wound while Toa broke out the med-light. "Is she alright?"

"I think so. It missed the bone."

"Here." He handed over the light.

"Thanks... And thanks also for the help back there."

"I do have a few questions when you're not too busy, of course."

"Of course," Thomas said, shining the light on the wound. "Just so you know, we're the good guys."

"I sure hope so... If you've got things under control, I should go help the others."

"I'm good. See Roberts, he's the one coordinating the action. He was on the Centurion and knows who you are."

"Roberts, the hovercraft!" Hawkins shouted into his communicator, a cannon blast just missing overhead. The next one would not. "Target the hovercraft on the right!"

"Rachael, are we online yet?" Roberts shouted in frustration over the incoming fire.

"No, and I don't know why!"

Toa ran up. "Can I help?"

"I can't make this thing work!"

"May I?"

"Be my guest," Roberts said and handed over the weapon.

Toa quickly examined it then pushed a button. "The safety was still on." He took aim at the hovercraft bearing down on Hawkins.

"Roberts!" Hawkins was heard to shout over the com system.

"Clear behind me?" Toa asked.

"Clear."

"Firing!"

The rocket impacted point-blank on the hovercraft's bow where dancing blue electricity enveloped the ship. The shields defeated, overloaded internal circuits caused all power to be lost. The craft fell like a rock. The crew just managed to run away before the ship burst into a giant fireball.

"That was cool," Toa said while Roberts reloaded.

"You're good to go."

Toa took aim at the second approaching hovercraft. "Clear?"

"Clear."

"Firing!"

A hit to the port side, the second hovercraft was thrown hard starboard and crashed into the remains of a downed building. The Captain helped the gunner run away before the ship was consumed by a series of explosions.

"Sergeant, move the remaining hovercraft back behind cover now!" the Colonel ordered.

"Yes, sir."

The Communications man ran forward. "Sir, I've got Sandor on tact two."

"Not now."

"He insists, sir."

"Damn it." The Colonel grabbed the communicator. "Mr. Sandor, I need you to clear this channel now."

"Colonel, dispatch the two remaining hovercraft to pick me up immediately."

"I can't do that, sir. We're outnumbered, and without those ships, there's little chance we can complete our mission."

"Colonel, this is not a request. It is an order. Do you understand or do I have to put someone in charge that does?"

"No sir. That's not necessary. The ships are on their way," he said then angrily threw the instrument back at his communications man. "Asshole."

"Oh, what hit me," Shara moaned, slowly coming out of her unconscious state.

"Nothing really," Thomas said with a smile. "Just a little disrupter blast set on kill."

"Oh, is that all." She raised her head slightly to look at the damage to her leg. "Now look what you've done to my new radiation suit."

Thomas switched off the lamp and admired his handy work. "There, good as new."

She tried to sit up then screamed in pain.

"Well, maybe not new," Thomas said with a grin when a blast from one of the departing hovercraft suddenly struck the ground just short of the trench. Thomas instinctively threw himself over Shara to protect her from the shower of dirt and rocks that followed. As it settled, he started to get up then stopped halfway as they came face to face. He wanted to stay there, to tell her how much he loved her, but… "I should go help the others."

She looked deeply into his eyes. She did not want him to go, but… "Yes, you should."

"Roberts," Rachael shouted, "the two remaining hovercraft are bugging out."

"Where to?"

"Stand by."

Crouching, Thomas ran down the trench to join Toa.

"Is Shara alright?" Roberts asked.

"She is a little sore, but otherwise, she'll be okay."

"Thank God."

"Really. What's the status?"

"Two hovercraft are down. We're tracking the other two."

"Thomas," Rachael said, "I show both of them headed toward Sandor, two blocks over and three up to the left of us."

"Got it," he said and handed Toa a disrupter pistol before grabbing another for himself. "Ready?"

"To do what?"

"To go get Sandor," he said, putting on a tactical wrist communicator.

"And why would I do that?"

"Well, if he's your boss, he probably wants you to save him."

Toa nodded. "That's probably true."

"So?"

"Lead the way."

Hunched over, Thomas raced down the trench, Toa on his heels. On exit, both men dodged the incoming Tactical Squad fire before diving behind the remains of a building's foundation.

"Not bad so far," Toa commented, catching his breath.

"Your glass half full?" Thomas asked, doing the same.

"Something like that."

Both men got up and ran full speed down the street to the next intersection and the safety of a partially destroyed wall. Checking for soldiers, seeing none, they stepped out into the street.

"Take cover!" Rachael suddenly shouted over Thomas's wrist communicator.

Both men instantly dove back to their left a split second before the ground they had been standing on exploded from a barrage of incoming disrupter blasts. "Rachael, where are they? Rachael? Rachael? Damn... Toa, how many do you think are out there?"

"Two?"

"Okay. I'll go to the right."

"Then how about I go to the left," Toa said with a grin.

Thomas shook his head then ran off, keeping behind the building remains. He was thankful his training had prepared him for a great many things, including urban combat. But no matter how real the setting or aggressive the opponent, everyone knew at the end of the exercise, they would be laughing and chiding one another over a cold beer. This was different. This was real, and the enemy was out to kill.

Thomas kept his movements purposely erratic, waiting, listening, moving randomly slow or fast, and scanning everywhere. He knew his opponents were doing the same. Sweat broke out on his brow. He hugged a wall then quickly looked around the corner, rapidly pulling his head back before someone could blow it off.

To the left, he suddenly heard a misplaced footstep. His disrupter set on stun, he rounded the corner and drew a bead on his enemy. His finger began to squeeze the trigger when his brain screamed hold fire, the image of Toa coming into focus.

Toa looked at Thomas then down and slowly shook his head only to spot a targeting laser moving up his pant leg from the side. He quickly jumped to his right before an incoming disrupter blast just missed him. Rolling upright, he opened fire on his now visible attacker. His first shot went wide, but not the second. The man screamed, struck square in the leg. The blast spun him around then dropped him on the ground where he stayed, unconscious.

Thomas saw a second soldier run down the road a block over on her way to Toa's position. The soldier spotted Thomas as well, but not in time. She flew backward, shot in the chest before she could fire. A second shot made sure she was unconscious.

Toa came forward. "Nice shot," he said, then suddenly aimed his disrupter at Thomas's head and fired. The blast flew just past Thomas's ear and struck down a third Tactical Squad soldier standing on the second story remains of a building.

Thomas looked casually behind him. "I thought you said there were only two."

"I guess I was wrong," Toa replied when the sound of hovercraft engines winding down to land was heard.

"Let's move."

Racing down the road, they came to a stop behind the ruins of a warehouse when two hovercraft flashed by.

"Now what?" Toa asked.

Thomas looked around, then up. "The street is a dead end. The only way out is past us, but with their shields up, we'll need to get at them from above."

"Agreed, but how?" Toa asked, then saw Thomas staring at the remains of a three-story building next to them. "You're not serious?"

"Afraid so," Thomas said on his way to the structure's fire escape.

"Damn."

"What the hell took you so long?" Sandor demanded of the Major as his hovercraft came to a stop.

"Our sensors don't work with all the background radiation. We had trouble finding you," the Major replied flatly, not at all happy to have left his men to rescue some worthless executive. "Sir, now that you're safe, I'd like to send the other ship back to reinforce our position."

"I'll tell you when I am safe," Sandor said in anger as he climbed into the copilot's seat. "Do you understand?"

"Yes, sir."

"Make sure you do. Now, get me to the transport."

"Yes, sir."

Up the fire escape, Thomas found the building to be of concrete and steel construction. The third story wall had shielded a sloped second story metal roof from the power plant's shockwave. He headed across it.

Toa reached the top of the fire escape, afraid to look down. A quarter of the way across the roof, he saw Thomas standing in front of an eight-meter long skylight devoid of glass. The roof above and below gone, only the narrow steel truss that ran the length of the skylight would allow passage to the other side. Coming up, looking nervously over the edge, he saw shards of glass embedded in the floor. Most appeared to be sticking straight up.

"Ready?" Thomas asked, stepping out on the beam.

"You're not going out there, are you?" Toa asked with uncommon concern in his voice.

Thomas looked back, surprised. "Why not?"

"Thomas, I can't."

"What?"

"I'm... I'm afraid of heights, okay?"

"You're what?"

"Have been since I was a little kid."

"But, you fly."

"That's different somehow. Don't ask me to explain it. I know it's dumb, but…" Toa said, shaking his head.

"You've got to do this."

"I know."

"Just don't look down."

"Now you tell me."

"Look," Thomas said, "just put your arms out to your side for balance and walk normally. Like this." He moved easily across the beam with a slight hop at the end. "Just like that."

"Thomas, I can't."

"Yes you can. Just concentrate."

"Sure, no problem," Toa said and took his first shaky step. "Just like that, sure." He carefully placed one foot in front of the other while his arms flailed in a feeble attempt to maintain his balance.

Too painful to watch, Thomas walked up to his section of the roof and carefully peered around the third story wall. "Hurry up. They're almost here."

"Be right there," Toa replied sarcastically. He was halfway across when his front foot somehow slipped, pitching him forward. He tried to calm himself, but couldn't. His mind filled with panic. Recovery impossible, his only alternative was to race to the end of the truss and hope he could maintain enough of his balance to make it. His first step covered one of the remaining three meters. The second covered even more before almost all control was lost. He knew the third would be his last, one way or another. With all his strength, he leaped for the roof and landed high on the panel next to the end of the truss. But the slope was too great. Desperately, he clawed for a handhold but was unable to find one before he slid toward the opening and the deadly chard-strewn floor below.

"Toa!" Thomas lunged for his hand, but just missed it. In horror, he saw his friend disappear out of sight. Quickly to the edge of the skylight opening, expecting the worst, he found Toa holding on to the bottom section of the truss. "Would you quit hanging around," he said, trying to hide his concern. "We've got a bad guy to catch."

"Sorry, it slipped my mind for a second," he replied and climbed up the truss. Thomas lent him a hand the last part of the way up. "Hey, I think I might be cured."

"Good, then you won't mind the next part of the plan," Thomas said on his way to the far end of the roof.

"What do you mean? Aren't we going to fire on them as they pass?

"Can't. The hovercrafts' shields will alter the path of the disrupter blasts. We won't know where to aim."

"So, what are we doing up here on the roof?" Toa asked, his eyes going wide. Thomas grinned. "No, you're not serious."

"You said you were cured," he said, timing the approach of the hovercraft nearest to them. Unfortunately, it was the one without Sandor.

"I said I might be cured."

"Same thing. Ready?"

"No!"

"Now!"

Both men raced down the remaining length of the roof and jumped off into space.

"Captain!" the hovercraft gunner shouted.

The pilot instinctively slammed the stick of the hovercraft hard port for a second, causing the ship to rotate onto its port side. Thomas and Toa landed on the ship's exposed starboard side then crawled quickly up to the rail before the hovercraft was righted, leaving both men dangling.

"Captain, the wall!"

The pilot again threw the stick hard port briefly to avoid a collision. In the process, Thomas and Toa were able to rotate themselves around the rail and into the open cockpit before the vessel was righted again. Thomas lunged for the Captain while Toa went for the strapped-in gunner when the Captain again pitched the craft, this time to starboard. Toa just managed to grab the mast of the disrupter cannon. Thomas clung onto the back of the copilot's chair before the ship was righted once more.

Out of his seat restraint, standing, the Captain drew a disrupter from his shoulder holster. Thomas lunged for the hand holding the pistol only to have the Captain counter with a devastating left cross. Sent flying on his back into the pilot's seat, Thomas looked up to see the disrupter aimed at his head.

"Time to die, asshole."

Thomas kicked the copilot's control stick hard starboard, putting the vessel on its side. The Captain tried to balance himself but failed. He fell screaming over the starboard rail onto the ground some four meters below. "I don't think so."

The hovercraft righted once again, Toa on his back, he continued to hold onto the mast with one hand while he grabbed the barrel of the disrupter cannon with the other. Swinging it wide, the handle caught the unsuspecting gunner in the back of the head, dropping him. Toa on his feet, a quick disconnect of the man's safety harness was followed by a hard push that sent the stunned gunner over the stern.

"You good?" Thomas called back, taking over the hovercraft's controls, buckling himself in.

Toa put on a spare harness then attached it. "Go."

Thomas powered the hovercraft forward in pursuit of Sandor.

"Major, I've lost visual contact with the other hovercraft," the gunner reported.

"I'll circle around."

"The hell you will," Sandor shouted. "Get me to the transport now!"

"But, sir?"

"Now, Major."

"Yes, sir."

"Great plan, Thomas," Toa shouted, the hovercraft rapidly moving past the remains of the warehouse sector, headed toward the spaceport.

"You didn't like it?" he yelled back, spotting Sandor.

"No."

"Major, the Dissenters have captured our other hovercraft!" the gunner shouted, having looked behind him.

"Open fire!"

"Yes, sir," he said and rotated his disrupter cannon into position.

"Transport," the Major yelled into his com system over the sound of outgoing fire, "take off now. We'll rendezvous on my signal."

"What the hell do you think you're doing, Major?" Sandor fumed.

"My job, sir. Now strap in," he said and turned hard starboard.

"Front shields are at maximum," Thomas shouted over the outgoing disrupter fire while he moved his hovercraft randomly up and down, to port and starboard to avoid being hit himself. "Target his engines."

"If you don't hold still for a second, I'll be lucky to hit the ship."

"They're gaining on us," Sandor shouted.

The Major scanned a three dimensional graphic of the area. "We're carrying more weight, but we can lose the other hovercraft in the cave."

"The what?"

Toa watched Sandor's hovercraft disappear underground. "That guy's nuts."

Thomas quickly called up his ship's chart. "There are three exits, all well separated. We'll lose Sandor if we don't go in after him."

"Great."

"Don't tell me you're afraid of the dark too," Thomas said as he dove the ship underground. In the darkness, their speed, the confined space, and the incoming disrupter fire all combined with raising his adrenalin level. One wrong move and it would be their ruin.

The Major headed toward one of the exits. "Gunny, fire at the cavern roof."

He rotated his cannon upward. "Firing!"

"Toa, I need to flip us over!"

Toa activated his harness' tractor beam. "Go."

Thomas put the hovercraft upside down for protection from the falling rocks, but... "I can't hold her much longer," he yelled, each blow from above, making it almost impossible to fly the ship.

Outside, the Major had pulled his ship to a stop. He watched the captured hovercraft exit the cavern upside down, crippled, barely in control. It didn't matter. "Fire!"

A direct hit, the captured ship on fire, the Major saw it momentarily disappear over a small ridge then become visible halfway across the lake. Flashing down the tarmac, it smashed into what was left of the spaceport's terminal building. A second and third explosion rocked the area.

Sandor watched the smoke rise from the crash site as they approached. "Nicely done, Major."

"Thank you, sir," the Major replied, for he couldn't agree more. The men he had just killed were murderers who deserved nothing better than to suffer a fate worse than that of their victims. His only regret was that they had died too quickly.

He flew over the wreckage that radiated out from the crash site for fifty meters in all directions. As expected, there were no survivors to be seen. Moving off, he activated his com system. "Transport, rendezvous at 134-166."

"Roger Major."

CHAPTER SIXTEEN

Unable to hold his breath any longer, Thomas burst to the surface of the lake and gasped for air. In front of him, the hovercraft with Sandor in it was disappearing to the east. Toa surfaced right behind him. "I thought they would never leave," Toa said, trying to catch his breath as they waded ashore.

"Neither did I," Thomas said, gasping.

"So do you think these things out ahead of time, or do you just kind of go with the flow?" Toa asked.

Thomas led the way up the low bank. "Planned to the last detail."

"Right... Now what?" Toa asked, taking off his harness. "No, wait, don't tell me. Let me guess. You've got a fighter stashed somewhere around here, and we're going to blast off after the transport. Am I right?"

Thomas pulled a remote control from his pocket and pushed the button. The cloak deactivated, the tri-wing fighter Hawkins had brought back earlier from the Black Market, suddenly appeared at the lake-end of the tarmac. He grinned. "How did you know?"

Toa just shook his head.

The Major entered the bridge of the transporter to see a starfield on the viewscreen. He was followed by his Gunny and Sandor. "We're heading for Kuril, sir," the Helmsman announced.

The Major made his way to the command chair. "Control, has the base been notified of our situation?" he asked of the only other soldier that had been left onboard the ship.

"Yes, sir. A squad of fighters is scheduled to arrive in one hour twenty minutes, followed by a Strike Force of 125 thirty minutes later."

"Excellent," Sandor said, standing next to the Major. "That should take care of the situation."

The officer bit his lip, suppressing the anger he felt, knowing he had been forced to leave his men behind.

"Sir," the Controller said, "I'm picking up an incoming communication."

"On speaker."

"Yes, sir."

"Theta Tactical Squad transport, this is Thomas Chandler. Return to the planet's surface immediately, or we will open fire."

"No," Sandor said in disbelief.

"Rear view on screen, now!" the Major ordered.

"Yes, sir."

The picture changed to show the tri-wing fighter screaming out of Sorel's upper atmosphere directly for them. Far more modern and technologically superior to the best Tactical Squad starfighter, three curves blended at the wing and empennage tips. At the interstices, just short of the tips, were well-stocked armament bays.

The Major activated the com from his command chair. "Chandler, this is Major Kangas. We are shorthanded and unarmed, repeat, unarmed. We will comply with your orders."

"You'll what?" Sandor shouted.

The Major slammed his fist down on the communication's button, deactivating the system. "Listen, Sandor, against my better judgment, I agreed to leave my men to save your sorry ass, so sit down, shut up and let me do my job. Is that clear?"

Sandor's face went flush. No one had talked to him like that and ultimately survived. But he needed this man and his skills for now. He would wait, but not long. "Then do your job."

The Major reactivated the comm system again. "Sorry, Chandler, we had a little... dissent onboard. We will comply with your request as soon as we program the navigational computer for re-entry. Until then, we will shut down our engines."

Thomas couldn't help but snicker as Toa checked his sensor screen from the single-seat attack center located in front of and below the pilot's position. "She's cut her engines as advertised."

"This is too easy," Thomas said, shaking his head. "The pilot of that hovercraft was too good to just give up like this. Scan for anything unusual."

"Right."

"Thomas?" Shara was heard to say over the com system.

"Go ahead, Shara."

She stood on Main Street. To the side, three Dissenters led the last of the Tactical Squad at disrupter point to the park to join their bound comrades. Other Dissenters were loading equipment on the Copernicus shuttle. "Thomas, the area is secure. The Tactical Squad are all accounted for and restrained."

"Is everyone alright?"

"Two of our people were hurt, but the Doc says it's not life-threatening. The rest of the injuries are minor, still… Get him, Thomas. Get Sandor."

He continued to power the fighter toward the transport. "We will."

"Thomas, it's a trap!" Toa shouted.

"Full power to the aft shields!" he ordered, throwing the stick hard starboard and pushing the throttles to full. A second later, the transport's main body exploded, sending fragments flying out in all directions. The fighter raced just ahead of the blast when an alarm for a weapons lock filled the cockpit.

The Major brought the transporter's separated command module in behind the fighter, its two outboard pods fully armed. "Fire!"

Thomas pulled back on the stick to climb his ship. The incoming disrupter beams flashed just under them. "Target her engines," he said, continuing his loop.

"You idiot, they're turning inside us!" Sandor yelled.

"Helm, bring," he started to say when disrupter blasts from the fighter rocked the command module. Alarms sounded as overloaded circuits began to fail. The Controller scanned his board. "Sir, I've lost power to the disrupters!"

"Helm, hard port. Gunny, fire all torpedoes."

The weapons pods on either side of the command module erupted. In rapid-fire, one torpedo after another sped away on its individual path to the fighter.

"Thomas!"

"I see them," he said and accelerated into a hard turn to port. "How many are there?"

Toa flashed up a three-dimensional scan of the surrounding space and the torpedoes tracks. "Seven. No, eight."

"Establish their command codes."

"I'll need some time."

"I know…" He moved the fighter erratically, trying to prevent the torpedoes from getting a lock on them.

Toa entered the necessary data into his computer. The screen came alive, displaying eight lines of ten numbers. Each began to rapidly cycle in a searching pattern.

"Toa, two dead ahead!"

He quickly turned his attention back to his attack computer and set up two separate solutions. "Can you hold steady?"

"Not for long," Thomas said when an alarm sounded a weapon's lock. "Toa?"

"Firing!"

Intense disrupter beams shot out aft from two of the fighter's weapons bays. Two fireballs marked the demise of the incoming threat when another alarm sounded. Thomas checked his screen. "Two more dead astern."

"Activating the magnetic grid… Go!"

Thomas spiraled the fighter, dispensing six satellite mines around a larger central one aft. Once in position, laser beams connected each of the orbs, forming a blue electronic web between the fighter and the incoming torpedoes. Thomas again held his ship on a straight course causing both torpedoes to slam full power into the energy field, exploding them on contact. "How are you doing on those codes?"

"Almost there," Toa said when two more alarms were heard. "Thomas, I show two torpedoes inbound, one starboard the other port," he said when another alarm sounded. "The command module has a missile lock! They've fired. Two are inbound starboard side!"

"What kind of tracking?"

"Infra-red."

"Fire on the starboard torpedo, first," Thomas said and banked the fighter to head straight for it.

"Firing!"

Thomas raced his ship up and over the starboard torpedo's explosion, then put it directly between his ship and the incoming portside torpedo, causing the portside torpedo to explode. He then held his breath as he cut his engines and watched the two incoming missiles flash just above and below the fighter on their way to the higher heat source. Two more massive explosions followed aft.

"I have the codes for the two remaining torpedoes."

"Jam them."

"Done," Toa said then checked his board. "Oh no!"

"What?"

"The torpedoes are going after the command module!"

"Can we intercept them?"

"Not in time."

"Major, the two remaining torpedoes have locked onto us!" the Controller shouted over an alarm.

"Establish new codes."

"I can't, sir. They're jammed."

"Helm, get us out of here!"

"Yes, sir."

Sandor suddenly rotated the command chair around to force the Major to look at him. "What are you doing? Destroy the fighter."

"Get out of my way, asshole," the Major said and pushed Sandor to the side on his way to the weapons station. "Gunny, can you get the disrupters back online?"

"Not in time, sir."

"Damn." He was no quitter, but then again, he was no fool.

"Thirty seconds to impact!" the Controller shouted.

THE DISSENTERS

The Major nodded. "Open the escape pod's inner door."

Standing next to the only pod as the door opened, Sandor entered then, without a second thought, shut the door before the others could get there.

"Sandor!" the Major shouted racing aft.

"Damn him," the Gunny said, joining the Major. He ripped off the pod's control panel and tried to electrically force the door open. "It's no good. He's locked it out!"

"Fifteen seconds to impact!" the Controller shouted.

The pod's automatic distress beacon and external lights deactivated, Sandor looked through the window in the door at the Major. A sadistic smile crossed his face while he activated the com system. "Goodbye, asshole, wasn't it?" he said with a laugh before he ejected the pod.

Helpless, Thomas and Toa could only watch the two torpedoes slam into the command module. A series of fiery explosions followed, marking its demise.

"Did anyone make it out?" Thomas asked.

"Not that I can tell," Toa replied.

"What a waste…"

Shara watched the Copernicus shuttle land once more and lower its aft ramp. The last of the Dissenters raced to load their equipment and weapons when Roberts ran up. "This should do it."

"It has to. We're running out of time."

"Right."

"Were you able to record our conversation with Sandor before shooting started?"

"No. The Tactical Squad jammed the frequency."

Shara slowly shook her head. "That's unfortunate."

"Does it matter if Sandor is dead?"

"We still need to clear our name."

"True…"

"Roberts," Keira called out, "I need your help."

"Coming."

Shara turned to watch the tri-wing land on Main Street. She saw Thomas get out, barely noticing Toa as he ran to help the others. No words were spoken. None were needed as Thomas took her in his arms and kissed her.

"Captain, I'm picking up an emergency beacon," the lead Tactical Squad fighter's Controller announced.
"Magnify."
"Yes, sir," he said, the escape pod appearing on his screen. "We're being hailed, sir."
Sandor appeared. "Good to see you, Captain."
"Mr. Sandor. Are you alright? Are others with you?"
"I am, but the others were killed by the Dissenters in their wanton attack on the transport."
"Damn them."

Her limp almost gone, the Copernicus safe once again in the nearby nebula, Shara headed into the mess to find Toa and Thomas and a cup of coffee. "Toa, thank you for your help back on the planet."
He nodded. "At first, things just didn't add up. Then when Sandor showed his true colors by ordering your executions, it was an easy decision to make."
She joined the two at the table. "Sandor was truly evil."
"Agreed," Thomas said. "So, what do you want to do now, Shara?"
"I want to expose Sandor using the recordings."
"Anonymously?" Toa asked.
She shook her head. "No, but just me."
"Do you think that wise?" Thomas asked. "You'll be a marked woman if they don't believe you."
Shara laughed. "I think I'm way past that…"
Thomas smiled. "True."
"As for the ore, I asked Chu to contact his father earlier. Mr. Lee is willing to store both the Copernicus and the ore in one of his secret salvage yards left over from the Corporate War. He will also act as our broker in the sale of the ore."
"That's fantastic," Thomas said.
"What ore?" Toa asked innocently.

"We discovered a new deposit of diamatron ore on Sorel just before you arrived on the planet. What was there is now onboard the Copernicus."

"Really? How much, if you don't mind my asking?"

"I'd say billions, with a capital B," Thomas replied.

"Wow!"

"I know," Shara said, "but if we can't prove our innocence…"

"Understood."

"To that end," Shara continued, "I thought we'd use some of the money to buy a new freighter."

Thomas nodded. "Sooner or later, someone will put two and two together and come looking for the Copernicus."

"Exactly. Mr. Lee was able to locate one for us on the planet Matee. I thought the three of us, Keira and Roberts, would go there to get her outfitted. Chu, Hawkins, and the rest of the Dissenters can take care of this ship and the ore."

"We can also monitor Theta's efforts to capture us as well," Thomas offered.

"Oh, yeah, that too…"

CHAPTER SEVENTEEN

Byron Walker sat at the anchor desk and watched the countdown from the floor controller. With five seconds to go, he tilted his head in preparation for his cue. Two, one, and the music started. His monitor showed the wide shot of the newsroom moving to a close up of him. "Good evening and welcome to the Theta Corporation News. I'm Byron Walker."

A picture of Sandor appeared over his left shoulder. "A day after T.A. Sandor's dramatic escape from a vicious attack by the Dissenters, an email was sent to the District High Court by Shara Lockett, the daughter of the late Corbin Lockett, founder of the Dissenters. In it, she accuses Mr. Sandor of being responsible for the destruction of the Sorel Colony. Bound by law to investigate, the District High Court just minutes ago issued a statement in which its members unanimously agreed that the allegations against Mr. Sandor were nothing more than yet another attack on the Theta Corporation by the Dissenters. For a live report, we go now to Win Chow at the Alpha District Courthouse. Win."

"Byron," Win said, the courthouse perfectly framed over his left shoulder. "I have with me now one of the Theta Corporation lawyers, Mr. Viken, who argued the case on behalf of Mr. Sandor." Win turned to his left as the camera pulled back to frame the two of them. "Mr. Viken, can you tell us just how serious this allegation was?"

"Well, the fact that it was made by Shara Lockett discounted its credibility right from the start, but we treat any attack on the Theta Corporation and its people very seriously."

"I see. And are you now free to talk about your defense?"

"Now that the Court has ruled, yes," he said with a slight

nod of his head. "There were actually two attachments to the correspondence the Court received. The first was a recording where the Dissenters claimed responsibility for altering the course of one of our ore ships in the Theta Shipping Lane via a buoy malfunction they induced. Shara Lockett asserted that Mr. Sandor had ordered that recording be selectively edited to where the Dissenters claimed they destroyed the Sorel Colony instead."

"Why did she think Mr. Sandor would do that?"

"She claimed the Sorel Mine was losing money and owed the miners a contract-end bonus and paid relocation. Ms. Lockett said that by Mr. Sandor ordering the destruction of the colony, he was not only able to get out from under that situation but, by blaming the Dissenters, he was also able to claim the insurance money."

"And how were you able to refute her claim?"

"Our investigators found the buoy malfunction was the result of a defective circuit board and not something purposely initiated by the Dissenters. As such, her claim was thrown out by the court."

"I see," Win said. "And the second attachment?"

"It was a recording from the Sorel power plant's security room. On it, Pendrac, a Supervisor for the Sorel Mine's manager, Lucian Merrick, was seen adjusting the power plant's controls just before the uncontained reaction. The associated text accused Mr. Sandor of approving the operation for the same reasons I gave earlier."

"And what was your argument to the court?"

"We claimed the recording was doctored. Through her job at the Sorel Mine, Shara Lockett had access to the security room and could easily have taken footage from before and shopped in Pendrac, the date and/or both. Of more importance, however, was that our investigators examined the Sorel power plant's security room and found the equipment had been destroyed by the uncontained reaction. As such, the second recording was also thrown out."

"Interesting. Did Ms. Lockett claim anything else?"

"No, but our investigation did discover additional information suggesting a motive for the Dissenter's destruction of the Sorel Colony," Viken volunteered.

"And what was that?"

"We obtained entries from Mr. Sandor's private files where he described his increasing suspicion that there was more diamatron ore being mined on Sorel than what was actually being reported by Mr. Merrick, but he could not prove it. These entries were made well before the uncontained reaction occurred. We believe Corbin Lockett discovered the stockpiled ore then quit so he could later obtain it for himself and the Dissenters."

"How so?"

"In his position as foreman, Corbin Lockett would have known that the Sorel Mine's claim would expire if a continual presence was not maintained by the Theta Corporation for ten days. By destroying the Sorel Colony then waiting the appropriate time, the Dissenters were able to take ownership of the Sorel Mine through the Phoenix Mining Company."

"But Corbin Lockett was killed before the discovery was announced," Win argued.

"He was, but his daughter, Shara, was not. She took over the Dissenters and is also one of the co-founders of the Phoenix Mining Company."

"And the attack on Mr. Sandor?"

"He went to Sorel with a Theta Tactical Squad detail to expose the Phoenix Mining Company's management as being Dissenters. When there, they were viciously attacked by the main Dissenter force with superior numbers and firepower. Mr. Sandor was lucky to have escaped with his life."

"And the stockpiled ore?"

"After the attack, evidence was found that showed the Dissenters had removed a large amount of ore from the planet before Mr. Sandor's arrival. We believe it was the stockpiled ore."

"An incredible story."

"It truly is."

"Thank you for your candor, Mr. Viken."

"You're welcome," he replied before the camera pushed in and once again captured only Win.

"There you have it, Byron. Not only has Mr. Sandor been found innocent, but it is now believed that the Dissenters' true motive behind the destruction of the Sorel Colony and the murder of the colonists was not in protest of the Theta Corporation, but was simple greed. For Theta Corporation News, I'm Win Chow."

Keira walked down to the end of the seedy bar and placed her drink tray down. "Two whiskey sours," she called out to the bartender before adjusting her skimpy server's dress. She looked at the viewscreen while she waited. The Theta Corporation News was on.

"A recording of the uncontained reaction that destroyed the Sorel Colony taken from a weather satellite in geosynchronous orbit above the colony has just been released," Byron said. "We offer it to you now. Parental guidance is advised."

The picture on the viewscreen changed to show the Sorel Colony from above. The mine and power plant were to the west. The colony to the east. A cloudless day, a blinding flash suddenly radiated out from the power plant. The camera did its best to compensate for the extreme brightness, but couldn't, and the picture went black. When it finally did return, a mushroom cloud was seen forming over what little was left of the colony below.

"Damn," slurred a man at the bar.

"Those Dissenters should be drawn and quartered," another said before downing a shot of whiskey in one gulp. "One more?" he asked the woman next to him.

"Sure," she replied, weaving slightly when the anchor reappeared.

"For a live report from the Sorel Colony, we go now to Michael Brannon. Michael."

The picture changed again to show Michael dressed in a radiation suit, standing in front of a mass of twisted metal and broken concrete. "Thank you, Byron. Those responsible for the destruction you see behind me are now the object of the largest man-hunt in the history of the Discovered Worlds. Although many of the details of that investigation remain secret, we have recently learned that a multi-functional task force has been formed and is very close to discovering the Dissenters' whereabouts. We will update you on any developments as soon as they become known. From Sorel, I'm Michael Brannon."

"Thank you, Michael," Byron said back on camera. "As a result of tonight's ruling by the District High Court, arrest warrants for the mass murder have been issued for three of the Dissenters."

Three pictures appeared on the screen. "They are Thomas Chandler, Shara Lockett, and Wendel 'Toa' Alesana," Byron said in a voice-over.

"And in a related story," Byron said once more back on camera, a picture of Sandor above his left shoulder, "it has been reported that Chairman Andrews of the Theta Corporation will announce the promotion of T.A. Sandor to Corporate Vice President of Operations at this evening's Theta Corporation Charity Ball. In that position, Mr. Sandor will report directly to the Chairman."

The excitement over, the patrons of the bar turned back to their drinks, the scenes of Sorel already forgotten. They had their own problems and conquests to worry about.

"Here you go, Keira," the bartender said, giving her the requested drinks.

"Thanks." She headed to the couple in the corner when a drunk yelled out from the back.

"Hey cutie, how about some service over here," a fat, bald man replete with fake gold chains on a thick bed of exposed chest hair called out.

Keira headed back to the bar. "Margie will be right there to take your order."

"That's not what I'm talking about, honey. How about you and I get out of here? I can put a smile on that pretty little face of yours that will last a week."

"Yeah, right," Keira said, unable to mask the disgust in her voice. Putting her drink tray away, she headed to the backroom. Thank God their time on Matee would only be for a couple more days.

With an hour for lunch, she quickly replaced her high heels with conventional walking shoes. She then draped a long, hooded overcoat over her for cover against the dark drizzle that never seemed to end in the city of Jartu. Out the rear door, she fell in step with the great unwashed on their way to a maze of tents and corrugated metal shacks that housed the city's open-air market. The smell of herbs and garlic beckoned her, but one sight of the steam tables with their thick soup of unidentified animal parts and her appetite quickly disappeared. Instead, she chose from a mixture of fruits and vegetables, selecting the ones least rotten.

"How much?"

The yellow-skinned man with epicanthic eyes stood behind the counter. He strained to see the face in the dark recess of the hood but failed. "Twenty-five," he finally said in broken English.

Keira quickly paid him then, with her grocery bag in hand, she once more joined the others in walking down the sidewalk, past the drunks and hookers with their broken English come-ons.

"Hey you, mister, mister," an approaching woman called out to the man just in front of her, wearing all black. The raincoat the woman had on suddenly changed from opaque to clear and exposed her large naked breasts underneath it. "You want jig jig? I very good. Not much money, heya?"

As the man stopped to stare at the woman's offer, Keira walked on in disgust. At the corner, she waited for the crossing traffic when an unseen drunk lying in the doorway of a boarded-up building reached out and grabbed her by the ankle. "Change... I need some change."

She quickly yanked her foot away, then ran across the street and ducked into a deserted alley. Halfway down it, a male voice called out from the shadows of the abandoned building in front of her. "Yo, my man."

She froze as he stepped out into the road. He was joined by another, also in his late teens. Both sported red mohawks and wore heavy black eye makeup. Their signature black leather vests, replete with a distinctive split devil's head patch, announced they were members of a fierce street gang known as the Mulu Warriors. The first man carried a baseball bat. The second twirled a butterfly knife with deadly precision.

Keira turned to run when a third youth appeared from the shadows to block her escape. "Hey, maintain, my brother," he said and drew a tomahawk from a holster strapped to his back. He began to walk toward her. "We just want the bag... and maybe anything else you got."

Keira slowly backed up until blocked by a building as the three converged on her.

"What's wrong, my man?" asked the Warrior with the bat. "We're not going to hurt you." An evil grin stretched across his face.

Each tried to peer beneath her hood. "Yo, drop the hood.

Now!" the male with the knife demanded.

Keira shifted the grocery bag to her left hand then did as instructed.

"Yo, mama!" the Warrior with the tomahawk exclaimed. "Alright, it's party time. Now, how about you take off," he started to say when Keira threw her grocery bag at the man with the knife then kicked out at the one with the tomahawk. Her foot caught him square in the crotch before she just barely ducked a roundhouse blow from the bat. From a crouch, she extended her right arm, and a miniature disrupter automatically sprang out of her sleeve and into her hand. She fired point-blank at the man with the bat, the impact lifting him off his feet and into instant unconsciousness. The man with the knife fell next before the tomahawk flashed just past her ear. Keira pivoted and fired again, purposely aiming for the man's crotch. She was pleased with her accuracy. "Party on."

From a darkened doorway, the man dressed in all black holstered his own disrupter and watched Keira gather up her groceries. He stayed hidden while she rushed down the alley.

Byron Walker sat at the anchor desk. "We go now to the Theta Corporation's Grand Ballroom and the annual Theta Corporation Charity Ball. Reporting live from this evening's gala event is our own social editor, April Van Borne. April."

"Thank you, Byron," she said from the balcony above the ballroom. Her coiffure was perfect, and her low-cut designer gown stunning. Theta's elite and their spouses, all dressed in formal attire, filled the vast room below. "A veritable who's who of top management from throughout the Theta Corporation have gathered here tonight to give back to the community," she said with excitement. "Dressed in their very finest, the champagne is flowing and the mood is festive, to say the least. Scheduled activities include a speech by Chairman Andrews then dancing till dawn," she said when the room lights began to dim. "Let's go now to Chairman Andrews."

Polite applause filled the ballroom as the music faded, and the Chairman moved behind a podium on a stage in the back. Sandor stood behind him to the side. "Thank you, ladies and gentlemen," the Chairman began. "Thank you all for coming tonight and making this affair such a great success. So, while I have you here..." He paused while those assembled politely laughed. "As you all know, success in business is bringing the right product to market on time and at cost. What all of you don't know, however, is that in the Operations community, this is never done without a battle. They are always complaining that they either don't have enough time or money or that the engineering requires changing or that their suppliers are late. Well, let me assure you the list is endless. So, the question is, how do they do it, besides padding their estimates?"

Polite laughter again filled the room.

"They do it with the strength of their people and those who manage them. We were all recently saddened by the untimely death of Suki Masuto. Her dedication to Theta and her leadership at the helm of the Operations organization will long be remembered. Replacing her was by no means a small task, and yet the other Board Members and I feel extremely confident that T.A. Sandor will not only maintain that organization's outstanding record but will take it to new heights. T.A."

Applause filled the Grand Ballroom. The Chairman yielded the podium to Sandor after a congratulatory handshake.

"Thank you, everyone," Sandor said, "especially Chairman Andrews and the Board for allowing me to serve in this capacity and for having the confidence in me to continue the tradition of quality that has so distinguished the Operations organization and the Theta Corporation.

Before I accepted this position, however, I made a special request of Chairman Andrew. I asked him to also allow me to continue to direct the Theta Corporation's efforts in apprehending and bringing to justice the Dissenters for their act of infamy at the Sorel Mining Colony. I am pleased to tell you tonight that Chairman Andrews graciously granted me permission to do so. And so I stand before you now and vow to do everything humanly possible to ensure that the senseless murder of 1638 men, women, and children will not go unpunished."

The assembly shouted their approval.

"Well, there you have it," April said in a voice loud enough to be heard over the applause for Sandor. "In an unprecedented move, a corporate officer has been appointed to lead the search for the Dissenters."

Toa turned off the viewscreen they had brought with them to the best apartment they could find in the condemned building the five Dissenters had chosen to stay in while their new freighter was being outfitted. "I thought Sandor still being alive was bad enough. Now he has total control," he said, dodging the drips coming from the ceiling on his way to the only dry spot in the room, the kitchen table.

"Get rid of us, and he's free," Shara said. "I wonder how long it will be until he's chairman."

Thomas, the only other one there at the moment, sat across from her. "Really…"

Keira headed down another dark alley and slowed her pace. She cautiously checked the shadows for any sign of movement when a cat jumped, screaming from a garbage can. The disrupter instantly in her hand, she was barely able to hold her fire. "Damn."

Her heart pounding, she retracted the weapon that was part of her cloak then ran the remaining distance to the condemned apartment building. Entering through a broken back door, she crossed the graffitied lobby to the sound of rodents scurrying across the broken tile floor. At the top of the grand stairs, she walked down a darkened hall to her left and stopped at the second door from the end on the right. There she pushed the doorbell.

Unseen, unheard, the man dressed in all black silently settled back into the shadows just down the hall from her. He pulled out a small directional recording device and aimed it at her.

Keira looked just above the door. "One alpha, two beta, lambda."

"Alpha?" she heard Shara ask.

"Yes."

A second later, a low hum was followed by the momentary appearance of a blue force field deactivating in front of the door at the end of the hall. Thomas opened the door. "Here, let me take that for you."

Keira walked down the remainder of the hall and handed him the grocery sack. "Thanks." Following her brother inside, she closed the door behind her while Shara reactivated the force field from a console to the side of the living room.

"How's the job?" Thomas asked.

"As good as the living conditions here," she replied sarcastically, noting they were running out of containers for the rainwater dripping from the ceiling.

"Any word on the Tactical Squad?" Toa asked.

Keira took off her shoes and began to massage her feet. "The latest rumor around the bar is that they're looking for us on Omicron."

"Good. How about the task force?"

"Pete, the local duty officer, came in, and after several very strong drinks, said the task force is all for show."

"Oh?"

"He said all that really happened was that some hotshot Hunter came in, asked a few questions then left."

Thomas bit into something that looked vaguely like an apple, but was sour. "I don't like the sound of that. In fact, I don't think you should go back to the bar. We don't need to risk any further exposure."

"Shouldn't I at least quit? I admit the possibility is remote, but what if they send someone out to look for me?"

"She's right, Thomas," Shara said. "I don't think we should do anything that could possibly call attention to ourselves."

He nodded. "Alright, but after tonight, quit."

"Believe me, you don't have to ask twice," Keira said with a laugh. "So, what's the status of the new ship?"

"They're ahead of schedule," Toa said and checked his watch. "In fact, Thomas, Roberts is probably already waiting for us."

"You're going to see Roberts?" Keira asked with new energy. "Maybe I should go with you."

Thomas put a disrupter in his belt then pulled a poncho over his head. "I thought you said you should go back to the bar to quit."

"Well, I... "

"Cheer up, Keira," Shara said, "we'll be out of here tomorrow and possibly clean again."

"I've been meaning to talk to you about that," Thomas said

with a grin.

"What? You're one to talk."

Toa finished putting his poncho on then looked at Shara. "How about I toss this walking armpit in the biggest puddle I see?"

She shook her head. "It won't help, Toa. That smell will have to be surgically removed."

"Not bad," Thomas replied. "Not bad at all. Now how about letting us out the backdoor?"

Shara checked the monitor then deactivated the rear door force field. "My pleasure. It will clear the air," she said, inwardly pleased. She was getting much better at Thomas and Toa's strange sense of humor.

Thomas opened the rear door. "Smells better out here, don't you think?" he said, then immediately shut it behind them.

Shara just shook her head and reactivated the rear door force field. "Your brother."

"Tell me about it. I had to grow up with Thomas."

"I'm sorry."

"Me too… Well, I'd better get going myself."

"How about I send Roberts to walk you home after your shift is over?"

"Well, if you really think you should," Keira said with a smile as she slipped her shoes back on.

Shara checked the monitor. The hall clear, she deactivated the front door force field. "Be careful."

"Yes, mother. See you."

She watched Keira walk down the hall on her monitor then reactivated the force field before absently staring at a picture of her and Thomas she had taped to the wall. Roberts had taken it on Sorel before Sandor's arrival when they were about as dirty and disgusting as anyone could get from the mining operation. Still, she couldn't help but smile.

Outside the building, Keira raised her hood against a smattering of rain then headed down the alley. Turning at the street, she almost ran into the only other person walking down the sidewalk. "Oh, I'm sorry," she said to a man dressed in all black.

"No, it's my fault," he replied with a friendly smile. "I'm afraid I wasn't watching where I was going. Say, I'm really lost.

Could you tell me if this is Central Avenue?"

"Yes it is."

The man's smile instantly gone, he pulled a disrupter from his pocket and aimed it at her head, the setting on kill. "Don't make a sound unless you want to die."

"But, you're mistaken."

The man grabbed Keira's right arm with his free hand, and automatically ejected the concealed disrupter. "I don't think so, Ms. Chandler," he said and adeptly removed the weapon from its mechanism.

"You have no right to do this to me."

"You had no right to kill the people on Sorel. Now move, or I'll drop you right here," he said and shoved her back toward the condemned building she had just left.

Thomas and Toa headed down a dark, deserted, rain-swept street to a corner deli. A sign visible through the bars on the front window declared the establishment was closed. The key in Thomas's hand proved otherwise. Money did have its advantages, and with their find on Sorel, they had more than anyone could ever hope for. It was enough that each of the Dissenters could quit and hopefully disappear beyond the reach of the law. But none had. The thought of always having to look over one's shoulder was prohibitive. The thought of the Prison Planet was terrifying. All wanted to clear their names. All wanted justice.

Thomas locked the barred door behind him then followed Toa to the back.

"Gentlemen," Roberts called out in the dim light. Before him was a sandwich and a bottle of beer.

Toa headed for the cooler. "How's the food today?"

"Quite good, actually."

Thomas joined Roberts at the small table. "So, where do we stand?"

"We finished loading the provisions a couple of hours ago. The diamatron crystals are to be delivered in about an hour. After that, we should be ready to go."

Toa brought three beers to the table with him. "Then, do you need us?"

"No, not really."

"Then we'll go get Shara and Keira and join you at the ship," Thomas said.

Roberts nodded. "Sounds good."

Keira and the Hunter walked in silence down the apartment's hall, his pistol in the small of her back. A hand on her shoulder brought her to a stop just in front of the door with the bell. "One wrong move and you're dead. Got it?" he whispered. Keira nodded while he moved in front of her. Crouching down out of view of the concealed camera, he took out the recorder from his pocket with his free hand. He next pushed the doorbell. "One alpha, two beta, lambda," Keira heard her own voice say.

"Alpha?" Shara asked over a hidden speaker.

"Yes," the recording replied.

"Ok. Stand by."

Keira saw the Hunter glance toward the now visible force field at the end of the hall and lashed out at him with her foot. "Shara, it's a trap!"

The Hunter dodged the intended blow then shot Keira in the shoulder. Turning, he raced for the apartment door when his screams suddenly filled the corridor. His left arm was trapped behind him in the dancing blue electricity of the reactivated force field. With all his strength, he somehow managed to pull it free when the apartment door burst open. Shara fired her disrupter at the figure rolling to his right but missed. The Hunter instantly returned fire then watched Shara fly backward into the room, blood flowing freely from her chest. But was she alone? Quickly up, in pain, he took cover behind the door jamb. A series of random penetrations into the opening gave him the confidence to rush into the room. A careful search showed the other rooms to be empty. She was obviously alone, but for how long? He had to move quickly despite his burned arm.

At the control station, he deactivated the front door force field and exited the apartment. With his good hand, he dragged Keira's unconscious body back inside then shut the door. But the effort was not without cost. His face covered with sweat, his breathing elevated and heavy, he slumped against the wall. The pain and loss of blood were taking their toll. With difficulty, with his good hand shaking, he removed an injector from a pack strapped to his waist and jammed it into his thigh. The reward was instantaneous, marked by a lazy smile in reaction to the powerful narcotic.

His energy temporarily renewed, he got to his feet again and reactivated the force field for the front door then moved to Shara. Her chest covered in blood, her breathing shallow, he took her pulse and found it weak. But then it really didn't matter if she lived or died. He was being paid to rid the worlds of scum like her any way possible. He next took a sample of Shara's blood and inserted it into a small DNA analyzer. Seconds later, her name appeared on the instrument. With a self-satisfied grin, he sat in the chair at the force field console and activated his communicator. "Theta Tactical Control, this is Zeta Three. I have a confirmed capture of Shara Lockett and Keira Chandler. Both are in critical condition."

"Roger, Zeta Three. What's your situation?"

"I'm alone in the suspects' apartment. My arm was caught in a force field on entry. I need medical attention and back-up."

"Stand by... Both have been dispatched to your coordinates. What of Thomas Chandler and Alesana?"

"Thomas Chandler was here but left. I'm not sure of," he started to say when Thomas and Toa suddenly appeared on the rear hallway monitor. "Wait, they're both returning." He terminated the transmission just before a doorbell rang.

"One alpha, two beta, lambda," Thomas's voice was heard to say over the speaker.

The Hunter brushed the sweat from his brow, uncertain what to say... Deciding to not say anything, he lowered the rear hall force field then moved behind a sofa for cover. With the two women, he was already a rich man. With these two, he would never have to work again.

The door opened, and he fired, but into an empty corridor. Two separate disrupter blasts were suddenly returned from either side of the doorway. He ducked the one. The other took out the room's only light.

Thomas and Toa quickly, silently entered the apartment under cover of darkness. His back up against the wall, Thomas held his breath and listened for what he could only assume was the Hunter when a figure quickly crossed in front of the security monitors on its way toward the kitchenette. Thomas fired then dove to his left only to have the Hunter fire back to that side of the flash.

Toa heard both shots, heard two short separate screams, but in the darkness, he was unwilling to believe either. He crawled toward the kitchenette, toward the second scream and found himself under the kitchen table. He stopped and listened, but heard only the sound of dripping water. He started to crawl forward out from under the table when a drop hit his hand. It was a drop that shouldn't be there! Turning instantly on his back, he repeatedly fired up through the table. The Hunter's screams filled the apartment before the man came crashing down on the floor next to him, unconscious.

"Thomas?" Toa called out cautiously. He was sure they had been attacked by only one, but... "Thomas?" No reply, he crawled to the emergency kit they had placed next to the back door and retrieved a light-stick. From behind an armchair, he activated the chemicals and tossed the stick into the center of the room. A careful probe confirmed the Hunter was alone. It also verified his worst nightmare.

Retrieving a medkit, he rushed to Thomas's side to find him unconscious and bleeding profusely from a disrupter blast to his right thigh. The med-light quickly activated, Toa propped it into position then retrieved a hypo of blood multiplier. A second shot of pain reliever was followed by a stimulant before he rushed to Shara.

"Toa," she said weakly. She tried to move, but only grimaced from the pain.

"It's okay, Shara. You're safe now," he said, a bio-scanner in hand.

"Shara," Thomas called out, the stimulant having taken hold. Despite his own pain, he managed to crawl across the floor to her, bringing the med-light with him.

With effort, she turned her head toward him. "Thomas, I'm so sorry," she said while Toa injected her with blood multiplier then a pain reliever before pulling back, giving her and Thomas time together.

"Lie still," Thomas said as he focused the light on her wound. "I'll get the Doc here soon."

"No, there's no time. I heard the Hunter call for backup."
Thomas looked into her eyes. "Shara..."

"Thomas, so many times I've wanted to tell you how much I love you."

"I've loved you from the first day we met."

"Thank you," she said, her eyes sparkling before her head slumped to one side, her breathing erratic.

"No," he moaned through his own tears before gently kissing her.

Toa stood back and stared at the Hunter in anger. He was tempted to end the man's life when out of the corner of his eye, he saw another body lying on the floor. "Oh my God!"

"What?"

"It's Keira!" he said and ran to her with the bio-scanner. "She's alive, but..."

"How bad is it?"

"She's been shot in the shoulder and has lost a lot of blood," he said on his way to the medkit.

"Can you save her?"

"I think so. I'll need the med-light."

Thomas nodded his grim understanding of triage. "Here."

Taking it, Toa focused it on Keira's shoulder then injected her with blood multiplier before again checking the bio scanner. "I need to get her to the Doc," he said when an alarm suddenly sounded from the force field's control station.

With considerable pain, Thomas crawled to the counter then the chair. Men with disrupters were cautiously approaching the apartment's front door. "It's the Hunter's backup. You've got to get Keira out of here now, out the back."

"You too, Thomas," he said, gathering her up in his arms.

"No. I'll only slow you down. Save Keira. Please!"

"But Thomas," Toa started to protest.

"There's no time. Please!"

Toa headed for the backdoor. He knew Thomas was right. Still... "Just remember, we'll be out there whenever."

"I know. Thank you." He watched Toa and Keira clear the backdoor then reactivated the force field. With what strength he had left, he crawled back to Shara. Tears fell from his eyes as he kissed her.

With Keira in his arms, Toa had entered a service stairwell and descended to the basement floor. Moving through a common kitchen to the second condemned tower of the complex, he descended one more flight of stairs to an empty underground parking garage. "Sorry about this," he said, laying her unconscious body gently down on the cement floor for a moment. He removed a remote from his pocket and disabled a cloaking device. An older, non-descript hovercraft suddenly appeared. Gathering Keira back up, he put her in the passenger seat then got in behind the controls. He was about to exit the garage when a police hovercraft with flashing lights raced by. His lights off, Toa nosed his hovercraft forward, enough to find the way clear. Lights on, he pulled out just before two more police hovercraft suddenly rounded the corner. He moved to the curb and stopped to make way. Holding his breath, he watched them race by. Exhaling, he joined traffic and headed toward Roberts and their awaiting ship.

CHAPTER EIGHTEEN

Sandor exited the maglev in front of Theta Corporate Headquarters and was instantly surrounded by a sea of reporters. "Mr. Sandor, Mr. Sandor, is it true you've captured one of the leaders of the Dissenters and killed another?"

Flanked by Theta security, Sandor smiled at the cameramen who walked backward in front of him. He purposely kept his pace slow for maximum exposure. "An official statement will be issued later tonight."

"But sir, haven't you personally taken charge of apprehending the Dissenters?"

"Yes, I have."

"Then, can you confirm the capture and death and give us their names?"

"Not at this time." He knew all too well the value of speculation by the media. He knew that by giving out the information a piece at a time, he could further exploit the Dissenters and remain in the spotlight. "To do so now could possibly place our own people in jeopardy."

"Mr. Sandor! Mr. Sandor!"

Off to one side of the lobby, Chairman Andrews stood talking with two of his staff when Sandor entered the building alone, the reporters held outside by security. The Chairman excused himself and crossed to the elevator and Sandor. "A fine job last night, T.A."

"Thank you, Mr. Chairman," he said as the executive elevator's door opened, and both men entered. "We were lucky."

"You're much too modest," the Chairman said, the elevator

quickly taking them to the top floor. "No, that was a well-conceived and executed plan. Damned unfortunate the other two got away."

The elevator door opened. "We have the area completely covered. Alesana and Keira Chandler shouldn't get far."

The Chairman patted Sandor on the back. "Excellent. Keep up the good work."

"Thank you, sir."

They walked off in opposite directions, Sandor to his new office, where he was greeted by his secretary. "Congratulations."

"Why thank you, Helen. Any word on Keira Chandler and Alesana?"

"No, sir, I'm afraid not."

Sandor nodded. He was torn between the continued exposures to the media that the Dissenters provided him and the potential danger they represented. But then it was all just a matter of timing. Ultimately, the Dissenters' demise was in his best interest. "Keep me posted."

"Yes, sir."

"Also, would you please ask Mr. Terac to come to my office now, if possible?"

"Chairman Andrews' pilot, sir?"

"That's the one."

Sandor headed into his inner office and shut the door. It was time to move on, time to find a fresh horse. He crossed to the bar and made himself a drink. He had completed his research and made his choice. If he was wrong, it would be a problem, but not something he couldn't overcome. Then again, he wasn't wrong.

The intercom sounded.

"Yes Helen?"

"Mr. Terac is here to see you, sir."

"Send him in, please."

"Yes, sir."

Sandor knew Terac to be a former football tight end, but to see him in person was impressive. His hand was like a rock as measured by his grip. "Mr. Terac."

"Mr. Sandor."

"Have a seat, won't you?" Sandor said and motioned to four leather chairs around a coffee table as he made his way to the bar.

"Would you like a drink?"

"Why yes, thank you, sir. Scotch, please, neat," he replied, surprised by the offer.

Sandor nodded and selected the proper glass. "I suppose you're a bit curious as to why I've asked you here."

"Yes, sir, I am."

"Then, I'll get right to it." He handed his guest the drink, then took a seat opposite him. "As one of Chairman Andrews' personal pilots, you have access to information not readily obtainable from, say, conventional sources. I would find that information of value. The question is, would you be willing to provide it to me, covertly, of course?"

"Is that all you would like, sir?" Terac asked simply.

Sandor smiled. It was as he expected. "That's up to you."

"Please continue."

"There may be times when it would be to my advantage to create a situation or eliminate a problem."

Terac nodded. "I understand."

"Do you? Just in case, let me make myself perfectly clear. I will tell you exactly what I want to be done, and you will do it without questioning my reasons or motive. In other words, I require blind loyalty. The price for any other behavior is, well, not in your best interest," Sandor said and searched Terac's face for a reaction. There was none to be seen.

"I fully understand, sir."

"Then, would such a position be of interest to you?"

"Knowledge is power, Mr. Sandor. It can also be a dangerous thing. The reward must, therefore, equal the risk."

"Yes, I quite agree," he said, inwardly pleased by the response. "Although not recorded, I will pay you four times what you are currently making. Also, you will receive certain bonuses for jobs well done."

Terac nodded.

"Then, do you accept?"

"Barring any type of sexual perversion, Yes, sir, I accept."

"Excellent. Please, follow me." Sandor got up and crossed to his desk. He opened a drawer and handed Terac a com-badge. "This unit is an exact replica of the one you're wearing except for a secondary receiver that only I can activate. When needed, you will feel a slight vibration."

Terac examined the unit. "Clever."

"Thank you. This way, please." Sandor headed to a bookcase that made up much of one wall of his new office. There he activated an unseen switch, and the center section of the case unexpectedly swung open to reveal a passage into an adjacent room. "In the future, you will enter through here. A motion detector and video camera will alert me to your presence. I will activate this door only when I'm alone. The other room is secure and posted as such. I have one keycard. Here is the only other."

Terac accepted the card.

"The only other person who knows about this panel," Sandor said, closing the case, "is Mr. Damon Palmer of the Palmer Construction Company. I want him eliminated."

"It will be my pleasure, sir."

Thomas sat in an isolation cell, the two-by-three-meter space devoid of windows or bars. A bunk, toilet, and sink were his only furnishings, but he failed to care. All he could think about was Shara… He had held her in his arms, only dimly aware of the shouting voices suddenly around him. The next thing he knew, he was face down on the apartment carpet with his hands forced behind him and cuffed. Roughly brought to his feet, he looked back to see the paramedics huddled over her. And then there was a hood over his head and only blackness…

When he arrived at the jail, he was told Shara had been killed by the Hunter. He knew the stages of grief far too well. Now, as before, he would use anger to reach acceptance, acceptance that Shara was dead, acceptance that he would do everything in his power to bring Sandor to justice.

The jail's Watch Commander looked at his monitor and saw Thomas just sitting inside his cell. "Things sure have changed since the Corporate War, haven't they Lieutenant?" he said, shaking his head.

"Yes, sir," the officer replied, the only other man in the office. "Maybe we could induce a power surge and take out the surveillance cameras."

"Much as I'd like to, this one is too hot. Any mark on that

pretty little face of his, and there would be hell to pay. No, he'll just have to wait for the prison barge to get what he deserves."

"Can I volunteer for that duty?"

"Really…"

Bertram J. Dykstra, the Corporate Vice President of Engineering, stood in front of Chairman Andrews and his fellow executive staff members. "As you all know, ten weeks ago, the Delta Corporation mounted a campaign that was nothing less than critical of our hovercraft line."

The Chairman looked beyond Dykstra to the chart on the viewscreen. A plot of Theta sales versus weeks for their hovercraft product line showed a noticeable decrease in revenue commensurate with the start of the Delta campaign.

Dykstra changed the chart. "Since we adopted a more aggressive advertising campaign of our own, one which exploited the holes in Delta's claims for their hovercraft, our sales have risen to near their previous high. It's still early days, but market analysis shows the gain corresponds directly to a decrease in Delta sales."

"Well done," the Chairman said. "You know, if it were anyone other than Delta, I'd say we should stop our campaign now. But as they're the ones who wanted to play hardball, how about we continue it just a little bit longer?"

A quick survey of the faces around the table showed only smiles and nods of approval.

"Alright, thanks, Bert," the Chairman said, accepting the silence as consensus. Delta had always been a thorn in Theta's side, and she deserved what was happening to her. Smear advertising was nothing more than poor form. But to use it based on false claims about your own product, claims that could easily be exposed and used against you, was just plain stupid.

Dykstra made way for the Chairman's chief aide, Renée Lafontaine. "That concludes our agenda for today," she said. "Please note that the next meeting will be held on the 14th at our regular time. Mr. Chairman, is there anything you would like to add?"

"No, that should cover it, Renée. Thank you, ladies and gentlemen. Good meeting." He got up from his chair and joined Sandor in leaving the room. "Any luck with capturing the other

Dissenters?"

"No, I'm afraid not, Mr. Chairman," he replied as they made their way out the door. "The Tactical Squad had the area completely covered, but Alesana and the Chandler girl still managed to get away. I'm being assured they won't get far."

"Good to hear. Well, have a good night," the Chairman said and headed off alone to his office.

"You too, sir," Sandor replied before walking to his. Locking the door behind him, he walked over to the bookcase and opened it. "Mr. Terac, nice of you to come so quickly."

"I was still in the building, sir."

"Please, have a seat. Scotch?" Sandor closed the bookcase and headed for the bar.

"Yes. Thank you, sir."

"I trust the financial arrangements meet with your approval?"

Terac accepted the offered drink. "Yes, sir, quite. Thank you again."

Sandor sat opposite Terac with a drink of his own. "Not a problem. Mr. Terac, are you a student of history?"

"No, sir, not really."

Sandor took a sip from his drink. "History tells us what those who recorded it either experienced or what they had been told was true, at times, even if it wasn't true. What I would like you to do is create evidence, as it were, to where those who view it later will reach the conclusion I want them to reach."

Terac nodded. "Interesting. Intriguing."

"Good. To that end, I would like you to hack into Bert Dykstra's computer."

Terac thought for a moment. "The best way would be to get his access code from the system's programmer before his untimely death."

Sandor smiled. "Excellent."

Byron Walker read from the teleprompter just above the camera from the Theta Nightly News anchor desk. "Two days after his dramatic capture, Thomas Chandler, one of the leaders of the Dissenters, was taken from his maximum-security holding cell to a heavily-armed shuttle bound for the Prison Planet. For a live update, we go to Win Chow. Win?"

"Thank you, Byron," Win said, the district's jail in view behind him. "The scene is quiet now, but earlier today, tension filled the air when Thomas Chandler was led across the jail courtyard under heavy security."

The picture changed to a recording of Thomas shuffling forward with shackles around his ankles and wrists restricting full movement. Six armed guards surrounded him while the Tactical Squad stood watch over the area from the jail walls above.

"Earlier," Win said in a voice-over, "the District High Court took less than an hour to reach a guilty verdict and sentence Chandler to the maximum penalty allowed by law, life without hope of parole on the Prison Planet."

The picture again changed to show the shuttle and its twelve fighter escort taking off from just outside the jail. Win continued his voice-over. "Most here feel the sentence was too lenient."

"Get up, asshole," Tate, the fat, unshaven guard shouted at the beaten figure lying huddled on the deck of the prison barge, free of his shackles. He slammed his foot into Thomas's side to punctuate the command.

Pain again racked Thomas's body. He wanted to scream but knew he couldn't give in. Once he did, all would be lost.

Zane, the slimmer of the two guards, pulled Thomas part way up by his sweat-drenched hair. He looked into what was left of Thomas's face. "Come on, you piece of," the man said through his broken and missing teeth.

Blood coming from his nose and mouth, Thomas looked at his tormentor through his blurred right eye, his left completely swollen shut. "Go to hell," he mumbled.

Zane smashed Thomas's head down hard on the deck then quickly pulled it back up again. "I think you got that all wrong, good buddy. It's you who's going to hell. This ain't even close."

"Here, Chandler, let's see if this fits," Tate said, coming forward. With considerable effort, he bent down to snap a collar around Thomas's neck. "Hope that's not too tight. Wouldn't want you to choke to death."

Zane laughed. "Better make sure it works, Tate."

"You're right..." With his fat hand, Tate pulled a remote from his pocket and activated the unit. A grin crossed his face as Thomas writhed on the deck, clutching at the collar that kept him from his next breath. "I think it's a perfect fit, don't you?"

"Couldn't be better," he replied when a Lieutenant entered the bay.

"The collar off now."

"Yes, sir," Tate said and half-heartedly deactivated the unit.

The Lieutenant walked over to Thomas, who lay gasping face down on the deck. He roughly rolled him over with his foot then looked directly at the guards. "You two are slipping. Get him ready for transport."

"Yes, sir," Zane replied with a smile. He grabbed Thomas by one arm while Tate took the other. "You heard the Lieutenant." They lifted him to his feet then shoved him toward a transport drone. Too weak to stand, Thomas crashed onto the deck only to be picked up and thrown forward once more.

The Lieutenant headed to the bay's control station. "I should let these two kill you, but that would be too humane compared to what you've got coming," he said when the com sounded.

The Lieutenant activated the system. "What?"

"We're in position, sir," the ship's Controller announced.

"Activate the com-link."

"Yes, sir."

Thomas looked at the viewscreen through his one good eye and saw a localized green, bullet-shaped force field extending up from the planet's surface into the upper atmosphere.

"Prison Colony Control, this is Prison Barge Three, do you read?" the Lieutenant asked.

"This is Prison Colony Control. Ready for the access code."

The Lieutenant activated a switch on the control panel, and a series of electronic pulses was immediately sent to the planet.

"This is Prison Colony Control. Your transmission has been verified. The field will remain open for thirty seconds, two minutes from now."

"Roger Control. Prison Barge Three out." The Lieutenant turned to his men. "Throw him in."

"Yes, sir," Tate replied.

Yanked off the deck, Thomas found himself flying headfirst into the back of a large drone. He collapsed in a bloody heap.

"I hope you take a long time to die, Chandler," the Lieutenant called out before he closed the drone's aft ramp.

Alone, Sandor sat in his office and watched yet another report on Chandler. It would all be over soon. The Tactical Squad had assured him they would apprehend the main Dissenter force in the next few days. Then everyone besides himself that possibly knew the truth about Sorel would be as good as dead. For as far as the Prison Planet was concerned, no one had ever lived long enough to serve out their sentence. A smile crossed his face.

Terac inserted the keycard 'obtained' from the lead Theta Corporation computer programmer into the computer terminal on his desk. It was after hours. Bert Dykstra and his secretary had left the building for the night. His fellow pilots were gone as well. He was all alone.

"Enter access code," the synthetic voice commanded.

"Five alpha, six beta, two," Terac said, the memory of the programmer's screams still fresh in his mind.

"Access approved, Mr. Dykstra," the computer stated.

A smile crossed Terac's face. "Computer, scan for a meeting held in the last thirty days between myself and Chairman Andrews where the Delta Corporation was discussed with only the two of us present."

"Entry noted as Chairman/Dykstra, B., Delta Corporation Strategy, File: 06282152-012."

"Computer, maintain the file, but delete its contents."

"Are you sure you want to delete the contents of Chairman/Dykstra, B., Delta Corporation Strategy, File 06282152-012, Mr. Dykstra?"

"Computer, yes."

"File 06282152-012's contents have been deleted."

"Computer, erase all record of this session happening, then end it."

"All record of this session happening has been erased," the

computer said before the screen went black.

The drone came to a hover two meters above the ground then automatically lowered its aft ramp before rotating to vertical. Thomas's bruised body was sent crashing face down onto the Prison Planet's surface before the ship took off.

With a low moan, he fought his way back to full consciousness to find the ground soft and the air oppressively hot and humid. With a groan, he slowly managed to turn onto his back. The swelling of his left eye down enough to once more use it, he found himself in the middle of a jungle clearing, the surrounding foliage thick in all directions. Overhead, a heavy dark cloud was moving off across a green sky! Then he remembered the force field, and it all depressingly made sense.

Movement, it was essential he try to move despite the pain. He needed to find food and shelter from... He shook his head. Many before him had been sentenced to the Prison Planet, and yet he appeared to be alone. Not good...

Knowing he needed to stand, to walk, with a grimace, he first sat up. With a shout of pain, he brought himself up on one knee. Three deep breaths and a scream later, he was upright, albeit shaky. He staggered to a nearby tree trunk for much-needed support. Taking the weight off one leg at a time, flexing stiff joints, he was encouraged as they started to loosen up. Letting go of the tree, his first few steps were slow, deliberate. The pain was still there, but fading almost exponentially. More steps brought a smile to his face. His limp, pronounced at first, was disappearing. It was time to explore his new world. Answers, he needed answers if he was to survive.

Moving to the edge of the clearing, he spotted a trail, one unnaturally clear of plant life. Moving down it, he found footprints in the mud. They appeared humanoid in shape, but with indentations extending from each of the toes as though made by claws. Almost half a meter ahead was a second set of prints, indentations of four small, tightly grouped parallel depressions located midway between the footprints at a slightly wider separation. He slowly shook his head. The marks were like nothing he had ever seen before.

Tracking the prints a few meters more down the trail,

something to the side caught his eye. It was a stake with a human skull on it. Beyond it was another, then a third. Each had a collar like the one he was wearing at its base. Again, not good...

A high-pitched wail in the distance sent a sudden chill down his spine. Knowing caution to be his best ally, he ran with some difficulty away from it when a second wail joined in. It too was from behind him, but closer. At a fork in the trail, he went to his left then barely managed to stop himself from flying off the edge of a ten-meter cliff that dropped sharply to a rock-lined riverbank below. His heart pounding, he ran back to the fork and headed down the path to his right when a crude arrow flashed past his ear. Despite his pain, he forced himself to run even faster.

More wailing was heard almost directly behind him. A glance over his shoulder showed his attacker pursuing him on both arms and legs in an ape-like manner, despite her human features. Obviously female, her drooling fangs and pitch-black eyes beneath ragged tufts of hair only heightened the fear he already felt. Again the path came to a fork, but more wails from up ahead, from his right, forced him back toward the river and the trap that had obviously been set.

His back to the cliff edge, Thomas quickly searched for something he could use as a weapon when the first of the monsters raced forward and tackled him to the ground. Straddling him, she screamed as her claws slashed toward his throat. He fended off two potentially lethal blows then connected with a right fist to her jaw. Stunned, the creature fell off to the side. Quickly to his feet, another monster rush upon him with a club in hand. He barely ducked the first swing then countered with a martial art kick, his heel blasting her exposed ribs. She fell screaming when a third demon launched herself at him, sending the two of them flying off the edge of the cliff. Separated in the fall, the bank thankfully replaced by a sheer rock wall, Thomas crashed into the cold darkness of the swiftly moving river. He quickly struggled to the surface then looked around when the monster suddenly burst to the surface, only centimeters in front of him. Screaming, her sharp claws dug into his shoulder and pulled him closer to her bared fangs. He grabbed her neck with both hands and squeezed it with all his might, but the act only enraged the creature further. Claws shredded his clothes, drawing more blood as the river transformed into teaming white water, the force of which suddenly ripped the two of them apart.

Swept to one side, Thomas saw his attacker smash hard into a rock then be pinned headfirst under a fallen tree before his own body went airborne. He crashed back down only to have the water jerk him to the side and lift him up. Again, he was slammed back down then rushed at break-neck speed between two massive rocks. Caught in the turbulence, his world suddenly went dark and cold. His body skipped hard off a submerged rock before he was caught in an upward surge. Flung high in the air, he gasped for air before plummeting back down. Fighting his way to the surface again, gasping, he just managed to push off a large rock with his feet only to be swept sideways and backward into yet another confluence of rock and water. With what little strength he had left, he rotated his body at the last possible second to bring himself into the centerline of the flow. The water viciously grabbed him, then spit him out over a three-meter waterfall.

Thomas found himself once more underwater, but this time it was very much different. This time he was surrounded by a welcomed calmness, the rapids thankfully behind him. Back up to the surface, he swam to the opposite bank and collapsed on the sand. On his back, exhausted, he tried to catch his breath when something suddenly came between him and the sun. His instincts told him to run, but four homemade spears pointed directly at his chest made him reconsider.

"Ta neh a wah," a woman's voice said. The apparent command was followed by her raising her spear slightly as though he was supposed to stand.

The language unknown, Thomas hoped he was right and silently got to his feet, the spears tracking his every move. Slowly, carefully he turned to put the sun at his side so he could see clearly. Standing before him were three human men and a woman around his age. All had black hair and brown eyes. All were partially clad in animal skins and carried a homemade knife. Two of the men had bow and arrows.

The woman his own height, the men a full head taller. All were well muscled. And all wore collars. But based on his own situation, what did that really mean?

"Sha cha," the woman ordered.

Thomas shook his head, not knowing what to do when the largest male quickly rotated his spear and jammed the butt into Thomas's stomach. "Sha cha."

Thomas fell to his knees in pain. "Go to hell."

A second spear crashed down hard on his shoulders, knocking him to the ground.

"Hold, Tovar," the woman commanded, surprisingly in English.

"Neh ha, Maren," Tovar replied, his spear poised to run Thomas through. "Te sa nemakeha hohone."

"Yes, but of his spirit, it appears strong." She knelt down in front of Thomas and grabbed him by the hair. She bent his head backward. "Of our help in you continuing to live, if desired, it would be best for you to cooperate."

"Let go of my hair," Thomas said. "Please."

The woman called Maren began to laugh. "Bring him," she ordered to the others and threw his head back down onto the sand.

Two of the men reached down and effortlessly lifted Thomas to his feet before escorting him to a blockhouse partially hidden by the jungle. They entered through heavy metal double doors set in one-meter thick concrete then stopped in a torch-lit barren lobby.

Maren turned to face Thomas. "Of your spirit, it is strong, but so am I and my brothers. Of your treatment, it will go easy for you if you answer my questions. Of what name are you called by?"

"Thomas Chandler."

"And of your crime, what is it?"

Thomas stared defiantly at the two brothers still holding him by each arm. Maren nodded. "Release him."

Both did as told, but did not move from either side of Thomas.

"I am accused of murdering 1638 inhabitants of a Theta Corporation mining colony on the planet Sorel."

"And of this act, did you do it?" she asked simply.

Thomas looked at her. "Does it matter?"

"Yes."

"Then, no. I did not do it."

"Then, of who did?"

"The Theta Corporation and a man named Sandor," Thomas said, surprised to see Maren's eyes suddenly narrow in anger.

She stared at him intently. "Of this Sandor, why would he destroy that which was his?"

"If I told you, I'm not sure you would believe me."

"Of our belief, it is with you, Thomas Chandler, for in this, we are surprisingly alike."

Thomas saw Maren was serious and nodded. "The Sorel Mine was losing money, but to shut it down would have meant paying the workers more than they were willing to. By destroying the colony, all costs were eliminated, and the insurance money was collected."

"And of you?"

"My family lived on Sorel. My mother and father were killed by Sandor, who blamed a group of people known as the Dissenters for his crime. When I learned the truth about Sorel, I joined the Dissenters to help expose Sandor. Unfortunately, he has so far proven to be more powerful."

Maren continued to stare at Thomas. "Of your words, they are as though your time for victory still exists."

"Yes. I still think that way," he said to the grunts of approval from Maren's brothers. "And you, Maren?"

She smiled at hearing her name. "Of our land on the northern continent of Tiree, it was wanted by a man said to be named Sandor, but of his offer to buy it, it was refused. Then, of a Theta man's body, it was later found on our land, dead by our methods, but not by our hand. Still, of the crime, we were convicted and sent to this place to die… Yes, of much we have in common, Thomas Chandler," she said her focus once more back on him. "Of joining us, you are welcome if that is what you desire."

"Thanks, I," he started to say when a distant eerie wail suddenly came from outside the blockhouse.

"Mutants!" Rah said.

"The door," Maren ordered.

Thomas ran past the others to see the black-eyed monsters swimming across the river. Turning back to the blockhouse, it was obvious that even with the strength of five, the doors could not be closed in time.

"Of what are you doing?" Maren yelled as Thomas ran past her back inside.

He grabbed a spear. "Buying time for you to shut the door."

Out into the clearing, the first Mutant rushed upon him screaming, brandishing a club. Her first swing nearly took his head off. The second came even closer when from a crouch, he rammed the butt of the spear into the underside of her jaw and put her on the ground. A second spear suddenly crashed down hard on the Mutant's head to make sure she stayed there. Thomas looked up to see Maren. "What are you doing?"

"Of the time, it is for fighting, not questions, Thomas Chandler," she said when another Mutant raced forward. Maren fended off a savage spear thrust that allowed Thomas to bring his own spear down hard across the attacker's back. But the blow only enraged the monster who viciously turned on him then screamed, the point of Maren's spear lodged in her side. "Of this, I wish it different," she said, pulling out the bloody weapon, "but of their recovery, it is too quick."

Two Mutants suddenly ran screaming from the nearby jungle. Maren ducked a deadly first swing from the lead demon's club. Thomas found himself slammed hard to the ground by the other. Drool dripped from her fangs as she lunged for his neck. He just managed to land a brutal left cross on her jaw, sending the Mutant reeling to his side.

Maren's attacker dead, she turned and buried her spear deep into the stomach of Thomas's monster. Screaming, the creature leaped up off the ground and began to pull the spear through her to get at Maren on the other end.

Back on his feet, Thomas was suddenly grabbed from behind in a bear hug by yet another Mutant. As he struggled just to breathe, a second monster raced forward, her spear leveled to run him through. He feigned left then quickly pivoted to his right. Two screams pierced the air, one in pain from the Mutant holding him, the other in frustration from the creature who continued to push her spear through her dead comrade to get to Thomas. Seizing the moment, he quickly recovered his own spear off the ground. With a rapid pivot, he sent its butt end into his attacker's temple, dropping her on the spot.

Maren struggled to retrieve her spear from the now-dead Mutant's body when another monster attacked her with a wicked swing of her club. She ducked just in time, but in so doing stumbled to the ground. Her escape blocked by the body of a Mutant slain earlier, she could only watch helplessly as the demon above her raised her club to strike a death blow. She heard the creature scream then saw her club fall harmlessly to the side. Lifeless eyes stared at her before the body fell away, Thomas's spear lodged in her back.

"Maren!" Tovar shouted from the only remaining open window, the doors closed.

"Thomas, follow," she said and raced off.

He started after her but fell hard when a Mutant's arrow struck him in the back of the leg. Fighting through the pain, he turned in time to catch his latest attacker tackle him. His strength almost gone, he somehow managed to throw her off to the side but knew it was only a matter of time. The monster knew it, too. Quick to her feet, she raised up to attack him when one of Rah's arrows struck the Mutant in her shoulder. She fell screaming.

"Thomas, now!" Maren shouted from inside the building.

He struggled to his feet, then used his spear as a crutch to limp forward. More of Rah's arrows filled the air. More Mutant screams were heard behind him. Nearly at the window, he saw Rah's eyes widen, smelled the stench of decay growing stronger from behind him. He suddenly dropped to one knee then thrust his spear backward with all his might. It met the resistance of flesh and bone. A scream pierced his ears as he again struggled to get to his feet. Upraised hands were met by others, stronger, that lifted him away from the madness.

Tovar secured the metal window cover while Maren bent over Thomas and pulled out the remains of a crude arrow from his leg. He met the pain silently, confirming what she already knew.

"Of our thanks, it is offered," Oden said. "Of you being a warrior, there is no doubt."

Thomas sat up and tore away a piece of his shirt to cover the bleeding hole in his leg. "Thank you for saving my life," he said when a new sound was suddenly heard from outside, one which resembled an air raid siren.

"Of this, it is all night," Tovar volunteered in reaction to the look on Thomas's face.

Maren offered Thomas a hand up. "Come, of rest chambers, they are below, away from the noise."

"But…"

Maren raised her hand to stop him. "Tomorrow, of answers, tomorrow. Of the time for rest, it is now."

CHAPTER NINETEEN

The sun down, the city bathed in dark and artificial light, the maglev slowed on the approach to the elevated platform then stopped. Doors on the left-hand side automatically opened to let the evening commuters eagerly rush down the exit ramp. Doors on the opposite side opened next to allow boarding. The cycle complete, all doors closed, the car moved on, leaving a very well-dressed woman to stand alone.

Despite the wide-brimmed hat that partially shielded her face from the harsh overhead lights, Terac could see the woman was extremely beautiful as he made his way to her from out of the shadows. "Any problems?"

"No, none," she replied, her tone implying she found the question insulting.

He nodded. "This way."

Down the ramp, they entered a stylish pub on the corner as a couple, but the reaction was still the same, the staring, both blatant and feebly disguised, the conversations suddenly interrupted in mid-sentence when she passed by. But then she was used to it and privately worried about the day it would no longer happen.

They walked the length of the bar, her gaze forward, his toward the crowd as though looking for a table. The restaurant was crowded as expected. With no seats to be found, they stopped near the end of the bar. Terac leaned in close and whispered in the woman's ear. "Two tables to my right. The partially bald man in the corporate suit seated by himself."

She took her time to casually survey the crowd, only glancing at the table in question. "Try to kiss me," she whispered back.

"What?"

"Just do it."

Terac did as asked only to receive a slap across the face for his trouble. "How dare you," she shouted, her voice loud enough to be heard at least two tables away. She glared at Terac, inwardly pleased to see true anger on the man's face. "Leave me alone!" she said then continued to stare after him as he stormed out the front door. With a troubled look on her face, she turned toward the pub's clientele and made eye contact with the partially bald man in the corporate suit seated by himself.

"Excuse me," the man said suddenly on his feet. "May I be of assistance?"

"That's very kind of you." She walked toward him. "If you don't mind, perhaps I could join you for a minute. I'm a little upset and..."

"Please, please have a seat," he said, pulled out the chair opposite his for her. "I'm Bert Dykstra."

"Karla Marlow, and thank you. Thank you so very much. I hope I'm not intruding."

Dykstra reclaimed his own chair. "No, not at all. I'm here by myself, and I'm not one to eavesdrop, but..."

She removed her coat to reveal a beautiful conservative black dress over a stunning figure. "I didn't want to go out with him, to begin with, but it was for a friend of a friend who is off-planet and... Well, I'm sure none of this makes any sense to you. Let's just say he was less than a gentleman."

Dykstra nodded his understanding. "Would a drink help?"

"You know," she said with a perfect smile, "that would be great. Thank you."

The Delta Corporation's Records Unit building rose skyward, its reflective glass walls slightly distorting the pattern of the city lights below. Beneath a maglev track, three men spoke in hushed voices. Each took turns looking around to make sure they were not being observed. "Half now, half later as we agreed," said the partially bald man in an overcoat. He handed over a briefcase to the taller of the two men, Benzu. He and his partner, Talief, were dressed in the Comptec jackets, complete with the identification badges he had been given them the day before.

Benzu quickly opened the briefcase. The contents were met with smiles before the case was closed.

"We'll meet you at the dock in two hours, Mr. Dykstra," Talief said.

"Right. Good luck." He shook each man's hand, then crossed the street and headed down the alley. Stopping in the shadows, the moon full, he carefully made his way unseen back to the street to covertly watch his new employees. They had gone to their parked hovercraft and exchanged the briefcase for the repair cases he had also provided them the other day. He watched them head to the Delta building's main entrance. Satisfied, Terac pulled at the corner of the Dykstra mask he had on.

The Delta Corporation's Records Unit guard watched the two men in matching company jackets enter the building and head toward him. He didn't recognize their names, but he was certainly familiar with their firm. Comptec, a member of the Delta Corporation, had serviced the Delta Records Unit's computers for years. "May I help you?"

Benzu pulled out his notepad. "We had a call that a... Ms. Dillan's computer was down."

"Hum, that's funny..." The guard checked the screen in front of him. "She didn't report it here."

"Maybe she forgot to tell you," Talief offered.

The guard shook his head. "That's not like Ms. Dillan. And without a report, I'm afraid I can't let you two up there."

"Is there any way you can reach her?" Talief asked.

The guard checked another monitor. "No, I'm afraid not. She's off-planet, due in some time tomorrow."

Benzu looked at his partner and shrugged. "Okay... Well, if there is something wrong, tell Ms. Dillan we can make it back here in about a week."

The guard looked at them with raised eyebrows. "A week?"

"I'm afraid so. We're working twelve-hour days as is. I'd say we'll be lucky to even be back by then."

The guard rubbed his chin. "I'd hate to face Ms. Dillan tomorrow if her computer is down."

"That bad?" Talief asked.

"Worse," the guard said with a slight chuckle. "Ah heck, go on up. Here's the keycard to her office, the eighteenth floor. As you get off the elevator, turn right then head down to the end of the hall. You'll see her name on the door on the left. But first, I need both of you to sign in."

Benzu swiped his ID card through the reader. "And I thought we could knock off early for a change and tie into some cold ones."

"Yeah. Just our luck," Talief replied.

"Sorry about that, gentlemen."

Talief took his turn at the reader. "We shouldn't be too long."

"Take your time. I'll just need you to sign out when you're done."

"Right. See you in a little bit."

Both men headed for the elevator and its open door. Inside, the door closed, and the car started up. "Maybe we should do this for a living," Talief said to his partner.

Benzu smiled. "Maybe so."

Still in the shadows, Terac saw the light in Ms. Dillan's office come on. Even though he was alone, he was careful to conceal the lighted dial of his watch from view. He noted the time.

Benzu connected the equipment inside his repair case to the nearest computer terminal in Ms. Dillan's office. Until the other night, he had only heard rumors of a Datascanner. Now, thanks to Dykstra, he would use the highly classified Theta Corporation property to download trillions of bits of information in mere minutes. But first, there was the access code to break. "How's it going?"

Talief watched the second piece of classified Theta technology rapidly cycle through the twelve place security code. First one, then another, and another green light appeared. "You should be in."

Benzu saw his own machine suddenly come alive. "I am." He pulled up the main directory. "Man, look at the size of these files!"

Talief moved to his partner's side. "Dykstra said he wanted everything from the D series."

Benzu shook his head. "I know, but even with this machine that will take over an hour."

"I say we get what we can in thirty minutes, then get out of here."

"I'm with you."

"Karla, are you sure you wouldn't rather go out for dinner?" Dykstra asked, paying for the cab. "It's not too late."

She called for the private elevator in the underground garage to number 207 of the Palisades Condominium complex. "I know, but... You don't mind, do you?"

"No, not at all," he said, the door opening. Seconds later, they were in Karla's condo's foyer. "I just don't want to put you to any trouble," he said, helping her out of her coat.

"Thank you... It's no trouble at all." She took her coat and hung it up in the closet. "Wine?"

"Please." He walked into the living room while she headed into the kitchen. He found it done in a tasteful blend of old and new works of expensive art. "You have some very impressive pieces here."

"Thank you." She joined him with two glasses. "My parents did rather well before they died, and as I was an only child, well, it's allowed me the pleasure of pursuing some of my passions."

He took the offered glass then stopped in front of an especially impressive painting. "An original Bata?"

"Yes."

"Very nice."

"Again, thank you," she said and took a seat on the couch while he sat across from her. "You know, after that incident in the bar tonight, I think I'll give up dating and join a convent."

Dykstra smiled. "I tried dating again after my wife died, but that was, to say the least, a disaster."

"She must have been very special."

"She was."

Karla kicked off her shoes and offered up a toast with her raised glass. "Then here's to hoping you find someone as wonderful as she was."

"Thank you," he said and raised his glass. Karla smiled a perfect smile in return.

Terac checked his watch again. It was time. He reached into his pocket and produced a portable communicator, one that would show that it was registered to Comptec.

"Good evening. Delta Records, may I help you?" he heard the guard say on the other end of the line.

"Good evening. This is Comptec calling to confirm a computer repair scheduled for a Ms. Dillan tomorrow at 14:30."

"Tomorrow?" the guard was heard to say in a voice that sounded suddenly uneasy.

"Yes, sir, at 14:30."

The guard accessed the log. "Excuse me, but do you have a Mr. Talief and a Mr. Benzu in your employ?"

Terac smiled in the dark. "No sir. Why do you ask?"

He never received an answer.

Talief stopped pacing long enough to look at his partner. "How much longer?"

"Relax. Nothing is going to happen," Benzu said when the lobby guard entered the room with a disrupter in hand.

"Hands up where I can see them!" the guard ordered. Two other guards quickly filed in behind him. They, too, had their weapons drawn.

Terac had earlier that evening defeated the lock to the Palisades Condominiums' unmanned security room located in the complex's underground garage. He had then erased the recording of his ever being there before setting up continuous loops of inactivity on select security cameras throughout the area. They were scheduled to go active at a predetermined time. He had next arranged to have Dykstra and Karla picked up from the pub by an associate in a hovercraft painted the same color and with the same signage as that of a local cab company.

Returning from outside the Delta Corporation's Records Unit building, Terac reentered the security room. A quick check revealed that his arrival and that of Karla with Dykstra had not been recorded. With a smile, he sat back to wait.

Dykstra lay in Karla's bed, watching her sleep. His attraction to her had been instantaneous, but the memories of his deceased wife had caused him to back away. Then, as though she had read his mind, she helped him talk about the guilt he felt, helped him bring it to consciousness. She had taken her time, had understood. And what was attractive became beautiful. Even making love seemed like the right thing to do. Damn, could he be falling in love? Now that would really be something.

His communicator unexpectedly sounded.

"Honey, what is it?" Karla asked, half awake.

"Nothing. Please go back to sleep." He got up and headed naked into the bathroom. Once inside, he shut the door and activated the unit. "Control, do you know what time it is?"

"Sorry, sir, but we have a priority one."

He nodded his acceptance of the situation. "Alright, I'm on my way."

"Yes, sir. Control out."

"What is it? Is something wrong?" Karla asked as he came out of the bathroom. She sat up in bed, the satin sheet slipping down, exposing her perfect breasts.

"It's something of an emergency at work. I have to go to the office."

"Oh no," she said with obvious disappointment. "Now, in the middle of the night?"

"I'm afraid so."

"This something of an emergency, do you have to be there right away?" she asked, a devilish grin crossing her face.

"Well, not right away. Why?"

"Well…"

Half dozing in the security shack, Terac was instantly awakened by his communicator. "Yes?"

"I'd like to order a taxi," Karla's voice was heard to say.

"Where and when?" he asked just in case Dykstra was listening.

"Palisades Condominiums underground garage, unit 207."

"The taxi is on its way."

"Thank you," he heard her say before she hung up.

Terac dialed his associate. "Now."

"Right."

Sitting back, Terac covertly watched his associate's partner arrive in the taxi that did not register on a monitor. Minutes later, Dykstra was whisked away. With a smile, Terac headed out of the security room to the private elevator. There, he stopped long enough to change the number back from 207 to 202 before he entered the car and pushed the up button.

"Honey, did you forget something?" Karla called out from the bedroom.

Terac entered, surprising her. "Oh, it's you," she said, her voice suddenly hard. She wrapped herself in the bedsheet and headed to the vanity.

"Well done."

She looked at his reflection in the mirror. "Did you bring the rest of the money?"

"Yes, and a bonus too."

"A bonus?" She turned to see Terac was holding a strange pistol in his hand. A split second later, a poisoned dart exploded her heart.

CHAPTER TWENTY

Bert Dykstra shook the hand of his unexpected visitor. "What can I do for you, Detective Davis?"

"Two men were caught late last night stealing data from the Delta Records Unit using classified Theta Corporation equipment. Both have identified you as the one who hired them."

Dykstra's brow furrowed. "That's ridiculous."

"We think so too, sir, but my Captain would like for you to come down to the station so we can clarify a few things and establish your innocence."

"Certainly," Dykstra said with an inward smile. In the old days, the criminal justice system and corruption were synonymous. Never mind what was right or wrong, for the right price, you could easily buy your innocence. But all that had changed after the Corporate War, due in great part to his own efforts. Judges, professional jurors, and the police were routinely subjected to a truth test. Any evidence of corruption, outside influence, or forced bias was punishable with time off up to dismissal. So it just wouldn't look good for him to refuse to go to the station. Besides, he was innocent.

Dykstra led the way to his outer office and his secretary. "I'm going to police headquarters. Have Mr. Viken from legal join me there, will you?"

"Yes, sir," his secretary replied, shocked.

"I assume you have a hovercraft waiting," Dykstra said on their way to a waiting elevator.

"Yes, sir," the detective replied, getting in the car. "Outside, in front."

"Then, this should be interesting…"

The elevator door closing, the car headed down to the main lobby. Crossing it in silence, the two men exited the building to find a sea of reporters waiting.

"Mr. Dykstra, is it true you hired the Delta Records burglars?" one shouted over the others asking their questions.

"No."

"Have they arrested you?"

"No," he said on his way into the waiting police hovercraft.

"But, Mr. Dykstra…"

"No!" Thomas shouted, a Mutant on top of him slashing the air, trying to tear him apart. "No!" he yelled again, the monster's claws ripping through his flesh. He screamed and tried to toss her off him but couldn't.

"Thomas!"

He looked to the side. "Maren!" he shouted when fangs suddenly plunged deep into his shoulder. Again, he screamed.

"Thomas!"

He saw Maren running toward him when a Mutant suddenly appeared above him, her club poised to smash his head in.

"Thomas!"

He watched Maren slam her foot into the monster, kicking her away. She then grabbed him by the shoulders and shook him. "Thomas… Thomas…"

Suddenly wide-awake, Thomas bolted straight up in bed, his heart pounding, unsure of where he was. When the fog finally cleared, he saw Maren in the torchlight, sitting next to him, holding him by the shoulders. "Maren… I…"

"Of the nightmares, they are common at first. Of the cause, it is thought to be a toxin in the Mutant's saliva. Of the effect, it will pass."

"God, I hope so. It was so real," Thomas said, trying to catch his breath. "Why do you call them Mutants?"

"Of words written below, they are not unlike our own. Of a warning for radiation, it often appears for weapons that were used," Maren said and slowly shook her head. "But of the bodies found here inside, they do not resemble those outside that kill."

"A nuclear war?" Thomas asked.

"Of that, it makes the most sense. Come, of all that I have just told you, you can see for yourself." She grabbed the torch she had brought with her and led the way out into the corridor. "Of non-Mutants, we have found no others until you, Thomas. Of the monsters, they kill, then eat all."

"Great…" They moved down a hallway to the sound of small animals scurrying away in the dark. "And this place allowed you to survive?"

"Yes. Of its existence, it was found before the night when the Mutants hunt. Of the door, it was closed, but only with the strength of four to give us life."

"But we were attacked while the sun was still up."

"Of the sound of your drone, it probably caused a Mutant nearby to awake. Of the monster's wail, it was then heard by others. Of the attack on us, it was my fault for seeking you out."

"I'm glad you did."

She shrugged her shoulders, then turned a corner and approached a large vault-like door.

"And these collars?"

"Of their preventing breathing, it occurs when you get too close to the green haze. Of retreat from the haze, the constriction stops," Maren explained, then pushed open the door and entered the chamber.

In the torchlight, Thomas saw two skeletons in tattered military uniforms handcuffed to separate control consoles. "Interesting…"

Maren shook her head. "Of any race being so foolish as to want to destroy themselves…"

"Agreed," he said on his way to one of the control boards. "Do you know what this symbol means?"

"Radiation."

"Then it was a nuclear war."

"A waste."

Thomas pointed to the writing below one of six circles, themselves arranged in a circle. "What does this say?"

"Of the symbol, it is for the number two, the same written on walls here."

Thomas moved his finger to the writing inside the number two circle. "And this?"

"Of the word, it means launched."

With an air of excitement, Thomas pointed to the only circle where the writing was different. "And this?"

"Of the word, it means present."

Thomas looked at Maren. "I think one of their nuclear missiles was never launched!"

"But of what use is that to us? Of the field, it is strong, and of missiles, we have no knowledge."

"I have such knowledge, and the field can resist attack from the outside, but not from the inside."

"What?"

"Have you heard of an electromagnetic pulse?"

"Of such things, do you talk about them to women you have just met?" she asked with a grin.

Thomas just shook his head and smiled. "If we can launch the missile and detonate it at the top of the force field, everything electronic inside of it should overload and fail, including the field and these collars."

Maren turned suddenly serious. "Freedom?"

"Yes. I talk of freedom."

"And of this, can you make it happen?"

"If we can locate the last missile and if it is still functional, there is a slim chance, but still a chance that we can make it happen."

Maren pointed to the circle representing the remaining missile. "Of this place, it is known, but…" She shook her head.

"But what?"

"Of the structure, it is a Mutant camp. Of the missile building itself, it is their shrine."

"Damn."

Dykstra slowly shook his head. It was just like in the old videos. Good cop, bad cop. The same questions asked over and over again in one form or another, the repeated probes for inconsistencies, the feeble attempts to wear him down. The idea was to get him to accidentally volunteer some piece of information that would eventually be his undoing. But one didn't rise to the top of the Theta Corporation by being slow on the uptake or wilting under pressure. He would play their game awhile longer, but not for much more. "I'll tell you once more, I don't know the people who you call Talief and Benzu."

"And you were where last night at 21:30?" the Captain asked.

"Maybe you should write it down, so you don't have to keep asking the same question," Dykstra offered. "I was in Karla Marlow's condominium, the Palisades, number 207."

"Come off it, Dykstra," the detective said. "Your buddies sold you out. You're walking on some pretty thin ice, and if I were you, I'd start telling the truth."

"Captain, this has been quite enough," Viken interrupted, having joined them a few minutes earlier. "Either you charge Mr. Dykstra, or we're walking out of here."

A policeman suddenly entered the room and said something in a low voice to the Captain. "Excuse me for a minute," the Captain said and left the interrogation room for his own office. There, he activated a viewscreen to find Davis standing in an empty apartment. "What have you got?"

"Captain, I'm in 207, the condominium Dykstra claims he was in last night. It's vacant, sir, not so much as a stick of furniture. The manager says it has been that way for about two months now."

"Interesting… Has anyone ever seen Karla Marlow or someone matching her description?"

Davis shook his head. "No, sir."

"And what about the neighbors?"

"One is on vacation. The others say they didn't see anything out of the ordinary."

"Security recordings?"

"Nothing on them for either the entrance to the complex or the underground garage."

"And the taxi Dykstra claims to have taken to and from there?"

"The company shows no record of either pick up."

"Ok, thanks, Davis. Come on back."

"Yes, sir."

The Captain ended the communication and headed back into the interrogation room. "Mr. Dykstra, you're under arrest for corporate spying."

"What?" Dykstra said in a barely audible whisper, his face going pale.

"That's right, Mr. Dykstra. It will be the Prison Planet for you if you're convicted."

"But I'm innocent."

"Gee, where have I heard that before?"

In the morning, the doors of Blockhouse Two were carefully opened, and the surrounding area searched. No Mutants were found, not even the dead from the previous attack. Thomas could only assume they had become the next meal for the survivors.

"Of the backwater, it is this way," Maren said and headed upriver.

The Mutant shrine downriver, all had agreed the best way in, and the fastest way out would be by raft. Thomas smiled on finding several logs floating in a shallow pool. "These will do quite nicely," he said and waded in. Maren followed while her brothers stood guard.

"Eight should do. This size would be best," Thomas said, selecting one around four meters in length and around thirty centimeters in diameter.

"Understood," Maren replied, spotting another log fitting the description.

Thomas moved his log to the bank. "What about the vines?"

"Of a type of tree found deeper in the jungle, but not far," Maren replied, pulling her log parallel to his, "they have the ones we have used for our bows. Of superior strength, they are also in abundance."

"Excellent."

Sandor locked his inner office door, then crossed the room and opened the bookcase. "Mr. Terac."

"Mr. Sandor."

"Have a seat. I think the show is about to end," Sandor said on his way to one of the chairs. Terac took the other. Dave Ackerman, the anchorman for the Delta Corporation Nightly News, was on the viewscreen.

"Repeating tonight's top story, Bertram J. Dykstra, a member of the executive staff of the Theta Corporation, was brought in for questioning by police early today for his alleged association with the break-in at the Delta Corporation's Records Unit last night. When asked about his innocence... Excuse me," Ackerman said, then put his hand to his ear to better hear the message coming in over his earwig. "We have just received word that Mr. Dykstra has now been officially charged with corporate spying. This is obviously quite a shock as it is widely believed that Mr. Dykstra is next in line to become chairman of the Theta Corporation."

Ackerman turned to face another camera. "For further details on this and other top stories of the day, please stay tuned for Delta News in Review, a comprehensive look at this week in the news. As for our show, thank you for watching. For the Delta Corporation Nightly News, I'm Dave Ackerman."

"Computer, viewscreen off," Sandor ordered. He turned to Terac, a smile on his face. "Please make your call now."

"Yes, sir."

"And we're out," the Delta News floor director shouted.

Ackerman's mannequin posture and fixed expression quickly faded. His agent came forward. "Nice show, Dave."

"Thanks," he replied in the middle of a stretch. "Damn strange about Dykstra, isn't it?"

"Very. Do you think he really did it?"

"I'm not sure, but I think I should cover this one personally, don't you?"

"My thoughts exactly," the agent said with a smile when Ackerman's communicator surprisingly sounded. Only a select few had the number.

"Ackerman."

"Please listen," an electronically distorted voice said. "Dykstra is not the end. Look to the top. All the way to the top."

"What? Who is this?"

"That's not important. The meeting records are," was heard before the call ended.

The raft complete with a tiller, hand, and footholds, Thomas and the Ba'ahs had waited until the next morning to make their way downstream. Thomas manned the tiller while the others sat, holding onto straps made out of vines. The water calm, the current moderate, they made good progress.

"Of the location, it is there next to the swamp that is just short of the white water," Maren said softly, pointing to a trail leading up a slight hill.

Thomas nodded and pushed on the tiller, bringing the raft to shore. Oden silently positioned himself to tie it off while Rah slipped ashore and crept along the trail. They waited in silence.

"Clear," Rah whispered upon his return.

Per the plan, Thomas and Maren stood guard while Oden secured the raft, and Tovar and Rah waded into the putrid swamp water. Grabbing handfuls of ooze, they rubbed it on themselves then each other before trading places with those onshore.

"This stuff stinks," Thomas whispered.

Maren reached down and grabbed another large handful of mud. "Of your own smell, it will cover it. Turn around." She slapped a glob of the slime on his back and rubbed it on those portions of his body not covered by the animal skins he'd been given earlier to wear. "There, of the Mutants, they cannot smell you now," she whispered. "Of my back, do it now."

He fished out a handful of the sludge and dumped it on top of her shoulders. "With pleasure."

The task complete, Oden quietly, cautiously led the way up the trail that wound through the thick of the jungle, the smell of death and decay growing ever stronger with each step. Less than three meters from a clearing, an upraised hand caused everyone to quietly seek cover.

From behind a large fern, Thomas looked out upon a blockhouse exactly like the one they had occupied. It was located in the center of a clearing. Crude ladders made their way to a flat roof where fifty or so Mutants, male and female, lay sleeping in the shade cast by the station's solar panels. Above them, the rungs of a tower holding an air raid siren were decorated with numerous collars. He turned to Maren and whispered. "The door and window coverings look rusted shut."

She pointed to the side of the blockhouse. "Of a ladder, one rises up out of the ground," she said when a signal from Oden brought everyone's attention to an approaching Mutant sentry. All held still, held their breath.

The Mutant's stench overpowering, even over the mud they wore, Thomas watched her walk directly in front of him with a spear in hand, then suddenly stop and anxiously sniff the air. He saw the monster's head snap around toward him, and her mouth start to drool. He knew any attempt to defend himself might bring the rest of the camp down on them, but still... He saw the Mutant's eyes grow large just before she charged toward him. He was just about to rise up and defend himself when the monster stabbed the ground with her spear a meter in front of him. A grunt of pleasure followed, a frog-like animal impaled on the end of the raised shaft. Thomas let out a long, slow sigh of relief as she moved off toward the blockhouse. With obvious satisfaction, she ripped off one of the animal's hind legs and began to devour it when a second sentry appeared sniffing the air. A brief scuffle ensued before the spoils were divided.

"Of their numbers, I count only two," Rah whispered.

"Agreed," Maren replied. "Of each, can they be taken where they stand without sound?"

Tovar looked at Rah. Both nodded.

"Do so."

Two arrows sliced through the air. Each severed the vocal cords of its victim on its way through their jugular. The Mutants collapsed dead on the ground. Maren turned to Thomas. "Go now."

Handing his spear to Rah, he silently, quickly made his way across the clearing then down the crude ladder to a concrete tunnel below. Skulls and collars marked the way to an open steel door and a darkened room. Inside, he pressed his back up against the wall then stopped to listen for any sign of his discovery. None heard, he started to move forward when a hand grabbed his shoulder.

"Thomas?"

"Damn, Maren," he whispered then struggled to regain his composure.

"Of being scared, it is good for a warrior every now and then," she said with a chuckle. "Of the missile's controls, have you found them?"

"Not yet…" On the off-chance, he ran his hand up against the wall and found a switch. The sudden introduction of artificial light caused both he and Maren to shield their eyes.

"Of this, how is it so?" she asked with a spear in hand.

"The panels on the roof catch the sun's energy," Thomas said, the odds improving. Now they were only a million to one against them. A quick scan of the room revealed the skeletal remains of two soldiers wearing the same uniforms as in Blockhouse Two. Each was handcuffed to separate, but identical control panels. "The same fail-safe system."

Maren shook her head. "Of this, I do not know of what you speak."

He made his way to the first of the two consoles. "Both people have to turn their keys at the same time to activate the missiles."

"Then, of the system, does it work?"

"Let's find out." Thomas threw the main power lever. Both consoles sprang to life. "I'll be damned. Maren, what does this say?" he said, pointing to a display.

"Of the words, they say something like time to launch."

Thomas rotated a dial one click. "And this?"

"Of the symbol, it is number one."

"And this?"

"Two."

"Great. And the units?"

"Of the value, it is about two minutes."

"Excellent," Thomas said and adjusted the dial before moving to a second display. "How about these?"

She pointed to the first of three displays. "Of this one, it says latitude." She moved her finger to the second. "Of this, it is for longitude, and of this, it is for elevation," she said, pointing to the third.

Thomas pointed to the first display and what appeared to be a number. "And this?"

"Of it, it means zed, nothing."

Thomas turned the dial one more notch. "And this?"

"Of this, it is one mar, a distance just short of a kilometer."

"Excellent."

She watched him adjust the dials across the board. "Of this, do you know how it works?"

"I think so if I've got the coordinate system right."

"And of the consequence, if you do not?"

"Then you won't have to worry anymore," he replied with a grin.

Maren forced Thomas to look her face to face. "Of this, do it right, Thomas."

"If you insist," he said before moving to the next control station. His grin suddenly disappeared. "Damn!"

"Of the problem, what is it?"

"The second key is missing. We can't launch without it."

"Then, of a search, we must conduct one."

"Agreed," he said when a large male Mutant suddenly burst through a previously unseen side door and screamed, his hands instantly over his eyes to shield them from the harsh light above. Maren quickly raced forward and ran him through with her spear. Thomas ran to shut the door when a second male started to enter. Thomas slammed his body into the door, pinning the monster's arm between it and the jamb. As the second Mutant screamed and pulled his wounded limb back, Thomas shut the door. Maren threw the locking bar in place.

"Thomas, of the key, is that it?" she asked, pointing to the decoration hanging from a vine around the dead Mutant's neck.

"I think so…" Bending down, he ripped the key free then headed to the second console. The key fit. "This just might work," he shouted over pounding coming from behind the locked side door. "Maren, when I say three, turn this key all the way toward me."

"Agreed."

He ran to the first console. "Ready, one, two, three."

Warning lights suddenly flashed throughout the room. An alarm sounded, and an alien computer voice made an announcement in an unknown tongue. Thomas activated the launch sequence. "Let's get out of here."

They raced back down the tunnel then up the ladder when an external alarm sounded. Startled Mutants jumped down from the roof, their claws slashing the air, ready to fight. First, one head, then another, and another turned to see Maren and Thomas sprint across the clearing. Drool began to drip from their fangs.

"Tovar, circle," Maren shouted before finding themselves suddenly surrounded by Mutants. Thomas recovered his spear then put his back to Maren and her brothers, their spears pointed out. She knew it was only a matter of time before they would all die when the air raid siren atop the blockhouse suddenly blasted out a warning from the Mutant's past. One by one, the monsters fell writhing on the ground, their hands over their ears, the sound they made matching that coming from above.

"Let's move!" Thomas shouted.

Jumping over the Mutant bodies, they ran alone back down the path for the raft. Quickly pushed from shore, Maren and her brothers grabbed for the hand-holds. Thomas took hold of the tiller then lodged his feet under the restraining straps. The rapidly increasing current plunging them toward the ominous rumble of the white water ahead, he pushed the tiller hard starboard to position the raft as the river narrowed to half its width before racing between two banks of rocks. "Hold on!"

Tovar's eyes grew wide as the raft was thrown high into the air then crashed back down with equal force. A wall of water slammed into him, doing its best to rip him from the make-shift craft. But he was stronger than any water. He would not suffer the associated disgrace.

Again, the river narrowed. Again, the raft picked up speed. The massive rocks that defined the edge of the river flashed by while those beneath the surface churned the already deadly torrent. Water and spray came from all directions.

"Thomas!" Maren shouted, a massive rock dead ahead coming at them from out of the mist.

"Jump!"

The empty raft rode high on the rock before being blasted into pieces.

In the water, the raging torrent sent Maren tumbling head over heels before it dragged her under. She struggled to the surface only to be caught again by the current that finally flung her up and over the top of a massive rock. She again gasped for air then crashed back down into the teaming white water. Turned backward, she found herself once more airborne. Again she came down hard, beyond the white water, but only fifty meters in front of the green haze! With newfound strength, she swam for shore.

Thomas staggered the final few meters in the shallows then collapsed on the riverbank. Trying to catch his breath, he looked upstream for the others and found all except Oden. A quick check downstream showed his new friend lying face down in a backwater, his collar aglow. "Oden!"

Not more than five meters from where he started, Thomas felt his own collar constrict but knew there was no option. He had to keep going. Running through the shallows, he reached down and began to drag Oden's unconscious body back upstream, out of range of the field's deadly effect. But time and distance were not on his side. His throat on fire, his lungs about to explode, there was still time to save himself, but not Oden. Still, he had to try... He had to... Then everything went black.

CHAPTER TWENTY ONE

Thomas suddenly sat upright, gasping, not sure where he was. Looking around, he found himself some twenty meters further upstream from where he last remembered being. To the other side of him were Maren, Rah, Tovar... and Oden!

"Of my brother's life, our thanks are offered for saving it," Maren said.

"Thank you for saving my own," he replied, his voice a little raw.

"Of value, you may still have some," she said with a chuckle before turning serious again. "Thomas, of a place where lives are not so often in need of saving, I would like to find it now. Of strength, if you have it once again, we should continue."

"Agreed." He got to his feet and followed Maren, who led the way up the river bank to a Mutant trail. That, in turn, led to a road that paralleled the force field a safe distance away.

"Thomas, of the time to launch, how much longer will it be?" Tovar asked from behind him.

"It should have gone off by now," he replied, shaking his head. They were getting further and further away from Blockhouse Two that had earlier saved their lives. If they kept going and the missile did not launch, it was doubtful they could make it back there before dark.

"Of this effort, it is our best, perhaps our only opportunity for freedom," Maren said as though reading his thoughts. "Of the risk, it is justified," she said when the deafening sound of the missile blasting off toward the heavens caused all to stop. Maren shielded her eyes against the sun to watch the exhaust plume rise high overhead. "Of how such a thing so deadly can appear almost beautiful, I find it fascinating."

"Of it being the potential means for our freedom, then it truly is a beautiful thing," Rah replied.

"Agreed," Tovar and Oden said at the same time.

"We need to take cover," Thomas said. "A clearing would be best."

"Of such a place, it is just around the bend in the road," she said and took off running. Ten seconds later, they came upon an open space short of where the road disappeared into the force field. "Of this place, it is where guards gather their armed vehicles before they patrol."

Thomas led the way to the center of the clearing, away from the trees. "Remember, stay down until I give you the all-clear."

"Agreed," Maren replied. She checked her brothers first then laid face down on the ground. She then shut and covered her eyes with her arm, just as Thomas had told them to do. After all, he was a warrior and deserved their respect.

His eyes closed and covered, Thomas could only pray he was right. He knew they could survive the flash from the warhead, but the effect of the force field on the shockwave from the blast was unknown. The electromagnetic pulse should overload the electronic controls inside the dome, but would it neutralize the field in time? If not, the shock wave would be focused directly down upon them. But as Maren had said, the risk was justified.

Even though the precautions, all knew the detonation had occurred. First a flash, then a deafening boom came from overhead. But both were quickly forgotten when gale-force winds suddenly blasted down on them from above, pressing their bodies into the soft jungle floor with almost suffocating force. Trees cracked and fell while pieces of the jungle flashed overhead with deadly velocity. And then it was suddenly calm again.

"All-clear."

First, to his feet, Tovar stared in the direction of the force field. "Of the green haze, it is truly gone!" he said with a smile.

Oden grabbed his collar and ripped the powerless device from his neck. "Maren, freedom."

She removed her own collar and threw it down on the ground in victory. "Freedom."

"We're not out of this yet," Thomas cautioned, his collar off as well.

"Agreed." She turned to where the force field had been. Beyond the previously contained jungle lay a desert canyon.

Thomas pointed to a small building between two spires in the distance. "Looks like a guard shack."

Maren nodded. "Agreed. Of transportation and provisions, both should be available if that is so."

"Of guards, they should be there as well," Oden cautioned.

Maren just shrugged. "Of guards after Mutants?"

"Agreed."

The five took off running from the cover of one rock to another until they were twenty meters from the back of the shack. Hidden from view, Thomas carefully surveyed the building. "I don't see anyone, but there's no telling how many may be inside."

"Then, of that, it must be determined," Maren said and looked to her brothers. Somehow, Rah and Tovar had managed to retain their bow and arrows despite the river's best efforts to separate them. "Of cover, supply it from here."

"Agreed," they said as she, Thomas, and Oden ran to the back of the shack.

A Lieutenant and private headed out the front door of the shack. Rounding the corner, they stopped just short of the back of the building and stared at the now visible jungle.

"How the hell is that possible, sir?" the private asked.

"Damned if I know, Hayes," he said before Thomas sprang out from behind the shack and rushed the Lieutenant. He landed a brutal right to the officer's jaw, knocking him out cold. In reaction, Hayes drew his disrupter, but Oden rushed toward him and deflected the shot. A punishing elbow to the face followed, sending the guard flying into an unconscious heap. Maren headed after the liberated weapon that had ended up behind the building.

"Hands up, you two," the first of two new armed guards commanded after rounding the corner and seeing only Thomas and Oden. "Well, I'll be damned, Zane. If it isn't Chandler," the fat guard exclaimed.

His partner smiled, exposing his broken and missing teeth. "I told you we should have killed him on the prison barge, Tate."

"Well, I guess we'll just have to correct that," he said when Maren suddenly appeared from behind the shack and fired the captured disrupter. Tate flew back from the impact, unconscious. Zane aimed his weapon at her when an arrow suddenly pierced his forearm and foiled the shot. A blow from Oden silenced the man's screams. Maren fired again at each of the four guards, making sure they were stunned.

"Maren," Oden said, returning from the other side of the cabin, "of others inside, there are none. Of vehicles, two exist in front."

"Rah, Tovar, come."

Both men appeared.

"Of the guards, place them in the cabin in case the Mutants come," Maren ordered. "Of any weapons and provisions the structure has to offer, liberate them and put them in the vehicles."

"Agreed."

Thomas grabbed the unconscious Lieutenant's ankles and began to drag him to the front of the cabin. "Not a bad shot, Maren."

"Of our need for you, it still remains," she said with a grin that quickly disappeared on seeing two open-air hovercraft. "Thomas, of these vehicles, we have no knowledge."

"We'll need both if we're to get far enough away."

"Of their operation, can it be learned quickly?"

"Yes."

"Then, of it, teach me," she said with determination.

"Alright." He hurriedly deposited the Lieutenant in the cabin then exited to find Maren already in the pilot's seat. "This is an anti-gravity vessel. To go up, you pull back on the stick." He pointed to the control device. "To go down, you push it forward. To go right, you move the stick slowly to the right. To go left, you move the stick slowly to the left."

"Understood."

"On the floor are two pedals. To go forward, you push down on the right one. To stop, you lift your foot off the right pedal and push down on the left one. Okay?"

"Agreed," Maren said, unconsciously nodding her head.

Thomas grabbed a helmet. "Put this on. It will allow us to talk with one another the whole time."

"Of that, it may be helpful," she said and lowered it over her head.

Once the provisions were stored, Thomas turned to the brothers. "Who wants to ride with your sister?"

There were no volunteers.

"Rah, now," Maren commanded.

"Agreed," he said and reluctantly came forward. Thomas strapped him in then headed to the other craft.

Maren looked at her passenger. "Of this, are you afraid?"

"No, but of this, it is not to my liking."

"Of my own feeling, it is much the same."

"Maren, can you hear me?" Thomas asked over the com-link.

"Yes."

"Push in the red button to activate the craft, then slowly pull back on the stick."

As the hovercraft came to life, Maren knew she was up to the task. And even though Thomas had told her to pull the stick back slowly, she was no child. She quickly pulled it all the way back.

"Maren!" Rah shouted as they shot straight up in the air.

"Maren, let go of the stick! Let go of the stick!" Thomas yelled over the com system.

Her panic caused her to pull the stick back even harder before she realized her error and let it go. As the hovercraft came to a sudden stop, she breathed a sigh of relief only to have it quickly replaced by panic after glancing over the rail. The ship was some thirty meters above the ground.

Getting in his own ship, Thomas climbed it to match Maren's elevation. He couldn't help but smile at the look on both her and Rah's face. Oden and Tovar were too preoccupied to notice. "Slowly, Maren. Always move the stick slowly."

"Agreed," she replied, still somewhat shaken.

"Alright, to go to the right, move the stick slowly to the right before bringing it back to the center after completing your turn. That's it. Good," Thomas said, her execution of the maneuver surprisingly smooth. "To go to the left, move the stick slowly to the left, then return it to center. That's good. Alright, to go down, push the stick slowly forward. Great, you're a natural."

"A child's toy. I wish to go forward now."

"Okay. Push the right pedal down slowly. The further you push it down, the faster you will go."

"Understood." She pushed the pedal down, but the instant acceleration threw her back in her seat. She braced herself by putting her right foot further down on the accelerator and pulling back on the stick.

"Maren!" Rah yelled as they raced upon a canyon spire directly in front of them.

"Maren, the left pedal, push it. Turn, turn!" Thomas shouted.

Fighting the panic, she jammed on the speed brakes then threw the stick hard to the right twice. The ship came to a stop mere meters from the side of the rock, but upside down.

Thomas climbed his ship another thirty meters then brought it next to hers when he noted the laughter from his own two passengers. "Oh yeah?"

"No, Thomas!" Oden shouted, suddenly finding himself upside down as well.

"Thomas, of this, we will not laugh again," Tovar yelled.

Maren looked over, and despite her green color, she managed a slight chuckle of her own.

"Okay, Maren, push the stick sharply to the side two times."

"Agreed." Doing so, she once again found both herself and her ship in an upright position.

Thomas did the same. "Now remember slow, deliberate movements except to rotate."

"Agreed," she replied and shook her head.

"You'll be alright," he said when a disrupter blast suddenly flashed over the bow of Thomas's ship. "Maren, take off. Head away from the guards!" he shouted and accelerated his ship forward. She powered her ship forward at forty-five degrees away from Thomas.

"Maren!" Rah shouted, an armed guard cruiser heading straight for them.

"Na cha te," she said and banked right.

Thomas pitched his ship erratically from side to side to dodge the incoming disrupter fire when a second guard ship appeared from the portside and forced him to follow the natural path of the box canyon.

"Thomas, of our course, they drive us where there is no escape. Of the walls, they are too high to get over."

"There's an opening between the two spires," he said, heading for it.

"Of its width, it is too narrow!"

"Possibly... Duck!" Thomas put the ship on its side, passing between the rocks with a good two centimeters to spare.

"Maren, hold steady," Rah yelled, her erratic movements only adding to the frustration he felt using the captured disrupter on the cruiser behind them.

"What you ask is difficult, but I will try," she replied with equal emotion.

Rah disconnected his seatbelt then stood among the incoming fire with his bow in hand. His first arrow went wide and high, but the second flew true, hitting the cruiser's helmsman in the shoulder. The ship lurched to port then crashed into a canyon wall before falling like a rock.

"Rah, sit!" She banked the hovercraft hard to port to miss the canyon wall then rotated it back only to find herself alone. "Rah!"

"Maren!"

"Rah?" She put the craft on its side and saw her brother hanging by one hand from his seatbelt.

"Of this, I still do not like it!" he yelled.

Maren slammed the stick to the side and flipped her brother rudely back into the craft. "Of my apology, it is offered."

"Thomas!" Tovar shouted, between shots with the foreign weapon. "Of two more ships, they are coming at us from my side."

"Thomas, of another ship, it is coming at us from ahead," Oden shouted.

"It's Maren," Thomas said, seeing a guard's cruiser directly behind her. "Maren, go to your right," he said, then followed after her.

She came out of her turn only to find two more guard ships headed straight for her. She turned again, this time to port. "Thomas, of only death, I fear it awaits us for our troubles."

"Not if I can help it," he replied while scanning the terrain in front of them. "There's a cave to your left. Head for it," he said, not ready to give up without a fight.

"Agreed," she replied when the sky was suddenly filled with disrupter blasts from above. One by one, the attacking guard ships fell victim to a tri-wing fighter that screamed overhead.

"Thomas, of what action should be taken?" Maren asked.

"Land your ship just outside the cave's entrance, then take cover behind it," he said with a smile.

"Agreed."

Thomas put his hovercraft down next to Maren's. His smile broadened on seeing the Copernicus shuttle flash overhead. It circled then landed some ten meters away.

"Thomas!" Keira shouted from the lowering aft ramp.

"Follow me!" He and the Ba'ahs ran to the safety of the shuttle while the fighter provided top cover. "Buckle up," Thomas shouted, the aft ramp coming up.

"Everyone good?" Keira asked from the controller's seat.

Thomas did a quick visual check. "We are. Go."

The former prisoners met the force of acceleration with joy as it pushed them into their seatbacks. Rah looked out a window and saw the planet's outer atmosphere fade into a brilliant starfield. "Freedom, Maren."

"Agreed," she said as Keira made her way aft and hugged her brother. Tears streamed down her face.

"Thank you," he said simply.

Toa, having put the shuttle on autopilot, came aft as well. "Good to see you again, Thomas," he said, shaking his hand.

"You did say you would be out there whenever."

Toa smiled. "We were getting ready to 'encourage' a guard or two to go in and get you when the force field suddenly dropped. Then, when the guard ships attacked two of their own ships, we knew it had to be you and quickly changed our plans."

Thomas grinned. "I'm glad you did. I'm not sure we could have lasted much longer. And as for us, Keira, Toa, this is Maren, Tovar, Rah, and Oden Ba'ah."

"Of our rescue, our thanks are offered," Maren said to Keira in a flat tone.

"Thank you for taking care of my brother."

"Brother?" Maren said, a smile suddenly crossing her face. "Of your brother's care, you are welcome."

"Oh, by the way, Thomas," Toa said, "those skins you're wearing really bring out the blue in your eyes. And that smell..."

"I've missed you too, Toa."

CHAPTER TWENTY TWO

"Good evening, ladies and gentlemen," Dave Ackerman said from the Delta Corporation News anchor desk. "In a follow-up to the arrest of Bertram Dykstra of the Theta Corporation, a press conference was held earlier in the day with T.A. Sandor, Vice President of Operations for the Theta Corporation. We offer a portion of that conference to you now for your consideration."

The picture changed to show Sandor at Theta Corporate Headquarters on the planet Kuril. Standing on stage at a podium, he pointed to one of several reporters sitting in front of him. Mr. Kuo."

"Mr. Sandor, as Mr. Dykstra has been charged with corporate spying, can you shed any light on the level of involvement of Theta Corporation itself?"

Sandor stiffened. "This news conference has been called to tell you about the latest progress on our efforts to apprehend the Dissenters."

"Then should I assume from your silence on the Dykstra matter that Theta has something to hide?"

"No, not at all," Sandor replied. "The Theta Corporation denies any involvement on the part of Mr. Dykstra or the corporation itself."

The reporters again shouted for Sandor's attention.

Sandor gestured to another of the reporters. "Mr. Ackerman."

"Mr. Sandor, are recordings made of all meetings held with Chairman Andrews?"

"Yes, but..."

"Then is the Theta Corporation planning to release any and all recordings to the District High Court where the Chairman and

Mr. Dykstra discussed the Delta Corporation, specifically the local Records Unit?"

Sandor's jaw tightened. "Again, my intent is to talk about the Dissenters."

"Yes, sir, but I'm asking if the recordings will be made available."

"No," Sandor replied curtly. "The recordings are highly proprietary and for that reason will not be released. Again, people, the Theta Corporation is not involved in the Delta Records Unit break-in, and there is no conspiracy. Mr. Dykstra has not even gone to trial, let alone been found guilty. And in no way is Chairman Andrews involved."

"If the District High Court requests the Theta Corporation's records," Ackerman persisted, "will they be furnished?"

Sandor was unable to mask his frustration. "Yes, of course, but this line of questioning is way off the mark."

"Mr. Sandor?"

"I have nothing further to say."

The reporters looked at one another with raised eyebrows as Sandor stormed off the stage.

"This evening," Ackerman said back on camera, "the District High Court did officially request any and all recordings of the meetings between Chairman Andrews and Mr. Dykstra where the Delta Corporation was discussed. For a live report, we now go to Roger Morphew at the Alpha District Courthouse. Roger."

Roger stood on the large steps leading up to an all-glass structure that was the District High Court building. "The Theta Corporation recordings were transmitted to the court about two hours ago, and we have just received word from a reliable source that one entry involving Mr. Dykstra and Chairman Andrews has been deleted. We will stand by here for any further details as they become known. For the Delta Corporation News team, I'm Roger Morphew."

"Thank you, Roger," Ackerman said once again back on camera. "In other news tonight," he said when Toa switched off the viewscreen in the mess of the Dissenter's new freighter, Veritas. "Unreal. All the way to the Chairman."

Keira, the only other in the room, sat at the table and shook her head. "Can't anyone be trusted anymore?"

"It must be the power. They must overload or something," Tao replied when the door opened, and the former prisoners entered. He found the transformation from the mud and skins amazing. Maren was stunningly beautiful, her brothers huge. All were well-built.

"Feel better?" Keira asked.

"You certainly smell better," Toa commented.

"Thank you," Thomas replied on his way to the table. "I forgot how nice it is to be clean."

Maren nodded as she and her brothers sat at the table. "Agreed. Of our time without that privilege, it was much longer."

"Much," Oden said.

"Coffee? Tea?" Toa asked.

"Of tea, that would be most appreciated," Maren said. Her brothers nodded.

Toa headed for the teapot and cups for their guests. "Did you see the news?"

"In the other room," Thomas replied. "Dykstra is under arrest for corporate spying, and Chairman Andrews is thought to be involved?"

"That's the implication," Keira replied, helping Toa with the cups.

"But what I don't understand," Thomas said, "is why break into the Delta Records Unit in the first place? What could they have possibly been after that would be of any value?"

"The obvious answer is information," Keira said.

"But what information?" Thomas questioned. "What could they have gotten that would justify the risk?"

Toa started pouring the tea. "Production quantities, investments?"

Thomas slowly shook his head. "Not likely. It was a Records Unit. Any information they have is old."

"So then why did they do it?" Keira asked.

"Thomas, of this man who was on stage, is he Sandor?" Maren asked.

"Yes," he replied, his tone cold.

Her eyes narrowed. "Then, of answers, look there."

"Agreed," Rah said. "Of Sandor, he leads where he wants you to go."

"Agreed," Tovar added. "Of his words, although they appeared emotional, they were well-planned."

Thomas looked around the table. "Did Sandor bring up the conspiracy, or did the reporters?"

"Sandor did," Toa offered. "He... damn."

"What?"

"While you were away, Sandor was promoted to Vice President of Operations for all of Theta. That puts him just behind Chairman Andrews and Dykstra."

Thomas looked down, lost in thought. "Sandor sets up Dykstra then works the conspiracy angle to take out Chairman Andrews so that he can become Chairman."

Keira shook her head. "We can't let that happen. We've got to do something."

"Thomas," Maren said, "of our land, it completes us, makes us who we are. Of our freedom, it will not be truly realized until our name is cleared, and our land is once more ours."

Maren's brothers all solemnly nodded.

"Of Sandor's exposure, it is also our best chance to make that happen," she continued. "Of our help in your quest, it is offered."

Thomas looked at the smiles on Toa and Keira's faces. "Then welcome to the Dissenters," he said with a smile of his own. "Now, all we need is a plan."

"Of what you have told us Thomas and of what we have just now learned," Maren said, "I have a suggestion."

"What's that?"

"Of Chairman Andrews, are his movements known, or can they be determined?"

"I would think so."

"Then of an unannounced visit to him, one is recommended where the suspicions of Sandor orchestrating all that has befallen both him and Dykstra are provided. Of the Chairman's subsequent investigation, it should also cast doubt on Sandor's claims against the Dissenters."

Thomas slowly nodded. "Agreed... Toa? Keira?"

"Agreed," they both replied.

Chairman Andrews and his chief aide entered the executive elevator alone. "Renée, we need to find out just what's going on."

"I agree, Mr. Chairman, but the bottom line is that we don't know how the deletion could have occurred. We've subjected everyone with possible access to the files to a security scan, and all passed with flying colors. The only other possibility was the system programmer, but it turns out he died in a boating accident awhile back."

The two exited into the building's basement and headed outside to a private maglev car, its customary four-man security detail standing by. "Well, I know I'm innocent," the Chairman said, "but given the evidence, I don't think too many people believe that right about now."

Renée shook her head. "Unfortunately, sir, I have to agree with you."

The Chairman stopped in front of the car. "If we don't come up with some answers soon, I'll lose Theta."

"We'll go over it all again tonight, sir. Maybe we missed something."

The Chairman nodded. "Don't stay too late."

"Yes, sir. Good night."

"Good night, Renée."

Out of sight, Rah used a newly acquired high powered scope to see Chairman Andrews get into mag-lev car number 454. He pulled out his secure communicator.

A dark, stormy night, Terac carefully moved inside an empty maglev car parked on a spur. With a bogus keycard, he made sure the car was operable then quickly turned it off so that the electronic emissions on what was supposed to be a cleared track were not detected by the Chairman's car.

Chairman Andrews sat back in his leather chair and absently watched the city lights rush by, lost in the events of the day. The whole thing was so damned impossible to believe. There was no way Dykstra was guilty, but he had no defensible alibi. And how could the record of his meeting with Dykstra have been deleted? No wonder the press thought there was a conspiracy. Who wouldn't?

"Your beer, sir," his butler Jerome said. He bent down with two freshly poured glasses of the Chairman's favorite ale on a silver tray.

"Thanks, Jerome. I can sure use it tonight," he said and took one of the glasses. Being the Chairman meant he had to be many things to many people, but deep down inside, he was still human. He liked a cold beer at the end of the day, and that was that. And he didn't like to drink alone, and that was also that. So when Jerome first took the job, he had to the man's ultimate surprise, asked him to join him in having a beer. Now they were more friends than employee and employer.

Jerome took the second glass and sat in the opposite chair. "The conspiracy talk, sir?"

"The conspiracy talk," he responded with an audible sigh. "The current thinking is that someone at Delta is out to get me, but I'll be damned if I can figure out who."

"Mr. Dykstra was framed, obviously, but who would also have had access to the Theta records?" Jerome asked. He had repeatedly considered all the possibilities, and each time, he had come up empty.

The Chairman slowly shook his head. "That I do not know."

Well concealed from view, Terac watched the Chairman's car speed by then disappear into the darkness of the night. He waited long enough to be outside the sensor range then again activated the car he was in. Without lights, he pulled it out onto the mainline for the Northern Bay track in pursuit of his prey.

Thomas, Toa, Maren, and Oden settled in the woods just above an unmanned power station for the Northern Bay maglev track. Toa ran an electronic scan. "The area is clear," he said in a lowered voice.

"Alright," Thomas said softly back. He turned and looked at Maren and Oden through his night-vision goggles. "Ready?"

"Yes," she replied, looking all around, still marveling at the technology that allowed her to see clearly in the dark of the night.

Oden nodded. "Ready."

While Toa held his position, Thomas led the way down the hill for the others, trying to be as quiet as possible. He knew that even though the area was shown to be unpopulated, caution was still their best friend. At the bottom of the ravine, but hidden in the woods, he scanned the area before they emerged out into the open. "Clear."

Oden, carrying a previously scorched section of the metal undercarriage from a maglev car, stopped some fifteen meters short of the power station and laid the part next to the track before heading back up into the woods. Thomas and Maren continued on to the power station's door to find it locked. "Of this, can it be opened?" she asked.

"Shouldn't be a problem." Thomas placed a black box over the lock mechanism. Seconds later, a distinctive click was heard, and the door opened freely. "After you."

Maren entered the building. "Of you, a gentleman?"

Thomas followed her in. "Every now and then," he said with a chuckle before locking the door behind him. "Is your headgear off?"

"Yes."

He turned the interior lights on then led the way to the control panel for the maglev track power. He scanned the display.

"Of this, is it as you had hoped?"

"Exactly."

"Toa?" Oden whispered.

"Over here."

He climbed the remaining meters then knelt beside Toa. "Of all, it is ready."

Toa activated a secure communicator. "We're all set here."

"We're ready here as well," Thomas replied.

"Alright. Stand by," came over the com system.

"Well, Maren, we should," Thomas started to say when the look on her face caused him to pause. "Is something wrong?"

Her eyes met his. "Of Shara Lockett's death, I am truly sorry. Of her life ending, does it still cause you pain?"

He looked at Maren then down at the floor. "Yes, it does... I think of her often."

"And of love, will you be able to experience it again?"

He looked back at Maren. Her directness was, at times, disturbing, but it was also one of the things that attracted him to her. Would he love again? It was a question he'd been afraid to ask himself. It was also one he knew he would have to answer sooner or later. Was it wrong to think of loving someone else so soon after Shara's death? Was grief infinite, or was it eventually overcome by loneliness? He looked back into Maren's eyes, glad to be with her. "Yes."

At first sight of the oncoming maglev's lights, Tovar ducked behind the solid concrete rail of the overpass. As the car moved under the structure, he rose up in time to see the 454 written on its top with his night-vision goggles. "Of 454, it has just passed my position," he announced into his secure communicator.

"Going to phase two," came the reply.

Taking off his goggles, Tovar started across the bridge when what sounded like another car following the Chairman's car without lights brought him to a stop. Walking back to where he had been, he checked the track but saw only the blackness of the night.

Toa watched the Chairman's car round the corner and activated his communicator. "Four, three, two, one. Now!"

The headlights on the car suddenly went out. Darkness was replaced by a shower of sparks from emergency brakes before the maglev came to a stop some twenty meters short of the power station.

"What the!" Terac said, his car suddenly going dead in the middle of nowhere. Getting out, he ran toward the bend in the track some hundred meters away. Hopefully, he could put eyes on the Chairman's car.

"Are you alright, Mr. Chairman?" his butler asked, emergency lights coming on.

"Yes, Jerome," he replied, finding the silver tray had been replaced by a disrupter. The other four, who had also sworn to protect the Chairman with their lives, had their weapons out as well. "Don't you think you're overdoing it a bit?"

"Perhaps, sir, but it never hurts to be prepared."

"You're right, of course," the Chairman said. He had decided long ago that although he was the leader of the worlds' largest corporation, he was by no means a security specialist. That was Jerome's real job. The butler position was just a cover. Together they had agreed that in all matters of security, Jerome would be in charge. He would continue to honor that agreement.

"Captain, what about communications?" Jerome asked.

"Nothing but static on all channels, sir. Must be the surrounding hills."

"Communicators?"

"They're still functional, but I'm not getting anyone."

One of the security detail, Mitchum, came forward. "Sir," I believe there's a power station just forward. Maybe we can bring the system back online."

Jerome looked at the Chairman.

"It's your call."

"Yes, sir... Alright, you and Jergens go check it out, but be careful. I don't like this."

"Yes, sir."

Both men put on overcoats and hats for protection against the worsening weather, then exited the car and headed outside with flashlights in hand.

"Mitchum, look." Jergens focused his light on a piece of metal lying next to the track just in front of them. "Look at those scorch marks."

"It must have fallen off another car and tripped a breaker. Think we can reboot the system?"

"Don't know why not..." They made their way to the power station to find the door locked. Jergens pulled out his disrupter and fired on the lock. A well-placed kick completed the task. Turning the lights on inside, they made their way to the control panel as the door closed automatically behind them.

"What do you think?" Mitchum asked.

"Breaker's tripped. All we have to do is," he said before a stun grenade suddenly exploded at their feet. Dancing blue electricity quickly engulfed both men. Writhing, they fell on the floor, unconscious. Thomas and Maren came out of hiding. Thomas removed Jergens' hat then put on the man's coat. "So far, so good."

Maren tucked her hair under Mitchum's hat, his coat already on. "Agreed."

Thomas restored the power to the track. "Ready?"

"No," she replied, then kissed Thomas. After all, she was from a matriarchal society… "Of being ready, I am now," she said with a smile.

"That's more like it," Jerome said as the car came back to life. He holstered his disrupter. The other two guards did the same before one of them opened the car's door for their returning comrades. "You two are in the wrong line of work."

Maren suddenly pulled the bodyguard out of the car and shot him point-blank with her weapon set on stun. Thomas stunned the second bodyguard on his way inside then pointed his disrupter at Jerome. "Hands up, now!"

Maren quickly entered behind Thomas and trained her weapon on the maglev Captain.

"Everyone do as they say," the Chairman said, calmly sitting in his chair.

"Captain, please come aft and lay down on the deck," Thomas ordered. "Jerome," he said, pleased by the look of surprise on the man's face on hearing his name. Thomas handed the butler a pair of shackles. "Please put these on the Captain, if you would. I have another pair for you."

Terac knew the distinctive flash of a disrupter when he saw one. What he did not know was what was going on. It certainly wasn't what he had planned. He pulled out his untraceable communicator only to find the lack of a signal. He suspected the surrounding hills. With the power to the track restored, he ran back to his car. Once there, he put it in reverse long enough to finally get a signal on his communicator. He called his contact.

"Yeah," came the harsh reply from the other end.

"Abort."

"And the money?"

"You'll be paid."

"Right."

Terac quickly terminated the transmission and called another number.

"Theta Maglev Security," the Duty Officer's voice was heard to say.

"Ah yes, I'd like to report ah, well, it looks like a hijacking."

"What is your location?"

"Ah... I'm above the Northern Bay track near kilometer post 128, and, ah, this car is stopped, and I thought I saw a disrupter blast and ah, well, damn, I thought I should call."

The Duty Officer punched the location into her console to identify the car in question. "Holy," she said and instantly activated an emergency alarm. "Excuse me, sir. Could I have your name, please?"

"Ah sure, ah... No, no, I don't want to get involved any more than I already am. Oh, hey, these guys have weapons," Terac said and purposely terminated the connection. He then moved his car forward again. Stopping just short of the bend in the track, he headed up into the surrounding woods.

While Maren handcuffed Jerome, Thomas approached Chairman Andrews. "Mr. Chairman, I'm Thomas Chandler."

The Chairman watched Thomas sit opposite him with practiced calm. "Mr. Chandler. You obviously don't want to kill me, or you would have done so long ago. And as for kidnapping me, we would not still be here. So that only leaves talking," he said while Toa, Oden, and Maren moved the stunned bodyguards back into the mag-lev car.

Thomas nodded his acceptance of the Chairman's abilities. "Sir, as impossible as this sounds, I'm going to ask you to try and ignore the circumstances and listen to what I have to say. Believe me, if there was any other way..."

"Are you going to try to convince me of the Dissenters' innocence?"

"Indirectly, but our main concern right now is the Delta break-in, and what we are convinced is a plot to remove you from office."

"You've gone to a lot of trouble to tell me the obvious. Many corporations would be more than happy to see that happen."

"Not other corporations, Mr. Chairman. From within."

The Chairman looked at Thomas, his eyes slightly narrowed. "Please explain."

"We believe Sandor is orchestrating the whole affair. If you and Mr. Dykstra are out of the way, he will be your successor in all probability."

"He's also the one responsible for your capture and conviction."

"Listen, we're trying to help you."

"Are you? Or are you trying to help yourselves at my expense? The courts certainly didn't believe you. Why should I?"

"Because if you don't, you'll lose Theta. He controls the media. He did with us, and he is doing it right now with you. It's his game and his rules, and he doesn't like to lose. Listen, all I ask is that you examine the facts. Look at what happened on Sorel assuming the Dissenters are innocent, and Sandor is guilty. Then do the same for your own situation, assuming Sandor is responsible instead of another corporation."

Toa suddenly raced back inside the car. "Thomas, we've got multiple Tactical Squad landcruisers approaching from the south."

"Take off. I'll join you in a second."

He turned back to face the Chairman. "Please think about what I've said. If you believe me or need our help, call this number, and we'll contact you." He handed the Chairman a card and the keys for the shackles. "Again, I'm sorry we had to meet this way."

Out of the car, Thomas raced down the tracks to the north as the first on the inbound Tactical Squad landcruisers rounded the corner from the south. The north side of the power station provided cover just in time from the incoming disrupter blasts when the Dissenter tri-wing fighter suddenly screamed overhead firing, its weapons on stun. One by one, the cruisers crashed to the ground, but more kept coming. A second pass followed before the Dissenter shuttle landed just around a bend in the track to the immediate north of the station.

"Of the number of landcruisers still functional, it is now over twenty," Maren shouted when small weapons fire erupted from the bank to their left.

"Hawkins, we're taking fire from the east," Toa shouted into his communicator.

"I'm on it."

The tri-wing again screamed overhead, laying down a spread pattern.

"Let's move!" Thomas yelled.

All raced for the shuttle when an incoming landcruiser cannon blast landed between Toa and Maren, knocking both to the ground. Oden rushed to his sister. Thomas helped Toa up as their fighter passed overhead once more, providing precious cover fire.

"It's my right ankle," Toa yelled through the pain.

"Put your arm around my shoulder."

"Alright, let's go."

With Maren's unconscious body in his arms, Oden started to run down the track when a landcruiser cannon blast struck him square in the back. The effect of the stun rapidly consuming him, it was all he could do to stagger to the side of the tracks and collapse behind a large rock.

With Tactical Squad disrupter blasts striking all around them, Thomas moved as best he could with Toa toward the shuttle. Roberts rushed past Keira as she laid down cover fire. "I've got Toa," Roberts said, Thomas, making the handoff.

"Thanks," Thomas said and raced back for Oden and Maren when again, the fighter screamed overhead. "Oden?"

"Here," he moaned.

Thomas ran to his side. "Save Maren," Oden said, then passed out.

"Hawkins," Thomas shouted into his communicator, hoisting Maren's limp body over his shoulder. "I'm by the big rock just south of the shuttle. I need cover fire."

"Here it comes."

Thomas heard the fighter approach, heard its disrupter's fire then ran to the shuttle and Roberts. "I'm going back for Oden," he said, again making the handoff.

Keira suddenly blocked his way. "You can't. They've overrun Oden's position."

"But I have to save him," Thomas pleaded.

"Thomas, there's nothing you can do."

The Tactical Squad Commander watched the shuttle disappear into the night under the tri-wing fighter's escort before turning his attention back to the Chairman's car. "Commander, I have the code," his communications man announced, running forward.

"It's about time." Even though the area was secure, those inside would not come out until given the proper access code. The Commander activated his communicator. "Theta One, the code is four, two, alpha, sigma."

"Thank you," came the reply before the car door opened. The Chairman alone came out then closed the door behind him. "Commander," he said and shook the man's hand, "you and your people did an excellent job."

"Thank you, Mr. Chairman. Do you have any idea who they were and/or what they wanted?"

"I'm afraid the answer to both questions is no, thanks to your timely arrival."

"I think that fortunate."

"I agree. Were you able to capture any of them?"

"One, sir," he replied as an officer came forward. "Excuse me for a moment, please, Mr. Chairman."

"Certainly."

"What have you got, Captain?"

"We're ready to transport the prisoner to the hospital."

"Has he regained consciousness yet?"

"No. Not yet, sir."

"I want answers as soon as possible."

"Yes, sir."

"Make sure his legs are secure," one of two medics attending an unconscious Oden said when the Captain approached the hovercraft's pilot from behind him.

"Lieutenant, take the prisoner to Theta Emergency Central."

Terac dropped the borrowed helmet's night visor in place then turned to face the Captain from the pilot's seat. "Yes, sir. Please stand clear."

From a distance, the Chairman watched the hovercraft carrying the prisoner rotate then accelerate back down the ravine. "Commander, I shall be most interested in finding out what you learn from the prisoner."

"Yes, sir."

CHAPTER TWENTY THREE

The sound of Sandor's heels on the cement floor echoed inside the abandoned warehouse as he made his way to the only illuminated room. There, he found Terac standing over a very large man strapped to an inclined table, his head angled down. "Has he said anything yet?"

Terac adjusted an electrode on Oden's forehead. "No, sir," he replied and moved back behind a makeshift control console.

Sandor joined him. "Does anyone else know you have him?"

Terac motioned with his head to the bodies of the two medics slumped in the parked hovercraft. Both had been shot in the chest. "No. There is also a Tactical Squad pilot. His body is in the hovercraft's boot."

Sandor nodded. "What level did you reach with the computer programmer?"

"At two, he was begging for mercy."

Sandor motioned to the controls. "May I?"

"Certainly, sir. Just one second…" Terac took a syringe off an adjacent table then jammed the needle into Oden's arm.

"What was that?" Sandor asked.

"A stimulant," Terac replied, then slapped Oden hard across the face three times to help him focus. "Are you ready to talk now?"

Oden slowly opened his eyes to see Terac's face next to his. "Of your hell, go to it."

Terac slammed his fist into Oden's injured shoulder. "No, you."

The pain excruciating, Oden wanted to scream, but knew to do so would show weakness. He would not be weak, he told himself when he started to shake uncontrollably.

"He's ready."

"Excellent." Sandor adjusted the control panel's microphone. "Who do you work for?" he began, his voice purposely distorted by an audio system to further induce fear in Oden's drugged mind. "Who do you work for?"

Oden remained silent.

Sandor responded by turning the power to level one. Oden's body began to jerk from the dancing blue electricity that surrounded him. "Are you a Dissenter? Are you a Dissenter? Who do you work for?" Still no reply, Sandor impatiently turned the power setting to level two.

Oden screamed from the intense pain but knew he would never give his captors what they wanted. Death was better than disgrace.

"Who do you work for?" Sandor yelled, intoxicated by the power. "Are you a Dissenter? Answer me, damn it!" he shouted, then turned the power setting to level three.

Oden's screams became continuous, the electricity turning from blue to white. "Any more and you'll kill him," Terac warned calmly.

"So be it," he yelled and increased the power to level four. "Are you a Dissenter? Are you a Dissenter? Damn it, tell me. Tell me!"

Oden's screams were suddenly replaced by convulsions. Then he quit moving altogether.

Sandor turned the power off to allow Terac access to the prisoner. "Is he dead?"

"No, but it's just a matter of time," Terac replied. "No one has ever made it past level three."

Sandor ran his fingers through his hair, then adjusted his coat. "No matter," he said, once again calm. "He wasn't going to talk, and we couldn't let him live."

Terac nodded. "Agreed. Do you think he is a Dissenter?"

"He matches the description of one of those who escaped with Chandler from the Prison Planet. He, his brothers, and sister could certainly have joined the Dissenters."

Terac looked at Sandor with raised eyebrows. "Do you think Chandler has figured out your plan?"

"No," Sandor said after a moment of thought. "He's probably still trying to convince anyone who will listen of their innocence on Sorel. But if I could link the Chairman to the Dissenters..."

"Is that necessary?" Terac asked innocently.

"Never underestimate the power of the Chairman," Sandor warned. "No, I need to take advantage of every opportunity that presents itself. To connect the Chairman with the Dissenters would certainly be his death knell."

The Chairman sat alone in the darkened study of his mansion located in a private reserve outside the city of Edo. It was a welcome break from the constant demands of the job most nights. Not this one... He stared out the window at the floodlit pools and woods beyond. The night's events had certainly been interesting, to say the least. But now it was time to take a more objective look at what had happened.

"You wanted to see me, sir?" Jerome asked from a half-opened door.

The Chairman rotated in his chair to face his butler. "I know it's late, but if you don't mind."

Jerome entered the room. "Not at all, sir. I'm afraid I'm not all that sleepy after the way I handled the situation earlier tonight." He took a seat opposite the Chairman's desk.

"Don't be hard on yourself. I was there and agreed with every move that was made. Besides, the past is the past, and the last time I checked, there still isn't anything we can do to change it. No, what we need to do now is to figure out what's to be learned from tonight's events."

"Yes, sir," Jerome replied. "Thank you, sir."

The Chairman nodded then leaned back in his chair. "So, tell me. What did you think of the attack from a planning and execution standpoint?"

"Well, they chose an unpopulated location and set up a plausible cause for the power outage so that we would think exactly what they wanted us to and let our guard down. They also covered the air space above and had an escape route ready to go so they could get out quickly if anything went wrong. All in all, I'd say it was just about perfect."

"I agree. So what went wrong?"

"A call to Security."

"From whom?"

"Unknown. The man wouldn't leave his name."

"So, we have a call from the middle of nowhere by someone who wouldn't identify himself. Did the Tactical Squad find anyone else in the area, a camper, or a hiker?"

"No, but they did find another maglev car on the track behind ours that was abandoned."

"Was that part of the Dissenter's plan?"

Jerome shifted slightly in his chair. "That's our current thinking, but now I'm not so sure that scenario makes sense. They needed to know where we were, of course, but that could have been done in several different ways. Better ways."

"Like an electronic bug?"

"No, our sensors would have picked it up. It would have had to have been something more basic."

"Like the number on top of my car?"

Jerome looked at the Chairman with raised eyebrows. "Observed from, say, an overpass?"

"Remember, you said Chandler's plan was better than good, and this scenario sounds consistent."

"Agreed."

"Then let's assume whoever was in the other car placed the call," the Chairman concluded. "Now, why?"

"To prevent the Dissenters from contacting you?"

"Well, that seems to me to be the most probable answer. Although not public knowledge, several people, including Sandor, know Chandler is no longer a resident of the Prison Planet. And if Sandor is truly at the bottom of this whole mess, he certainly wouldn't want Chandler to contact me for fear that I just might look further into the Sorel affair and explore any options to the already accepted facts. So to prevent that, he has someone follow me and report any out of the ordinary behavior."

"Makes sense," Jerome said. "So, where did the man go?"

"If I was him, I would have blended in with the Tactical Squad. Were there any reported losses or people missing?"

"No sir."

"Well then," the Chairman started to say when the com sounded. "Yes?"

"Mr. Sandor calling, sir," an unseen voice announced.

"Interesting. Please hold a minute... Jerome, I'd like you to hear this, but I don't want Sandor to know you're here. Just stand over there out of view."

"Yes, sir," Jerome said and moved into position.

"Put Mr. Sandor through, please."

"Yes, sir." The viewscreen on the far wall came alive to show Sandor in his office.

"Working late tonight, T.A.?"

"Yes, sir. I'm sorry to disturb you, Mr. Chairman, but I just heard about the attack and wanted to make sure you were alright."

"I'm fine, thank you," the Chairman replied with an outward smile. "Unfortunately, it's all part of the job."

"Unfortunately... Do you know who attacked you and what they wanted?"

"I was hoping you would tell me."

"Sir?" Sandor replied, somewhat confused.

"Do you know if the prisoner has talked yet?"

"Oh, I'm afraid I have some bad news for you there, sir."

"Bad news?"

"Yes, sir," Sandor said with a nod. "The hovercraft with the prisoner on board crashed in the Meadowlands. There were no survivors."

"I see... Has the Tactical Squad determined the cause of the crash yet?"

"No sir. There was very little left after the fire that followed."

"Damn." The Chairman shook his head, lost in thought.

"Sir, about this attack..."

"Yes?" he said, his attention back on Sandor.

"Security believes it was carried out by members of the Dissenters. They've asked me to express their concern that if word gets out about what happened tonight, it might compromise their efforts to apprehend them."

"I see. Yes, yes, I quite agree. But how do you propose to keep the attack from the media?"

"I thought that we could tell them it was a readiness drill to see how well the Tactical Squad would perform in an emergency."

"An excellent idea, T.A. See to it, will you?"

"Yes, sir. Well, I'm glad you're safe, Mr. Chairman."

"Goodnight, T.A., and thank you for calling."

"You're welcome, sir. Goodnight."

The viewscreen blank, the Chairman turned in his chair to see Jerome come out of the shadows. "Well, what do you think?"

"I think the pilot of that hovercraft was killed by our caller, who then took his place. I also think the man works for Sandor."

"Why, Sandor?"

"Motive and opportunity both here and with the Dykstra affair."

"Go on."

"I think our caller later killed the two medics and got what information he could out of the prisoner before killing him. He then staged a fiery crash to get rid of the evidence, including the body of the original pilot of the hovercraft."

The Chairman leaned back in his chair and removed the card he'd been given earlier that night by Thomas Chandler from his pocket. "That does seem to be the only logical conclusion that fits all the facts."

Thomas sat alone in the mess of the Veritas. He knew he shouldn't be angry with himself for leaving Oden behind, but…

Maren entered to find him looking at her, shaking his head. "Maren, I'm so sorry. I should have saved Oden."

"Thomas, hold. Of your current feelings of guilt, they are both not helpful, nor are they deserved. Of Oden, he knew the risk and accepted it. Of his death, it was with honor."

"But I could have saved him."

"No, of that you are wrong. Of any attempt on your part, it would have cost you not only your own life but those of the other Dissenters over time."

He slowly nodded. "I suppose you are right."

"Of this, I am."

Hawkins suddenly entered the room, excited. "Thomas, we've just received a message from Jerome. The Chairman wants us to set up a meeting."

"Excellent... Have Chu contact his father using his family's code. We need his help again."

"Then, you have a plan?"

Thomas just smiled.

The Chairman sat in his office and stared out the window at the morning sun with an inward smile. For the first time, he had an enemy with a face, an enemy he could study, fight, and defeat. But caution was the key. He had to make sure Sandor remained in the dark. He had to maintain the current state of confusion.

"Mr. Dykstra is here to see you, sir," his secretary announced over the com.

"Send him in please and hold all my calls."

"Yes, sir."

His attire was fresh, but Dykstra's face was worn. Still, he managed a smile as he crossed the room to meet the Chairman halfway and shake hands.

"Bert, how are you?"

"Well, quite frankly, I'm confused and frustrated, but I still have enough of my mind left to thank you for getting me out on bail. I don't think I could have taken much more."

"I'm just sorry we couldn't have gotten you out sooner."

Dykstra nodded. "I wish I knew what was going on."

"Me too," the Chairman said. "How about a little fresh air?"

"Sure," Dykstra replied in a tone reflecting his confusion with such an odd request. He followed the Chairman outside.

The Chairman leaned on the balcony rail and looked out over the city, away from his office. "Bert, this is going to sound pretty strange, but for reasons of security, when you talk, face away from the office. There are no recording devices out here, but I wouldn't put lip-reading past him."

Dykstra stared at the Chairman and saw the man was serious. He did as instructed. "Him?"

The Chairman smiled. "Listen, Bert, I know you're innocent."

"Thanks. I can't tell you how nice it is to hear that."

"I also know you were set up."

"You also know who did it and why, don't you?"

The Chairman nodded. "As for why, he wants you gone. He's also using you to get to me, to remove me from office."

"The rumors of a conspiracy. Your reported involvement. It makes sense, but who?"

"Sandor."

"Sandor!" Dykstra felt his face go flush with anger. His mind raced. "Of course, we're gone, and he's in," Bert said, the pieces falling into place. "That bastard. Does he know you suspect him?"

"No, not so far, and he mustn't find out."

It was Dykstra's turn to nod. "Can he be stopped?"

"Easily, but I lose Theta in the process, and that's not something I'm willing to do, at least not yet."

"Then I assume there's another way, a not so easy way."

"There is," the Chairman said and smiled, "but I need your help."

"Name it."

"It may involve going outside the law."

Dykstra chuckled. "They can only send me to the Prison Planet once."

"That's certainly true," the Chairman said with a laugh. "Do you remember the business about the Dissenters?"

"1638 people dead is hard to forget. Sandor... Oh my God! He destroyed Sorel for the profit?"

"Initially, yes, but ultimately, I think it was done for the power. Remember, Sandor was the one who exposed the Dissenters, and as a result, I put him where he is today," the Chairman said and slowly shook his head. "Bert, the other night, I received a visit from Thomas Chandler."

"I thought he was on the Prison Planet."

"The keyword is *was*. Chandler is a very resourceful man. At any rate, he's volunteered the Dissenters' help in exposing Sandor."

Dykstra thought for a moment. "Do you need their help? Can't we link Sandor to the sabotage of the Sorel Colony without him?"

The Chairman shook his head. "I don't think so. The District High Court has already ruled on all the evidence we currently have, and besides, there's no direct link back to Sandor anyway."

"How about our own people?"

"It's hard to know who to trust. If I choose one of Sandor's people, Sandor would definitely have the upper hand."

"Do you think Chandler can be trusted, or is he just trying to use you?"

The Chairman shrugged. "I think he's trying to expose Sandor, and I'm his best bet to do that. So in a way, yes, he's using me. I also think he can be trusted."

"But what if you're linked to the Dissenters?"

"Instant destruction. But compared to a slow death by Sandor's hand, there really isn't much of a choice when you think about it. Besides, as I see it, the Dissenters are the bait Sandor won't be able to resist."

"True... So how can I help?"

The Chairman smiled.

Chu had piloted the Veritas' shuttle to a distant part of space, well off the beaten path.

"Thomas, Mr. Lee's shuttle is inbound," Hawkins reported. "We're being hailed."

"Put him on the viewscreen... Mr. Lee, I'm Thomas Chandler. Thank you for coming so quickly."

"It is a pleasure to finally meet you, Mr. Chandler. I was excited to hear about your upcoming meeting and wish to help any way I can."

"Thank you. It is very much appreciated. As Chu has told you, we need several fighters and a small, armed, warp-capable transport if possible."

"Then, please turn your camera to view the space in front of you."

With a smile, Chu did as asked. A massive yard holding more than a thousand military ships of all types and sizes from the Corporate War suddenly appeared from behind a cloak.

"My God!" Hawkins exclaimed.

"Very impressive," Thomas said as Mr. Lee appeared back on the viewscreen.

"As I told Hawkins earlier, I was able to patent my storage concept for the salvage business and sell it to those heading up Corporate Rule. They had a great deal of inventory they wanted to keep, just in case. This is one of eleven such yards I hold the maintenance contract for. Given the involvement of the Chairman of the Theta Corporation, my thinking is those in charge will not miss some of their inventory," Mr. Lee said with a smile.

Thomas smiled in return. "I completely agree."

"Good, then please follow me."

"Chu, you could have told us about the yard earlier," Hawkins said.

"And ruin the surprise?" he replied when an opening appeared in the surrounding force field.

"The sheer size is incredible as are its contents," Thomas offered.

"I first saw it when I was a little kid and was blown away," Chu said, following his father's ship on the way to one of the many spacecraft carriers in storage. The ship's design consisted of twelve hangars connected to a central hub in a vertical plane. "My father keeps a hangar on one of the carriers in each yard functional to act as his base of operations," he said, passing through the carrier's active force field and landing next to his father's ship.

Thomas lowered the aft ramp then followed Hawkins and Chu out onto the hangar deck. "Mr. Lee," Thomas said, shaking the man's hand. To one side were what looked like unused corporate fighters from the war. Of a blended wing-to-body design, armaments were housed in a recessed arched bay below the vessel's centerline. The pilot and copilot sat forward in tandem, one slightly below the other. "This just keeps getting better."

"These fighters were ready to go into service when the war ended," Mr. Lee said with a smile. "Will they meet your needs?"

"Yes. Very much so."

"Good. As for the armed transport," Mr. Lee said, turning around and heading to a candidate ship, "there is one here that you might like. The earlier models were not capable of warp speed. This model is, but was not released for service in time."

Her aft ramp already down, the party entered the box-like vessel to find seating for eight. "Forward firing disrupters?" Thomas asked.

"Yes. The transport also has a mine dispenser."

"And the mines?"

"They are available but will have to be loaded, however."

"How long will that take? We're a little short on time."

"An hour at the most."

"Excellent."

"There are also modern spacesuits unless you prefer the ones I provided earlier."

Thomas couldn't help but laugh. "The modern ones, please."

From his private mag-lev car, the Chairman saw the Edo Regional Spaceport appear in the distance. An all too familiar sight, it was built to make the comings and goings of Theta's top executives more convenient. He would now use that to his advantage.

Dykstra came out of the car's bathroom wearing a mask of the Chairman's face. "Well, what do you think?"

"I think you're the most handsome person I've ever seen," the Chairman said with a chuckle. "How's it feel?"

"Ah, I don't want to ruin the surprise."

The Chairman got up and headed into the bathroom. "That good, huh?"

The incredible Mr. Lee had told them about Space Station 575. Located just outside the Lambda Asteroid Field, it had been abandoned as a remnant of the Corporate War. Its location no longer of importance, the cost to relocate and modernize it prohibitive, the station was long forgotten by almost all, making it perfect for a meeting.

After recharging Module One's power generator, Toa sat at its controls, the other two modules of the station uninhabitable. "We're all set."

Thomas nodded, lost in thought... So, was the Chairman a man of his word? Was he going to come alone or bring the Tactical Squad down upon them? The risk was extreme. The decision not to involve the main Dissenter force in the meeting was the right one. Still… "I feel like a sitting duck."

"Me too, but we've got to trust him," Toa said.

"I know."

Concealed in a darkened hanger across the tarmac from the Chairman's ship, the Tactical Squad Commander watched the Chairman's mag-lev car pull to a stop in front of the corporate hangar. "I hope you are right about this, Mr. Sandor."

Sandor just smiled.

The Chairman followed Dykstra out of the car and walked over to his private spacecraft. "Hopefully, this won't take too long," Dykstra appeared to say.

The Chairman appeared to nod. "Call if you need help."

"Will do." The two shook hands before what appeared to be Dykstra got on the ship, and what appeared to be the Chairman returned to the mag-lev.

"Edo Regional Control, this is Theta One," the pilot announced into the ship's com system. "Requesting clearance for takeoff."

"Roger, Theta One. You are cleared for runway one nine."

"Runway one nine. Roger, Control. Theta One, out... We're ready, sir."

The Chairman removed his Dykstra mask. "Alright, Mr. Terac, proceed."

Sandor watched the Chairman's ship head down the runway and blast off for the cosmos when a Lieutenant came forward. "Commander, I have a confirmed visual that the Chairman did not board the ship. Only Mr. Dykstra did."

Sandor smiled. "Send in your men, Commander."

"Yes, sir."

Bert Dykstra came out of the bathroom of the Chairman's car after removing the mask and destroying it. He reached for a drink when four Theta Tactical Squad soldiers entered armed. "Hands up!" a Captain shouted, pointing his disrupter at Dykstra while his men searched the car.

"Clear."

"Clear."

"Search him."

One of the soldiers came away with Dykstra's identification and handed it to his Captain. "Sorry about that, Mr. Dykstra," the officer said. "You can put your hands down."

"Care to tell me what this is all about, Captain?" Dykstra asked in a less than pleasant tone.

"Yes, sir. We just received word of an imminent threat against Chairman Andrews. We were dispatched to escort him to safety and did not know who you were, sir."

"He just took off."

"Thank you, sir. Sorry to have bothered you," the Captain said before he and his men departed.

Dykstra slowly shook his head, then activated the car's com.

"Yes, sir?"

"Take me to the research center's hangar now."

"Yes, sir."

Chairman Andrews never failed to marvel at being in the heavens. The troubles of man seemed to pale compared to the beauty and brilliance of the countless stars set in a pitch-black background.

"Sir, per our flight plan, we should reach the planet Matee in about four hours and twenty minutes."

"I'm sorry, Mr. Terac. I failed to tell you earlier, but there's been a change of plans. Please head to 112-883-221 at the outer marker."

"Yes, sir," he said and pushed a series of pads on his control console.

"Commander, the tracking device onboard the Chairman's ship has just gone active. She's changed course and is now heading for the Natie Asteroid Field."

"Control, launch Alpha One."

Sandor watched the small scout ship without lights lift off from the field and streak after the Chairman's ship. Move and counter move.

Toa surveyed his tactical screen. "Thomas, I'm getting an intermittent signal, possibly a ship closing on the Chairman's."

"Any ID?"

"Nothing. My guess is that it's either an electronic shadow or a ship running without their signal beacon."

"Any bets?"

"Not a chance."

The Chairman was briefly startled by the gentle vibration from the secure communicator attached to his wrist. "Mr. Terac, our friends want us to change course again." He read the display. "Head to 115-871-333."

"That's inside the field, sir."

"Interesting."

"Yes, sir." Terac slowed then carefully proceeded down a channel framed by the asteroids. "Sir, look!" Ahead, a ship lay motionless in front of them. She was the identical make and model as the Chairman's ship. "A decoy?"

"Probably. I can only assume we're being followed."

Terac scanned his panel. "Sensors show nothing behind us, sir."

"Well, I hope you're right. If not, we may have taken this little trip for nothing. Please pass the ship and continue on this heading, Mr. Terac."

"Yes, sir," he replied and entered in the additional commands.

The Controller looked up from his monitor. "Commander, I've lost the tracking signal onboard the Chairman's ship."

Sandor stared at the Commander. "What does that mean?" he asked, his tone less than friendly.

"A moment, Mr. Sandor." The Commander made his way to the control station. "Does Alpha One have visual?"

"She lost visual when the Chairman's ship first entered the asteroid field but has since reacquired her, sir."

The Commander thought for a second. "Notify all ships to go to full sensor sweep."

"Captain, there she is," the Controller of the Tactical Squad's transport Andromeda announced seeing what appeared to be Theta One emerging from the asteroid field.

"Magnify the image."

"Yes, sir."

The Captain watched the ship ahead exit the field and run starboard side to. He activated his com system. "Andromeda to base."

Sandor stood behind the Commander's chair, a frown on his face.

"Go ahead, Andromeda," replied the Commander.

"Sir, a ship is approaching us that is the same make and model as the Chairman's ship, but her starboard light is green, repeat green. The scout ship is behind her."

"Understood. Control out."

"Commander, what's going on?" Sandor demanded, his eyes narrowed in anger.

"We covertly changed the starboard light on the Chairman's ship to blue."

"Then, you've lost them?"

"Only for the moment. Control, have all ships go to full sensor sweep."

"Thomas, the shadow is gone."

"Send the final coordinates."

The Chairman's secure communicator vibrated again. "Mr. Terac, please head 122-899-453."

"Yes, sir." He altered course and checked his charts. "Sir, there appears to be an old space station on this heading. My records show it abandoned."

"An excellent place for a meeting, wouldn't you say?"

"Yes, sir."

"Alpha Three to Control," came over the hanger's com system.

"Control."

"We've picked up two momentary transmissions from the tracking device onboard the Chairman's ship. The positions were 122-899-453 and 114-874-661."

"Roger. Stand by, Alpha Three."

The Commander called up the appropriate chart and drew a straight line between the two points. It led to the three modules that made up Space Station 575. "There, Mr. Sandor, there's your target. I'd bet my life on it."

"Thank you, Commander," Sandor said calmly, knowing that the man already had.

CHAPTER TWENTY FOUR

As they made their way through one of two transfer chambers, Terac stayed in the background while Chairman Andrews came forward and offered his hand. "Mr. Alesana, Mr. Chandler."

"Mr. Chairman," Toa said in greeting.

"Thank you for coming, sir," Thomas said.

"I found our encounter the other night to be most... interesting."

Thomas smiled. "This way, please." He led the way to a table and chairs in the center of the room. Toa headed to the station's control console.

"Is the whole station operational?" the Chairman asked, taking a seat.

"No, sir," Thomas replied. "Just this module."

"Then you two are alone?"

"I saw no need to expose the others."

"I quite agree," the Chairman said when an alarm suddenly sounded. Toa quickly scanned the sensors. "Twelve pod-wing fighters and an armed frigate are headed this way!"

Thomas stared hard at the man across from him. "Is this your solution, Mr. Chairman? Capture us to take the heat off back home?"

The Chairman looked wide-eyed at Thomas. "I give you my word. I had nothing to do with any of this."

Toa deactivated the alarm. "Thomas, incoming message."

"On screen."

"Station 575, this is the Theta Tactical Squad. Prepare to be boarded. Any resistance and we will open fire."

"What shall we do?" the Chairman asked.

"Put your hands up," Terac ordered his disrupter set on kill and aimed at Toa's head.

"Terac, what are you doing?" the Chairman demanded.

"Sealing your fate," he said with a grin. "The both of you, move against the far wall now. You too," he said to Toa and roughly pushed him forward. Behind him, the Tactical Squad Commander and two of his men came through the second transfer chamber door. Each had their weapon drawn. "We're alone, and they're unarmed," Terac reported.

"Well done," the Commander offered.

"Yes, well done, Mr. Terac," Sandor echoed on entry into the module. "Interesting company you're keeping these days, Mr. Chairman."

Thomas's jaw tightened. Despite the situation, he wanted to lash out at Sandor, but...

The Chairman started to walk forward. A raised Tactical Squad disrupter brought him to a stop. "Commander, this isn't what you think."

"Actually, you're right," Sandor interjected. "It isn't what he thinks. It's what the people will think, isn't that right, Chandler?"

"Commander," the Chairman said before Thomas could answer. "Am I being detained?"

"Yes, sir."

"On what charge?"

"Aiding and abetting a known fugitive for starters, sir."

"The Chairman of the Theta Corporation in a clandestine meeting with the Dissenters," Sandor mused. "Who would have thought?"

"No one will ever believe you, Sandor," Thomas said as he stood against the wall, Terac's weapon aimed at him and Toa.

"Of course they will. Remember, I'm the one in charge of apprehending the Dissenters and their accomplices."

"Commander," Thomas said, "the truth is that Sandor framed Dykstra and is now trying to move the Chairman out so that he can take over Theta."

Sandor smiled. "A fanciful story, especially coming from a mass murderer. But once again there is no evidence to support your claim, is there?"

"There is concerning Sorel," Thomas shot back.

Sandor shook his head. "Come on, Chandler, that's getting a bit old, isn't it?"

"You're right," the Chairman said, taking over the conversation. "Not only is it getting old, but it doesn't make any sense."

"What do you mean?" Sandor asked, suddenly defensive.

"I reviewed Chandler's argument," he said calmly. "There were so many other options."

"Such as?"

"New equipment could have been brought in to increase productivity and hence profit for one."

Sandor began to pace. "I totally disagree. Predictions showed less than one percent of the ore remained."

"Ore predictions usually aren't worth a damn," the Chairman countered. "The Phoenix Mining Company's claim pretty much proved that."

Sandor glared at the Chairman, his eyes narrowed. "We were losing our ass at Sorel. Projected contract-end and relocation costs alone were staggering."

The Chairman stared off in the distance. "Reduce overhead and labor to maintain an adequate profit margin," he said calmly.

"Damn right. And with the insurance money, I couldn't lose." Sandor said, defiant, determined to win the argument, determined to show his skill, his prowess.

The Chairman's head suddenly snapped back around, his focus on Sandor. "You couldn't lose?"

"What?"

"You said you couldn't lose," the Chairman replied. "Did you hear that, Commander?"

"Yes, sir, I did," the man said, suddenly finding it very uncomfortable to be holding the most powerful man in the Discovered Worlds at disrupter point.

"Think, Commander," the Chairman pressed, "who has told you all you know about this situation, what he wants you to know?"

"Enough," Sandor shouted. "Don't listen to him Commander. He's just trying to weasel his way out of this."

The Commander turned and unconsciously aimed his disrupter at Sandor. "I'm not so sure about that, Mr. Sandor," he said before a disrupter blast from Terac suddenly sliced through the air, striking the Commander in the shoulder. Terac's next shot ripped apart one soldier's chest before two more shots were heard. Terac fell stunned from one. The second soldier fell dead from the other.

Thomas lunged for Terac's weapon when Sandor blasted it away using the recovered the Commander's weapon.

"Back up!" Sandor shouted while he adjusted his weapon to kill. "Back to where you were. Now!"

Thomas, the Chairman, and Toa did as ordered.

"That's right. Nice and easy. Well, Mr. Chairman, a good try, but I'm afraid it can only end one way."

"You only know one way, don't you, Sandor?" the Chairman said, his tone meant to antagonize.

"You sanctimonious bastard. You can't see, can you? 1638 people, such a small, insignificant price to pay for power. You're weak. Dykstra's weak. It was too easy to frame him then accuse you. You don't belong anymore."

"And you think you can lead Theta better?"

"You're damn right I can. And I will. But first..." Sandor turned and fired, killing Terac instantly.

Thomas shook his head in disgust. "A little knowledge can be a dangerous thing."

"How true, Mr. Chandler, but then you'll be next to find out," Sandor said when an arrow suddenly flashed through the air, striking the disrupter from Sandor's hand. Tovar quickly reloaded, but his second shot found only the transfer chamber's door as Sandor closed it behind him.

Maren rushed in with a disrupter in hand. "Thomas, of the sound of weapons, it caused us concern. Of the decision to decloak, it was made."

"I'm glad you did," he said on his way to a medkit, then the fallen Commander. Tovar headed to the soldiers while the Chairman checked Terac.

Maren looked down at the Commander's unconscious body. "Of his life, will it continue?"

Thomas checked the kit's scanner. "Yes. There's only minor damage. A pressure bandage should do for now," he said, pulling one out of the kit and placing it on the wound.

"Thomas, of both soldiers, they are dead," Tovar reported.

"Terac is dead too," the Chairman said, joining the others.

"Then I suggest we get to our ship while we still can."

"Of the Commander, I will carry him," Tovar offered, lifting the officer up and putting him over his shoulder before running with the others to the station's hangar.

"Get us out of here!" Sandor yelled to the frigate's Controller.

"But sir, what about the Commander and the others?"

"Dead. All dead. It was a trap. The Dissenters ambushed us before we knew what happened. Now move, damn it!"

The Controller broke the connection with the docking ring then raced the frigate away from the station while Sandor assumed the command chair. "Give me ship-to-ship communications."

"Go ahead, sir."

"This is Sandor. Your Commander has been killed in a trap set by the Dissenters. As soon as we clear, bring all weapons to bear on the station's module."

Even though the module's shields were activate, those in the station were still barely able to maintain their balance amidst the incoming disrupter fire from the Tactical Squad. Finally inside the transport, Toa jumped into the controller's seat. "I don't think the station can take much more," he shouted, bringing the ship to life. "Shields are at full."

Another round of disrupter fire momentarily kept Maren from her seat at the helm, a position that she had bested both Academy grads at over the past few days. Thomas moved to the weapons console while Tovar buckled the unconscious Commander in a rear seat. He strapped in next to him. The Chairman attached his restraint for the seat across the aisle from Tovar.

"Activate the hangar doors," Thomas said.

Toa repeatedly inputted the command for the door, but nothing happened. "They're stuck."

"Then let me help you with that," Thomas said with a smile. "Firing!"

Sandor sat back with a grin at the sight of the fleet's weapons bearing down on the station's defenses. Soon he would be the next Theta chairman.

"The module's shields are down to ten percent."

"Continue firing," Sandor ordered before a series of explosions suddenly ripped the module apart.

"A transport!" the Controller shouted, the ship seen speeding just ahead of the massive fireball on its way into the asteroid field.

"After them," Sandor shouted, coming halfway out of his chair.

"Can we get away?" the Chairman asked, the concern in his voice obvious.

Thomas stared at the tactical screen. "I don't know," he said before an incoming disrupter blast rocked the ship, knocking out the viewscreen. "Toa, reroute auxiliary power."

"Of this, do it quickly," Maren said, flying blind. She turned the transport and hoped her memory of what lay in front of them was accurate.

Toa feverishly pushed a series of pads on his control board then looked up. The system flickered momentarily then finally sprung to life. An asteroid filled most of the screen.

"Maren!" Thomas shouted.

She instantly put the transport on its side then raced it between two more asteroids.

"Computer," Sandor said, "identify the transport type ahead of us, their weapons and speed capability,"

"The transport is a class T-20 from the Corporate War. In standard configuration, she has forward firing disrupters and is not capable of warp."

A grin crossed his face. The Chairman would not get far.

Another disrupter blast nearly knocked Toa from his seat. "Shields are at 80 percent," Toa reported.

Thomas scanned the tactical screen but saw nothing. "Where is she?"

"Behind the asteroid directly to the port," the Chairman said, looking out his porthole.

"Maren, take us 90 degrees starboard. Toa, launch the mines."

"That will give them a straight shot at us!" the Chairman exclaimed.

"Hopefully," Thomas replied with a smile.

"Here she comes," Toa announced just before the Tactical Squad fighter's left engine pod disappeared. The power imbalance threw her into the nearest asteroid.

"Maren, head to," Thomas started to say when an incoming disrupter blast suddenly flashed across their bow. "Hard starboard."

She rounded an asteroid only to have the ship rocked again, this time by disrupter fire from both the port and starboard.

Toa quickly scanned his panel. "Shields are at fifty-four percent," he said when more alarms sounded. "Two more ships are closing on us from below."

Thomas looked to the tactical screen. "We're boxed in," he said when the ship was hit again. A new alarm sounded.

Toa scanned his board. "Our warp drive is offline!"

"See if you can fix it."

"Right," Toa said and raced aft.

Thomas turned to the Chairman. "Care to take over the controller's position?"

"It's been a while," he said on his way forward.

"Thomas, of an opening, one exists through the second asteroid to port," Maren announced.

"Go for it."

The Chairman looked at Maren wide-eyed. "We won't fit!"

"Then, of worries, you will no longer have any," she said and climbed the transport straight for the large rock. At the entrance to the tunnel, she threw the ship into a tight spiral then followed the maneuver with a sharp dive that brought them through the hole unscathed.

The Chairman looked at her in amazement. "Where did you learn to fly like that?"

"Learn?"

"Control, status?" Sandor demanded.
"The transport has exited the field and is making a run for Gamma Nebula," he replied, their own ship coming free of the asteroids. "She'll be in range in seconds."
"Then destroy it. For your Commander."
"My pleasure, sir."

Thomas checked his tactical screen. Eleven pod wing fighters and an armed frigate were closing in on them.
"Our shields are at twenty percent," the Chairman announced.
"Toa, how much longer?" Thomas asked.
On his back, his head buried under the warp drive system, he feverishly continued checking each module, trying to find the bad one. "I'm not sure," he said when a new threat alarm suddenly sounded.
"Eight fighters are inbound," the Chairman announced. "They're from the Corporate War!"
Roberts suddenly appeared on the viewscreen from the helm of one of the fighters. In front of him was Rachael at the controller's station. "Like some help?"
Thomas smiled. "Well, we had things pretty much under control, but as long as you are here."

The frigate still pursuing the transport, the two fighter forces opened fire on one another in classic dogfight style.
"Target his engines," Roberts said to Rachael, bringing his ship in behind a Tactical Squad fighter. He thought it almost artistic the way the two ships weaved their way through space, move and counter-move punctuated by bursts of light. But art was something to be appreciated and treasured over time. This was a deadly game.
A tone suddenly sounded. "Firing!" Rachael shouted.

"Keira, I've got one on my tail. I can't shake him!" she heard Hawkins shout over her com system, his ship taking yet another volley. "Aft shields are at 45 percent!"

"Pull up, Hawkins," she shouted then watched his ship move through her sites, bringing the Tactical Squad's ship to bear. A tone was heard. "Control, fire!"

A series of disrupter blasts raced forward. A massive explosion left the Theta ship minus a starboard engine. The fuselage trailed a shower of sparks behind it when a collision alarm suddenly sounded. Keira looked to starboard to see a crippled pod-wing fighter heading straight for them, out of control. She threw the stick hard forward then held her breath as the Tactical Squad ship passed harmlessly overhead and ironically slammed into the port side engine of another less fortunate enemy ship.

"Destroy the transport, damn it!" Sandor yelled, his well-practiced calm replaced by anger brought on by frustration.

"I can't get a lock, sir," the Controller replied, the transport moving erratically.

Sandor slammed his fist down on the arm of his chair. "I don't want any of your excuses. Eliminate the transport now!"

"Marsh, dive!" Roberts shouted over his com system, driving his fighter forward as fast as it could go. "Are we in range of the pursuing fighter yet?"

"Almost," Rachael said when Marsh's ship suddenly exploded before their eyes. "I've got a lock!"

"Fire!" Roberts watched a torpedo take out the port engine of the Tactical Squad fighter when his own ship was suddenly blasted. He instantly went high and to port.

"Shields are at 35 percent!" Rachael shouted through the smoke from a console fire. "She's got a lock on us!" she said before another salvo nearly took their ship apart. "Our weapons systems are down!" Rachael yelled when the ship was blasted yet again. "Our shields are gone as well!"

Roberts searched for an answer, but there was nothing left. "Hold on!" he shouted and dove the ship when a torpedo suddenly flashed overhead and ripped away the attacking Theta fighter's starboard engine pod.

"Roberts, you two okay?" Keira was heard to ask.

"We are. Thanks."

"No problem," she replied and raced her fighter up over his ship. "Stay below me. We'll cover you with our shields," she said when an alarm suddenly sounded.

"One coming up on our port side!" her Controller shouted just before a missile suddenly flashed by and took out one of the approaching Tactical Squad fighter's engines.

"I thought I'd return the favor," she heard Hawkins say over the com system.

"Thomas, one of the Tactical Squad fighters has broken free and is on an intercept course," the Chairman shouted over a new alarm.

"Maren, turn directly into the approaching ship," he ordered, putting Sandor's frigate astern and in harm's way if the fighter fired and missed.

"Agreed"

The Chairman's eyes grew wide again. He couldn't help but recall the old videos where they had called the game they were playing chicken. Back then, he thought suicide was a better name. Now he was sure of it.

"Thomas, of this course, how long do you wish it held?"

"Longer than they do."

"Agreed," she replied with a grin.

"I'll fire as they break off."

The Chairman turned and looked at Thomas. "What if they don't break off?"

It was Thomas's turn to grin.

"Impact, in fifteen seconds," the Chairman said, beginning to squirm. He knew Maren would not back off. He just hoped a like-minded counterpart wasn't flying the Tactical Squad fighter. "Ten."

Thomas looked at the viewscreen and the approaching ship that occupied more and more of it with each passing second. At first, he had felt confident, but now... "Maintain course."

"Five... Four... Three... They're off!"

"Firing!"

Sandor barely noticed the pod wing fighter streak past them, her engines on fire. His attention was fixed on only one thing, the destruction of the transport in front of them. "Fire!"

Again the Dissenter transport was rocked, the blast throwing those inside back in their seats. Smoke came from select consoles.
"Toa!"

"Mr. Sandor, their shields are down!" the Controller announced.
"Then, fire!"
Two disrupter blasts raced from the ship and headed harmlessly into open space, the transport no longer there. "What the?
"She's gone to warp, sir!"
"But you said she wasn't capable of warp," Sandor stammered.
"I've got them," the Controller announced.
"Then, after them, damn it."

"Sandor is still following us, Thomas," the Chairman said.
"What's her speed?"
"Warp 1.0."
"And ours?"
"1.15."
"Then we should be able to make the nebula," Thomas said when a harsh pulsating alarm suddenly filled the flight deck. The Chairman studied his board. "The warp drive is causing our power plant's containment field to destabilize. We've got to take it offline now, or we'll blow up!"
"Drop us out of warp," Thomas ordered. "Everyone, spacesuits on, conformal setting. Tovar, put one on the Commander as well."
"Agreed."
Thomas activated his suit then checked to make sure everyone else had done so as well. "Maren, full stop, then turn us 180 degrees."
"Agreed."

"Mr. Chairman, internal pressure to zero."

"At zero."

"Toa, open the side door and leave it open. Everyone, form a single file in front of the open door and abandon ship. When you're 500 meters from the ship, attach a tractor beam to her, but only long enough to stop your forward motion."

The Commander still unconscious, Tovar deactivated the man's tractor beam, making it easy for him to move him around as he floated free. He then moved to the head of the line and turned around so he would face the ship after his exit. Toa was next in line, facing him. Tovar turned his tractor beam off. "Toa, push me."

Toa did as asked then repeated the process.

"And of you, Thomas?" Maren asked, the last in line.

"I'll be right behind you," he said and pushed her out into space. "Computer, give me a countdown for when the approaching frigate will come out of warp starting now."

"Ten point seven seconds," the computer announced.

"Computer, establish a course that passes just above the approaching frigate after she comes out of warp."

"Course established."

Thomas did a quick mental calculation. "Computer, accelerate to one quarter light speed after the approaching frigate comes out of warp. On acceleration, disengage this ship's power plant containment field," he ordered, the irony of using an uncontained reaction against Sandor's ship not lost on him. He moved in front of the open door.

"Acknowledged. Five seconds."

Thomas pushed the button to disable his tractor beam, but the system malfunctioned. Instead of flying out into space, he was still held to the deck.

"Four seconds."

"Damn..." He desperately pushed the reset button for the tractor beam.

"Three seconds."

"Come on. Come on!" Thomas said, sweat forming on his brow.

"Two seconds."

Suddenly floating, Thomas grabbed the door jamb and pulled himself as hard as he could out into space, slightly spinning himself in the process.

"One second."

Only ten meters away from the transport, Thomas saw the ship literally disappear in a burst of speed. A split-second later, he shielded his eyes from the massive explosion that consumed their transport. "Everyone, switch your suit's force field to the spherical setting now!" he said, doing so himself just before the shockwave hit. The instant acceleration and associated turbulence tossed him hard inside the bubble, but its shape shed most of the energy while keeping the flying debris a sufficient distance away from his body. As it passed, he shook his head, trying to clear it when he saw Sandor's ship. Her engines dark, the explosion of his ship had sent the frigate speeding in his direction. Projecting the ship's course on the inside of his force field bubble, with his index finger, he moved the tractor beam's sites onto it and activated the system. The instant acceleration made him smile. "Toa, status?" he asked as he started to pull himself toward Sandor's ship.

"We're all a little shaken and spread out, but otherwise okay... What now?"

"I've locked onto Sandor's ship. I'm going to go after him before he can get away and spin things to his advantage again."

"Understood."

Returning his spacesuit back to its conformal setting, another tractor beam allowed Thomas to pull himself to the ship's outer transfer chamber door. Opening it, he entered. On its close, he activated the chamber itself. A screen showed the ship was on emergency power, but otherwise intact. Three life forms beside himself were also shown to be on board, alive. "Computer, emergency stop."

Engaged forward gas jets threw Thomas a bit off-balance, but he recovered as the atmosphere in the chamber was restored. His spacesuit deactivated, he pulled a disrupter from his backpack and took cover behind the side of the inner door before opening it. Unchallenged, he started to make his way out then instantly pulled back just before a disrupter blast flashed by his head. Weighing his chances with a direct charge, he noticed the reflection of the Tactical Squad soldier in the outer door's window. Seeing the man suddenly move to take cover closer in, Thomas turned and fired. Caught in the open, the soldier screamed before falling on the deck unconscious.

Carefully, cautiously, Thomas moved forward, searching, seeking when the sound of a footstep made him pull back into the recess of a door. A soldier with disrupter at the ready turned the other way giving Thomas an open shot. The man screamed then fell unconscious as Sandor suddenly raced up from behind Thomas with a makeshift club in hand. Seeing Sandor out of the corner of his eye at the last second, Thomas tried to block the blow with his right arm. The club came down hard, breaking Thomas's wrist, the one holding his disrupter. As he screamed and dropped the weapon, Sandor lunged for it, but despite his pain, Thomas slammed his body into Sandor's before the man could get to it.

Quickly recovering, Sandor swung his club wildly at Thomas's head. He somehow managed to duck the blow before rising back up and landing a left cross to Sandor's chin. The blow only further fueling Sandor's rage, he swung the club again. Again he missed, this time embedding the weapon in an electronic stack. Sparks flying, Sandor unable to pull the club free, Thomas pivoted and kicked him in the stomach. But Sandor quickly recovered and turned back on Thomas. He grabbed him by the neck with both hands and began to choke him. "Time to die, Chandler."

With his good hand, Thomas reached up and grabbed the little and ring fingers of Sandor's right hand, then bent them back as fast, hard, and far as he could until he heard them pop out of their joints. As Sandor screamed in pain, his grip on Thomas's neck lessened. A backhand to Sandor's face caused him to let go. A massive left cross sent Sandor reeling backward, falling next to the disrupter. He grabbed it with his left hand. "That will be enough of that, Chandler."

Thomas pulled back slightly. "Even you should know you're through, Sandor."

"That's where you're wrong," he said, awkwardly working his way back up to his feet, keeping the weapon trained on Thomas. "After you're dead, your friends and the Chairman will be nothing more than target practice, and the Theta Corporation will be mine."

"I don't think so," Thomas said, feigning to his right, drawing Sandor's unnatural left-handed shot in that direction before pivoting and kicking him in the ribs. As the man flew back, Thomas moved in. His left fist came down hard on Sandor's left wrist, causing the disrupter to fall onto the deck. Sandor screaming, Thomas landed a left to the man's stomach that doubled him over. A devastating uppercut stood him up before a following roundhouse put him back down on the deck, bruised, bloody and unconscious.

His own breathing hard and rapid, Thomas lorded over his tormentor. Consumed with bloodlust, he readied himself to finish the job, to end the man's life, but… He slowly pulled back and stared down at the pathetic man in front of him, his mind clearing. He would not sink to his level…

Securing his disrupter, he stunned Sandor then accessed his communicator. "Toa, I've got him. I've got Sandor."

"Excellent. Dykstra just showed up. We'll join you soon."

"Right…" Thomas looked down at Sandor. It was finally over, but… He thought about all the pain and suffering the man had caused. The thought about the colony, all the Dissenters they had lost along the way, his parents and Shara. He started to cry.

CHAPTER TWENTY FIVE

Thomas lay in his bunk on board the Veritas. Sandor was in jail. He and the rest of the Dissenters had surrendered and were now confined to the ship, under guard, waiting for the court to decide their fate. They were certainly guilty of destroying property and injuring a few people along the way, but now that the truth was finally known, he hoped the scales would balance. A return trip to the Prison Planet was certainly within the realm of possibility. Still...

With a deep sigh, he sat up and turned on the viewscreen. The Theta Corporation News was on. Byron Walker was at the anchor desk with a mug shot of Sandor above his left shoulder.

"... For a live report, we go now to Win Chow at the Alpha District Courthouse," Byron said. "Win."

Win stood in front of an illuminated fountain. "Byron, I have with me one of the Theta Corporation lawyers, Mr. Viken, who argued the case on behalf of the Theta Corporation against Mr. Sandor." Win turned to his left as the camera pulled back to frame the two of them. "Mr. Viken, quite a turn of events since the last time we spoke."

"Agreed. As it turns out, much of the evidence we used earlier to defend Mr. Sandor was actually manufactured by him in a well-thought-out plan to become the next Chairman of the Theta Corporation."

"And now that the Court has convicted Mr. Sandor, are you free to share with us the details of your prosecution?"

Viken nodded. "Yes. After Mr. Dykstra was arrested for corporate spying and the rumor was spread that Chairman Andrews was involved, the Chairman's suspicions fell on Sandor. Sandor had the means, motive, and the opportunity to create not only the situation Mr. Dykstra and he were in, but the destruction of the Sorel Mining Colony as well. To understand Sorel better, the Chairman met with the Dissenters under a 'flag of truce,' so to speak. The Dissenters were more than willing to produce the original recordings of the copies Shara Lockett had sent earlier. The Chairman then secretly hired an independent investigation team to look into what had happened at each site. For the Buoy 19 malfunction, their review of the entire shipping lane guidance system showed the defective circuit board was introduced after the attack."

"And the Sorel power plant recording?"

"They determined the damage to the room and its equipment occurred after the uncontained reaction as the result of an accelerant."

"And was that enough for an arrest warrant against Sandor?" Win asked.

"Unfortunately, no. In both cases, there was no way to directly tie in Sandor. But it was enough for Chairman Andrews to set up a sting operation with the Dissenters agreeing to act as bait. When Sandor was convinced that he had the upper hand, he actually bragged about destroying the Sorel Colony, framing Mr. Dykstra, and setting up Chairman Andrews as the one who ordered the Delta Records break-in. That conversation was both recorded as well as witnessed."

"And what about the Dissenters?" Win asked. "It seems like they have been the victims throughout all of this."

"Agreed. The Dissenters have elected to throw themselves on the mercy of the court. I should also mention that Chairman Andrews has asked us to drop all charges we have against them and lend our support to their defense."

"Admirable… Thank you once again, Mr. Viken, for your candor."

"My pleasure," he said before the camera pushed in to frame only Win.

"There you have it, Byron. Sandor destroyed the Sorel Colony and blamed the Dissenters for his crime."

Thomas turned off the viewscreen and laid back down on his bunk. He had had enough of Sandor.

Thomas, Toa said, suddenly sticking his head inside the room. "The High Court has handed down their ruling. The Chairman is going to announce it in a couple minutes."

"Finally," he said, getting up and following Toa the short distance into the cargo bay. At the far end, a viewscreen had been set up. Armed guards stood ever vigilant.

"Thomas, Toa," Maren called out.

"Ready for a return trip to the Prison Planet?" Thomas asked, the two of them joining her, Tovar and Rah.

Maren shook her head. "Of that, justice would not be served."

"Agreed," Rah said.

His shackles off, Sandor was handed off to the Prison Barge detention area where two new guards, Tate and Zane, were waiting for him. Another prisoner had preceded his arrival. The man lay in a heap on the deck, his face bloody and swollen. "Gentlemen, I can only anticipate you have malice on your minds for me as well."

"If you mean are we going to beat the crap out of you," Tate said, clenching his fist, a grin on his face, "you couldn't be more right."

"You do know that I'm a wealthy man, don't you?"

"So?" Zane said, relaxing slightly.

Sandor smiled. "I am more than willing to make it financially worth your while if you do not harm me."

"And how do you propose to do that?"

"I will give you the numbers to a bank account so that you can verify the funds are available. I will then give you the password just before we reach the Prison Planet if I remain unharmed."

"The Lieutenant will know something's up when he comes down here to send you to the surface and finds you're not near dead."

"Then the three of you will be wealthy men."

"And what if we just beat the password out of you," Tate said.

"You stand the risk of me not telling you what it is. So, what is more important to you, the beating, or wealth?"

Zane looked at Tate, who escorted Sandor to a chair in front of a computer terminal. "The account number, please, Mr. Sandor."

"Mr. Chairman, it's time."

"Thanks, Renée." Chairman Andrews walked to the podium on the same stage Sandor had used earlier to convince the Discovered Worlds of the Dissenters' guilt. He now had to ask the people to trust him that the destruction of Sorel was the isolated act of a deranged individual and not the Theta Corporation.

"Ladies and gentlemen, too often, the worlds have seen what an individual with an insane hunger for power is willing to do. Too often, these people had left pain, suffering, and death in their wake before they were stopped. Sandor was no exception. I know there is no way to replace the loved ones lost or remove the deep emotional scars that have resulted from his inexcusable actions, but I pledge to you now that the Theta Corporation will do everything possible to help those so brutally affected."

As anticipated, sporadic applause was heard. Most of those in attendance gave their neighbors skeptical glances. The Chairman understood why.

"I know that many of you have too often heard that the abuse of power must never be allowed to happen again. Then, too often, little or nothing was done about it. This time, however, it will be different. I am pleased to announce tonight that the Theta Corporation has joined with the other Ruling Corporations of the Discovered Worlds to create a Corporate Oversight Service, an independent agency under the law enforcement umbrella. Its purpose will be to review any and all complaints concerning the misuse of power by any corporation and/or their members and bring those found guilty of a crime to justice."

The applause was stronger, barely.

"And finally, I would like to offer a public apology to the Dissenters. Themselves the victims of Sandor's evil, they relentlessly fought to prove their innocence and expose the truth. I know there is no way to repay them for those they have lost or the injustices they have suffered, but I am very pleased to announce tonight that all charges against the members of the Dissenters have been dropped by the District High Court. Also, the convictions of all their members already found guilty have been overturned. To the Dissenters, I offer my congratulations and my thanks."

None of the Dissenters heard the reaction at the Theta Amphitheater over the shouts for joy in the Veritas's cargo bay. Some broke down crying. Others embraced their neighbors while the Tactical Squad quietly took their leave. The wait had been agonizing, the tension thick, but with the announcement, the relief was complete. Thomas shook Toa's hand. "Well done."

"You too."

"Congratulations, Thomas Chandler," Maren said with a grin before hugging him. "Of our thanks, they are offered."

"As are mine for all you and your family have done. I just wish Oden were here."

"Of the same, it can be said for all the others who died by Sandor's hand, especially your parents and Shara."

Thomas nodded. "Agreed."

"Thomas!" Keira called out, coming forward with Roberts, tears in her eyes. She hugged him.

"Tears of joy?" he asked with a suspicious smile.

"Roberts just proposed. We're getting married."

"Congratulations. "I couldn't be happier for the two of you."

"Thank you," she said first to Thomas and then to Toa and the Ba'ahs when Bert Dykstra suddenly appeared out of nowhere.

Surprised, Thomas shook the man's hand. "Mr. Dykstra, to what do we owe the honor?"

"Chairman Andrews and I would like to show our appreciation to the Dissenters for all you have done," he said and gestured to tables of hors d'oeuvres and a bar that were being rolled into the bay. "I think you'll find the wine to be some of the finest. It's from the Ba'ah's cellar."

"Our wine?" Maren asked, surprised if not a bit angered.

Dykstra smiled. "We borrowed a few bottles while we still owned your property."

"Still?" she asked, her eyes going wide.

Dykstra's smile grew larger. "Your land has been returned to you and your family."

Maren shook Dykstra's hand. Her brothers followed her lead.

"Of our thanks, they are offered," Tovar said.

"It's the least we could do for all you've done. Shall we?" Dykstra said and led the way to the tables. Toa, Thomas, and Maren lagged behind.

"Of plans for your future Toa," Maren asked, "have you made any?"

A smile crossed his face. "I'm finally going to go home and visit my family."

"Then, of them, they are truly the fortunate ones."

"Thank you."

"Toa," Hawkins called out from across the bay. Standing next to Rachael, he held up a glass of wine.

Toa smiled. "If you will excuse me…"

"Certainly," Thomas said. "Maren, I meant to tell you. The rest of the Dissenters have all agreed to give Toa, you and your brothers, including Oden, and Mr. Lee an equal share of our proceeds from the diamatron ore we discovered on Sorel for all the help you have given us."

"Of that, you do not have to do it, Thomas," she said in all honesty.

"It is something we all want to do. Besides, it will probably come in handy in restoring your land to its former glory after your absence."

"Then, of our thanks, they are offered… And of you, Thomas, what will you do now?"

He suddenly realized that for the first time in a long time, he was actually free to do anything he wanted to, to go anywhere he wanted to go. And with his share of the money from the Phoenix Mining Company, he could do just that for the rest of his life. "You know, I really haven't given it much thought."

She took his hand in hers. "Of further discussion of this over a glass of our wine, it is suggested."

"Agreed."

The drone hovered just above the surface of the Prison Planet then rotated up. Unharmed, Sandor slid down feet first then rolled after hitting the ground to keep from breaking any bones.

His fellow prisoner fell hard then stayed there for a minute before staggering to his feet. Surrounded by jungle, he found the heat and humidity oppressive, but…

In the distance, an eerie high-pitched wail was suddenly heard, one that cut into Sandor's very soul. It was followed by another then another when, coming out of the shadows, he saw one of the Mutants. Her claws slashed the air while drool dripped from her fangs. His fellow prisoner tried to run as best he could, but only made it a few steps before the monster attacked. His screams were short-lived as in an instant, the Mutant had buried her fangs in his neck. Blood dripping from her mouth, she turned and focused her full attention on Sandor.

THE END

Made in the USA
Monee, IL
08 January 2020